FRANK DELANEY

TELLING THE PICTURES

LONDON NEW YORK SYDNEY TORONTO

This edition published 1993
by BCA
by arrangement with Harper Collins

Copyright © Frank Delaney 1993

The Author asserts the moral right to
be identified as the author of this work

CN 5890

Printed an bound in Germany
by Graphischer Großbetrieb Pößneck GmbH
A member of the Mohndruck printing group

FOR SOPHIE

PART ONE

PROLOGUE

In Belfast, in 1942, lived Belle, a mill-girl with a gift. Every morning at work, she enthralled people with the story of the film she saw last night. In her apron and turban-tied headscarf she climbed on the table of the spinning-room in Rufus Street, and dramatised, in her own sharp accent, the passions of Hollywood. With her wide eyes and her wit, and her hands weaving gestures like a magician casting spells, she pierced the overcast of their long, dirty workdays.

They all knew Belle, and her circumstances, her morose household: the MacKnights had suffered an outrage in Belle's childhood. Only Belle had never been told what had happened – everybody knew that too. But how could she not have heard the whispers: they continued long after the funeral? Leonard, the other child of the family, knew the whole story, and he seemed as angry as Belle seemed good-natured: Superintendent Crawford, responsible for Leonard's division of the Special Reserve Constabulary, had often had to caution him, tone him down. Belle never seemed to enquire what had happened to make Leonard like that; or had made her mother so religious. Belle never asked those questions: anyone could have told her: the loving Aunt Sandra, or run-off-at-the-mouth Uncle Jed, a hundred neighbours.

The Rufus Street women talked about Belle as if she were family, and their view of her had become a kind of control. By discussing her, they maintained her innocence, these women devoid of compunctions. By saying how they liked the girl, loved her, and without asking whether she wanted or needed it, they gave Belle their protection like a tribe with a pubescent daughter. In their company, she lived their view of her, and by now, in her twenty-fourth year, she had created a pattern of naive behaviour: enthusiastic about fashion – 'style' as they called it; abreast of every new cosmetic product; ahead of every new film months before it

11

arrived; and, seemingly, never touched by any of the mill's carnal banter.

'See you, Belle, d'you know what, there's'nt one ounce of dirt in you.'

So, by keeping her as a kind of mascot, they let her shine among them, these tough, menial women who had husbands at war, or, if lucky, among the many in the 'reserved occupations', those trades essential to the war effort. Openly, the mill-women hoped out loud that Belle might be the one to break out, to get away and 'do well'. They all had husbands and children and tiny, badly-appointed houses, and they all had the grinding difficulty of making ends meet on savagely low wages, earned in denigrating surroundings. Belle, though, if lucky, might go through life without the pettiness and hardship they had all known forever. Like some impresario with a wonderful dancer or singer, they were forever looking for someone among them who could be raised above their own lives; who would marry above her and them; someone the world would never rain on, someone they could be proud of, could talk about without envy, who would live out the dreams they dreamed, and Belle, they said, had that sort of refinement about her.

For the moment, while she and they waited for Mr Right, Belle could continue to bring them the platinum blondes and the glamour from her nights at the cinema: Claudette Colbert's hair, was she wearing it up this time?

Most of these women could rarely afford to go to the pictures, and so, they took up small collections, once, maybe twice a week, in order that Belle could have the best seat in Belfast, so that she, a spinner, could join the men in suits and the women in costumes, and sit equal to them in red plush. A halfpenny between two or three or four women, loan and loan about, bought Belle, their delegate to the class above them, a night of quality.

They considered these collections good value for money when, next day, Belle began by describing to them the clothes of the women in the queues. In her conscientiousness, Belle always went early, and stood in the foyer as if waiting for someone. There she saw without looking the hats, gloves, bags, shoes.

She never described an 'outfit' without the accessories: 'If I did that,' she said, 'it'd be like telling you a story and not giving the beginning or the end.' Then, the Fashion Bulletin delivered, and

12

having dealt with Questions From The Audience, she brought to them what they really had been waiting for – the whole screen itself: the long shadows on high walls, footsteps on lonely streets; the devil-may-care raised eyebrows of Errol Flynn, his moustache painted on by Lucifer himself; Paulette Goddard's hips, sometimes outlined in a brocade skirt; Ray Milland's hair-oil, and his eyes always about to smile; Dolores del Rio in *Lancer Spy*, her hair parted in the middle like the Duchess of Windsor's, and as black-sleeked as a crow: Mae West in *My Little Chickadee* with her curls like a nest of little fat blonde coil-springs piling all over her head. Belle brought it all right into the Long Room, and into the sheds that passed for canteens, and into the Women's Necessary, with only three lavatory cubicles for nearly four hundred women. There, waiting her turn for one of the three mirrors, in the dim lighting of a few naked low-wattage bulbs, as they lit and held a match for someone putting on her lipstick, or as the spinners borrowed cold cream from each other to try and abate the ferocious chilblains up to the elbow and another day ahead of them drawing the rough yarn through the water, or Belle herself smearing Vaseline on the hard skin at the heel of her hand to soften her 'spinner's welt', she would announce the title of last night's epic, and as a trailer call out another chapter from her Stories of the Stars.

'Miscellaneous facts,' she would cry, flinging out an arm and laughing: 'Deanna Durbin – from the Child of Our Hearts to the Woman We Love'; or – with a twist of mockery – 'The Romance of Clark Gable and Carole Lombard has been a long and rocky one but, as the old novel says, Love always finds a way.' All of this she knew verbatim from *Picturegoer*, and her cousin in Canada sent her *Modern Screen* and she kept them all, and she had at least four *Picture Show Annual*s, and as for newspaper advertisements – 'Miss Judy Garland – the Princess of Pep!'

No matter how the spinning-women swathed her in the dreams they had for her, Belle worked hard. She may have been their star, but she sought no leeway. In a task where speed hallmarked the excellent, she could be one of the swiftest at her stand, ranging along that big machine, fore and aft, whipping the rove up and evenly through, not always waiting for one of the children to come and doff the full bobbins of thread, always quick to see whether a colleague at a nearby stand had come to grief. And never a hair out of place, never a smudge of oil on the cheekbone, never a cut finger nor a bruised wrist.

Before the war, when they began an hour earlier at six o'clock in the morning, Belle came in among the first. On the way home she had time to talk to the children, or time to visit some beginner laid up at home with the mill headache they all got in the first few days. She visited retired spinners, old, worn women; she cheered young wives with their babies and ill-tempered husbands. Always in good humour she clacked into work on her high heels, greetings everywhere. Among all the women in the mill, Belle MacKnight was the most widely known, and liked. Her starry picture-telling brought her to the attention of all departments, and dislike of her was rare. Nobody complained if she talked too much, or tried to 'posh' her accent, or seemed always to be washing her hands. Information about her, when the time came, abounded: how they talked and talked of her, how they fought for her, how confidently they gave their view of her tragedy as if it were Belle's own perception – and the *Belfast Telegraph* report began, 'She could tell the pictures better than the silver screen itself – but then along came a man with a silver tongue.'

1

On Monday evening, 17 August 1942, Belle checked Mrs McKibbin-next-door's newspaper again. 'War 51st week of 3rd year; Blackout times 9.24 p.m. to 5.33 a.m.' In the street beneath, children shouted, 'Queenie, queenie, whose the ball?' Belle slanted the page to the window, and murmured, 'Half-past seven, and they say it runs for nearly four hours, dear God, that's a quarter to twelve.'

She put the paper down, and peered once more at the cutting from Saturday's *Telegraph* stuck into the frame of her mirror. 'The film is still showing in London where every day huge queues stretch to the doors starting at eight o'clock in the morning.'

All the afternoon had been taken up with the excitement of her going. She waved her red ticket in one hand, and from the other read the R. S. Littlewood clipping aloud to them. 'At each performance hosts of people have to be turned away. This of course beats every record. The nearest approach was that of *Ben-Hur* which ran for forty-nine weeks at the Tivoli in the silent days.' One of the weavers had heard a rumour that the street was going to be closed off, the police were expecting such crowds, and Janice said she would ask Malcolm, whose beat took him near the Ritz: Janice said she never before took up such a quick collection for Belle – the four and ninepence no bother.

'God, Belle, youse'll have to dress up,' Alice MacKechnie said.

'Oh, aye, new knickers,' said Janice, speaking at top speed as usual, and they cheered.

'We should all be going, Belle,' said Gloria, who shared Belle's stand.

'Not at one and nine the cheapest,' said Dilly Curslow who was always going to funerals.

=

Now Belle looked in the mirror itself, between R. S. Littlewood's cutting and the photograph of Leslie Howard.

'What'll you wear, Belle?' Gloria had asked, walking home.

Belle had sighed, 'I wish I had a navy skirt.'

Alone, Belle stood back from the mirror, and raised her arms in front of her and murmured at herself: 'Is that jumper sat right?'

She fingered the knit, the red, her best colour, newly ironed after another wash; she raised the jumper high, then turned to create the poise of a profile.

'What time are you going to be back, Belle?'

Up through the open bedroom door climbed the edgy question. Belle pressed her tongue hard to her teeth and sucked in irritation. 'I mean, are you going to be late? In the blackout and that?'

'There's a bit of moonlight, isn't there?' she replied loudly, and pulled the jumper down and smoothed it, hip and other hip. In the drawer she rooted for the powder and lipstick hidden at the bottom of a cardboard box full of gloves.

Her mother walked from the kitchen table to the foot of the stairs.

'And anyway, Belle, that picture isn't supposed to be good for man nor beast, there's no morals in it, Belle.'

'Mam, where's my good headsquare?' She put her hands out to straighten the mirror, then leaned to it so that her face filled it.

'Nor there's no good, Belle, in being out and bombs dropping all over the place.'

'Mam, Uncle Jed saw it in London on his way back and he said it was great.' Belle stood upright again.

'And you forgot to do Leonard's uniform boots before you went out, he'd to do them himself, so he had.'

'Mam, is it in your drawer, is it? I left it below in the press, but 'twas gone outa there.'

'The Reverend MacCreagh is after writing to the Lord Mayor, so he is; he's saying it shouldn't be got into Belfast, a picture like that. There's all kinds of people giving out about it.'

'Ah, Mam!' Belle's voice grew exasperated. 'I've no headsquare, now. Oh, I have it! Here 'tis.' She laid the found headsquare on the bed behind her.

Next, Belle tore a corner from Mrs McKibbin-next-door's newspaper, the sports page, twisted it into a funnel the way the sweetshop did with six for a penny, dropped some powder in the paper twist, and re-lidded the powder box, which sighed a little dust. She barked her thigh off the edge of the drawer, and tried again to address her mother.

'Leonard wasn't bothered, was he?' she called down. 'He keeps his boots real clean anyway.'

Edith's tenaciousness swept her always beyond mollification.

'This is the fifth picture this month, Belle,' she persisted, 'and today's only, what, we're only on the seventeenth of the month?'

Belle shook out the headsquare.

Edith often built her aggression out of hopelessness: 'And what's it all for, Belle, filling your head with all them old pictures? All them false feelings.'

The headsquare draped the back of Belle's head in strawberries, with their green leaves curling up in tendrils. She slipped the paper twist of powder into her waistband and shoved the lipstick far up her sleeve into the crook of her elbow.

'What time is it down there, Mam?'

The reluctant reply said, 'Ten to seven.'

'God, I'd better shake myself.'

'Belle, the Lord's name is for prayer, not for haste.'

The back door clattered; Belle stretched her neck to look down the stairs, then tiptoed across the small landing and at Lennie's window looked down into the yard; her mother entered the privy. Belle ran back into her room, whipped a pair of lavender lace gloves from the box, plucked the cutting from the mirror-frame, whooshed downstairs, and called through the open back door, 'I'm off, Mam.'

'Can't you wait 'til I have a look and see if you're all right?'

'I can't, no, Mam. Sure I'm dead late.' She whipped out through the front door into empty Pretoria Street.

At the corner she glanced again at the newspaper cutting, her eyes dancing along the phrases. '. . . It has already made eight million pounds in America alone, where it is still showing in its third year of general release. When a picture does this kind of thing, criticism becomes unnecessary. It means that not only here is a masterpiece of production and of storytelling, which *Gone with the Wind* most certainly is; there must be a mysterious something else about it which draws the public irresistibly, and makes

17

the fact that it is four hours long an advantage rather than otherwise . . .'

Two men, supervised by a third, heaved sandbags off a dray truck in Ormeau Avenue.

'What about ye, Belle?' the supervisor called.

'Ach, Sammie, how are you yourself? Listen, d'you know what time it is?'

Sammie drew out a watch. 'Stroke o' seven, Belle.'

Belle walked on. The notice on the church board said, 'The Lord Shall be Unto Thee an Everlasting Light.'

Two queues, one long, one much shorter, approached the Ritz like a pincer movement. Belle slipped between them like an official.

'There y'are, Geordie.'

The commissionaire, in his maroon coat with gold braid, said, 'Ah, Belle, sure I wouldn't doubt you. D'you know what I said to myself, I said – I bet Belle'll be first in? I could have won money off of myself.'

Belle said, indicating the queues, 'There's your Christmas bonus, Geordie.'

'Don't be talking to me. We should be showing this picture at eight o'clock in the morning. There's people come in here the night from Dungannon, would you believe that, from Dungannon? You'd swear there was no war on.'

'I've a ticket, Geordie.' Belle pointed towards the interior.

'Course you have, Belle, but you'll have to stand around a wee while, like, when you come out again. Just for show like.'

'I'm only going to powder my nose.' They smiled at each other.

She climbed the shiny stairs, past the terracotta obelisks and their Egyptian electric lamps, to the bakelite-black door with the illuminated sign 'LADIES' overhead. Alone at the long mirror, she drew the lipstick from her sleeve and the twist of paper containing the powder from her waistband. At the bottom of her bag she had a small puff from an old powder-compact; Gloria had taught her to put the powder on before the lipstick – Belle used to do it the other way round, and then got her lips covered in dust and grains. She patted the powder into the planes of her cheeks and jaws. Wetting the lipstick in a fat slope across her lower lip, she pursed her mouth up and down to get an even spread.

In the 'Reserved' queue, several women wore suits, or their good blouses and skirts. Soldiers and officers had come out in uniforms, including three Americans, one with an umbrella, teased by his friends. 'Any fool can carry an umbrella on a wet day.' He brandished it. 'Only a wise man brings his on a fine day.' The people nearby laughed, in the general air of things. It was a warm evening, and cloudless, with no air-raid warnings. Belle walked slowly along them, as if expecting to see friends.

'Ach hallo, Belle, sure I knew you'd be here.'
   'Hallo, Lily. Isn't this all great?'
   'We'd never show it without you.' The usherette took Belle's ticket, tore it in half, returned one section to Belle and spiked the other half through a nail onto a long cord. 'Look at the length of my string tonight Belle did you ever see the like we're going to be jaded after all this and I've no flat shoes Belle my legs'll be sore over.'
   'I'm that excited, Lily.'
   'Belle I've two of your *Picturegoer*s so I have I was going to call up one evening if your mother's away out.'
   People called greetings from row to row in the dim lighting: 'Is that you!?' and, 'Are you here, too?'
   Belle held down the fat seat, and lowered herself. She shook out her hair and folded her headsquare as small as safety, checking the pattern to see which was inside out. Then she slipped the headsquare into the side-pocket of her handbag, a zipped isolation ward free from the leakages of powder or lipstick. Last, she drew the lace gloves off with the deliberateness of a countess, and laid them on the closed bag. She began to fold her cardigan: 'A third inwards along one side; then fold that sleeve lengthways; next, the same for the opposite side; and then the final third – one, two, three folds up from the bottom': Joan Crawford's maid's tip in *Modern Screen*'s 'How to Travel Well'.
   Assembled, she rested her shoulders and, by turning her head as if flexing her neck, checked the people on either side. When she knew them, or found them comfortable, they all compared

memories of films enjoyed, or their favourite cinema. Belle had seen Deanna Durbin here in *First Love*; and Maureen O'Hara and Charles Laughton in *The Hunchback of Notre Dame*; and Bette Davis in *Dark Victory*. Although, as she had said to somebody before the curtains parted the night she came here to Robert Donat in *Goodbye Mr Chips*, this was not to take away from the Royal in Arthur Square where she saw Tyrone Power and Alice Faye in *Rose of Washington Square*, or the Coliseum and Nelson Eddy and Jeannette MacDonald in *The Girl of the Golden West*. These conversations only took place when Belle felt certain they would never think her a spinning-girl.

The Pathe cock stood in his ring of laurels, then gurgled his loud, child's-farmyard cry. White letters on a shadow-powered background claimed, 'Prime Minister in the Middle East.' The newsreel's posh voice hammered out: 'A Lockheed Hudson touches down at a secret aerodrome. Bringing the mysterious Mr Bullfinch. No disguise, but a fine collection of hats and clothing, for the secret visit to the Middle East. General Auchinleck greets the Prime Minister at the start of his electric visit to the Egyptian war zone. Mr Churchill straightway goes up the line making personal contact with South African fighting men, as a very important part of his busy programme.'

The picture flickered and changed: a different triangle of the hot dark sky, a wider stripe of desert sands. Cheerily, the nasal jingoism drilled on. 'Travelling up to El Alamein, the Prime Minister made a point of chatting with a gun crew. Men of the Royal Artillery regiment, doing stout work with a four point five.' Soldiers in the cinema cheered the portly hero on the screen with his white solar topee and cigar, striding firm and fat along the lines of soldiers; the sun blared down in black-and-white, and tall, deferring, moustached men, in shorts and peaked caps, saluted with many elbows.

As the newsreel ended, a natural hubbub began, silenced when the curtains flowed open once more. The screen brightened; a large close-up tree appeared, with a rustic fence beneath it, and a great golden sky, and in riverboat lettering the word OVERTURE. Violins caught their breath and established their themes.

For the two minutes of music, Belle sat there, gazing at the molten clouds and the dark branches. That afternoon, she had whipped them up at work. 'Scarlett O'Hara is supposed to have a seventeen-and-a-half-inch waist, but Vivien Leigh, she had a twenty-two-inch waist, and all the girls, every last one of them, were laced into corsets nearly six inches tighter than their own waists so that their bosoms would not droop.'

Enid Mulcaghey, with the bloodshot eye, shouted, 'Jesus, I'll try that!' Belle laughed too.

'And the dressmakers made four thousand and ninety-eight costumes,' said Belle.

'*Simplicity* patterns, oh, aye,' hooted Janice.

Then Belle stunned them into wondering exchanges: 'There's one dress they made twenty-seven identical copies of, in case it was always getting damaged, 'cause there's a big fire that Vivien Leigh has to escape from.'

Blinking with excitement, Belle shifted and smoothed her skirt beneath her thighs. The cinema dropped into quiet; the hiss of the film began, then drums rolled, and bells clanged behind the screen. A white, leaf-dappled signboard materialised, swaying gently in a sunny breeze. *A Selznick International Picture*. Beneath the sign stood a mansion, white and colonnaded, with trees, shrubs, lawns; then the mystical name, *Metro-Goldwyn-Mayer*, and the statement, *Margaret Mitchell's Story of the Old South*. And from right to left across the screen, flying slowly like old, great, white swans, came the mighty words, GONE WITH THE WIND.

Exotic names rolled up. The music changed; a slaves' chorus hummed without lyrics, 'Look away. Look away. Look away, Dixieland'. Belle screwed her eyes to concentrate on the scrolled words; 'There was a land of Cavaliers and Cotton-fields called the Old South. Here in this pretty world, Gallantry took its last bow . . . last ever to be seen of Knights and their Ladies Fair, of Master and of Slave.' Belle's lips licked up the words, and soundlessly mouthed: 'Look for it only in books, for it is no more than a dream remembered. A Civilisation Gone With the Wind . . .'

The light from the screen technicolored her face with a soft wash of pastel; Belle, like a maiden, folded her hands in her lap. Above, the projectionist's dusty beam flowed out through those tiny windows, and, broad above her head, delivered all the faces, all the landscapes, to the screen.

Belle leaned forward, ready to devour. Vivien Leigh's face came into full view on the steps of the magnolia-framed verandah where she flounced at the Tarleton boys.

'Fiddle-de-dee! War. War. War,' said Scarlett mock-crossly. 'This war talk's spoiling all the fun at every party this spring. I get so bored I could scream.' She pouted, using pretended severity as a flirting tool. 'Besides. There isn't going to be any war.'

As Scarlett performed her shrill and whirling cavorting with the Tarleton boys, a dog snoozed upon the verandah behind her; a horse stood still with perfect patience; Belle MacKnight watched and watched. When she first wore this evening's clothes, she spoke as she always did, an inventory to her mirror: 'Jumper: home-knit, red wool: total cost five shillings; skirt, cut from a *Woman and Home* pattern, in a classic style: grey serge: cost fifteen shillings; shoes – twice heeled and twice soled, had been Aunt Sandra's, when new cost nineteen shillings and elevenpence; no stockings; wedges of fresh cardboard to give that brassiere the support it used to have; knickers, a little darned, I can't help that, can I?'

The Tarleton boy says, 'But you're giving us all your waltzes at the Ball tonight, aren't you?' and, desperate puppy, pleads for himself and his brother: thus Scarlett begins the first of the night's coquetries. All faces bask gaudy in the glow. A camera filming only Belle's face would have had to focus tightly to follow in her tiny expressions the flow of the film's tides – empathy, danger, coyness, defiance. Pout followed smile, followed grimace.

Outside the cinema, Belfast exhaled a little in the slow aftermath of a warm August day; in which several of the city's men died impersonally elsewhere, blown apart by Hitler's shells; in which voices at secret meetings declared once again, as they had done every Monday night since September 1939, that England's difficulty was Ireland's opportunity, and even if they keep hanging us as they did with Thomas Williams in July, God rest his soul and God Save Ireland, we will strike again, and again – and again.

Far away from the red clay of Georgia, far from the flying flags of nineteenth-century Atlanta, Edith MacKnight, the long-term and devastated widow, the sour-devout Presbyterian mother in her terraced house in Pretoria Street, darned her son's socks and her daughter's work apron, and eventually drew Mrs McKibbin-next-door's newspaper towards her to catch up on the news of the war and the local war effort, while there was still light in the last of the evening's rays.

Which also lit the long roofs of the linen mill where the Blackwoods, father Nesbit and son Gordon, watched as two of their friends, from shipbuilding families, slugged it out in a game of five-card draw poker for stakes higher than had ever before been played at night in the back offices of Rufus Street.

On another terraced street of tiny houses, in this city that some knighted proprietors still liked to call *Linenopolis*, a youngish man, six feet three inches tall, sat on his iron-framed bed in a silent house reading *Riders of the Purple Sage*. Soon he put the book down and fetched cold water from downstairs and a basin; he washed his face, arms and armpits, and shaved before bedtime. He bent and poked the corner of a wetted towel between each of his toes.

During the *Intermission* Belle did not move. As all others stretched and yawned, and walked up and down the aisles, or stood to flail their arms, she sat rubbing one palm into the other. Although flanked by homely-looking women, she spoke to nobody, nor did either woman seek to speak to her. The couple directly in front looked back at her, one, then the other: Belle stared a stiff enquiry at each in turn, and they returned quickly ahead.

When the lights dimmed for the second half, Belle dropped back into her trance. After the words 'Tomorrow is another day', as Scarlett stood against the light-dripping sky above Tara, and the music played people back to earth, Belle sat longest of all: her hands unclasped only when she stood for the cracked recording of 'God Save the King'. As she waited her turn to leave the aisle, she drew on the lavender lace gloves.

Belle saw Geordie in his Ritz commissionaire's braid looking all around him. She slipped towards the crowded doors; still she spoke to nobody. The clock in the foyer said twenty minutes to twelve. Shiny-eyed from the powerful colours of Georgia, people bumped into each other and smiled in the half-light melee outside the cinema. Darkness had fallen an hour and a half ago, but it had the gloaming of the far north in summer, and gave enough light to walk home by. One or two policemen warned about 'No cigarettes now,' and 'Remember now, no flashlamps please.' Belle slipped free, and within a moment reached the mouth of a drab, indifferent street that led her to home.

Lennie's bicycle blocked the hallway, ever making silent entry a problem. She stepped straight into the kitchen and felt the range: the fire had been let go out: behind her, Edith had laid the table for breakfast: a spread of newspapers covered all the crockery, and other pages soaked up a pool of water near the back door. Belle saluted the large framed-without-glass Union-Jacked photograph, *The King & Queen*, over the mantelpiece: 'Colonel Rhett Butler reporting!' From the meatsafe cupboard she took a jug of milk. 'Melanie Hamilton! What a surprise to run into you here.' She stood, sipping the milk from the jug. 'Frankly my dear, I don't *give* a damn!' and said aloud, 'Why did he say it that way, why didn't he say, "I don't give a *damn*"?' She returned the jug to its place. 'I don't *give* a damn?' Eyes accustomed to the dark, she grasped her gloves and bag and climbed the stairs to bed.

Edith had drawn the curtains over any possible chink of light from the MacKnight household. Belle had said on that first night of the blackout, 'Well, they'll never find this house so, them German bombers' – especially as Edith installed those new low-wattage bulbs in all the sockets. They gave Belle barely enough light to look in her mirror and smile, 'Fiddle-de-dee.'

She began to undress, kicking off her shoes: a toenail cut a neighbouring toe – she hacked off the hurtful shard of nail with her thumb. Elbowing downwards, she burrowed out of the jumper. She clambered her nightdress up over her head, resting it on her shoulders until she undid her straps and freed them, then let the nightdress slip down until it reached below the hem of her skirt; under cover of the nightdress she completed her undressing.

Belle stood on tiptoe to view the folds of her own nightdress from the waist downwards, and whirled a little to see whether any crinoline effect could be achieved. Her coat hung behind the door, and she reached for it, tiptoed downstairs, unbolted the back door and walked the few paces to the privy: her bare feet crinkled at the feel of the crushed cinders of the yard. Enough light remained in the sky for her to see the way; she knew it by touch, from winter nights, from rain, from frost and chill mornings. Sitting on the cold board of the privy, she heard not a murmur from the dark city. She could gauge from the sounds she made below her how soon the privy bucket would need emptying. Her toes wiggled in the packed cinder dust underfoot. Belle wagged her head and said half-aloud, 'Rhett Butler, if you think I'll marry you just to pay for that bonnet, well, I will no such thing!'

On cold feet, she re-entered her tiny bedroom, stood on the small frayed bedside mat. The narrow bed was plump with cushions. They lay together in mounds of pink and mauve, round and puffy, and a small square one, and a prosperous rectangular one; about ten cushions in all, and all gleamed with the satin sheen of a down-at-heel sultan's divan.

One had a red heart at the centre, one a ruched flower, one had little ribbons flying away, one had a pair of birds. All of these had been made by Belle herself, in long evenings when the picture-houses, holding films for more than a week, had no change of programme to offer her. She sewed the cushions from fabric begged, borrowed, stolen and bought at sales, crepe-de-Chine, brocade, grosgrain, shantung, velveteen, sateen, and stuffed with linen scraps smuggled home from Blackwoods. Edith grizzled repeatedly that Belle never finished them fully, left them with the backs tacked together in loose stitches: the stuffing frequently slipped out.

Once, Belle attempted to appliqué some of the photographs from *Modern Screen* on the front, but the paper of the magazine, even when she backed it with cardboard, proved too flimsy and slippery to be sewn into the fabric easily. She heaped her cushions onto the floor, drew down the sheet and climbed into bed.

At a quarter past six, Edith called. Belle, sticky-eyed, fetched a basin of hot water from the black kettle on the kitchen range.

'Mind you hurry with that basin.' Edith as usual had washed and dressed and opened up the house. 'Leonard'll be shaving.'

Upstairs, Belle flicked a small wood splinter from her foot, washed slowly, and mouthed to the mirror: 'Rhett Butler, you are the meanest, most aggravatin' – ' Still in her nightdress, but with shoes on, she took the basin back downstairs, emptied the water in the yard outside the back door and restored the basin to its place in the kitchen.

'Is Lennie out there?'

Edith replied, 'No, he's not fully down yet,' and exclaiming satisfiedly Belle hurried to the privy.

Back in her room, Belle dressed as modestly as she had undressed, putting on her underwear under the nightdress, and then the mended work-blouse and brown skirt. No powder, no lipstick, yet she patted her face as if she were a star at make-up, then tied a plaid scarf into a turban, the mill-woman's tribal head-dress. She knelt to get from under the bed the toilet water she had given Edith at Christmas but which Edith had returned, saying she found it 'unsuitable'. Puffballs of fluff floated on the floorboards past the inner bedlegs.

On the street below a noise erupted, heavy cracking at a door. From her window, Belle saw two policemen addressing a young man. In his shirtsleeves, he blinked in the morning sunlight: one officer grabbed him by the arm. Belle opened her window silently. The older of the two policemen told the young man, 'Go put on your coat.' He queried it, and the younger officer hit him with an open palm, as a schoolmaster might over-cuff an unruly boy.

'Go on now,' said Sergeant McCusker again, 'get your coat, it'll be easier.'

Downstairs, Belle asked, 'Who's after doing what?'

'They shouldn't be living on this street anyways, they should be with their own side.' Edith patrolled the lace curtains. 'Leonard, what's that about?'

His hair-oil gleaming, Lennie stamped down the stairs. 'He came back last night.'

'Did you tell on him?' asked Belle.

'Course I did.'

'Their sort,' said Edith. 'Sure they have to hang them to keep them right.' She returned from the window to slice bread.

'Hey, what about Clark Gable, Belle?' asked Lennie, crumbs flying from his mouth.

'What about him?' asked Belle.

'I heard you're in love with Clark Gable?'

Edith cut in, 'No joke, Leonard, that's five pictures in a fortnight she's went to.'

Belle stood, making her sandwiches.

'Oh, aye. Clark Gable.' Lennie laughed.

'Such talk.' Edith poked his arm with the handle of the breadknife.

'A lot o' people goes to the pictures.' Belle said it neither defiantly nor apologetically.

Lennie said, 'Oh, aye, they do. If they have the money.'

Edith said, 'Aye, people with nothin' in their heads. And no fear or love o' the Lord. A lot o' them pictures is blasphemous.'

Lennie drank more tea. 'Clark Gable. He's the boy. Belle, get's the egg, will you?'

Belle moved patiently from her sandwich-making and fetched Lennie's egg from the pan.

'Proteen. That's the word. Proteen.' Lennie said it again. 'Pro. Teen.'

Belle asked him, 'Is this a quiz? For money?'

'In the paper. Soldiers' food. Pro-teen. Energy, they says.'

Edith sliced him some more bread. 'This war talk. Dead meat. That's what youse'd all get. And be.'

'No, Mam, I'd be gettin' chicken. I'd be in the lap of luxury. And a bit of travel. An' life.'

'An' a bit of death. What are you saying, Leonard MacKnight? Anyone'd think you were still tryin' to enlist.'

'My chest's not that bad, Mam. And there was lots glad to get outa Blackwoods an' put on a uniform.'

'And they'll be buried in it. You watch. It'll be the Somme all over again.'

'Ach, it won't, Mam.'

Belle said, 'You're reserved anyway, you can't go.'

'They'll be letting reserved jobs go soon, wait 'til you'll see. Anyway, Mam, sure if I went, our film star here could come an' wave me off with a white handkerchief.' Lennie rose. 'Isn't that right, Film Star?'

'Let me alone, you.'

Leonard found his jacket; Edith stood before him, straightened the lapels.

Now Belle sat at breakfast; Edith cleared Lennie's dishes.

'What time did you get in last night, Belle?'

'Late.'

'I know it was late, but what time?'

'Late.'

'And there a blackout and God knows what else. Belle, are you ever going to get sense? When I was your age I was settled and married, not going to the pictures every chance I got.'

'There wasn't any pictures then, Mam.' Belle stared at the wall and licked jam from a finger.

'No, aye, but there was dances, I could have frittered away easily. Look at you. You've not a sign of marriage on you.'

'No.' Belle stared without intent at the curtains.

'I was talking to Reverend MacCreagh about you, and he was saying . . .'

'Would you leave me finish my breakfast?' Belle retouched her turban.

'He was saying . . .' Edith was not to be interrupted; therefore Belle sucked a tooth, took her mug of tea and slice of bread and climbed the stairs again.

She sat on the edge of her bed and surveyed: the cushions on the floor; her cinema magazines, photographs, cigarette cards of the stars; her collection of bladdered perfume bottles that her mother always wished to throw out. Belle defended them as if they were children, saying she liked their gold lacework and their red colours and their little brass nozzles.

2

The Blackwoods made a point of hiring ex-servicemen to police the mill doors. Most had suffered: those wounded in the Great War bore the *cachet* of having been among the few Ulstermen to return from the Somme and Ypres. Older ones carried a different venerability – from the Boer War, and even the Crimea. These men satisfied practically, as well as sentimentally: Rufus Street, with many disenchanted employees, had theft, arson, fights – among both sexes; practical jokes taken too far; love affairs gone jealous; a suicide two years ago. Although women had always formed the majority, and especially now in wartime, all security staff remained male; despite repeated requests from the union representatives who had neither power nor influence, 'problems' – of either sex – were addressed by these ex-servicemen.

'There y'are, Belle, did you enjoy last night?'

'God, Billy, news travels fast!' Belle smiled. 'You were talking to Geordie Craig?'

'Aye, he dropped in a pair of tickets on the way home. What about it anyway, Belle, should me and the wife go?'

'Don't miss it, Billy. It's great.'

In 1918, Nesbit Blackwood's father said, 'Another war soon'; he insisted that they look for wider markets and the Blackwood blue label grew famous. In Canada, Australia, the United States, their luxury damask sold well, with designs of shamrocks, round towers, Celtic crosses for the Irish-American expatriates and romantics. Nesbit's friends teased him: 'All this Catholic and Republican stuff?'

He laughed back, 'The Blackwoods were always as interested in the half-crown as the Crown.' To heighten the joke he would point to their most successful line ever: *The Half-Crown Tablecloth – in every Ulster home.* 'Even Catholics,' he said, 'can afford to fork out half a crown for a tablecloth.'

In eighty years, Blackwoods Linen Mills had changed little: few mechanical innovations ever reached Rufus Street. The family defended this to their friends and competitors, the Boyds, the Cruisemans, the Andersons, as an investment in the population, using workforce as plant. Nesbit, who smiled incessantly but hired notably vicious overseers, produced two steadfast defences.

'We're not old-fashioned. We're not reactionary. Old standards – that's what people want. We have stronger cloth,' he beamed. 'And,' he argued, 'Belfast depends on the likes of us. Look at the families we keep in work. Mechanisation's bad for workforces. Very bad.'

Moments before seven o'clock on the morning of Tuesday, 18 August, Belle tied on the hessian apron all the women wore, and joined the hundreds drifting in chatter towards the Long Room and its ranks and rows of machines. Her 'pair', Gloria, had not yet arrived. From the women's waists, their 'pickers' hung on strings, powerful long steel points, employed to free at great speed the rove of flaxweave if snagged in the big rollers. Six months ago, Gloria had lost a fingernail when her pickers got caught in a roller and dragged her forward.

Belle stood on her own bench, calling, waving, receiving greetings.

'Belle! Belle! Did you go?'

'Belle, Vivien Leigh's clothes?!'

'Belle! Leslie Howard?!'

'What about ye, Belle?'

'Janice, it was great. I thought about ye, the clothes. Get Malcolm to take you.'

Settling to the day's work usually took up to twenty minutes, to the fury of the overseers. The room cracked and whirred into action. All around Belle, the women, seeming to keep their heads down, waited until the rhythm of their work seemed settled, at which point the male overseers, at about twenty past seven, marched off to breakfast, led by 'Black' Bingham, their hard chief.

Gloria, who had crept along the floor on hands and knees to avoid her lateness being observed, scrambled up beside Belle.

'Jesus, Belle, I can't get up these mornings, so I can't.'

A small boy ran towards Belle, a bobbin in either hand. She flung out a hand to catch him.

'Come here to me, Tommy Crawford, are you going to marry me or aren't you?' He squealed and wriggled away, ran off.

'Listen, Belle, did you hear about Jenny MacIlwain?'

'No. What about her?'

'Well, I dunno, there's some big old thing going on, I only heard it last night, Andy was telling me his Mam heard it from Nettie Taylor's husband.'

'What happened?'

'Well, she's seeing some fella here, and he's married like, I think 'tis that big buck, Dougherty. And they were caught in here the other night by ould Blackwood himself.'

'Ooh, God!' Belle said. 'I never liked that fella Dougherty.'

'His wife is always expecting,' said Gloria, who had a sage air.

A whistle blew. Janice, the doffing-mistress, stood on her table to look out the high window down the corridor. When all seemed clear, she turned around and sang out, 'C'mon, Belle.'

The women began to stop work. Machines moaned to a halt. A last remaining spinning-master on his way out of the room called, 'Don't youse blame me if youse all get the sack!'

'Away to hell!' they told him.

Belle ran to the top of the rows of machines, and clambered to the high chair from which Janice surveyed the room: she acknowledged the calls with smiles and pretty-pretty mock curtseys. The women stepped into the aisles, leaned against the high machines and settled to listen.

Belle began. 'Picture of the week. *Gone with the Wind*, starring Vivien Leigh. And Clark Gable as a visitor from Charleston, Rhett Butler.'

'Wooo-ooh!' they chorused.

'And Leslie Howard and Olivia de Havilland. In technicolor. A David O. Selznick production. Directed by Victor Fleming.' She clapped her hands. 'Listen. *Picture Show*, see them, they did a whole pull-out on the picture when it came out first, and they said Victor Fleming was the handsomest man in Hollywood, that he had more than a bit of the Red Indian in him, and all the women were mad about him.'

Gloria shouted, 'Why wasn't he in the picture, so?' Belle flapped a hand at her, and continued merrily, 'Do you know what? There's somebody in it called "Butterfly MacQueen",' and she sat back, assured of their joy.

'That's it, Annie,' they called in their laughter to Annie MacQueen, who had just heard her husband in Belgium was hurt in the chest, but was all right. 'You're "Butterfly" now!' and Annie waved her arms like wings, Annie who spoke little. One of the weavers said something about her to someone else one day, and it got back to Annie, something about her brother being 'the father of his own nephew'. Annie attacked, and was suspended without pay for two months: she nearly starved: the girl whose cheekbone she broke never came back to work, nor near the mill again.

Belle tightened the strands of her apron. 'There's a Hamilton in it too,' she teased.

'Whooo-hoooo! Jen! Jen!' they looked around and chanted. 'What's she called, Belle, what's she called?'

Belle timed it like a comedian. 'She's called – Aunt Pittypat Hamilton.'

With her audience now safely in delight, Belle settled down – actressy, all fingers, curls and flutters, and began. 'There's this big house, you see, and 'tis called Tara, 'tis a real mansion like, and 'tis in the middle of real rich land, there's trees an' cattle and ploughed fields, 'tis like a chocolate box. Or a picture off of a calendar, and there's hundreds an' hundreds of slaves in the cotton-fields.'

A woman called out, 'Slaves! Jesus! Just like we'rselves!'

Everybody laughed. Belle knew their timing and her own, and she waited.

'And this plantation is owned by a man called O'Hara.'

Another interruption brought louder laughter: 'Oh, a Catholic. A Papist! A real Taig!' Ann Hamill, married at twenty-two, lost her first husband on the Somme in 1916; remarried a man ten years younger and now, at forty-eight, was awaiting news from France or anywhere, she did not know where he was, no letter for nine weeks.

Belle smiled again. It usually took some minutes before the story won them over into silence. 'And he has a wife and three daughters and one of 'em is called – Scarlett O'Hara. An' that's Vivien Leigh. The first thing you see is Vivien, that's Scarlett, and she's sitting on the steps of Tara with her bonnet and her big skirt.'

Belle, with a vivacious wave downwards, gestured to show how Scarlett was dressed. 'Her dress has about two hundred ribbons and flounces on, and she has a bonnet on the back of her head –'

A shouted question: 'What colour is her clothes, Belle?'

Alice MacKechnie had always worked, always would, just as well, because now she had to; no husband, killed at Dunkirk, and four sons, the oldest sixteen; her squint – in both eyes – brought mockery to her children in school, and her second son, tougher than the others, had already been spoken to by the police.

'Alice, 'tis – cream like, sort of creamy pink. The O'Haras is very rich. And Vivien Leigh, she has big green eyes, and dark hair, and she's a terrible flirt, so she is, but she really wants to marry Ashley Wilkes, her neighbour. Only he's going to marry Melanie Hamilton, she's Olivia de Havilland, and she's beautiful. Sleek hair on her. But Scarlett hates her.'

Belle put her hands on her hips and her head on one side, and pouted the quotation, 'Melanie Hamilton is a pale-faced, mealy-mouthed ninny, and I hate her!'

They laughed.

'Now.' Again, she waited for them. 'There's two houses involved at the beginning. There's Tara where the O'Haras live, and there's Twelve Oaks where the Wilkeses live, and there's two young fellas, they're chatting to Scarlett trying to get a dance with her that night over at Twelve Oaks. Y'see. 'Cause Scarlett' – Belle wagged a knowing finger – 'she's going to be at the ball and the barbecue.'

'Whassa a barbecue when 'tis at home?'

The other women rushed to hush the squeaky questioner, Sibby Kemp from Cupar Street, who had had to marry, and was seven months pregnant when she did, and then her husband got his foot caught beneath his own dray and could no longer work.

'A big party,' said Belle, 'where they all eat out in the open air and they dance and they take drink. So anyway, they're asking Scarlett will she dance with them, and she says to them that she might and then she might not, 'cause it looks like she's all taken up for the evening especially if Ashley Wilkes is going to be there.

And they tell her that it doesn't matter a rap to them 'cause they heard that Ashley Wilkes isn't going to be dancing with anyone except his cousin Melanie Hamilton, and of course Scarlett flounces off and she's only livid on account of fancying Ashley Wilkes, and she scoots away from your two lads.'

'She can send 'em over to us,' called Janie Mitchison, who had been a beauty, they said. She had six children and one dead, and she could work faster than any woman in the room and her own husband did not speak to her for weeks at a time.

'Anyway. The next thing is, Scarlett hears a voice calling her and 'tis her servant like, who's as black as the cinders in our back yard, and as fat as Maggie Henderson into the bargain, and she's at the top window and she's yelling at Scarlett to come away on in and put on her cardigan or something 'cause she'll catch her death of cold, and Scarlett says straight out she will not, not for no one, and away she goes, and who's coming towards her on a big white horse, galloping and galloping, only her own father, Patrick O'Hara.'

The morning sun over Belfast lit the high windows in Blackwoods, and sunbeams with dancing dust projected into the long, dim room. These rays, these industrial Jacob's Ladders, caught the whiteness of Belle's overall beneath the coarse hessian apron, and touched the lilac plaid in her knot-tied headscarf. As she perched on the high chair, in a cobbler's squat, one knee under her, her arms flung out to emphasise a point, or to illuminate a gesture made by Scarlett O'Hara, she glowed like a favourite. Beneath her, and down along the room, the women stood, or leaned, hands on hips, or arms folded, their faces following her eyes and eyebrows, their mouths pursing with her words, as Belle's own lips had mouthed with the words when she watched them on the screen.

An inspection of the room, a slow walk down the rows and rows of women, reveals coarse faces, roughened skin and tongues, women who had worked too long and women still young, but whose freshness had been assaulted by too much harsh labour too soon and too desperately. They gazed at Belle enthralled, agreeing to be magicked by her storytelling, following their headscarved pied piper and her fluttering hands ever deeper into the sweet long-ago of the old American South.

=

34

Far down, at the bottom right-hand corner, a door had been pushed gently ajar, by a listener standing there. He wore a bleach-white apron, and silvery armbands puckered the sleeves of his blue shirt. Now he took a pace forward into her full view, and he and Belle registered each other's gaze. After a short listen he stepped backwards through the doorway and vanished as swiftly and silently as he had appeared.

Belle craned a little to see him go. She paused, recovered, then gathering force, stood on the table and called out to the room, and across her face danced all the scenes, the dialogue, the players and the little and great amazements of *Gone with the Wind*.

Enid Mulcaghey – 'not able to say two words without cursing' – swore all the time. 'The Three Annes', as they were called, Anne Stevenson, Anne Acheson and Anne Byers (who always got everything wrong), went everywhere together; when one took a toilet break all three did; their periods began within a day of each other; Anne Byers's husband was a first cousin of Anne Acheson's; Anne Stevenson used to go out with Anne Byers's brother until she married George Stevenson who was now driving a lorry in Kent in the RAF. Edith Millar, they said, had airs; she lived near Belle, round the corner in Capetown Street, they often walked home together, or bumped into each other in the morning. She confided in Belle once that her husband's brother was interested in her, and Belle, not knowing what to say, told Janice, and Janice, so unlike her for once, said it back to Edith Millar who was cool with Belle for a while but now they were friendly once more, even though Edith did not confide in Belle again. 'If only they'd put a bit of whitewash on this room,' Edith often said to Belle.

This morning they all stared with smiling approval as Belle stood, rearing her head like a centaur. 'And he gets off the horse, the Da does, and he calls her "Katy Scarlett O'Hara" – that's exactly how he says it – "Katy Scarlett O'Hara" and she makes up to him like a little girl, and of course I forgot to say she's wearing a little red belt only that size.' Belle pinched her hands in a small marvelling circle.

'And they start talking about Ashley Wilkes, and of course her father sees what's eating at Scarlett, and he gets out of her that she is dead keen on Ashley Wilkes, and he tells her, "Katy Scarlett

O'Hara", he tells her that Ashley Wilkes – he has it "on good authority from Melanie Hamilton's own father", that Ashley Wilkes is going to marry Melanie Hamilton, "them Wilkeses always marry their cousins." And he says to Scarlett that anyway he'd be the wrong man for Scarlett and it didn't matter who Scarlett married as long as it was a Southerner.'

A jeer rose, and Enid Mulcaghey shouted, 'I bet he never said that. Sure who'd marry a fucking southerner?'

Janice called out a reprimand, 'Enid!' and Belle said, 'No, they meant an American Southerner, from the deep South like, not from down south here.'

Enid shouted back, 'But you said them fuckers were Irish?'

'Oh, aye,' Belle reassured her, 'but they're Irish-American. Only they call theirselves Irish, and as a matter of fact the next thing her father says to Scarlett is that the thing she'll always have to remember when she's marrying anyone is the land, is that as long as you're Irish anywhere, 'tis the land is the thing to watch out for.'

Enid was about to shout again when the double doors at the top of the room opened behind Belle.

'Good morning, Mrs Gillespie. More pictures, I see?'

Belle gasped, 'Oh, God,' and began to slide down off the table, one hand over her mouth, the other hand fixing her headscarf.

'Good morning, sir,' said Janice, a little confused.

'And what is it this morning, Mrs Gillespie?' Nesbit beamed.

'Ould Blackwood's smile,' said Sibby Kemp, 'there's never anything behind it except his teeth.'

'*Gone with the Wind*, sir.'

'Oh is it now?' He called after Belle who had legged it down the aisle, hoping to lose herself in the reassembling women. 'Is it any good?'

Belle reached her machine and Gloria hissed, 'He wants you to answer him.'

Belle turned and saw Nesbit Blackwood smiling, surrounded by a team of men, some in suits, some in white coats.

'Is it any good?' he called again.

Belle stood, flustered, pawing her sleeves. 'Oh 'tis, sir, 'tis great.'

'Would my wife like it?'

'Oh, aye, she would, sir, the clothes is lovely.'

Belle sat down and blushed; Nesbit Blackwood waved a smiling hand and the room went back to work. He turned to Janice.

'Mrs Gillespie, you remember my son, Gordon?'

'Oh, aye, sir, I do.'

'On leave, Mrs Gillespie, and his mother, I have to say, is delighted.'

Janice put out a hand. 'Hallo again, Mr Blackwood. Sure my own brother was in the Fusiliers.'

Gordon Blackwood shook her hand. 'How did you know my regiment?' he asked, not displeased.

'The doffing-mistress knows everything,' said his father. 'It's her business to, isn't that right, Mrs Gillespie?'

'Well, sure we all have to keep an eye on things, sir, don't we?'

The group began to walk down between the banks of machines, glancing to right and left. In the corners of the room farthest away from them, abusive whispers floated, heard only by the overseers tagging behind. 'Away to hell, Blackwood, you wee shite.'

Enid Mulcaghey always gave cause for alarm to the women nearest her, when she swore and not inaudibly, 'Oul' arsehole Blackwood and his scrawny wife.'

This morning Enid said, louder than usual, 'I bet his oul' arse smiles, too.'

Nesbit perked a head but seemed not sure of what he heard; Gordon turned as if he had registered something too. Bingham, his ear tuned to all the Rufus Street nuances, walked across to Enid's place and said, 'Shut yer beak.'

Enid replied, 'If any of youse were any kind of fucking men, youse'd be off fighting Hitler, so youse would.'

Several other Blackwoods overseers now copied Bingham's famous Chinese burn. He grabbed Enid's bare forearm, and swift as a snake, made her yelp, in a screwtwist of her flesh. Enid, built like a vat, had tears in her eyes and could not cool the arm quickly enough to shout after him. When the party reached the end of the room and stood at the door where the white-aproned, silver-armed stranger had gazed at Belle, Nesbit Blackwood looked back and smiled to Janice, 'Enough pictures for today, Mrs Gillespie, all right, I s'pose?'

Janice replied, 'All right, sir.' The doors closed behind them, swallowing Bingham's big trousers last of all.

After a moment or two, Alma Robinson, who had a brass voice, roared above the whirr-whirr of the bobbins, 'We should get holda that cub, someone. Follow Nettie. Tell us again, Enid.'

All cheered at the reference: Enid told the tale. Nesbit Blackwood's brother, Desmond, had married beneath him, Nettie Crawford, a weaver. Nettie came back to the mill the day after the honeymoon last May twelve months, drove up in Nesbit's car, and Billy Crawford, her own brother, Blackwood's chauffeur, driving her. In the open air, hundreds of the girls, eating their piece and having their smoke, jeered.

'We shouted at her, "Look at you, Lady Muck!" and – "Here's your five Woodbines, gimme back me knickers." And Nettie, she looked down her nose at us, and she only withering us. "If I wasn't a lady," she says, "I'd come down there and beat the shite outa the lot a' yez."'

When the laughing ended, and some rhythms of work returned, Belle concentrated hard for several minutes. Then, as they crossed from one side to the other of the machine, she asked while knitting her brows at her work, 'Who was that fella, Gloria?'

'Blackwood's young lad. Gordon. Same as the rest of 'em. Wee pig.'

Belle said, 'No, not him. The other fella.'

'What other fella?' Gloria looked at Belle – who stopped in mid-sentence and inspected the welt on her hand.

'My hands is getting like boards, Gloria. Look at yours, yours is better. The fella at the door at the back, with the blue shirt and the spotless apron.'

Gloria, deflected by Belle's nonchalance, said, 'I never seen him. What was he like?'

Belle said, 'About thirty. Bit more maybe. Big lad. He had lovely silver armbands on him.'

Gloria wondered, 'Armbands? I don't know. He must be a new lapper or something? Ask Dodie, she knows all them lappers.'

The room worked on through the morning.

'Come here to me you, Peter MacDade, that's going to hurt me one day soon, so it is,' Belle called to the mechanic as he passed her machine.

'What's up with ya, Belle?' He slid across to put an arm around Belle's waist. 'Fair exchange no robbery, you give me a squeeze and I'll fix your oul' machine.'

'See you? You're off your brains so you are.' Belle pushed him away.

'How'ya, Gloria,' he winked.

'I'll tell your wife on you, so I will,' said Gloria.

The klaxon hailed the morning's end. In the wait for the lavatories, a big, red-haired girl asked Belle, 'How d'you get your hair up like that?'

Belle said, 'I seen it on Loretta Young. She wore it up at the front here, and here' – Belle patted her own forehead – 'in a great picture, *The Lady from Cheyenne.* You part it here with water' – she indicated – 'and then you have to use about five hairclips, and you sort of spin it up 'til you can catch it all.' Belle held her piece between her knees, trying not to crush the sandwiches, as she raised her hands tracing the loops on her hair. 'It takes a while. I'll show you if you like.'

The girl watched, her arms folded. 'A real job, so it is?' she enquired.

'You get used to it,' replied Belle.

They followed the throng of women down the wide passageway to a great, dim room.

'Here y'are, Belle. Over here, Belle!' Anne Acheson called. Children sat with women, all eating bread brought from home and wrapped in newspaper.

Presently, men sloped in; some wore their caps; they leaned against the walls, talking, pulling at the packets to see what food their wives, mothers or sisters had packed. The women squatted on the floor, or distributed themselves about such furniture as could be made comfortable; one large lapping-table, discarded because of a shredded plank in the very centre, took several girls sitting around its perimeter, their legs swinging. Crumbs and gibes flew; newspaper wrappings were crushed and pelted at walls or each other, and then, in a hazy unison, with match-flames as brief and blue as kingfishers, they lit up, and as with one sigh exhaled the first cigarette drag. The buzz of their talk changed its key, into a more relaxed drone, still punctuated by the occasional burst of laughter or a jeer filled with the inflections of disbelief – 'Go you on out of that, I don't believe you!'

At last someone enquired, 'Are yeh all right there yet, Belle?' and their star, who had been leaning with Janice against a lopsided cupboard, straightened herself, and said, 'Where d'ye want it?' at which a man shouted, 'Anywhere you have it, Belle,' to more jeers. With a prance, Belle came to the old table, climbed gingerly towards the gashed centre and began.

'Where were we?'

'Tara!' shouted one woman.

'Her oul' fella,' shouted another.

'Oh, aye.' To compose herself, Belle drew her hands together like a nun and then flung them apart.

The mill-women slowly rearranged their positions to get the best view possible, an informal amphitheatre around her legs, and she blazed high above them, sometimes an arm akimbo, sometimes her face thrust forward, sometimes both hands applied coquettishly to the back of her headscarf. She had a repertoire of gestures; she whipped her apron to and fro like a can-can dancer; she sashayed a step forward, then back to make a point, she stamped a foot, clapped a hand, made them start.

'And her father says to Scarlett, "You listen here to me, Katy Scarlett O'Hara, so you do, you're not to be wanting that fellow Ashley to marry you when you could have any fella you want." And he takes Scarlett by the arm, and honest to God you'd swear it was Moses showing the Israelites the Promised Land, he takes her up to the top of a hill, and he shows her all the land around Tara.'

A wide entrance gaped into the room, wide enough to take the large trolleys that voyaged through the mill. The sun's beams lit the floor just in front of this opening, making it difficult to identify the person who had just entered. He stepped softly in, and stood in the doorway, framed and large. The sunrays' reflection on his white apron illuminated him like a warrior arrived at court: his shadow thrust itself forward along the brown planking. Only Belle saw him; her height on the table gave her a different trajectory of vision against the light. She looked at him and, as he folded his arms, she lost her concentration.

Belle broke off. 'To be continued in our next,' she chirped.

How they chorused. 'Aw, Belle, Belle! Belle, c'mon.'

'Greedy pigs,' she wagged at them. 'Anyway this picture's the best value ever – 'tis going to take weeks to tell.'

3

'Powse,' said Gene Comerford to Gordon Blackwood in the Lapping Room. 'They call it "powse", the dust, off the cloth. Some call it "pouce".'

'Whewp!' said Gordon, fisting his nostrils. 'Ngngngngnging! My nose is full of it.'

He opened a door, sending a swirl through the white dusty atmosphere. Ten men in shirtsleeves with armbands and aprons worked at long mahogany tables. The high room, with its long sunny windows, had the wood-panelled feel of a medieval work-shop, and the camaraderie of a guild. On each side-table rested the lapping-sticks, long, thick, ebony sticks tapering to a brass-clad point. But lapping had begun to fade: in the linen industry of the past, the lapping-sticks had been sceptres to the elite princes, who measured and folded linen crisp as ice, 'the princess of cloth'. The last war, and this one, obliged them to come down in the world and roll the coarser cloth for uniforms.

Ernest MacCloskey said to Gordon, 'Some days it gets very thick. It isn't bad when you can open the windows this time of the year.'

'That's why we have them spittoons,' Lennie MacKnight said, pointing at the brass cuspidors gleaming on the floor: one or two had milky spit in them.

He heaved a bale of khaki twill, and began to mark off measurements.

'Tour of duty?' Lennie asked Gordon.

'Yes. Sort of. My father says I shouldn't waste all my home leave playing golf.'

Lennie asked, 'Interestin'?'

'Which, the tour of duty or the golf?' Everybody duly chuckled, and then Gordon took Lennie's point seriously. 'Yes. Very. I like this part particularly. That's why I asked to come in here.'

'Sure we coulda had it made a reserved occupation for you too,' Ernest MacCloskey said. 'There's aprons hanging up there.'

Gordon looked and said, 'No, I like soldiering. Oh, that's a good idea.' He took off his blazer, crossed to the apron cupboard, and asked, 'Any specially?'

Ernest said, 'That one with the green birds stitched on it, that's John Barrow's, he's away sick, put that one on.'

'Bring you luck, he's the best we have,' John Macintosh coughed.

Lennie agreed, 'Oh, aye, John Barrow, he's a genius, so he is.'

'I remember you as a wee fella,' John Macintosh said in his heavy wheezing. 'Feathery wee get you were, tearin' at everythin',' and Gordon smiled.

'You're like your father when you smile,' said Ernest, 'but you've a great look of your mother.'

Gordon drew on the apron. 'Goodness, that's lovely cloth.' He pinched it, rubbed it between thumb and forefinger. 'Now, who is everybody?'

Ernest MacCloskey said, 'You know Macko, old Macintosh here, he's as old as the hills by now. That's Archie, the fellow with the quiff, Archie Heavey. That's Montana Campbell over there. That's Lennie . . .'

Gene Comerford, holding out a hand which Gordon took, said, 'I'm new here. Gene.'

'Nice armbands,' said Gordon, 'not real silver, are they?'

'Tin,' said Archie. 'He's from down south. The tinkers made 'em for him.'

Gene, smiling, said, 'Strange people working in this place.'

Archie replied, 'If they were only working itself.' All laughed good-naturedly.

'That's true enough,' said Gordon, 'when I came through one of the spinning-rooms over there, they were telling the story of *Gone with the Wind*.'

'Mind out there,' Archie cut in, and pointed to Lennie, 'that's his sister, Belle, she's the picture-teller.'

'Is that so?' asked Gordon, turning to Lennie, who, pleased, replied, 'That's true, that's our Belle.'

'She's very good at it, isn't she?' Gordon remarked interrogatively.

'Why wouldn't she be? She's always away in a daydream. Clark Gable. James Stewart.' Lennie made a gesture with his eyebrows indicating hopelessness.

'So that's your sister, is it?' Gordon said again.

'Aye, so.'

Montana interrupted. 'She has a problem with her stomach, so she has.'

Gordon asked politely, 'Oh? What?'

Montana said, 'She won't let anyone lie on it.'

As everyone laughed, Lennie picked up a lapper's stick and advanced mock-threateningly on Montana.

'Lads, back now to your tables or this man'll be cutting our wage,' said Ernest. 'Here.' He handed Gordon one end of a roll. 'No, thumb here, hand flat over here.'

Gene, who joined in the measuring, asked Gordon, 'I suppose you're an officer?'

'Oh, indeed. I have two weeks' leave. What about yourself?'

'No, I'm staying put.'

Lennie said, 'Good job there's no conscription.'

'I wouldn't be here if there was conscription,' said Gene.

Lennie ignored him. 'Anyways, your sort doesn't fight proper. Youse don't even have uniforms.'

Gordon asked, puzzled, 'His sort?'; then, as the gist of the taunt dawned, he smiled, 'Oh, yes, of course.'

Gene, pleasantly refusing to get riled, said to Gordon, 'He knows all about uniforms. He's a reserve policeman. Guards you at night, in your bed.'

To which Gordon replied, amid general laughter, 'Oh, I'd better tell him where I'll be.'

Lennie said to Gene, 'You're dodging the column, so you are. Your kind is cowards. Always were. Youse can only shoot from behind ditches.'

Gordon asked Lennie, not unkindly, 'Why aren't you overseas?'

Archie cut in, practised at heading off trouble, 'My friend Sammy, he can't go neither.'

Gordon asked, 'Why not?'

'His eyes.'

'What's wrong with his eyes?'

'Well . . .' Archie had taken Gordon captive, and the others smiled in anticipation. 'He's two black eyes on him.'

Gordon asked, 'What happened?'

Archie put down his roll of linen. 'I'll tell you if you want to know. When he got the first one, I says to him, "Heh, Sammy, what happened tae you?" An' he says to me, "Archie, wasn't I in the chapel Sunday, and there was a woman kneelin' in front of me. A big strong woman, she was. An' her skirt was all caught up in the Glens of Antrim, you know like."' Archie stopped and explained, 'That's the folds of her backside,' he said, explanatorily curving a gesture.

Ernest interposed in vain, 'Now, Archibald. No obscenity, if you please?'

Archie continued, encouraged by Gordon's smiling look. 'An' this poor woman, she looked awful uncomfortable, and Sammy says to me, "So I reaches out an' I tugs the skirt back out – out to make her comfortable like, and you know, make her skirt even –"' Archie demonstrated elaborately, draping a length of linen over his own buttocks: he had all his audience with him. 'Says Sammy, "And she turns back and fetches me a black eye wi' her fist." I laughs, so I does, out loud into his face and eyes, but Sammy says to me, "Archie, this is no laughin' matter."'

Gene smiled to Gordon, 'He never told you this is a long story.'

'Will it be over by the end of the war?' asked Gordon, surveying these men who smiled and who would never answer back.

Archie continued, gaining speed. 'So the next week, in comes Sammy again, and this time the other eye is black, and I says to him, "'Name o' God, Sammy, what did you do tae yersel' this time?" and I laughs. An' he says to me, "Archie, this is no laughin' matter," and he says, "Archie, wasn't I in the church again a' Sunday, and there was the same woman and she had the same problem, you know, th'oul' skirt, and the man beside me, he done the same neighbourly thing as I done, he reaches out and pulls out the folds o' the skirt from her arse. Only an' I knowin' full well what was goin' tae happen to him, I reaches out and tucks the skirt back in, pushes it right in, like, and she turns round and sees 'tis me and hits me another dig, and that's how I got the second black eye."'

All roared with laughter: Ernest MacCloskey finalised.

'Come on now, lads. Mm? Mmmm? Have a bit o' decency about youse. Mmmm? Come on, the Lord can hear youse. "Neither filthiness nor foolish talking, nor jesting, which are not convenient." Do youse not know your Ephesians? Come on now. Mmmm?'

Ernest cleared his throat and began to sing:

> 'On a hill far away
> Stood an old rugged cross,
> The emblem of suffering and shame.'

The lappers joined in:

> 'And I love that old cross
> Where the dearest and best
> For a world of lost sinners was slain.
> So I'll cherish the old rugged cross,
> Till my trophies at last I lay down;
> I will cling to the old rugged cross,
> And exchange it some day for a crown.'

Gordon asked Gene, 'Where did a Roman Catholic like you learn to sing good a Protestant hymn?'

Gene grinned, 'Ach, sure I fell into bad company.'

Montana of the sideburns contributed, 'Aye, an' he's still in it.'

Gene reached up his hands and hiked his apron loose at the neckband: his blue shirt had two maps of black sweat at the armpits: next, he swept dust from the ginger hairs on the backs of his hands and continued, 'I worked down in Tyrone for a long time.'

Gordon piped, 'Not at Judy Cruiseman's?'

'D'you know her, so?'

'Oh, indeed. She's coming to our house tonight.'

Gene said, 'They were good employers.' He leaned back to get something from a shelf behind him, and turned the action into a means of leaving the table.

Archie indicated Gene's back, and said in a low voice to Gordon, 'He's keen on the union – you know, workers' rights and that.'

Gordon looked at Gene's back. 'Seems a nice chap, though.'

Ernest leaned over. 'Well liked. Mmmm? Well liked already.

Made a good early impression. Always important. Mmmm? And he's Godfearing. Mm? He is. Godfearing.'

Ten years earlier, in 1932, Gene Comerford was twenty-four. That year, they had an exceptionally warm June in County Tyrone. The bees made enough honey to last two years; tables and chairs could stay out all night – only the tablecloths and cushions were taken in, to avoid the heavy dew; nobody could recall a heavier crop of redcurrants on the four old bushes in the kitchen garden.

One such afternoon, Judith Cruiseman and the farm manager, Mr Caldwell, were having one of their many 'disputations', as she liked to call them.

'But if there never have been boundaries drawn, Mr Caldwell, how can you say for sure? I mean, from what I can see, and Dr Porteous agrees with me, we could be in Clogher parish. Or Clogherny? Or Donacavey, couldn't we?'

No matter how warm the day, Mr Caldwell never perspired. 'I always go on local wisdom, and for as long as any of us can remember –'

She interrupted. 'Ah, is local wisdom always accurate though, Mr Caldwell?'

'Always near the truth, at any rate.'

'But why then does Dr Porteous agree with me?'

Mr Caldwell chuckled. 'Because he's a Fermanagh man.'

'That doesn't explain anything,' she arched.

'But it explains a lot.' They laughed.

Mr Caldwell and Dr Porteous drank together. When Dr Porteous got to his third whiskey – and Mr Caldwell often took him that far – Dr Porteous relaxed and told secrets. This enabled Mr Caldwell to become 'the most discreet man in the county', as Richard Cruiseman called him; the remark came a few days after Mr Caldwell had first walked in upon one of Lady Cruiseman's bouts of flailing tears, with her husband standing there distant and powerless. In those days, Mr Caldwell never looked at Lady Cruiseman's feet.

Then, only last year, on the very first day of 1931, Dr Porteous had begun to confirm what he, Mr Caldwell, had long suspected. They had met to consider the Cruisemans' New Year party – which she had again left early and tempestuously.

'She's a butterfly in winter,' said Dr Porteous.

Mr Caldwell, accustomed to Dr Porteous's ellipses, nodded.

'Of course,' said Dr Porteous, 'and you will understand immediately – the French would have a way of dealing with these things.'

'Blind eye, sort of thing?' asked Mr Caldwell.

Dr Porteous said, 'Yes, that sort of thing. They. Well. They – develop – their women. Bring them out of the chrysalis.'

'So – even a French – *husband*?'

'Oh, yes, yes. Did you ever hear me mention my cousin Pang? Pang Porteous? He had a French wife. Blind eye? Whooh? He wore an eye-patch if you ask me.'

Mr Caldwell rarely shared his Dr Porteous conversations, certainly not his Cruiseman discussions, with Mrs Caldwell, who did not like Lady Cruiseman, and always waited up until her husband came back after an evening spent doing the accounts at Fintown House.

'Her mouth's too loose for my liking,' Mrs Caldwell told her own sister. In any case, Mr Caldwell had managed very tactfully to ease the account books off the Cruiseman bedroom floor, getting the unwieldier ones first to a table in the corridor, and then to the largely unused upstairs salon, which had now become what Lady Cruiseman called 'the Treasury'. It was Mr Caldwell who suggested – and supervised the transfer of – all that spare furniture stacked up in the stable down at the dower house.

'And isn't this the only office you've ever been in, Mr Caldwell, with hundred-year-old silk curtains?' Lady Cruiseman asked, when they finished the restoration of the salon. 'Napoleon had the same pattern. Did you know that? Little bugger.'

Today, the breeze lifted the edge of the tablecloth, and ruffled the hem of her long primrose skirt.

'I'll tell you what, so.' Mr Caldwell settled the matter. 'Why don't we ask Canon Meldrum to come over one afternoon and bring some old diocesan maps with him. Because.' He tapped the table. 'I happen to know that the Church of Ireland documented itself thoroughly. If anything even better than the Church of England did.'

'Now, Mr Caldwell, you and Richard both. Yes, you'd both rob me of my arguments, wouldn't you?'

'Your "disputations"?'

She laughed. 'My disputations, yes.'

He looked at his watch. 'Time. The interview,' he said.

'Interview?' She stared at him for a moment. 'Oh. Bloody Alicia Black. Is today the seventeenth? Yes, it is. No, I hadn't forgotten, I mean I had, but I hadn't.' Both smiled. 'But you might remind me a bit.'

Mr Caldwell reached into his satchel. 'I brought back Mrs Black's letter. Do you want to read it again?'

'No – just remind me of . . . of that main thing she said.' Lady Cruiseman aired her fingers and looked at them.

Mr Caldwell did not need glasses, never would. 'This is the bit I think you mean. Mrs Black says, "The thing that impressed me most about the fellow was his intelligence. He has no education beyond fourteen years of age, and as you know my own preferences regarding keeping people in their place and so on, I was more than pleasantly surprised at his capacity, his general cheerfulness and his all-round good behaviour. It would not surprise me to learn that he might be a bit of a rogue, but in his time here he never got disorderly, and the fact that he is easy on the eye is always a help no matter where a man comes from." And Mrs Black ends by saying, "I would not be letting him go if it weren't for –"'

Lady Cruiseman cut in, 'Yes, yes, don't bother, "If it weren't for the fact that my poor husband died, and I am rapidly getting penniless and poor me, poor, poor me, who is going to look after me now?" Honestly, Mr Caldwell, I'm fond of Alicia Black, but she gives me an ache.'

Mr Caldwell folded the letter and offered it. 'I suppose you had better keep it by you.' He smirked. 'You don't have to read it again.'

Lady Cruiseman took it, slid it under her side-plate. 'Are you going back to the Treasury?' She half-rose, looking at her feet in the grass.

'Well, yes – but he's waiting.'

'Oh, my God. Still, I'm ready. I'll see him here. Can you ask Nin to bring a fresh pot of tea? Should I offer him some? Do you want to interview him with me?'

'One. His references are good and he's been travelling.' Mr Caldwell ticked his fingers. 'So. Two – tea, no harm in that. And three, no, I have seen him already, a strong fellow, and besides if he's for the mill rather than for the farm, it's Mr Duncan he should be dealing with.'

'He might be for both – the mill and the farm. But if you've seen him . . . ?'

Mr Caldwell rose. 'I'll direct him.'

'Don't forget to ask Canon Meldrum,' she called. Mr Caldwell waved a hand and laughed without turning to look back. Lady Cruiseman relaxed in her chair and listened to the warm silence of the afternoon. A bee buzzed in the flowers along the crevices of the stone steps. Pretending to raise her face to the sun, she watched the terrace doors keenly, although any distant observer would have sworn that her eyes were closed fast against the glare. She had practised this angle since a girl – how to lean back, get the sun on her face, almost close her eyes, yet see everything going on around her.

They emerged side by side, Nin with the tray, and the man, hands clasped behind his back.

'Now, Milady,' Nin announced from several feet away, and Lady Cruiseman sat up, affected an adjustment of her hat and smoothed her skirt. 'This is him, Milady.'

She squinted up quickly, looked away, did not offer her hand. 'How do you do?'

The man said, 'Very well, thanks.'

Lady Cruiseman said, 'Would you like a cup of tea?'

'All right so, thanks.' He stood with his hands behind his back.

'Sit down.' She waved him to Mr Caldwell's chair, and he sat carefully.

'Take off your jacket if you want, this is a very hot June, isn't it?' He did not move.

'I'm fine as I am, thanks.'

'Was it hot down in Sligo?'

'It was.'

She pushed the teacup towards him a little, obliging him to reach across the crowded table. 'There is milk and sugar. Do you like lemon cake?'

'I don't know.'

She stared at him. 'In case you are uncomfortable calling me nothing, better call me "ma'am". Cut him a slice, Nin. What did you call Mrs Black?'

'I called her "ma'am" – ma'am,' and he smiled at the play on words.

'You are very well spoken. And very well spoken of. How is Mrs Black? Thank you, Nin, fine.'

'She is a bit – reduced, ma'am.'

'That's a good word. "Reduced. A bit reduced." Yes, that sounds like Alicia. So reduced that she never gave you lemon cake?'

'But we had great fruitcake, ma'am.' Nin chugged back to the house.

Lady Cruiseman smiled. 'Loyal, aren't you.' He said nothing and she continued, 'Now you have milk, sugar and lemon cake, so shall we start. Remind me of your name.'

'Comerford, ma'am.'

'You make it sound like "comfort"?'

'No, ma'am, "Comerford". I spell it C-O-M-E-R-F-O-R-D.'

Lady Cruiseman laughed aloud. 'Do you? And how does the rest of the world spell it, Mr C-O-M-E-R-F-O-R-D?'

He allowed himself to smile.

'What is your first name?'

'My first name is Eugene, but they call me Gene.'

'Gene? As in "genial"? Comerford – as in "comfort". How old are you, Mr Genial Comfort?'

'Twenty-four, ma'am.'

Lady Cruiseman leaned forward a little and said, 'How old am I, though?'

He looked at her.

'Oh-ho, so you're not put out by the question, are you, Mr C-O-M-E-R-F-O-R-D?'

He rallied with simplicity. 'Mrs Black told me you were very young. But very capable.'

'Oh dear. "Capable." The murderous word. "Capable" – but not of joy. How long were you with Mrs Black?'

'Eight years, ma'am.'

'Since you were a child?'

'Well nearly, ma'am. I worked for farmers down at home before that.'

'Where's home?'

'A place called Deanstown, ma'am. In south Tipperary.'

Lady Cruiseman said, 'I've only been down south once, to

County Kildare to a hunt ball, it was freezing cold and they could not keep the food warm. My husband has friends down there. Do you know the Battersbys?'

'I don't, ma'am, no.'

'My husband knows them. I find them too tolerant. They like everything and everyone. Com – er – ford?' She drew the word out. 'I don't think we've ever had a southerner around here before. They tend to get treated with suspicion.'

Gene Comerford blushed a little.

'Why are you blushing?'

'Mrs Black told me that might be the case all right, ma'am.'

"And you have no fear of that?'

'No, ma'am. I'm a hard worker, and I'm told the North of Ireland likes hard workers.'

'Yes. We do. We do.' Lady Cruiseman spoke as if thinking of something else. 'Are you a Roman Catholic? Yes, you must be, with a name like Eugene. And Comerford. But where did a Roman Catholic like you learn to speak in such an educated manner?'

'I don't know, ma'am. I read a lot.'

She allowed a silence to fall, and she inspected him relentlessly across the table. He attended diligently to the lemon cake, then drank some tea and replaced the cup on the saucer without a chink.

Nor could any other sound be heard. A pair of kestrels, about to hatch four eggs in a nest high on the side of the stableyard wall, had killed off the pigeons. The stream, normally a bubbling creature, had declined in the heatwave, a trickle amid the watercresses; in its sedges, the mud had caked and cracked like a miniature desert. Gene Comerford's cup clinked on his saucer.

Lady Cruiseman spoke again, suddenly asking, 'Have you always had curly hair?'

'Since I was a small fellow, ma'am. They used to tell me that my mother put Curli-top in the soup.'

'Curli-top?! What's that?'

'It was nothing, ma'am, it never existed, it was a joke they made up. Like, as if there was a powder that made your hair go curly. If you took it in your soup or your tea or that.'

'Curli-top?!' Lady Cruiseman laughed again, then straightened her face abruptly. 'You never guessed my age.'

'You're twenty-eight, ma'am.'

'Almost twenty-nine. And since she seems to have told you everything, did Mrs Black also tell you about this?' Lady Cruiseman rose, walked around the corner of the table and displayed her surgical boot. 'That, Mr Eu-Gene C-O-M-E-R-F-O-R-D, is what they call a club foot. I was born with it. What do you think of that?'

'An aunt of my own had one, ma'am.'

'My,' said Lady Cruiseman, 'you are a citizen of the world. An aunt with a club foot.' She grew brisker. 'We got an excellent reference, as you know, from Mrs Black. Do you have another?'

'I've an old one, ma'am.'

'From whom?'

'From my own schoolmaster, ma'am.' He drew a fresh envelope from an inside pocket; this he handed to Lady Cruiseman, and from it she drew a considerably older envelope; inside sat a blue letter.

TO WHOM IT MAY CONCERN

Eugene Patrick Comerford was a pupil at this school from September 1912 to July 1922. During this period he was a pupil of the late Miss Bourke in the Junior Classroom, and then he became my pupil in the Senior Classroom. He left this school with not a blemish on his character. My colleague and I felt regret that he would never have the opportunity for further education. All his time at school was exemplarily conducted – never late, never troublesome, the first to answer questions, a pleasure to teach. I feel it a bounden duty upon me to state that he is likely to give the most conscientious and intelligent service possible to anyone wishing to employ him.

> Thomas Kane, Principal,
> Deanstown National School,
> 10 March 1925.

'Well, well, well,' said Lady Cruiseman, tucking the reference back in the two envelopes, and putting it under her plate alongside Mrs Black's letter. 'I expect you read that every night of your life, do you?'

'He gave me that, ma'am, when I was going up to Sligo to look for the job at Mrs Black's.'

'And they tell me you are interested in cloth?'

'I am, ma'am.'

'Do you know anything about linen?'

'No, ma'am, but I'd love to.'

'Well, Mr Comerford, Fintown is the last linen mill almost of any size outside of Belfast. I think you had better see Mr Duncan. He will, I warn you, ask some very searching questions, he has very fixed views. But I think you will be able to handle him. And I also think you should spend some time up here at the house. Do you know anything about flowers?'

'I know very little, ma'am, about flowers, but I love the look of them.'

'You say you read?' Lady Cruiseman had risen and was walking her slow, lumpy walk up the lawn to the house. She tapped her hand with the references of Gene Comerford. 'What do you read? Do you read poetry?'

'I do, ma'am.'

'Like what?'

'How d'you mean, ma'am?'

'Name one. Speak. Say one.'

For the first time, he looked discommoded. 'D'you mean – recite one?'

'Yes. Recite.'

He stopped. 'Here, ma'am?'

'Why not?' He swallowed, looked away, looked back again, and with a grave formality, began, '*Lord Ullin's Daughter* by Thomas Campbell.'

'Lord Ullin? Who was he?' she cut in.

'I don't know, ma'am,' he replied, and pressed on:

> '*A Chieftain to the Highlands bound*
> *Cries, "Boatman, do not tarry!*
> *And I'll give thee a silver pound*
> *To row us o'er the ferry.*
> *O I'm the chief of Ulva's isle,*
> *And this Lord Ullin's daughter."*'

Lady Cruiseman waved a hand, though not unpleasantly: 'That's enough, that's enough!' They had reached the limestone steps beneath the terrace, and she snapped, 'Give me your arm.' He looked at her blankly.

'God, are you deaf?! Hold out your arm so that I can lean on it to get myself up the first step!'

He put his arm out at right angles.

'No! Like this!' and brusquely she rearranged his forearm.

Her arm draped over his, as a white cloth over a waiter's, young Lady Cruiseman leaned on him heavily and the pair walked ill-assortedly up the steps to the terrace. There she pitched the arm away from her as if casting off a mooring-rope.

'I expect Mr Caldwell is waiting in the Treasury and if so he will take you to the mill to meet Mr Duncan. Now remember, Comerford, do not be afraid of Mr Duncan.' They entered the cool hall with the long pampas grass in the umbrella stands inside the french windows. 'Mr Caldwell! Mr Caldwell! We're here.'

The farm manager appeared at the curve of the broad landing.

'Mr Caldwell, I think it is time that Comerford went to the mill. I've decided to engage him. Mrs Black's word is as good as the next woman's. I presume you have lodgings in mind for him.'

Lady Cruiseman turned away and limped to the wide doorway of the drawing-room, calling over her shoulder, 'Did my husband say what time he would be back?'

Mr Caldwell spoke thoughtfully. 'I expect he'll be here about six or so, we have to go and see that breeder, the Sinclair man, at some stage.'

'Yes, the Sinclair man.' Lady Cruiseman turned from inside the sitting-room and found Gene Comerford in her line of vision. 'Speaking of breeding, I take it you are not married, Comerford?' Mr Caldwell smiled at the joke, and Gene Comerford smiled a little too. 'No, ma'am, I'm not.'

'Goodbye,' she tuned, and closed the door.

It took a mile from the Cruiseman house to the gate of the mill; Richard Cruiseman's father was fond of saying, 'It is exactly one thousand seven hundred and sixty statute yards, one statute mile, that is Scottish precision for you.'

Fintown House has survived, in different ownership today. Nothing remains of the mill. The millrace may easily be traced, and eventually becomes a pleasant small river; a rusted spur of the machinery that operated the millwheel still protrudes from one of the remaining walls. Schoolchildren who come here from Omagh, Tyrone's county town, are given the project of tracing the size of Fintown Mill from the ruins of the building. Easier in winter; the foundations and stubs of walls get hidden in the long grasses of summer. Ground naked with frost sometimes yields the kernel of a shuttle, or a fragment from an old hackling-table, a few of the high thin metal teeth through which the rough fibres of the flax had been combed like a mermaid's hair. In other ways, Nature will not let Fintown forget: the farmed headlands still sprout the tall, fibrous flax; in spring it flickers in the hedgerows, the blue flowers as pretty as embroidery.

'The first thing you have to learn,' Robert Duncan said to Gene Comerford, as they climbed the mill's wooden outside stairs, 'is your history, and once you learn your history you will learn your second thing, which is your manners.'

'Yes, sir.'

Inside, they sat in Mr Duncan's office, with pieces of cloth in various stages of development splayed on the table.

Mr Duncan said, 'I', tapping himself on the chest, 'am a Scot. I fought with the Argylls. I would fight again. I am a Presbyterian. I do not like the Pope of Rome. I find him a dishonest person, himself. My family came here from Argyllshire in 1604. My brother George works the farm we have owned since then. Your kind, Papists, Sinn Feiners, Republicans as they call themselves, they all call us "planters" or "settlers". To us that term is offensive. Do you understand that?'

'Yes, sir.' Gene held Mr Duncan's gaze.

Mr Duncan said, 'We believe we have worked the land here harder than ever your kind would have done if it was left in your hands. It was taken from your kind because you were lazy, dirty, you were treacherous to the Crown. We are hardworking, God-fearing and loyal. Do you understand that?'

Gene nodded his head deeply, once.

Mr Duncan said, 'Even to this day the Roman Catholics don't keep their houses clean.' He peered at Gene, found no reaction.

Mr Duncan said, 'I run my mill the way my forefathers ran their farm. Everyone has to work hard. Everyone is treated fair. On the King's birthday we sing "God Save the King" and I will expect

56

you to learn the words and sing it too. Will that be difficult for you?'

Mr Duncan said, without waiting for an answer, 'It should not be difficult if you have your manners. If I was in your country and that was the only thing to do, to sing your national anthem, even though I do not agree with it, "The Soldier's Song", isn't that what they call it, then I would sing it. Do you know that? That probably surprises you?'

Gene simply listened.

'If the only job I could find was in a building that flew your Tricolour, I would work there, just as we fly the Union Jack here. It is raised in the morning when we come in and it is lowered in the evening when we leave and in the winter it is lowered at sundown because it is an insult to any national flag to leave it flying after dark, just as it is an insult to any national flag to let it touch the ground when you are running it up or hauling it down, did you know that about flags?'

Gene said, 'I did not, sir.'

Mr Duncan said, 'You see, that is what is meant by manners. "Manners maketh man." Did you ever hear that saying?'

'No, sir.'

'In the same way' – Mr Duncan pronounced 'same' so that it sounded like 'saye-em' – 'in the saye-em way it is bad manners to discuss religion or politics so there will be no discussion here of religion or politics. Do you understand that?' Mr Duncan pronounced 'understand' as 'ontdherstand'.

Gene nodded gravely.

'If you get those lessons right, you'll do bravely here, you will be working directly under my eye, and every six months or so I will be the one to tell you how you are getting on, and if you are not doing all right, I'll tell you long before that. We have a hundred and eight people here and very few fights and I don't want any starting now. Do you ontdherstand that?'

Mr Duncan said, 'Let me tell you one more thing. I had a man here, a decent man called Victor Hannah.' Mr Duncan touched the mole at the side of his nose, tested the point of the little hair it sprouted. 'Victor Hannah was a big man, about six foot two, about your size, maybe a little heavier. He had black hair and it was going grey along here.'

Mr Duncan touched his own temple; Mr Duncan touched himself a lot while speaking. 'Now Victor Hannah taught every young fellow who came through here in his time, and I'm telling you that every master weaver from here to Magherafelt, even if he's no longer in the weaving trade, will tell you that he learned his weaving from Victor Hannah. Victor Hannah had one of the biggest funerals ever seen in the County Tyrone. And d'you know what happened to Victor Hannah?'

Mr Duncan rose in some agitation, the belt with implements clanking at his wide shiny hip.

'I'll tell you what happened to Victor Hannah. He was a man in his late fifties then, and he married a young wife, a Ferguson girl, she was from Omagh, aye, and she was what you'd call "a wee pretty". They had two young children. Seeing the way things was going, there was boys around here who wasn't going to be good for anything ever but trouble. Republicans. Roman Catholics. So, Victor Hannah comes up to me one day and he says to me, "Mr Duncan" – although he called me by my first name if we met outside – "Mr Duncan, would you have any objections to my joining the Reserve Constabulary?" And I says I would not, I'd not have an objection.'

Mr Duncan took out a small pocket-knife and began to pare the skin at the borders of his fingernails.

'We had to get him time off for a bit of training and so on, but he did, and he put on the uniform and he went on patrol as a B Special at weekends and in the evenings. A big, decent man, a face as open on him as a clean dinner-plate. He was a very well-known man as you can imagine about the place and he was no sooner in the uniform than one night, two boys called to his door, two strange boys, they had a motorbike, and his wife answered the door, and one of the children near her, and them two men hit past her into Victor Hannah's kitchen and they shot him at his own table, and he having the bread halfway to his mouth, there was blood on the butter afterwards, she told me.'

Mr Duncan put down the pocket-knife. 'Them two boys with the gun got away, they got down to Monaghan, we heard after, and they were never caught for it. Were you ever in Monaghan yourself?'

Gene, looking alarmed for the first time, said, 'No, oh no, sir, I was never in Monaghan.'

Ten years; ten years winter and summer Gene Comerford worked in Fintown; ten years and two months before he came to Belfast in August 1942. He learned the linen trade in Fintown, and came to love the cloth and all its fancies, and how to master them, and the step-by-step progression from tough plant to austere and exquisite cloth: he rubbed both between his thumb and fingers with natural and interested sensuality. In the same period, he also became a competent flower gardener, and this brought upon him a complication not of his making. From it sprang his undoing.

4

At about five o'clock every day, the Rufus Street doors were locked from the inside by the security men, in case anyone tried to slip out early. At six they opened them, and the hordes barged out. (In winter, Blackwoods sometimes closed earlier, but only because the workers' hands became too cold for competence.)

The ex-servicemen eyed for thieves in the emptying tide. Nesbit smiled at them, saying no great theft could take place: 'Not large parcels of cloth, anyway. Dribs and drabs maybe' – yet he provided a high raised platform in the entrance hall from which the security men could frown down on all those passing beneath their boots.

Only the elite lappers left work earlier, and Lennie usually reached home at least fifteen minutes before Belle. She, and Janice, or Gloria, often walked together, chattering like birds.

'What I'll, what I'll do,' Gloria, who had legs straight and thin as drainpipes, often turned full face to the person she addressed, 'when I'm married, is, I'll comb his hair. Every night. I'll get a dear comb, say three and sixpenceworth, with a handle, and I'll stand behind his chair and he eating his tea, and I'll comb, he'll have to grow his hair, and I'll cut the tripes outa him if he goes baldy.'

Janice, one of those people who had come from the womb with an expression of disbelief on her face, said, 'You will an' all. The first time he effs you blind out of it, the comb'll fly outa your hand. Don't I know it?'

Belle had the longest stride of the three. 'My fella'll buy me a leather suitcase. Did Malcolm ever buy you a leather suitcase, Janice, I mean before you were married?'

'And not since either,' said Janice. 'Where would I go with it?'

Over the years Belle learned how Janice and her husband spent the evening – food, the washing of clothes, visiting, Malcolm's night duty, their shoes.

60

'Janice, does Malcolm take off his big boots when he comes in? Do you be awake? Does he wear old slippers or anything? Did you get that taste for shoes from him, you always have great shoes and a shine on them the whole time? Does he eat all his tea? How many slices of bread would he take if he was real hungry? Does he drink a second mug of tea, see Leonard, he spills his down his front, you should see him at soup? When you get into the bed is it cold? What month of the year do you stop taking the hotwater bottle into the bed with you?'

Gloria had innumerable, somewhat zoological relatives. 'See my Auntie Mamie? She had two husbands and the second one she married, she was my mother's oldest sister, my Auntie Mamie, she was twenty-four when my mother was born, and that second husband, she married him deliberately and he a cripple already, so's she could go out dancing and dance with who she wanted, and he sitting there watching her and saying, "More power to you, Mamie, Jayzes if I could dance, I'd dance the legs off ya."'Cause her first husband, he was an oul' hoor, a blaggard, he wouldn't let her talk to the postman nor nothing.'

Janice and Malcolm had no children, a conversational vacuum. Lennie, who counted himself Malcolm's closest friend, took offence at Edith saying, 'Sure doesn't everyone know why they've no children, 'tisn't Janice's fault.'

Which sent Belle, then sixteen, to Alice MacKechnie next day; 'Alice, is there any such a thing as men not being able to have children? As well as women, like?'

Alice looked at her and said, 'Don't you be going asking that to Janice Gillespie.'

They still danced, Malcolm and Janice, not every week, but more than all other couples they knew who, once married, danced once a year at most. Those who disapproved, or envied, justified this extravagance easily: 'They haven't chick nor child, and two packets of wages coming in, that's why they're the way they are.'

On the way home that Tuesday evening, the girls' talk still glowed with Vivien Leigh.

'A'course,' remarked Gloria, 'if you had, if you had them pillars on your own house, you could be sat out there in the coolness.'

Janice retorted, 'Bess Cable was saying 'twould be a great place for a clothesline.' They giggled.

Belle asked, 'By the way, Janice, who was that fella?'

'Who?' Janice asked, pronouncing the word like a thin owl. 'Huwww?'

'Did you see him at all? Gloria didn't either.'

'No, where?' Janice turned to look at Belle. 'Not like you to spot a man, Belle.'

'Just before ould Blackwood came up into our room this morning. There was this man looking in at us. Down at the door, near where Dolly Walker is.'

'I never seen him.'

'Nor me,' said Gloria. 'I never seen him.'

Belle said, 'He had silver armbands. And his apron that spotless. He was there again at dinner time.'

Janice said, 'Apron? He must be a new lapper or something?'

Belle said, 'I don't know. He's red-haired, a bit.'

Janice said, 'He sounds like a Taig. Ask Lennie.'

Belle said, 'God, Janice, I'll do no such thing, you know the smart answer I'd get.'

All three women and all of their colleagues lived in near identical circumstances. Some, like Belle and Janice – but not Gloria – lived in a 'parlour house', with a room in addition to the kitchen and scullery. Others, but not Belle, lived on streets to which running water had come. At least Edith remained meticulous about the thickness of curtaining in the scullery, drawn shut for a 'standing-up bath'. Fifteen shillings down, five shillings a month bought furniture. Nobody took a tram to work – they walked; when the war began they joked that up to then cash was all that was rationed.

That sunlit afternoon, of the day when it all began to advance on Belle, men stood at street corners, still loose from the shipyards where their workplaces had not yet been restored after German bombs. A few gibed at the homegoing women: 'Over here to me!' or 'This wall's real soft.'

The three women walked on.

Edith had her hat on, but not her coat.

Belle asked her, 'Are you going or coming?'

Edith, a little spry this evening, said, 'There's a whole new parcel in. Them Scripture leaflets. I'm going around to unpack them and put them out for Sunday.'

'This is only Tuesday.'

'But them parcels causes a lot of dirt. And the paper's worse, the war has all the good paper gone, they're nearly wrapped in straw.'

'What is there to do?' asked Belle.

'There's darning. But you're not good at that, leave it.' Edith draped a coat over an arm. 'Your tea is there, Belle. Are you going over to Janice?'

'Only for a while. I have to take that skirt back to Auntie Sandra.'

Edith said, 'Mind yourself with Jed back. He'll be talking the hind leg off himself.'

Belle said, 'You don't need your coat, you'll bake.'

'It could be cold coming home.'

Edith held her handbag as others carry a bucket. As she closed the door, Belle said to Lennie's dour face, 'You're in good order, too, who stole your bun?'

'Shut you up and eat your tea.'

They sat side by side, sister and plump younger brother. Lennie's face shone from his evening scrub, the suspenders to hold up his police trousers flopped like a brace of flat tails either side of his hips.

'What time you going on duty?'

'Soon as Malcolm comes for me.'

Belle cut a slice of the bread and heaped butter and jam on it, then cut the bread diagonally into two triangles.

Lennie watched the bread into her mouth, his own slice wadded into one cheek. 'Why don't you cut it straight across like everyone else?'

'You're always saying that. And anyway I'm not a wee pig like some.' They munched in silence.

Belle asked, 'Young Blackwood's back.'

'Aye, he's for us.'

'He looks like a racing-driver.'

'Aye. He's an officer. His father shoved him on to us off his leave, 'cause we're so short-handed. We're even after taking on a Taig.'

'A Taig lapper? Oul' Blackwood must be going soft.'

'Aye.'

'What's he like?'

'He's a big fella, a bit of a Fancy Dan, he has silver armbands.'

Belle quickened her look at Lennie. 'Where's he from?'

'Down south. But he's after coming from Cruisemans. They're friends of oul' Blackwood. He was down in Fintown with years.'

Belle said, 'There was never a Catholic lapper before, was there?'

Heavy footfalls clinked outside; the front door opened.

'There y'are, Belle.'

'Ah, Malcolm.' Belle rose. 'You'll take a cup of tea?'

'No, Belle, I won't, thanks, I'm only after mine.'

Lennie slurped to a finish, and stood. Whenever Malcolm and Lennie stood side by side in the kitchen, Edith said they nearly looked like an army on their own, in their uniforms and polished boots.

Lennie said, shrugging on his tunic, 'I was only saying, we have a Taig at Blackwoods.'

Malcolm said, 'Go you on?! Where?'

Belle chimed, in a mimic-strict tone, 'Now Leonard, "Don't spread rumours, spread Velveeta the delicious cheese food that spreads like butter."'

'Aye, Belle,' said Malcolm. 'Careless talk costs lives.'

Belle smiled and continued the game; 'Is your hair a halo of loveliness, Malcolm?'

He grinned. 'Hey, Belle, what about *Gone with the Wind*, Janice was saying you were on your best.'

'Ah, it's a great story, Malcolm. Will you go?'

'Aye, her birthday's coming, so 'tis. And I've a bit extra on account of the air raids, like.'

Lennie asked, 'Was there bombers over Dungannon? Somebody was saying there was.'

'No. You wouldn't know. There's rumours like snuff at the minute.'

The men left, with Malcolm smiling over his shoulder, 'All right so, Belle?'

Belle reached into the cupboard above the range and took out the skirt for Aunt Sandra, found some brown paper, wrapped the skirt in it. She took some sugar from the bowl on the table, poured it into an old blue bag folded in the drawer of the kitchen table. Their side of the street had fallen into shadow when she closed the door behind her.

Overlooking Helen's Bay at Bangor, the Blackwoods held a small dinner-party to celebrate Gordon's homecoming on leave.

'They're late,' said Valerie Blackwood.

'They're all late,' replied Nesbit.

'All the more for us to drink,' said Gordon, and as his mother looked at him disapprovingly added, 'Dad learned his drinking in the army, didn't you, Dad?'

Nesbit smiled and said, as if repeating a quotation, 'I must not deny that which has happened in my life.'

'I'm not surprised at the Cruisemans being late, although Judy said she wanted to do some shopping. But Desmond?' Valerie frowned.

Nesbit winked at Gordon and said, 'Nettie's probably delayed him while they were getting ready.'

'Nesbit!'

He protested. 'Well, they are newly-weds?'

'He's too old to be called a newly-wed,' said Valerie, sitting down again.

'Well, technically speaking,' began Nesbit, 'he is very recently married –'

'His age, Nesbit. You make him sound lovesick. He's fifty!'

Gordon asked, 'Am I to call her "Aunt Nettie"? Wheeeee!' He laughed.

'You have to be civil to her, Gordon. Your father doesn't like her.'

Nesbit raised a disputing eyebrow, but said nothing. Valerie continued, 'I hope she doesn't disgrace us in front of Judy Cruiseman.'

Gordon remarked, 'I bet Richard Cruiseman'll like her. Look, Dad!' The men rose from their chairs on the wooden verandah and watched a troopship steam slowly in.

'Is she full or empty?' asked Nesbit.

Gordon reached for the ever-ready binoculars, viewed stock-still and concluded, 'Repair job. She's limping.'

The doorbell rang. Nesbit looked at his watch. 'Well, Mother, you said seven for half-past and here it is half-past.'

'Dad,' groaned Gordon, 'you say that every – single – time.' He rose to answer the door.

Valerie said, 'No. Mrs MacCloskey will let them in.'

The gale of talk began far back inside the house in the hall.

'Has Uncle Desmond changed?' said Gordon to his father.

'Oh, of course, I forgot. You haven't seen the two hunting as a pair.'

Nesbit alone had believed it when Desmond announced he would marry Nettie Crawford from Rhodesia Street. Many knew they had been seen together: a hotel in Newcastle; a party, it was said amazedly, in Enniskillen. Traditionally the Blackwood men relished selective and clandestine flings with the prettiest mill-girls – 'But we don't marry them,' said their mother. If it came to grief, they paid, no fuss. This, though, said the watchers, might be something new. When Valerie left the room that Sunday afternoon, Desmond justified, 'You know me, Nesbit. Golf. Enjoyment.'

'Drink and big tits,' said Nesbit, but he did not say it sourly, and Desmond, who never took offence, laughed.

Valerie, almost in tears, said when Desmond had gone, 'But she's a – *weaver*, Nesbit. I mean – a *mill-girl!*'

'But at least,' offered Nesbit in mitigation, 'they're too old to have children.'

'But I had Patricia Hark lined up for him,' said Valerie. 'And you knew that. Oh, Nesbit, he's an oaf and you should tell him so.'

Nesbit raised an eyebrow and Valerie said immediately, 'I'm sorry. I take that back.'

Nesbit sailed past her comment with, 'It has happened before, dear. Climb the family tree.'

'I know. But everybody said it would never happen again.'

'I'll concede this much,' said Nesbit. 'It is the only time I have ever been glad that Mother's dead.'

Nettie bounced towards them; she had never worn underwear stiff enough to subdue her nipples.

'Ah, look at the lot of youse,' she greeted.

When Gordon asked next morning, 'Mother, what were you

wincing at?' she replied thoughtfully, 'I think it was the yellow.'

'The hair or the dress?' rejoined Gordon.

'There y'are, Nesbit,' said Nettie. 'I've not seen you since the wedding. D'you know I was saying to Des on the way over, I can't get used to calling you "Nesbit", sure we used to call you "the oul' bollicks".'

'Here I am indeed,' and he leaned forward to kiss her, organising his shoulder to brush against her breast.

'Evening, Valerie,' said Desmond. 'Sorry we're late.'

'We're late for everything these days, we'd be late for our own funerals, wouldn't we, Des?' She pronounced her husband's name 'Dayz'; until Nettie met him his name had never been shortened.

'Drink?' asked Nesbit.

'I will, surely, Nes. Although we had one or two, didn't we, Des? Des is after putting a drinks press –'

'Cabinet,' he corrected.

'– Drinks cabinet in our bedroom. That's why we're late.' She heaved a giggle. 'Now are you Gordon, you are, sure we didn't meet, did we, you were away for the wedding? I'm Nettie.'

'You're not the only ones late,' said Valerie, 'the Cruisemans are to come yet.'

'I'll have to give you a kiss, Gordon, they say you should always kiss a soldier and he home on leave, for good luck.' Nettie kissed Gordon on the cheek, planking lipstick on his white flesh. 'You're awful like your Da, so you are. Hey, Nesbit, we're winning, so we are.'

Gordon raised an eyebrow.

Nettie explained. 'The air-raid shelters. There's people near my mother afraid of their lives to go back into their own houses.'

Nesbit contributed. 'The campaign, you know. She' – he flattened a palm in her direction: he still had difficulty calling her 'Nettie' – 'has been leading the campaign for shelters for the Shankill.'

'Come on, Nesbit, and the Antrim Road, what's left of it,' Nettie said.

Valerie entered the conversation. 'How is York Street?'

Blackwoods' biggest rival had received a direct hit in the German blitz sixteen months earlier. One entire wall of the mill had

67

collapsed on a row of houses in its shadow, killing a legion of occupants.

Desmond said to Nesbit, 'Thanks for the Anderson.'

Nettie said, 'I feel guilty, so I do. And we the lucky ones. The whole city should have them.'

'Where are you going to put it?' asked Valerie. 'That lovely garden. Is there a place to dig a shelter in? Desmond, your father and mother will turn in their graves if you dig up any of those flower-beds.'

'Hey, d'you know what?' exclaimed Nettie, acknowledging the whiskey Nesbit poured. '*Gone with the Wind* is on, who's goin' to see it, we should all go a night, I'm dyin' to see it.'

'We're showing it already,' said Nesbit drily.

Gordon looked puzzled for a moment, then laughed, 'Oh, yes. This morning.' He turned to Nettie. 'One of the spinning-women, this morning, when I was in at Rufus Street, she was telling them all the story.'

Nesbit looked at Desmond and said wryly, 'In direct contravention, needless to say.' To Gordon he explained, 'They're not supposed to talk during the work.'

Nettie chipped in. 'Away your arse, they've to breathe don't they?'

As she arranged herself in a garden chair, Nesbit said, 'What's that girl's name? You know, the way they tell the pictures?'

'Oh, it's probably Belle, is it?' asked Nettie. And as Nesbit and Gordon nodded, Nettie went on, 'Sure I know Belle well, sure she lives around the corner from us. She's a friend of my sister's. Belle's great at that, so she is. Awful sad girl.' She turned to Valerie, 'I mean she's no husband nor no sign of one, and that awful thing with her father, and she a wee girl at the time. Och, Belle's great.' Nettie gave Gordon a dig in the arm, 'You should say hallo to Belle, so you should, she's a grand-looking girl.'

Nesbit, stooping by Valerie's drink, hissed quietly, 'Don't', thereby heading off a gaffe and a possible spat. The day before the wedding, Valerie had said, 'Your Matron of Honour, is she a – mill-girl –?' and Nettie said, 'Your arse, she reared the six children she has.'

Instead, Valerie now said, 'I wonder what's keeping the Cruisemans?'

Nettie said, 'Is she the one with the club foot and rarin' to go?'

'Nettie!' laughed Desmond.

'That's only what you told me, sure boys will be boys, won't they, Val?' said Nettie. 'Hey, I got you two oranges, so I did, from a wee woman on the Newtownards Road.' She fished them out of her bag. All present handed the oranges one to another, as if they had been amulets; then they sat back and drank.

At that same moment, Belle was lifted off her feet and kissed near the ear. 'Belle, Belle, the lovely Belle, the best Belle that ever rang.' Uncle Jed sang and put her down. 'God, the rations isn't making you any lighter.'

'When did you get back?' Belle laughed.

'The night before last.'

'Did you do well?'

'Do well? Man dear, herself is smelling like a hotel, wait 'til you smell her with all the perfumes I brought her.'

'Perfumes, no less?'

'Aye and I brought your mother soap – so's she'll think I think she needs it, like.'

Belle roared with laughter. 'Oh aye, Uncle Jed, and she'll wash with it too, don't you know. Away off, it'd have to be carbolic.'

'I thought it might give that ould MacCreagh a kick in the carbolics when she's helping him down there.'

'Jed!' Aunt Sandra appeared. 'Isn't he terrible? What'll we do with him?' Face like a bird, she smiled at Belle over her spectacles, then admonished her husband again; 'And don't be saying things like that about Belle's mother.'

'Ach, 'tis the cold old squeeze he'd get off of her, so 'tis.'

'You're looking famous, Uncle Jed.'

Jed beamed and sang, '"Mr Can't: what I suffer from is lack of energy. Mr Can: what you suffer from is lack of Eno's liver salts." Come on in, Belle. I've brandy here.'

'Uncle Jed, sure I never drank brandy in my life.'

'There's a first time for everything.'

'But what'll I do if I get drunk?'

'You'll do the same as myself, you'll dance and you'll sing and you'll tell stories and you'll get a good squeeze off of some fella, isn't that right there, Sandie? C'mon, Belle, sit down tell us how are you. What are you up to; are you beatin' the fellas off with your cap?'

He fetched two glasses, then looked at his wife. 'Ach, break out this oncet?'

Aunt Sandra smiled, and said, 'I won't, but I'll watch the two of youse,' and Jed grinned at Belle and said, 'Keep an eye on us. That's what she means.' He held the bottle to the light. 'I brung this back. Never dropped it. Few close shaves, but –' and they laughed.

Sandra asked Belle, 'I hear you were at *Gone with the Wind*, were you?'

'Oh, it's great, Aunt Sandra. The clothes. And 'tis a great story. Clark Gable. He's like you'd write away for him.'

Uncle Jed handed Belle her glass and, putting his own to his lips, said, 'Here's to the Free French. That's what they're all saying over there. All them French lassies.' He winked.

Belle sniffed her glass. 'I don't know about this, Uncle Jed, so I don't.'

'Ach, not a bother on yeh, Belle, throw it back.'

Sandra interrupted, as she drew chairs together. 'Do no such of a thing, Belle, he got me drunk the first time I ever clapped an eye on him and he told me it was a cordial we were drinking.' Sandra hunched her shoulders in gleeful embarrassment. 'Rum he gave me. And I got stocious drunk.'

'Uncle Jed,' said Belle, 'I want to know the whole thing, how did you get on, where were you and all?'

'D'you know what, Belle?' He rubbed the nicotine-stained fingers together. 'I brung back over a thousand pound.'

'He did so,' Sandra confirmed.

'You did not?!' said Belle.

'Aye, I did so.'

'Oh, he did, he did.'

'Well! What did you say, Aunt Sandra?'

'Sure what could I say, Belle, he gave me the whole lot into my hand. I went down to the bank on Royal Avenue and I like a millionairess.'

'She'll have the fur coat next,' said Jed.

'Indeed nor I won't,' said Sandra, 'for I'll have to watch every penny of that, sure he'll be taking off again soon.'

'You're not telling me a word of it so far,' said Belle. She took the first sip of brandy in her life, and blinked and haw-ed outwards, 'God. 'S'hot, isn't it?'

'The cockles of your heart,' he grinned.

During the late nineteen-twenties, in a kind of sociological curio, several Belfast and Glasgow workmen became full-time gamblers in the casinos of the French Riviera. The first of them, Billy Hunter, had been in the skeleton crew of a new ship bound for fitting-out in Marseilles. In a card-game with other sailors, he won several hundred pounds. They told him he should try the tables with his luck in, and took him to the Casino in Nice in a borrowed dinner jacket. In the shipyards, Billy Hunter checked the calibrations in the building of the huge engine-room boilers. A folk artist among his mates, he took his great skill at figures for granted, as natural a gift as water-divining or playing the melodeon.

Watching the roulette table in Marseilles, Billy Hunter asked the others whether any pattern could be discerned in the way the ball fell among the numbers? A rich and crestfallen Dutchman overheard him, sensed the powerful natural quirk. He paid for Billy's lodgings, never left his side for days, sensing a winning system in the air. The Dutchman, like all gamblers, pushed hope farther than hope wished to be pushed, and when luck and hope departed arm-in-arm, decided to recruit science instead. On a large sketch-pad the man, who owned an engineering firm, drew a roulette wheel. Billy, a man who possessed no unfocused conversation, asked many clarifying questions, and hammered scraps of paper with pieces of pencil. On their first night together, they played nothing, but at a sidewalk table at three o'clock in the morning, Billy showed his new friend the outlines of something.

'I'm basing it on repetition. Do you know what repetition is?' asked Billy instructively, as if other commonplaces of life, such as indifference, or deafness, or forgetfulness, had never existed in Holland. 'No matter how many holes on the board,' said Billy, 'there's only the two colours. Red and black.'

'I've been here before,' said the Dutchman without spirit.

'D'you come every year?' Billy looked at him.

'No. Not that.' The Dutchman, weary, did not amplify. 'Go on. Explain.'

Billy said, 'No. I'll play it for you tomorrow night.'

The Dutchman shook his head. 'We do the afternoon. Quieter.'

Alone, Billy Hunter sat up until nine o'clock in the morning calculating and recalculating the odds.

That afternoon, at the tables in Nice, among the old ladies and inveterate hopers, with Billy nudging and the Dutchman placing, they won more money than the Dutchman had ever gambled. And that night, the next, and the next they won so massively that the management invited them to dine, fed them cognac, in order to keep them from the tables. Billy Hunter gave nothing away either in tips or information; he did not even give the full details of his new system to his friend, just stood beside him and told him how to play.

Billy Hunter and his Dutchman then went to Monte Carlo and in three nights won over sixty thousand pounds apiece, to add to the thirty thousand each from Nice. On their return to Marseilles, they were asked to leave on the fourth night: the word had gone out. The Dutchman went home to his house by the sea in Noordwijk, and Billy Hunter never answered his letters. Back in Belfast he opened two betting shops – and agreed to coach any of his old colleagues in what he called 'matters of chance'. Four tried Billy's system; each made money; all gave Billy his fifty per cent and his expenses – he always travelled with them and helped them to play. All, Uncle Jed among them, left the shipyard and became professional gamblers.

'Belle, y'see' – Uncle Jed leaned forward – 'I never learned Billy's system fully, he wouldn't let you play it often enough to let you do that. I could only remember parts of it and then other times it'd nearly all come to me in a flash and when that happens that's when I makes the money.'

'But what was it like, Uncle Jed? My Mam never let me ask you before.' Belle had seen Joan Crawford fall in love on the Riviera in *Heart of Gold*. 'I mean, is it like in the pictures?'

'Oh, very like, Belle, I mean, there's palm trees – they've no monkeys or coconuts, mind. And the casinos is all white and that, and there's great finery. I bought a pair of glasses and I changed combing my hair so's they wouldn't recognise me every night, and I kept takin' my winnings in small amounts so's they wouldn't get suspicious. And I moved on to the next casino. I mean you have to plan it, like.'

Sandra interrupted, 'He won't tell me how much he won altogether.'

'What's up with you? Haven't you money in the bank?' The brandy was making Uncle Jed irritable: Belle's cheeks had begun to flush.

Valerie of the large eyes said, 'No, Nesbit, we can't start without them.'

Gordon asked, 'How are they going to get enough petrol to drive from Fintown to Belfast?'

'Strings?' enquired Desmond.

'Aye, pullin' strings,' agreed Nettie. 'Oh, Val, did you know Betty Coker, she was a spinner, too, a'course you wouldn't know her, how would you, well, d'you know her daughter's after getting married in a dress made out of a German flag that was captured somewhere?'

Nobody heard the car, and all started at the vigorous apparition of Lady Cruiseman in the french windows saying, 'Voilà! We have landed!' and then, 'Gordon! How nice!' Behind her Valerie's housekeeper, Mrs MacCloskey, wife of Ernest in the Lapping Room, helped with the hat, and the veil took a little detaching.

Nesbit, after the pair of kisses from Judy, came forward to shake Dr Porteous's hand. Lady Cruiseman, seeing Gordon's puzzlement, explained, 'No Richard. London. Delays. Hush hush. And Dr Porteous has his emergency rations. Extra petrol. And I wanted to come up anyway. There is some chance that Richard will get in tomorrow, may even be on a boat now. How long do you have, my dear? Are there still mines in Belfast Lough?'

'Another two weeks,' said Gordon.

'Luxury. Luxury!' – at which Gordon blushed.

Lady Cruiseman said, 'Oh, the bridegroom, the blessed Desmond – and you must be The Wife, are you?' She held out her cheek to Desmond and her hand to Nettie and they got it wrong, which made everybody laugh.

'Judy,' Nesbit hovered. 'Would it be all right if we ate more or less straightaway?'

'I know, I know, we're terribly late, you know what the hospitality is like at Donald West's.' Nesbit and his wife exchanged glances, and Lady Cruiseman picked it up. 'Gaffe! Gaffe! Gaffe! I wasn't meant to have said we were anywhere else,' she sang out.

'Come on, Judy, come in and sit down.' Nesbit Blackwood steered her.

'Nesbit, I have a question to ask you before we sit, and in private; is that all right?' she asked Valerie.

'We'll go in ahead,' smiled Nesbit. 'One minute, that's all you're allowed, Judy.'

In the large hall, by the dining-room door, Lady Cruiseman then sat on the iron-bound chest, saying, 'Ooph, cold on the bottom.' Looking up she said, 'Now, Nesbit, you can guess.'

'I can't actually,' he said, his eyes wandering from her lips to her bosom and back again.

'Well,' she said with arch finality, 'it's about my recommendation. I want to know how he is getting on, and whether you are looking after him well.'

Nesbit looked at her as if he could not make out what she was talking about, and then it dawned. 'Oh, the lapper, the Roman Catholic. Oh. Gosh.' He smiled. 'Why are you so keen to know?'

'Keep your dirty little mind out of this, Nesbit. How is he?'

'Oh, Judy, give him a chance, he's only started. I haven't even met him yet.'

'Well, you do not yet know what I mean, but – I want progress reports from you. Not from anyone else. From you. Repeat, Nesbit, repeat. From you. And it is not what you think.'

'One minute you said,' said Valerie, who had stepped unheard into their earshot, 'and your one minute is up. Come along.'

'To be truthful, Nesbit, though I have no evidence, I have qualms about him. Qualms, Nesbit, qualms. And you know me, qualms have always been my friends.'

'Judy, he only started the other day.'

'Nesbit – don't protest. I have never been a comfortable receiver of protest. I am only saying. Peepers peeled? All right?' She opened her eyes wide and swivelled them to and fro. 'Enemy within, Nesbit. Peepers peeled. Eyes right, so to speak.'

The others trooped past where Nesbit and Judy talked. Dr Porteous adjusted his folded pocket handkerchief and told Valerie he really had more petrol than he needed, but you never know the day. Nettie took Gordon's arm and he clumsily managed both their glasses.

'Gordon, my mother used to clean in houses like this.' Behind her, Desmond laughed.

Judy looked after them. 'Yellow. And hair to match. The colour of the invader,' she said.

At table, Judy clutched Nesbit's arm, stroked Gordon's hair, told Desmond he looked 'virile. Yes. A good word. Virile. Richard hates the word, he says I'm the only woman he has ever known who can use classical allusions and language pejoratively. I said to him, "Richard, go away and read something, and come back then and argue with me," and do you know what he said? He said precisely nothing. I don't mean he said the words, "Precisely nothing," I mean that no sound came out of his mouth. Nesbit, will we have a linen industry left after this war? Uncle Eric says no.'

Nesbit laughed again. 'Judy, you always do that, you switch horses in midstream. Of course we will, all this uniform and military shirt business is only going to show them how we can meet our orders on time. We will thrive. Thrive.'

Judy said, 'And Uncle Eric's opinion?'

Desmond dismissed it. 'Oh, the Heckwrights were always pessimists, Judy. Present company excepted, of course.'

Judy pressed on. 'We are having difficulty. No workforce. If we lose many men to Mr Hitler we will have to close down or employ Catholics.'

Valerie said, 'Not much of a choice, really?'

'No,' replied Judy, 'they dig in. I've heard they have tunnels under their streets up here, is that right, Nesbit?'

Nettie said, 'I heard that too.'

Gordon said, 'But that new fellow you sent to us, he's a Catholic?'

Nesbit laughed. 'Yes, his eyes are very close together.'

Judy said, 'Gordon, I was foolish enough to do Alicia Black a good turn. Valerie, do you know Alicia Black?'

'Isn't she Angela Weir's cousin or something?' puzzled Valerie.

'She may be Mr Hitler's cousin for all I know, Valerie, but never do her a good turn, she has the heart of a blancmange. And we all know how silly a blancmange is. Oh-oh-oh-ohoh,

75

bubbubbububububllle' – at which Judy gave her quivering,
fluttering impression of Alicia Black.

In ten minutes, it would be too dark to recognise anyone. Even
now, Belle had to look twice. The girl proved quicker.

'Oh, hallo,' she said with swift friendliness. 'Is this where you
are?'

Belle recognised her: 'I could say the same to you.'

'I'm after coming out of there.' She pointed to the house directly
across the street from Belle, where the commotion had taken place
at breakfast. 'That's my auntie's.'

'Your auntie's?'

'My first cousin, her son, he was lifted this morning. He was
away down south and they got him.'

'Oh? For what?'

'For nothing. They want to ask him questions. I came over to
be with her. I'm frozen from her. The house is as cold as a cave.'
The girl lowered her forehead to peer at Belle's face. 'Your hair's
different again. My name's Noreen. Were you at the pictures
again?'

Belle smiled at her. 'I wish I was.'

'Hi-i-i-i, I wish I could go every night, but you'd need a fella
for that. A big buck with a wallet. And I don't see ne'er a sign of
one.' She looked around like quicksilver. 'If you see one will you
shout after me?'

Belle laughed. The girl, slightly shorter than Belle, used her
hands a lot, which jiggled the handbag over her arm. 'Great the
way you tell them pictures – Belle, aren't you? – is it hard to
learn?'

'No, I could teach you if you like.'

'That'd be great. I goes a lot.'

'Did you see it yet?'

Noreen shook her head, giggled. 'No, I'm dying to. But 'tis
nearly the same as seeing it listening to you. All them clothes of
Vivien Leigh's. Did you ever see a picture called *The Trial of
Mary Dugan*?'

'Norma Shearer?'

'That's nearly my favourite picture.'

'You're a bit like her,' said Belle. 'Her hair's great too.'

'It takes me ages to wash it, and everybody thinks I dyes it,' said Noreen. 'I says to them, oh, aye, red chalk, I goes out to a quarry down near Newry, that's where I'm from and I comes back with canvas bags full of red chalk and I hammers it down into a powder and whewsh, in I rubs it.' She pummelled a hand to her skull.

Belle laughed again. 'Lovely colour, though. That was her first talkie, did you know?' Belle looked up and down the street.

'Was it?! Norma Shearer?' Noreen also fidgeted a little, and said, 'Well, there's the dark. See you, so, Belle.' She gave Belle a little wave and vanished around the corner of Pretoria Street.

Gene had almost undressed for bed. Now, arms folded, he stood back inside the hallway, reluctant. 'You still haven't said who sent you.'

The young man replied, 'You'd be great value. Great use.' He leaned against the jamb of the door on Waterford Street, a match in his teeth. 'I mean, you could be. Great use.'

'But who sent you?'

'It doesn't matter, sure I'm here, aren't I?'

'But – I'd like to know.'

'There's no need to know. You know that. No need to know.' The young man looked away, down the street 'Sure don't we all know each other under the skin.'

'I don't know you from Adam.' Gene stood upright, as if any relaxation in his posture might invite the stranger in. A knock at the door, that was all, no letter, no nothing. Mrs MacCartan answered and then called him and disappeared into the kitchen, closing the door behind her.

'No, but I know you.'

'Where did you meet me?'

The stranger said, 'I didn't, but I know all about you. That reference you have, that gets you all the jobs.'

'How do you know about that?' Gene asked.

'I know about the man who wrote it. I read his book. I have it. *The War for Independence*. You know.'

'I never read it yet,' said Gene.

'Listen, my name is Joe.'

He put out his hand and Gene shook it gingerly.

'Very pleased to meet you,' said Joe. He stepped in a little. 'Listen, you're living on your own, a few of us meet for a few drinks now and again, you know.'

'No, I don't know.'

'You do now. We've a lot in common.' Joe had moved so invasively forward that Gene stepped back to the newel-post of the stairs.

Gene asked, 'How do you mean?'

'Well, don't you believe in a United Ireland?'

Gene nodded. 'I do.'

'Passionately?' asked Joe.

'Yes. I think – historically, that is, it should all be the same. North and south. I can't deny that.'

'Well, there you are. That's what I think too. And so does all of us, I mean all of us that I'm asking you to come and meet. That's what we talk about.'

Gene shook his head. 'I don't ever go to political meetings up here.'

'These are language meetings, they're good sport.'

'But all the same,' said Gene.

'Anyways, I'll call for you,' said Joe.

Gene knocked on the kitchen door.

'Mrs MacCartan, who was he?'

She did not look up. 'I'm baking for the morning. Who?'

'That young fellow?'

'You mean to say you don't know him?' – her head did not turn. 'I never saw him before.'

'Well he knows you. He said to me, "Is Gene here, Mrs Mac-Cartan?" I said you were.'

'Do you know him?' Gene asked.

'No, I never saw him before.'

'But he knew your name?'

Mrs MacCartan turned away. 'They know everybody's name. And right they should. They're all we have on our side.'

Belle reached for the string and pulled the key out through the letterbox; instead, the door loosened under the slight pressure – it had not been locked.

'What's that you have there?' asked Edith, indicating the box.

'I don't know. Uncle Jed brought it to me. From France.'

'Come over here to me. Let me smell your breath. You were drinking.' Edith rose from the chair and put on her most incredulous expression, of which she had a number.

'Aye. He gave me brandy.'

Lanky and menacing in her stride across the floor, Edith hit her so hard on the cheek that Belle did not feel the stinging force of the blow for a second or so, not in time to stop the second on exactly the same spot. This time Belle stepped back and yelled, 'You stop that you.'

Edith came after her. 'Drink! Inside this house! You'll eat soap, so you will! You'll wash out your dirty stomach!'

She grabbed Belle's arm and tried to force down her guard, mother and daughter of equal height.

'I will not. And you'll not hit me again' – but Edith did. This time Belle managed to deflect the blow with her forearm. Again Belle shouted, 'You stoppit, you!' She made it to the stairs, a position she knew she could defend.

'Shut you up, d'you want all Christendom to hear you?'

'They'll know what you're like! They'll know what you're like!' Belle had never stopped using the childhood ploy.

'You're filthy, you are. Drink in this God-loving house.'

'Touch me once more and I'll kick your head. Like I kicked Lennie's. Remember?'

Edith backed off. 'You're getting to be dirt, you are.'

Belle counter-attacked again. 'Why are you always in a temper when you come back after being with oul' MacCreagh?'

Edith reached through the banisters and grabbed the parcel.

She had it in her hands, paper torn, and the crimson knickers held aloft before Belle could reach her. Edith dropped them on the floor, recoiling her fingers from them as if burnt by a devil, then kicked them as Belle came charging down the stairs. When Belle bent to retrieve them, Edith kicked again, stamping obliquely on Belle's hand. Belle yelped in pain, yet retrieved the silken gift.

'God have mercy on you.'

Belle shouted, 'Go on, pray! Pray! That's all youse are good for.'

Edith looked at her and spat, 'Ha! "Youse"! "Youse"! Where's your fine picture talk now? You that gibes at your own brother for saying "youse"!'

Belle bunched the garment in her fist, drew it out of sight behind her back and began, 'Well anyway, you're always like this after –'

'After what?' Edith began to advance again. Belle, on whose cheek red splodges had begun to spread, turned and ran up the stairs, closed her bedroom door, stuck the chair under the doorknob.

The house subsided. Belle stood at the mirror inspecting her cheeks, turning each side of her face. She opened her eyes wide to see whether they contained tears.

'Do you know, I have not been in a kitchen for so long.' Judy Cruiseman spread her arms. 'No, just water dear, the coolness of it. Will we be bombed tonight, Nesbit?'

'Not out here.'

'You mean Mr Hitler does not find Bangor strategically crucial? Oh dear!'

Gordon laughed more than the remark warranted.

'And as for your new sister-in-law, Valerie. H'mmmmmmm!' Judy tossed the shawl about her shoulders, reached for her stick again. 'Isn't she what they call "a caution"?'

Valerie, who could be dry when required, said, 'I'm the one who has to teach her petit point.'

When their laughter subsided, Judy said, 'I am off to my cool virgin couch. Valerie, may I have a silk coverlet?'

Valerie replied, 'I asked Mrs MacCloskey to put out something in lawn – or very light linen.'

Judy said, 'Thank you. I want as little as possible near my skin on these warm nights' – and blew kisses to the men.

At a quarter to one, the last light went out in the Blackwood house. At one o'clock, a shot was fired at a pair of patrolling policemen by the sandbags on the corner of Glengall Street. The unseen gunman had cycled slowly down the slope. One of the men, the elderly Special Constable, got a scratch on his left hand, from the chip of stone sent flying by the bullet as it hit the wall behind them. When the policemen reached the station at Donegall Pass, Malcolm Gillespie, Janice's husband, fetched the first-aid kit and dressed the man's scratch, while Lennie, Belle's brother, listened again to their account of the incident.

Walking home, Lennie said to Malcolm, 'You'd have thought after hanging one of them last month, the IRA'd cop on and get sense somewhere? Or that they'd all get outa the place?'

Malcolm replied, 'No. One of the detectives was saying what they do is they bring in new blood.'

'New blood?' echoed Lennie. 'Eh?'

5

Janice reached Belle's machine.

'C'mere you. I want to talk to you.'

Belle, who had avoided her, stood out in the aisle. Janice asked, 'What happened to your face?'

'Can you see it?'

'Look at me. Am I blind, am I? Was it your Ma?'

'Aye. My Uncle Jed's back, and he gave me brandy to drink and he brung me a present of underwear.'

'Belle, 'tis none of my business, but you shouldn't be getting hit by your own mother and you a grown woman.'

Belle grimaced. 'You know what they say. "Don't let jangled nerves wreck your life," Janice.'

Janice smiled and complied. 'We'll have to get you a husband so we will.'

'You mean like Gloria said the last time, "So's he can hit me instead of my mother doing it"?' Both laughed.

At the end of a quiet day, Belle waited for the mirror. Women milled around, reaching over each other's shoulders to pile their hessian aprons on the table in the corridor.

'Here's a dot of powder, Belle,' said Nell Calen, and nodded hopefully, but Belle, accustomed to Nell's habit of giving something in order to gain information, merely thanked her and accepted.

Noreen brushed by. 'I'm going to my auntie's, in case I get into a good humour. Are you going home, Belle?'

Belle nodded, and Noreen said, 'I'll hang on so.'

Gloria watched Noreen go towards the lavatory cubicles and asked Belle, 'What was that one wanting? Warehouse doll.'

Belle replied, 'Her auntie lives on our street.'

'I never trust them Taigs, Belle.'

'Ach, Gloria, she seems like a nice wee one. 'Tisn't her fault what she was born.'

The few Catholic mill-women, all on rougher work, promoted their own isolation in preference to enduring it. As a stitcher, an exception, Noreen had greater confidence, born of her deftness, and of working in a comfortable room. Convent-educated, she hemstitched handkerchiefs, embroidered tablecloths and napkins: prejudice had been overcome when she first showed them her 'Rose with Two Leaves'; now they even trusted her with 'Bunch of Grapes'. Spinners despised these 'warehouse dolls', thought them soft, contemned their daintiness, ill fitted to typical mill marriages. As Noreen made her way back towards Belle, a commotion had broken out somewhere in the crowd of women, and Belle climbed on a table to see.

'What's up?' Gloria asked Belle's shins.

Belle reported, 'Someone's after faintin'.'

Gloria replied, 'I bet 'tis Maisie Hanna, maybe. She had a baby the day before yesterday.'

Belle jumped down to the floor; Noreen stood by, greeted coolly by Gloria who held the mirror for Belle to fix her hair. As Gloria left, and the crowd began to thin, Noreen, pawing her hair in the mirror, asked, 'Do you always wear gloves?'

Belle replied, 'They're kind of a weakness with me.'

Noreen quipped, 'Aye, you never know what fella's hand you'd have to hold.'

Belle laughed. 'No. I started doing it on account of Vivien Leigh. *Picture Show* says that she never travels without forty pairs of gloves in her luggage.'

Noreen asked, 'How d'you know a lot about Vivien Leigh and them?'

'I have a cousin in Canada and she sends me *Modern Screen*. And I get *Picturegoer and Film Weekly* myself, 'tis only tuppence. They have everybody in them. Paulette Goddard, she's supposed to have the most perfect figure in the world, and she was all palsy-walsy with Charlie Chaplin. And Katharine Hepburn, she was nearly going to be Scarlett O'Hara but Clark Gable hates her. I can lend you them, I have the *Photoplay Combined with Movie Mirror* for April, the war's taking them longer to come in the post.'

The girls walked through the front hall, past the high raised platforms of the security men, who called, 'Bye, Belle.'

In the bright sunshine, Noreen said, 'I love all that, the film stars.'

'Same here. They're great company.'

Belle looked around. 'Where's Janice 'n' Gloria gone to?'

Noreen asked, 'Could we go some night? What's on? I mean, I know *Gone with the Wind*'s on, but sure we'd never get in?'

'Give it a couple of weeks, and there's going to be matinées, if they knew there wasn't going to be air-raids.'

Noreen waxed. 'I love them air-raids, Belle. I'm never frightened. I'd never fear that a bomb'd land straight on my head. Wouldn't it be a scream if it did? You'd hear the whistle and you'd look up and there's this big thing falling straight down on top of you. And you'd say to yourself, "God, that's a bomb, so it is." My auntie says she'd catch it and shove it up oul' Blackwood.'

Belle laughed again. 'That's a scream.'

They walked on. 'Oh,' Belle said. 'There's a picture called *The Women*, that's Norma Shearer and Joan Crawford and Rosalind Russell.'

Noreen asked, 'Is there men in it?'

'Oh, there is, buckets of them. Oh, d'you know who's on Saturday night too, Greta Garbo? She always washes her face in rainwater. She's in *Ninotchka*. That's supposed to be real funny.'

'In rainwater? Jesus, she'd have awful clean hair around here. Will we go to that?'

Belle nodded. 'First time she ever laughed in a picture.'

Noreen said, 'Is she from Belfast, if she don't laugh often?'

'Oh.' Belle stopped. 'There's a real, good sad one on, *Wuthering Heights*, with Merle Oberon, she's lovely, and it's real tragic, like. I seen it before.'

The girls parted. Belle removed her gloves, hid them up her sleeves and squared her shoulders towards any sullen echoes of last night.

Albert and Darkie, two of Lennie's friends, sat in the kitchen.

'Make us tea, Belle, wouldya?' asked Lennie.

Belle began to cut sandwiches. When Edith came downstairs, Belle, wordless but sparky in her movements, boiled an egg for her, and toasted some bread on the long fork in front of the range.

Lennie's friends took the attention away from Belle. Edith listened enthralled to the conversation; two years earlier, Albert's father, a prison warder, had attended the hanging of Gerald MacCarthy.

'He was saying that at the last minute, your fella was asked, did he repent, like, had he any remorse, and all he said was, "God Save Ireland," and my oul' lad said to him, "Hey, boys, he'll have to save something – for he's not savin' you, is he?" and your boy said, "Up the Republic," and my oul' lad says to him, "No, son, 'tis up you," and up he goes. The oul' lad says you could hear the snap of his neck a whole street away, and oul' Pierpoint, that's the hangman, he looks down the trapdoor and says, "Boys, we done that fella well."'

Edith asked, 'Did your boy not pray?'

Albert replied, 'Oh, aye, I s'pose he did, like he had the priest there, but as my oul' lad says to him, "What good's the Pope of Rome to you now, eh, sonny?"'

Darkie remarked, 'There was a boy down our way, and he known the priest, like, who visited this same boy.' Darkie hastened to explain, 'This priest, like, he has a cousin married across, like, and he was telling them that your boy was saying to him, he'd do it all again, like.'

The conversation quickened. Edith asked, 'How many of them will they have to hang?'

Lennie contributed. 'Malcolm was saying the Superintendent told them we're to look out for new blood. That's what he said.'

'Aye,' said Darkie, ''tis like the Japs. For every one of them gets hanged there's ten more waiting to shoot, like.'

Lennie continued, 'And we're all warned to be watching out for them.'

Edith concluded, 'And we watching out for Germans as well. How're we going to watch out for everything? And there's Mrs Elderton telling me today that her mother's neighbour found a body in the rubble of the house next door, and it what, sixteen months after the big bombs. The dog found it.'

Belle listened, arms folded, leaning against the sill of the back window.

Darkie said, 'Aye, that blitz. Fierce. Aye.'

Lennie said, 'We have a fella I'm watching, a new lapper. He's a big fella, from down south, Malcolm says to keep an eye on him.'

Edith, watching Belle open her mouth to contribute, found a way back to her daughter by interrupting.

'Are you going to wash your hair the night, Belle? There's a spare egg.' Then, drawing her coat to her, Edith wandered towards the front door and out.

It rained all next morning, bringing dim light to the spinners' long room. Rain irritated them all: the noise on the galvanised tin roof drowned conversation. Janice heard the scream first: Belle from her stand could not see – then she went to the edge of the pass and looked along. Two of the women had caught Willie Cooper, and were holding him down to take his trousers off: one brandished a small pot of blue dye. The spinners nearby, glad of the diversion, looked on, cheering and laughing. Janice caught Belle's enquiring eyebrow, and shrugged. Belle and Janice disagreed over these ritual games, in which the women often painted the younger boys' genitals with a dye that washed off after days, even though they told the victim it lasted forever. Belle thought it cruel, Janice felt it stopped the women fighting each other, a fact ever more desirable since Elsie Keatinge lost an eye the day the Gallacher sisters ganged up on her.

Belle walked down the pass and said gently, 'Oy, oy, go on, girls, leave him go, sure he's only a wee fella.'

'Fuck off, Belle, 'tis only sport.'

''Tis no sport for him, is it, Willie? Come on.' She took his arm. They released him with a parting clip on the ear; Belle stooped and helped him fix his waistband.

'Come on, now,' she said, 'are you all right there?'

He wept profusely, stood, confused. Belle went across to the stand of the older culprit. 'Jinny, he's too young for that. He's too quiet a lad.'

'Away to fuck, Belle.'

Belle turned back, and said to the boy, 'Come on, I'll have a bobbin ready for you'; she stood him beside her stand until her rove was spun.

Janice said to her at the dinner break, 'Belle, give us another blast, will you. 'Tis awful restless today.'

The rain had stopped; Belle finished her piece, brushed crumbs off her apron and climbed on the broken table in the idle 'canteen' room. Cigarette smoke rose, soft blue.

'Where'd I stop?' she asked.

Several voices told her the story so far.

'Scarlett married that ould fool of a fella Charles and he died of the measles.'

'Pneumonia,' she corrected.

'Well, he didn't die like a soldier anyways.'

Another voice said, 'And Scarlett didn't want to wear mourning so she didn't.'

Alice MacKechnie said, 'She meets your man Clark Gable again.'

The women chorused, 'Oh aye, tell us that again, Belle.'

'What bit?'

Gloria said, 'Where he brings her a green bonnet and won't kiss her. To spite her.'

Enid Mulcaghey called out, 'No, fuck that. Where he gives a hundred and fifty dollars in gold to dance with Scarlett and everyone's livid 'cause she's in mourning.'

'Listen,' said Belle, 'if I have to keep telling you the same bits over and over, sure we'll never get it finished so we won't.'

'Go on, Belle, tell us about the gold.'

Belle grinned. 'No, I will not, I'll go on,' she said in a mock-prissy voice, and standing with her legs crossed, and folding her arms as if leaning against something, she began.

'The war's on. Right?'

'Right,' they shouted.

'And Scarlett is a widow. Right?'

'Right.'

'Only she's not a very sincere widow, is she?'

Enid Mulcaghey shouted, 'She don't give a tinker's fuck!'

Another voice shouted, 'But she would if she could get one –' to laughter.

'Listen here to me!' said Belle, in mock anger, 'which of you is telling this story?'

'Aye, shut up, all of youse!' said Enid, the worst offender.

Belle continued. 'Anyway, there's this big bazaar just the very same as us for the war effort, only 'tis in Atlanta and not in the Ulster Hall.'

'Up Hitler – with a bomb!' sang one woman.

Belle said, 'Anyway, the lists comes out. Of the names of all the people killed in the war. Right? And Scarlett gets her hands on it.'

'What was she wearin'?' came a shout.

Enid shouted, 'You're thick as shit, wasn't she a widow?'

Belle confirmed. 'Aye, she was wearing black, though she never wanted to.'

Men had drifted to the doorway. One shouted, 'Was she a real widow: was she wearin' black drawers?'

'Go you home outa this, Montana Campbell,' shouted Janice, 'you dirty get.'

Montana replied as he did to everything, 'Giddyap.'

Belle never discovered what all the other women knew about Montana – that he said 'Giddyap' to all the women. If they rose to his bait and asked what he meant by 'Giddyap', he would explain with eagerness in terms of mounting and riding.

A chorus of 'Whooo-hoo!' went up from around the room.

Belle said, 'And then Scarlett, she reads down the list and there's "Wendell", she reads out, and she reads the name "White", and she reads the name of "Williams", and she reads "Wilson", and the name of "Workman". And all of a sudden Melanie stops her and says – "Scarlett," and she has tears in her eyes, "Scarlett, you're after going past 'Ashley Wilkes'. His name isn't on the thing at all at all. So he mustn't be dead!" and they're delighted with theirselves. And at that very minute, who comes up alongside Scarlett on his horse only –' Belle drew herself up to her full height, flung out a dramatic hand. 'Ladies and Gentlemen. Our friend from Charleston. Captain Rhett Butler!' – and all the women cheered.

Letting the cheers die their own natural death, Belle then drew her voice down into a hush. 'Of course, Scarlett doesn't know what to say to him, and he's looking at her real funny – and he rides up real close, and –' Belle half-crouched and thrust her head forward confidentially, as if holding a pair of reins, 'and he edges the ould horse right up alongside her.'

Montana shouted, 'Giddyap,' and broke the spell.

Enid Mulcaghey rushed at him. 'Ah, fuck off you.'

'Away to hell, you brown bollicks.' Two more women rose and

ran at him and Montana cantered away through the door. Belle waited for the room to subside and resumed.

'So Scarlett turns her head so's he can't talk to her and what does your man Rhett Butler do?'

She held the pause until all the women had fallen silent, spellbound once more. Belle looked over and saw, standing in the doorway alongside Gordon Blackwood, the man in the silver armbands. He smiled in approval and leaned against the jamb admiring her performance.

'He says, real sarcastic-like –' Leaning forward, she held the hush. 'Clark says, "So – Ashley Wilkes is still alive to come home to the women who love him – both of them" and he rides off. Well, Scarlett is only hopping at him.' Belle clapped her hands. 'God, you should'a seen the face on her. She was like a Scotch terrier.' Belle gathered her work-skirts as if they were a Southern belle's day-gown and stamped her foot on the tabletop.

Even Montana, back once more at the doorway, was moved to silence as Belle swung to and fro in the tiny space within the big dishevelled room, saying, 'Oh, Rhett Butler! You aggravatin' varmint!'

The rain swept back, and thundered on the tin roof like applause.

An hour later, the invitation came. News of it ran through the spinning-room like wildfire. They teased Belle, calling her 'Nettie', and 'Mrs Blackwood'. Janice saw it happen. On a tour of inspection, Gordon passed through the room in his father's wake, turned quickly, bent and whispered something to Belle; Gordon's action was so swift that he had fallen in step behind his father again without his lightning move ever having been noticed.

'What happened?' asked Janice when she got Belle alone in the queue at the lavatories.

'He invited me, Janice. Gordon Blackwood invited me. That's for fact. He says, "Monday evening next. The twenty-fourth of August." He nearly said "Nineteen forty-two", he was that exact. "Six o'clock," he says. "A drink upstairs. In the offices. Just you and me," he says. "All right?" That's all he said, Janice, he didn't give me time to say yes, aye or no.'

Janice looked at her. 'God, Belle? But you've no clothes?'

'I can't refuse, Janice, can I?'

'Gloria's telling everyone,' said Janice.

'Aye. She says she heard every word.'

Gloria stood at the cubicle door while Belle sat. Belle pointed down. 'Look at the darns on them knickers, Janice.' The two women began to giggle.

'You're not going up there with darns on your knickers,' said Gloria. 'That's one thing.'

'Gloria – "I was a hitchhiker in the highway of love until I used Listerine." Right?'

'Go on out of that.'

'Tell you what,' and Belle started to laugh again. 'I'll wear the ones Uncle Jed gave me.'

Janice asked, 'Did your Ma say anything more last night? Or hit you again?'

'No.'

'Are you going to tell her?'

'I will no such thing.'

The Chief Constable, who had prepared the documentation in anticipation of Stormont's request, enumerated the seven gunshot incidents so far that year. 'Although flesh wounds have been the most serious recorded,' he observed, 'only good fortune and the darkness of the blackout prevented the certain deaths of officers. We cannot postpone debating an increased patrol force, nor can we delay the issue of blanket search warrants, now that we know several guns have been used, rather than the same one over and over.'

The Civil Servant told him, 'You'll not get the search warrant. Too sensitive. The first thing we'd have is Dublin saying it just goes to prove we regard "the minority population as enemies even though they are citizens like anyone else". You can hear De Valera saying it, can't you?'

Late that evening, the sound of breaking glass drew no attention; any possible listener lived five hundred yards away, along the shore. Two men stepped back into the dripping shrubbery. Nothing materialised, no dog barking, no shout from inside. Eventually, the smaller hoisted himself through the window and fought softly through the blackout curtains. Outside, the other waited, and then was beckoned to the opening front door. A shaded flashlamp lit their way along the white carpet. Beyond the silver and the crystal glass, outside the smaller drawing-room, they found it: a tall cabinet full of guns. No need to break the glass: open the shaky tall door carefully. One excellent Purdey under-and-over; one single-barrel shotgun, one new .303 rifle, and one service revolver, although it seemed the pin had been flattened. They hastened, although they could have taken all evening and all night, and all the following day; the Richardsons had left Crawfordsburn for the weekend, and gone to Fermanagh.

On Saturday afternoon, Gene Comerford boarded a tram, then signed on at the city library. The man who took his form asked for 'specific interests', and Gene, vague for a moment, was given directions to History, then Poetry and Fiction.

'My name's Norman McCullough, and if you can't find anything, I'm over there, usually. Do you read a lot?'

'An awful lot.'

'It's very restful. Or do you read for learning?'

'Well,' Gene blushed. 'The two, I suppose.'

'Yes, yes.'

Gene spent an hour in the bookstacks, then returned to the desk with *The Oxford Book of English Verse*.

'Oh, look, I'm awfully sorry,' said Norman McCullough, 'but we can't give that out, that's what they call a library copy, you can only read that on the premises.'

'Oh, that's all right. I mean, if I wanted to copy anything?'

'Of course, of course. You could copy out what you like. That's what the tables are here for, to sit and read after all.' Norman McCullough asked, 'Is there anything in particular . . . ?'

Gene replied, 'No, yes, I mean several things, I'm looking for that thing that says, "a rose-red city twice as old as Time". That's one of them.'

'"Half as old as Time"?' Norman McCullough corrected kindly. 'No, that's not in there.' He took the book gently from Gene's hands and showed him the alphabetical index of poets. 'That was written a hundred years ago by a man I think called Burgon or Burgeon. Do you want it badly?'

Gene replied, 'No, I'd just like to have it. I'd like to read it all, that's all I know of it.'

'Isn't it annoying when a thing like that sticks in your head,' said Norman McCullough, 'isn't it annoying?' He took one of the pens from his top pocket and, making a note, said, 'I'll have a look for it if it's all the same to you. I'd say you'll be in again?'

'I will. Often,' smiled Gene.

'You're not from here? Needless to say?'

'No,' said Gene. 'Down south, I think you'd say.'

'I would, I would. I'm a great reader myself. I'm just finishing that man Sitwell, d'you know him at all, very – well, really, eccentric, very.' Norman McCullough nodded at Gene.

Gene walked to a table with the *Oxford Book of English Verse* and sat there for an hour and more, flicking, stopping, going back, going forward, checking the index of first lines. He stopped at 'There is a garden in her face/Where roses and white lilies blow'. He shook his head, and read the poem through, then read it again. Lady Cruiseman had said the next morning, as they walked down the gravel pathway, 'I have a poetry book in this house somewhere, you're welcome to look at it. A Palgrave': and then quoted the line.

After Gene's first, alarming meeting with Mr Duncan that hot day ten years ago, Mr Caldwell said, 'You will have no proper mill-work to learn until the harvesting and the retting, because you're beginning at the beginning, and that's not for another six weeks or so.'

'Retting?' asked Gene.

'They'll tell you. And your two hands'll know all about it. And your spine. First you're to go up to the house in the morning and Milady will give you your job in the garden. You've the rest of the day off.'

'What time?'

'Go up early. Eight o'clock, I'd say, but sometimes she rises with the lark.'

That first afternoon, the directions he was given took Gene along a narrow road tall with Queen Anne's Lace. He had his heavy suitcase in one hand, and in the other a sack of possessions. Made of old flourbags by some loving hand somewhere, the sack had a draw-string inserted at the top, and when the sunlight caught it, the dyed name of the flour millers, 'Johnston Mooney & O'Brien', materialised inside a faded red circle.

'Blue suit, somewhat shiny with age; brown shoes, a little cracked but well-polished; a white shirt, spotlessly clean, with no collar, no tie'; these details Lady Cruiseman ticked off to her husband at dinner.

'Where is he lodging?'

'The MacAuleys.'

Richard Cruiseman nodded in satisfaction. 'Like with like.'

'Yes, Richard, *status quo* maintained,' she said.

'Don't be acid.'

'A good cottage,' Mr Caldwell had told Gene Comerford, 'in fact, a very good cottage.'

'What he means by that,' said Michael MacAuley, 'is we're supposed to be better nor some other cottages inhabited by Catholics. There's always a double meaning up here when they're talking about us.'

Michael MacAuley next commented, 'Good man yourself for the job, I mean, for getting it. I never worked. Before the war they promised me and I going into the army in 1914 there'd be a job here for me when I got back, over at old Basil Brooke's place or something. I never got it. In eighteen years since, I never got a job off any of them. The wife works at Fintown now and again, the Cruisemans likes her baking.'

And Michael MacAuley asked Gene, 'Is that fed and found? Eleven shillings a week fed and found? Aye, well the weavers that come through here, the journeymen like, they make good money. Down south, now, would you make more nor that?'

Gene said it depended, but the farmers paid very little.

'Aye, farmers always pays very little. Do you know what I'm going to tell you, and I told every man who ever crossed this threshold the very same thing? I never had a pay packet in my life. In my whole life,' said Michael MacAuley.

Gene shook his head. 'That's terrible.'

'And I forty-two years old now. Never a one. Not a one.'

Gene said, 'I often heard it was like that all right up here.'

Mrs MacAuley said, 'You're fixed up though, that's because you're easy on the eye, them rich Protestant women always hires men who's easy on the eye, but they'd never hire a wee scut of a fella like him there.' Her husband nodded in sympathy.

'Did you – never – do anything about it?' Gene cut his slice of bread and butter carefully in half.

Michael MacAuley started. 'Oh, no, no. Nor would we. Would we, Mammy?' he asked his wife.

She said darkly, 'I know what I'd like to do. To the lot of them. Them that keeps able-bodied men out of work. And they're always saying the Catholics is dirty – but I know about her, so I do. That one.'

'No, Mammy, no.' Alarmed, Michael MacAuley looked at Gene. 'You have to keep your mouth shut around here, so you do. And I mean, the likes of you, you'll have to keep your mouth shut tight so you will. I mean, they'll be looking out for you, and you from down south.'

'What did she say to you anyway?' asked Mary MacAuley.

Gene looked at her, and waited for his comprehension to arrive, and Mary MacAuley said, 'Herself. The one.'

'Oh. Mrs – Lady – Cruiseman. She said that I was a big strong fella.'

The MacAuleys laughed.

'Hi-hi, she did say that, I'd say' – and Michael MacAuley chuckled.

In answer to Lady Cruiseman's question, 'Why so early?', Gene said next morning, 'Because Mr Caldwell said you were often up with the lark.'

'Did he?'

They walked, Gene being careful to go slowly in time with her, along a long stripe of grass, to a rough area where the clay had cracked in the crazy heatwave.

'I'm going to turn this into a rockery. I've wanted to for years, only I never found anyone who might be able to help me.' She stopped and squinted up at him. 'Did you know I went to Cambridge? So you needn't think I'm some rich ninny. I was one of the first women to go. I read Classics.'

Gene inclined his head to listen.

'Cambridge is a university in England, and they never ever let women in there and I was one of the first. To "read" means to "study". So if I say to you I "read Classics", it means I studied Greek and Latin poets and thinkers.' She sneezed in the early morning sunshine.

'What are you going to plant in here, ma'am?'

She squinted again and mimicked his accent. 'What are you going to plant in here, ma'am?' Gene stood with his hands behind his back, unmoved.

'I don't know yet, "Mr Com-fort".' She drawled the words. 'What about "beds of violets and myrtles and all olfactory crops"?' When he made no reply, but looked all round, she said, 'Do you know Horace, Mr Comfort?'

'I don't, ma'am.'

'Hah!' she said. 'But you didn't say "Horace who?", did you?'

'Why would I say that, ma'am?'

'You would say it if you didn't know. That's why, "Mr Com-fort".' She sang a little when teasing.

'We never learned him fully, ma'am.'

She turned away. 'How old were you when you left school?'

'Fourteen, ma'am.'

She turned back. 'Well, Mr Bloody Comfort, a "Taig", as they call your lot, from the south, and you knew who Horace was in primary school! I can see you're the kind might get above himself.'

Gene had been poking the dry earth with his booted toe, as if measuring where to begin digging. He turned to her and drew a deep breath.

'Ma'am, I never get above myself, and I never will. I keep myself to myself, and I do my work. That's the only way I can live.' She stepped back.

'Don't you talk to me like that.'

'I'm only telling you the truth,' he said quietly, then dropped his hands by his sides and waited for her next remarks. In a gesture of agitation she rubbed her hands down along the fronts of her hip-bones, stared into Gene's unflinching face, then subsided by looking away. When she spoke again, her tone had a mollifying ring.

'Well, it's just that we don't get intelligent Catholics around here.'

Richard Cruiseman, dressing and gazing out of the window, saw his wife in her lavender dress. As he looked, he saw her draw her hands down her hips, and the new man straighten from his stoop and turn to look at his wife. Too far away to hear; too far away to see the expressions on their faces; Judy arguing again. Richard Cruiseman leaned on the windowsill and looked all around, at the long border of jewelled lupins and pastel sweet-pea, and the glistening leaves of the espaliers on the brick wall, at the soft-iced footprints in the dew of the lawn. As Richard watched, the new man bent to listen to Judy, then turned to the pile of stones across by the kitchen-garden gate and began to heft them over to the open ground where Judy said she wanted the rockery.

6

And after all, while Belle held her breath, Monday afternoon came. As women raced for the doorways, a tight group stayed behind to involve themselves in Belle's big event. Janice took charge. She ordered the mirror taken off the lavatory wall and fetched to the window in the Long Room, where Belle might dress by the strong late sunlight. Alice MacKechnie polished the mirror with spit and a sleeve.

'Are you going to be another Nettie, Belle?' she asked.

'Would you marry a Blackwood, Alice?' retorted Janice.

Enid said, 'I'd take his money and get to fuck out of it. And if he came after me I'd get my brother on him.'

Gloria did the unwrapping and laid the clothes out on Janice's sleek oak worktable, draping the red blouse that Belle had saved so hard for on the arms of Janice's high chair.

While one kept watch lest a man drift by, they dressed Belle communally. Her shoulders white, she turned her back to them and strapped on the harness of Gloria's new bra, on its first outing: 'A "wonderful item", Belle, that's what my sister called it'; Janice's good cream slip, rarely worn since her wedding ten years ago, foamed down over her head; then, with glee, Belle flourished the garment that immediately became known as 'Uncle Jed's knickers'. The women scrutinised, stretched it across their palms.

'I can just see anyone's oul' fella if they were brought home to them. They'd say, "Youse'll catch your death of cold in them", so they would,' said Alice.

Janice said, 'I don't know. At the same time I think they'd love 'em.'

Gloria said, 'On somebody else. See if, if you wore 'em. See my father of a Monday when the washin''s on the line. He's a scream to watch. I'm always hopin' the wind'll slap knickers into his face.

You'd want to see him goin' out the yard, he's like he's dancing – dodging the clothesline.' She bobbed in mimicry.

Anne Millar brought a skirt she had only worn twice; 'There, Belle, see, there's a bit of a kick-out in it.'

Alice Costelloe's silk scarf was her aunt's, and had come from Spain; Belle had her own good shoes, with a fairish high heel, and she 'oooh-ed' at, most precious of all now, silk stockings. Still in their wrapper and never yet worn, the best Bradmola made, Alice MacKechnie said she refused them to her own sister but Belle should wear them and if she knew Belle they would come back without a brack on them.

Belle felt them. 'God. They're silky. The feel of them. I often wondered is that what some place like Egypt feels like?'

Calamity approached: how was she going to keep the stockings up? They examined the knickers. Resourceful Janice said, 'They have a bit of a leg in them and the stockings could hitch, but you'll have to walk awful slow'; they laughed until Alice wheezed.

Not one of them had a sixpence, or a coin of any kind; Gloria ran over to Tommy Best, the mechanic, and he gave her four small washers, and no questions asked. Gloria pulled the ribbon hem loose from the knicker leg and threaded twists of linen threads, to which she tied the washers. They brushed Belle's hair, they painted her nails, they pulled her straps back high, and they dabbed her with rouge; they turned her round and round like a painted clockwork doll.

'This is what they do to the film stars,' said Belle, as flushed with attention as with rouge, and there she stood, finishing off her own lipstick, and they stood back to admire her.

'How are the stockings?' asked Janice, and Gloria went down on one knee and checked under Belle's skirt, trying not to ruffle the line of it in front. Gloria rose, saying, 'I declare to God, Belle, if he gets his hand in there he'll think 'tis in the shipyards he's in, with them washers' – and they creased with laughter.

'He won't be looking in up there,' said Janice firmly.

'He might. Isn't he a Blackwood?' said Gloria.

'All the same,' said Belle.

'Lift your skirt,' said Janice, and they all stood back to inspect.

'No, that's fine,' said Janice, 'and they'll stay up.'

'You've no giggle gap,' said Gloria. Belle looked at her blankly.

'Shut up, Gloria. Pull down that skirt, Belle, and have one more look at yourself in the mirror,' said Janice, turning Belle to the light. Belle stood as they held the mirror for her, and then arranged herself so that she filled the mirror, shutting out the dingy room, and shutting out the door tilting off its bottom hinge, and beyond it, shutting out the condensation-wet walls of the lavatory with its filthy washbasins.

'I wish I had a ribbon for my hair,' said Belle.

'A red ribbon'd set it off grand,' said Alice, who had straight and lank hair.

'It'd give him the wrong idea,' said Janice.

'He'll have that anyway,' said Gloria. 'Go on, Belle, you'll be late.'

'And if you meet that oul' hairpin, Rita Boyd, she works up there,' chimed in Anne Millar, 'and if she tells you you're looking great – you'd better come back and we'll have to dress you all over again.'

Belle sashayed away from them on her adventure, carrying light about her, it seemed, down the long dark spinning-room with the silent machines, by the empty bobbins like a vast army of little white soldiers, under the wheels and cranks and metal riggings of the overhead apparatus. The steel pillars threw shadows across the floor, as Belle dodged the water of the cleaners left in pools as usual. She walked carefully, poised without teetering, partly because of the knickers, and partly because Hollywood decreed. As she reached the wide door at the far end, she peered around a bank of machines like a child playing hide-and-seek, and waved.

Alice called after her, 'Belle, you watch yourself.'

Janice called after her, 'I'll bring your real clothes home with me. Be sure an' drop in.'

Enid shouted, 'Don't forget. Use your knees and elbows if he's too frisky.'

'Enid!' reprimanded Janice.

Belle vanished, her acknowledging hand folded away by the dusk of the doorway. The women, thoughtful as a group portrait, stood and gazed at the empty distance.

Janice said, 'She's old enough but.'

Gloria said, 'Aye – but she never heard of the giggle gap.'

Anne Millar said, 'Nor me. What is it?'

Enid snorted. 'Jesus, where were you with all these years?'

Janice smiled and said, 'You know – the gap where the skin is. Between the end of your knickers and the tops of your stockings.'

Anne said, 'Does it tickle or something?'

Gloria said, 'No, but if a fella gets his hand up that far, he's laughing.'

Out of sight, Belle stopped in the empty mill, leaned against a wall and closed her eyes. She blinked rapidly, breath anxiously deep: she recovered, and walked tentatively on, to the offices upstairs. Some time ago, a doffing-mistress, Janice's predecessor, perceived that Belle had enough intelligence to get a job in the offices and Miss MacAllister had said as much to Edith, and called Belle up for a talk one afternoon, but nothing came of it.

Wrinkling her nostrils at the smells of polish and brand-new linen, Belle tiptoed cautiously down a long ramp into an area where the floor, highly polished at the edges, wore a large, square, multi-coloured carpet. A table, narrow as an altar, ran along one wall, and on this lay half-unfurled tablecloths, dressed with napkins. The damask glistened: Celtic knots whorled slowly all around the borders, and lovely intertwining lines roamed down the centre to a large panel on which a shamrock and crown intertwined. Ancient Round Towers sat at each damasked corner; the accompanying napkins had hand-stitched borders. Belle, rarely seeing the end product of her own raw work so exquisitely revealed, paused to gaze. Two other boxes, their contents arranged outwards, contained hem-stitched linen sheets and their pillowcases; on a brass stand of the sort seen in a draper's window, stood a mannequin torso with an epauletted military shirt, and a placard at the bottom which read, *The Best for the Best! The Fusilier's Shirt*: and in smaller copperplate, 'The Blackwood Family are pleased that the Fusiliers have demanded – and been granted – the right to wear only the *Grade One Militia*, the very same military shirt that beat the Kaiser!'

As Belle inspected, a door opened and a woman emerged, small and fast-walking, with glasses. She peered at Belle: 'Do you want something?' – then checked herself and said, 'Oh, no, it's all right. Down there,' and pointed to the corridor.

Belle walked on, climbed broad steps to a long plateau; the

carpet ended. Her heels now clicked on the polished wood. A door on her right whipped open with a suddenness startling to anyone walking by, and a voice said, 'Well, Miss Southern Belle?'

Gordon Blackwood stood in the doorway. She offered to shake hands, but he took the hand and kissed it.

'Nice perfume. What is it – "Meadows of France"? "Arabian Nights"?'

'Cusson's Number One Lavender Water, I got it at Anderson and MacAuleys.' She withdrew her hand and rotated it a few times as if it had been pleasantly stung.

'Come in, come in, have you ever been up here before?'

'No. What is it?'

'This – is the boardroom.'

Belle looked around at the panelled wall, the portraits, and the long table of voluptuous mahogany, and said, 'God, I'd never be bored here.'

Gordon threw back his head and laughed, 'No, no, no! The "board". The "board" of the company, the people that own and run it. My father. My uncle. And Mr Heckwright. Those people. Not bored from doing nothing.'

'Oh, sorry.'

'Don't be, don't be. No. Lovely. Lovely and fresh. Do you know Mr Heckwright?'

'I seen him. Isn't he the fella with the fat white face?'

Gordon laughed again. 'And the horn-rimmed glasses. What else do you know about him? No, don't answer that. G 'n' T?'

'Beggin' your pardon, Mr Blackwood?'

'Gordon. Gin and tonic?' Then he looked at the bottle on the table and laughed, 'Yes, you see, Gordon's gin', and showed her the label.

'Do they make that for you, yourself?'

He said, 'Yes, but they don't know it', and when he saw she didn't get the joke he said, 'What I meant was, call me "Gordon", not "Mr Blackwood". I nearly had to look around to see who you were talking to. Do you like gin?'

'Och, ach, I don't know, I only had brandy the other day.'

'Expensive tastes. Would you prefer a brandy?'

He reached towards the cabinet.

'God, no. Not now.'

'I agree,' he said, and misread again, 'too early. Brandy's for after dinner, isn't it? Say "when".' He poured.

'When what?'

'When you've had enough.'

'Sure how'll I know that 'til I had enough?'

Again Gordon found this extremely funny, and, still laughing, gestured Belle to a leather chair; he handed her a glass half full of gin. Judy Cruiseman's father-in-law once accused the young Nesbit Blackwood of 'exercising a tawdry *droit de seigneur*'.

'Tonic?' Without waiting, he squirted from the siphon. 'Gin's best with only a little tonic.'

He had already prepared his own glass, and with authoritative courtesy, he drew up a chair squarely opposite Belle and sat.

'Well, now – how are the pictures?'

'Great.'

'Chin-chin,' and he raised his glass to her and drank.

'Very well, thank you,' Belle said, with the air of someone who did not know what to say, but she too drank, and her face flattened in recoil at the strength and bitterness of the drink.

'Is Brian Donlevy on in anything?' Gordon asked.

'He's a Belfastman.' Belle held the drink in both hands which rested on her lap.

'He's a close friend of my parents.'

'Get away with you!'

'Would you like to meet him?'

Belle said, 'He's supposed to be lovely.'

'I'm sure he'd love to hear you telling a picture he's in.'

'God, no, I'd die!' Belle flapped a hand. 'He's going to be in *Down Went McGinty*.'

'No!' said Gordon in delighted incredulousness.

''Tis comin' next week, no, the week after.'

'Is it true,' began Gordon: his father had taught him, 'You can flatter someone by the kind of question you ask them.' 'Is it true,' he asked Belle, 'that your colleagues often like your version of the pictures better?'

'I often change things.'

'How's your drink? What kind of things?'

'Things I don't like. This gin's bitter, so it is.'

'Oh, would you prefer de Kuyper's? Or Cork? I have both.'

'No. The other one was smoother and hotter, my Uncle Jed's. The brandy. I'm thinking of changing *Gone with the Wind*. The bit with Melanie dyin'.'

'There's a drink called gin and bitter. At your service, madam.' Gordon, in his chair, bowed from the waist exaggeratedly. 'I hear that's what Clark Gable does.'

'He's lovely. He's Rhett Butler.'

Gordon drank at length. 'Ooh. I was thirsty.' He rose, took off his jacket, went to the tray, and poured into his glass again. He waved the gin bottle at Belle, and asked, 'Ready?' Like an obedient child, she held out her still almost half-full glass. Gordon finished pouring and sat down, surveying Belle. Such circumstances provided the closest social contact a Blackwood ever had with a spinner, a doffer or any of the other manual mill-workers. 'Ownership,' said his grandfather at a famous linen guilds meeting, 'has to be total or it is nothing.'

'Now. Will you tell me a picture?'

Belle looked down to avoid his fixed gaze.

Gordon said, 'I invited you here for a private performance.'

'This is a lovely glass.'

'Come on. It would be like having my own cinema.'

'Sure you've enough money to buy the Ritz itself. You could see the pictures free every night.'

'Miss Southern Belle!' He feigned indignation, then abandoned it. 'Did anyone ever tell you you look a bit like Princess Elizabeth?'

'She's younger than me. She's eight years younger.'

'All right. You're shy. I understand. What were you telling them at work today? I didn't get a chance to hear you.' Gordon rose again and began to pace.

'Still *Gone with the Wind*.'

'Yes, but what part of it?'

'We're not far into it.'

'Tell me a bit. Or would you like to wait a while, think about it?'

'I'll have to stand up.'

Gordon took the silver cigarette box and the table lighter and lit up; Belle declined.

'All right' – he blew the smoke, then he came to his chair, sat back and ostentatiously arranged himself like an eager audience.

Belle, standing, looked down into her glass. Gordon asked, 'Do you need a little extra fortification?'

Belle looked at him in alarm. 'What's after happening?' Gingerly she looked down at her stockings.

'No. What do you mean? I meant – do you want a little more in your glass?'

'No, no.' She drank and coughed. 'I think 'tis going to me head. Youse'll have to carry me out.' Belle blinked.

'Right. I'm waiting.'

Belle said, 'I need both hands.' He took the glass from her and rested it on the table.

'You're a quick drinker,' he said.

She eased her hair out from behind her left ear; then, hands clasped, she began.

'Y'see, Scarlett O'Hara, she's the girl, like, she still wants to marry Ashley Wilkes, even though he's after marrying Melanie Hamilton, and at the same time she's delighted 'cause she's after reading in the newspapers that he's not dead at all in the war –'

'– I know that feeling,' cut in Gordon.

Belle paused, waiting for him to say more, but he waved her on: 'Sorry.'

'And then Ashley comes home on leave.'

'Oh, just like myself.'

In drink, Belle hit her stride early. 'And they have a great time, only Scarlett is watching Ashley and Melanie all the time and she's dead jealous of Melanie, 'cause Scarlett was always crazy about Ashley who didn't marry her. Anyway, the day comes when Ashley has to go back to the war. And Melanie is too upset to see him off and she has to lie down, so Scarlett waits for Ashley in the hall and down the stairs he comes and he's tying on his sword.'

'An officer and a gentleman,' said Gordon, 'only a few of us left.'

'Scarlett, she rushes up to him and she says to him, "Oh, Ashley."' Belle made a mournful face. '"Ashley, I want to talk to youse, so I do."' Belle held out her hands beseechingly, as if Gordon had been Ashley. 'And he's standing on the stairs and he says, "Ach, what about ye, Scarlett, how yeh doin', are yeh well?" – see, he's trying, like, he's trying to ignore, to not pretend, that she's keen on him.'

Gordon rose, circled to the back of his chair, upon which he leaned forward.

Belle continued. 'And Scarlett says, "Come here to me, Ashley Wilkes, for I have something I want to say to youse," and she takes him by the arm. And he says to her, "Well, that's a funny thing, Scarlett, for I have something to say to youse."' Nervous in Gordon's presence, Belle's accent flattened, lost any sheen she had ever tried to apply: the alcohol loosened her further.

Apparently rapt, Gordon moved around his leather chair, and advanced a pace at a time towards Belle, who retreated and began to use the boardroom table as a prop, splaying her hands on the shiny surface and cocking her hip along the table's edge.

'And she puts her hand on his arm and he looks down at her.'

Gordon reached Belle and stood right in front of her, looking hard up into her eyes.

'She says, "Sure what am I going to do without youse at all, Ashley Wilkes? Sure I'm going to be lost without youse, amn't I?"'

Gordon reached forward, took one of Belle's hands and caressed it in both of his.

Belle faltered, yet pressed on, eyeing Gordon stroking her hand, then averting her eyes, concentrating on her story.

'Anyways, Ashley bends down and he kisses the top of Scarlett's head, only she grabs him and kisses him on the lips –'

Gordon stroked and stroked Belle's hand.

She gulped, 'And Ashley, and his wife above in the bed, he doesn't want the kiss to be like that, and he tries to pull back out of it, only he gives in to it for a bit –'

Belle tried and failed to remove her hand from Gordon's insistent massage. Her voice acquired a shrill edge; as she faltered again, Gordon darted a question: 'Why did he resist her kiss?'

'Well, like – he's not married to her or anything . . .'

'But people kiss even if they're not married. Don't they, Belle?' He lowered his voice.

'I don't rightly know off, I think – I think . . . the pictures is different.'

Still gripping her hand, Gordon put out his other hand and encased Belle's left breast, as if reaching for a football. Belle looked down at his splayed fingers. Gordon squeezed a little, and whispered with a smile, 'Don't they?'

Belle said, 'Don't they what?'

'Kiss? If they're not married?'

She stepped back. 'No. Stop.'

'They do!'

'They don't do that.' With her head she indicated Gordon's hand.

'But other pictures?'

'They don't.'

'My brother told me Hedy Lamarr wears no clothes.' Gordon pressed the breast again, as if honking the rubber bulb of an old car-horn.

'But that was only in one picture, *Ecstasy*. An' that was never shown in Belfast.'

'Still. As I say. People do it.'

'I never seen people do it.' Belle tore his hands away in a brushing-off gesture.

Gordon reached once more, both palms this time, up, open and curved. Gazing at her bosom he said, 'That doesn't mean they don't do it.'

Belle retreated farther. 'But I never seen anyone do it.' She shook her head, in a mixture of vigour and uncertainty, and conveyed such a strong air of confusion that Gordon dropped his hands to his sides. A stand-off silence fell. Belle looked around the room. She changed the subject.

'All them – paintings?'

'Ancestors. Here.'

Gordon, accepting the slowing-down of the momentum, walked past Belle, over to where the line of portraits in oils began. Belle followed him.

'These are all Blackwoods. They're my mother's family, too, my father and my mother are distant cousins. My mother's maiden name is Blackwood. Her father and uncle owned this place, then they sold it, and then strangely enough my father's father bought it back.'

'Lovely clothes they're all wearin'.'

'That's Uncle Alec, my grandfather's brother. He was a general in the Boer War, then he came back and ran the mill at Rampartstown. That's his wife. She was a famous pianist. Played for the King.'

'That's a fox fur she's wearing.'

'Oh, here, this one will interest you. This is Auntie Jenny, she was a great character. Now, she was a mill-girl too. Also from a little terraced house. So you see, Belle. She captured a Blackwood heart, Donald's, he's another of my grandfather's brothers. She only died a few years ago. You see? It can happen.'

'A mill-girl?' Belle looked at him for the first time since he pawed her. 'Like – like Nettie?'

'Oh, you all know all about Nettie,' and Gordon laughed.

He led the way to their chairs, and began to refill Belle's glass: she shook her head. He lit a cigarette and blew the smoke cloudily, then stared at her in intense silence.

'Are you all right . . . ?' he asked.

'Oh, aye.'

'You tell the pictures very well.'

Belle made no comment.

'What's your favourite love scene?'

'Why d'you want to know that for?'

'Just interested.' He dragged, inhaled, flared his nostrils with the exhaling smoke.

Belle lowered her head and looked in the glass, which she did not raise to her lips.

'I mean,' he continued, 'who isn't interested in love?'

Belle spoke almost in a whisper. '*Wuthering Heights.*'

'*Wuthering Heights?* Oh, yes.' He blew smoke again and said with some aggression, 'Surely you can tell me some of that!'

Belle began to obey.

'The man, he's called Heathcliff, he never gets over that the girl, she's called Cathy, she married someone else but now she's dyin' of love for him, like.'

Tears stood in Belle's eyes. She shook her head as if clearing her thoughts, stood up, plonked the glass on the table and walked to the end of the room, where, with her back to Gordon, she wiped her eyes, sniffed.

Gordon rose, and like a dancing-master pranced slowly down the room. Belle did not turn around, but kept telling her story.

'An' she says to him, "Oh, Heathcliff, Heathcliff," an' he looks at her . . . she's lyin' there . . .'

Gordon stood behind Belle, placed a hand on her waist, began to trace the rise of her hip. She spoke on.

'He bent down to her in the bed, an' he says to her . . .'

Gordon lifted the hair at the back of Belle's neck and kissed her nape. He pressed his crotch to her hip hard, then wound an arm around her waist to the front and turned her around. She would not look at him.

'Lift your face.'

She did but kept the eyes downcast.

'They always, always, kiss in the pictures. Do-you. Hear-me?'

He adjusted the angle of Belle's jaw and held her cheek so that her mouth could not escape, then pushed his mouth at her closed lips. Belle did not move, and he flicked her lips with his tongue. He still did not notice her tears, and then he manoeuvred her so that she stood leaning backwards, with both hands resting on the table behind her. He pressed her to sit, and with his hands on the table, he trapped Belle within the arena of his arms.

'Film star! Southern Belle!' he whispered, arching down to press the length of his body against her length.

Belle, her shoulders and upper back flat on the table, turned her head away to avoid Gordon's mouth. So Gordon pressed his mouth to Belle's neck, then raised his hands from the table and traced them down her face. She stopped, closed her eyes; his hands continued to her neck, then her shoulders. Belle tried to lift a hand to wipe her eyes but could not get the hand through Gordon's arm.

'They always.' Gordon kissed. 'Always.' Gordon kissed again. 'Kiss.' His hands crawled down along her face and neck. 'In the pictures.'

When he reached Belle's breasts, she lay still. Gordon opened the top button of the red blouse, her year's savings. Then the next button. 'Film star,' he whispered. Then the next button. Gloria's white bra began to appear. Belle turned her head away to one side; Gordon neither looked nor cared: he gazed at the next button, undid it, then the next, then the sixth, tugged the blouse from the waistband until it fell open. He laid his head softly upon Belle's cleavage and whispered, 'Belle, Belle, Southern Belle.' Belle sniffed, tipped her head back as the tears began to flow towards each ear. Gordon kissed the top of each breast, then hauled one breast from its cup.

108

'You're not French,' he whispered, 'they never have such lovely fat nipples.' As he bent to kiss, Belle said, 'Oh, no. Please.'

'Oh, yes, please.'

'No.'

'Yes.'

'No, Mr Blackwood.'

'Yes, Miss MacKnight. And that's an order.'

Belle began to sob loudly, and Gordon said, 'Shhhhhhh, shhhhhh.' Belle sobbed louder. Gordon, as if hoping to silence her, pressed her harder to the table. He knocked her feet off balance, then forced her to lie splayed in front of him.

'No, no, no' – the sob became a wail.

'Ah, Belle, Belle! Belle the film star.' He reached forward, trying to ease Gloria's new bra downwards.

'No. No.' Her voice rose.

'Shhhhhhh, shhhhhh. Please.'

'Don't. Gordon. Don't. I never –'

'Never what? No? I don't believe it.' He stepped back a little. 'But you're, I mean you're a mill-girl –'

'I never – had anything to do with . . . men . . .'

Belle, with a huge effort, began to struggle upright, tried to duck under Gordon's arms and fell off the table, to her hands and knees on the floor. He put his arms around her from behind, hands clutching her breasts, and began to lift her.

'No, no. Please! PLEASE!' By now she had begun to shout.

'Oy, oy, oy. No shouting. Not playing the game.'

'I said. Please.' Belle, her back to Gordon, began to struggle, her front askew. The volume rose. 'PLEASE, Mr Blackwood!'

'It's. Gordon.' He gritted his teeth. 'Come on. Come. On.'

'No. Please.'

He tightened his grip and she struggled harder.

'Come on. You're not a child.' He took one arm away and thrust it up under her skirt from behind.

Belle yelped. 'Let go. Please! Oh, please! Stop. Oh, God. Help me!'

He released his grip; Belle scrambled up and ran for the door. Gordon, nonplussed, did not react for a moment, then took off after her, but she had opened the door and was in the corridor. At the top of the stairs he caught her again from behind and she wailed, 'No, ah, God, no, please, please, ah, God!' They struggled down the stairs like a hopeless swordfight, their cries and grunts echoing in the high vaulted walls. At the first landing he held her, again from behind, and in an awkward grip which further pulled apart her clothes from the front. Their shadows danced high, high across the stairwell.

'Let me go. Please. Jesus! Please!'

'Come on. I said. You're not a child.'

Then Gordon froze. A big face looked up the stairs at them, the auburn-red hair illuminated in the window's light. A finger pointed from an outstretched arm like a general's command.

'Let her go.' The man did not raise his voice, no need to in that wide echoing stairwell.

'It's all right,' said Gordon, 'we're only playing.'

'Play a different game.'

Gordon released Belle who pulled her clothing together and went down the stairs awkwardly.

He called down, 'Don't get the wrong impression.'

'Don't *give* the wrong impression,' said Gene Comerford. Less curtly, he looked at Belle: 'Are you all right?'

'I left my bag.'

'Get it.' He climbed the stairs towards Gordon who was straightening a shirt-cuff.

'Her bag?' asked Gordon. 'Of course, of course. I'll get it.'

Gordon walked back towards the boardroom, with Gene following some considered paces behind. As Gene stood at the door of the boardroom, Gordon, bending to find Belle's bag beside her chair, said, 'It was only a bit of fun.'

Gene said, 'For who?'

Gordon handed him the bag and said, 'You won't say anything – will you?'

Gene took the bag and walked away, then in mid-corridor turned back and said, 'Just because you hire people – you don't own them. Slavery's gone out.'

Gene said to Belle, 'Do you live far away?' She had turned her face to the wall in order to complete her restoration.

'No. I always walk it. Pretoria Street, but I have to go to my friend's house first. She's near too.'

He said, 'I'll walk with you.'

Autumn sunlight had poured amber into the evening streets. Belle, unsteady in the shoes and the stockings suspendered with metal washers, half-sobbed, 'I s'pose I'll be sacked now.'

Gene said firmly, 'No. You won't.'

'Ach, how would you know? 'Tis always happening. It happened with your man's father. And his uncle. And his grandfather. It happened to – to Shirley West, and to Ruby Magee. We didn't know for ages why.' She stopped in a shop doorway, and raised her forearm to her wailing face; he stood watching as she wept, her face deep in the forearm of the red blouse.

After some long seconds, he took her arm.

'It won't happen to you.'

'Sure how would you know?'

'Because I saw what he was at, and he knows it. He won't do a thing. Bullies are always cowards.'

They walked in silence. Belle stopped once more and wept, again with the forearm held up to her face, a sleeve to cry on. Each time he stood by, patient and undemanding. When they moved on, he walked close enough to touch her shoulder occasionally with his. She guided him to Janice's street. Nearing the door, he asked, 'Are you all right now?'

Belle said, 'No, or yes, thanks, sort of.' For a second she hesitated as if she might once more break, but she straightened.

The children playing at the lamp-post looked with curiosity at tall Belle and her big calm companion in his white shirt, the navy-blue jacket folded over his arm. Janice, emerging with a basin to scrub a windowsill, saw Belle's tearstained face.

'Eh, what's up? Malcolm!' she called so urgently that her husband appeared instantly, the tunic of his uniform relaxedly open.

Gene spoke. 'She had a bit of a barney.' Then, looking at Janice, asked, 'You're the doffing-mistress, aren't you?'

'And who are you when you're at home?'

'I'm new, I'm in the Lapping Room.'

Malcolm walked forward. 'What about ye, Belle, what's up?'

'Come on in,' said Janice. 'Quick. Quick.'

Malcolm looked on curiously as Janice said to Gene, 'You too.'

Inside, Belle sat on a kitchen chair, and roared and moaned: they all stood awkwardly and Malcolm sat down.

111

'Janice, he tried to take my clothes off,' Belle said with a wild snivel.

Even though Gene flinched, Janice never misunderstood for a second.

'I was afraid of that. Them Blackwoods.' She looked at Gene. 'Where did you come in?'

'I was going home. I was late, and trying to find the night door. She came running down the stairs.'

Belle said, 'Gordon ran off out of the way when he saw him.'

Malcolm stood and shook hands with Gene. 'I'm Malcolm Gillespie, and thanks very much. Belle, she's a great friend of ours.'

'Oh, you're welcome. Sure we have to have the pictures told to us tomorrow.' Gene smiled.

'Did you have your tea?' asked Janice.

'Grand thanks, no, I have to go on,' said Gene. 'It'll be waiting for me.'

'Thanks again,' said Malcolm. 'Any harm asking where are you from?'

Gene replied, 'Down south. But I was working down in Fintown for a long time.'

Gene turned to Belle. 'You're all right now?'

As he left, Belle came to the doorway and asked quietly, 'You won't tell anyone – that you saw me with my clothes open.'

Gene shook his head and said gravely, 'I saw nothing anyway.' Then as he stepped away, he turned and said, 'It'd be nice to talk to you again. Sometime, when you're over all this, maybe?'

'Aye. It would.'

He said, 'I'll ask you,' and walked away.

In the gleaming small kitchen, the black range shiny, the china dogs on the mantel cheap lustrous-bronze, they sat and listened as Belle haltingly described the incident. Janice made soothing sounds – 'Awww, awww, awwww. Awwww, Belle.' Malcolm stood by Janice's side in his uniform, whippet-thin.

'D'you want to change into your own clothes?' Janice asked.

'I will,' and Belle wandered up to Janice's room.

Janice whispered to her husband, 'How are we going to find out how much he did to her?'

'Ask her.'

'Ach, I can't ask her straight out.'

As they pondered and murmured, Belle returned, sat to drink the tea.

Janice asked, 'And how did the washers go?'

Belle smiled wanly. 'They held up great, Janice, even when I was running away from him.'

Janice smiled in relief. 'And the nylons?'

'Alice was right, there isn't a mark on them, I put them back in their box.'

Malcolm stood and patted Belle's shoulder.

'Malkie, what time are you going on duty?' Janice asked. 'I mean, can you walk over home with Belle?'

'I'm going on now,' he said, 'but sure I'll come back for her in half an hour,' and he departed, giving Belle a warm wink.

Janice said as he left, 'How d'you feel?'

'Astray. The drink made me dizzy, and at the same time, when he put his hand on my skin, Janice, I can't say honestly I hated it, even though I didn't like him doing it, although I liked him a bit – you know?'

'You mean to tell me you never had a fella put his hand up your jaxie before?'

'No.'

'I never thought of warning you, although Gloria said we should.'

'Janice, if that's what I have to do to get a husband, I don't want to get married.'

Janice laughed. 'Ah, Belle. God help your head. There's other ways of getting married besides having young Blackwood slobbering over you.'

'Janice, will he sack me?'

'They done it before.'

'Your man, the lapper fella, he was awful nice, he says they won't sack me, he says Gordon Blackwood'll keep his mouth shut because another fella seen him.'

'He might so.'

'Janice, what am I going to do if my Ma finds out?'

'I'll put Malkie on her, so I will.' They laughed and Belle began to calm down.

'He's a fine big fella, that lapper, isn't he?' said Janice. 'Some of them Catholics is big fellas. When you were upstairs, Malkie said he was probably the first southerner ever inside this door.'

'He couldn't have been nicer to me,' said Belle, and there they left it.

Malcolm and Belle arrived at Belle's house five minutes before blackout time: Edith was arranging her famous blackout curtains.

'She'll soon not live here at all the rate she's going,' said Edith.

'Aye, but she's great company for Janice of an evening and I out,' insisted Malcolm, and Edith demurred no further.

'Leonard's down at his pigeons,' she said, 'go you down and say hallo to him.'

'I will so.' Malcolm touched the peak of his cap and left.

Edith looked at her daughter and asked, 'Are you feeling all right, Belle?'

'I am a'course, Mam.'

Edith peered across the dim kitchen. 'Is your eyes red?'

'There was powse everywhere today. Listen, I'm going to make tea, who wants it?'

Edith shook her head. 'I've things to do, Belle. I've no time to be drinking tea.'

Belle sat on her bed. From between the pages of last year's *Picture Show*, the one with Errol Flynn on the cover kneeling in front of Bette Davis in *The Private Lives of Elizabeth and Essex*, Belle took an envelope, and from it selected with her thumb the piece of paper it contained. She had salvaged it on the day after the funeral, when Lennie was given her father's pocket-watch, and as he opened it, a paper disc fell out. On one side, it bore an advertisement for the watchmakers, *Grahames on the Antrim Road*; on the other side, the date it was sold to her father, 17 June 1907, a date she knew to be his twenty-fifth birthday; this side also bore instructions on the care and winding of the watch, which was to be returned for cleaning every two years. A narrow strip all around the perimeter was divided into fifty compartments, one for every two years of the owner's life, and the series of figures – '09', '11', '13', '15', up to '25' – testified that her father had indeed returned the watch for cleaning every two years, including the year he died.

Belle's eyes turned to the only open space on the watch-paper, where, amid all the boxes and instructions, her father had written in tiny but powerful ink, 'Isabel, born 12.10.'18'.

Next day, Belle resisted all enquiries: Janice warned her to smile and say to everyone, 'What you don't know won't trouble you.' Suspicions were aroused when she refused to tell the pictures, but Janice allayed those with the usual gesture of hands spread in a grimace, the code they used across the room to indicate a woman having a period, and Belle sat quietly.

When permission was granted to open all the windows, the violent noise of the Long Room thinned. Gordon Blackwood appeared and specifically allowed himself to be seen seeking Belle out.

Janice greeted him courteously, calling to his ear, 'She's there, Mr Blackwood, no – over there,' and watched hawk-eyed as Gordon picked his way through the machines. He stood to Belle.

'Look. I am terribly sorry.' He spoke so that no one else could hear. 'I really am.'

Belle had the presence of mind to smile at him so that Gloria beside her would not grow suspicious. Gordon continued, 'I really like you. I do apologise. I was drunk. No hard feelings. All right?'

'All right.' Belle smiled again and Gordon left, and above the machine noise the women went 'Woooooo! Belle! Wooooooo!!'

Gordon returned to the Lapping Room and watched until he found Gene in an isolated moment.

'I went to her and I apologised,' said Gordon, fingering his moustache and looking up at Gene. 'I went to her first thing this morning and said I was sorry. And I am sorry.'

Gene said nothing, continued polishing his lapping-stick.

Gordon pressed on in an anxious whisper, 'And I think I should apologise to you too, I mean I am sorry that you should have to get involved in such a thing. It was all my fault and I hope you'll accept my apology.'

Gene replied, 'Oh, you don't have to apologise to me, but the thing is – I think you had it wrong, some of those girls are very moral.'

Gordon said, 'I know that now.' His anxiety mounted. 'Do you think an apology is enough, I mean should I do something more, should I offer her some money or something?'

'Only if you really want to insult her,' said Gene. 'Let the hare sit. Watch it, here's her brother.'

As Lennie drew near them, Gene changed the subject audibly. 'Ebony usually. Sometimes they're made of oak, black bog-oak' – he held the long tapering stick to the light and rubbed the sharp brass-pointed ferrule – 'and some have been in families for five or six generations. I was given this when I was leaving Fintown. It belonged to a famous old guy down there, he died at the Somme and they had held on to it and they gave it to me.'

Lennie cut in, 'They must have thought a lot of you?'

Gene said, 'Maybe.'

Lennie said, 'Maybe what?'

'Maybe they did.'

'Maybe they did what?'

'Maybe they did think a lot of me.' Lennie looked at the stick and walked away. Across the lapping-table he said, 'You have it very highly polished. You look like a man used to polishing things. Do you know how to clean a gun?'

Gene replied, 'Your own lapping-stick is well polished.'

Lennie replied, 'I'm used to cleaning a gun. That's why I know.'

Archie defused matters by saying, 'Aye, I'm always saying to the missus you can't beat a well-polished lapping-stick.'

Gordon, trying to settle this flare-up, said to Lennie and the Lapping Room in general, 'You haven't seen this man's particulars. I have. From Cruisemans.'

'I have a great set of particulars myself,' said Montana, and the issue subsided in laughter.

7

Belle exhaled a soft 'Ahhh!' at the trailer for *Down Went McGinty*.

Noreen asked, 'What's up?'

Belle said, 'That's Brian Donlevy, he's a –'

'He's a what?'

Belle, retrieving, said, 'He's a Belfastman.'

Pathe Gazette took them overseas. 'Malta Receives its George Cross.'

'God, Belle, there's not goin' to be enough men left to go round, so there's not.'

A woman behind said, 'Shhhh!'

'Malta's glorious resistance to the enemy is suitably honoured.' Same jaunty voice. 'In the bomb-battered Palace Square, Valetta. When Lord Gort, VC, Governor and Commander-in-Chief, presents the people of Malta with their George Cross.' A band played, and men with insignia relished their own soldiering. Olive-skinned boys watched with dark eyes full of guns and drums.

When the break came before the big picture, Belle remarked to Noreen, 'The first rule is always buy the best seats, and that way nobody round you is talking.'

Wuthering Heights began. The girls settled down in their seats, bathed in expectation. Noreen took the hint, and never said another word: she gripped the arm of her seat in passion when Laurence Olivier, the returned and triumphant Heathcliff, strode into the house of the Lintons, and as dark as from Hades, took Merle Oberon back into his soul. The house lights came up, and Noreen's face glowed. She smiled with the ruefulness of someone ambushed by artificially induced emotion.

'I'm staying at my auntie's the night,' she told Belle in the foyer, and they set out to walk home together.

Noreen said, 'My heart's lepping out through my mouth.'

Sometimes she grunted after she spoke. 'They're still up there, I'd bet you,' she said to Belle. 'Unnh.'

'You mean – up on the rocks, and the moors and all, still walking around?' Belle's question nonetheless wished to agree with Noreen.

'Aye,' said Noreen. She linked Belle's arm. They walked in silence.

''Tis their teeth I'm always looking at,' said Noreen, 'how they ever get them perfect like that. We have terrible teeth. Our whole family.'

They crossed Ormeau Avenue, turned the next corner and into the dim mouth of Pretoria Street. 'D'you think I'll ever know how to do it, Belle?' Walking in the middle of the deserted street, one of the war's few luxuries, they had reached both their houses.

Belle leaned against a quenched street-lamp.

''Course you will. 'Tis only practice.'

'But how's it start, like?'

'The first thing is, you follow the picture all the way through.'

'But I'd never remember.'

'No, all you have to do is remember what you liked yourself. That's what you tell 'em mainly.'

'Why's that?' Noreen grunted again: 'Unnnh?'

''Cause they're the things you'll be the most excited about yourself. And then you watch their faces.'

'Why?'

'Did you ever tell a story to a child? Same thing.' Belle hugged herself; a breeze from the docks slipped through the street. 'And there's all kinds of other tricks.'

Noreen asked, 'How d'you mean – tricks?'

Belle said tranquilly, 'Well, little other stories. Like, me telling *Wuthering Heights* when it came here first two years ago, and saying that Merle Oberon's real name was Estelle Thompson and that Leslie Howard nearly left his wife for her. Or telling *Gone with the Wind* and sayin' that Olivia de Havilland was Joan Fontaine's sister, that makes 'em think what kind of family was that, like, compared to any of our own.'

Noreen stood directly in front of Belle, looking as closely as the gloom would allow. She asked, 'If there's something you didn't like, would you tell it anyway?'

'No. I'd never tell cowboy pictures. Or gangsters. I never told

118

a picture with a gun in it. A war picture's different. But I'd never say a thing about a picture where one fella kills another to his face, like.'

'Even if 'twas very exciting?'

Belle knew about these things and her tone showed it. 'No. The thing they're after in the mill is love. They want kisses and all the clothes, and women pretending they're not interested in men, only they're real interested. Only they don't want the men to find out, they want the men to chase them, like. Women's only interested in love.'

'How,' asked Noreen, her voice tinged with daring, 'would you tell a kiss?'

Belle pondered. 'We-ell. There's a great kiss in *Gone with the Wind*, the first kiss between Clark Gable and Vivien Leigh. It doesn't come for ages. I mean, he threatens her he'll kiss her and then he says no he won't for a while, and then he only kisses her first when he's going off to join the army, and Scarlett, she's trying to get back to Tara and Atlanta is in flames – here, hold this.' Belle handed her little bag and gloves to Noreen. She stood away from the lamp-post.

'And they're standing there against the sky glowing red as a fire and he takes his hat off.' Belle paused elaborately. 'Now. I never know whether a man kissing a girl takes his hat off outa good manners or because he's afraid it'll fall offa his head when he bends down. The man always has to be bigger than the girl, or else 'twon't work. So Clark puts his arms down so's he grips her – here.' Belle put her hands back to the high small of her own back. 'Just under the shoulder-blades –' She leaned forward to show Noreen the position of Clark Gable's hands. 'Enid Mulcaghey always wants to know where the grip is. And Vivien Leigh, she puts her hands up around his neck, she looks as if she's trying to hold on to him, but you could also say she's getting ready for a kiss, she has the angle right.'

Belle then raised her arms and tilted her face upwards beseechingly. She indicated with her hand planed out flat the difference in corresponding heights between Rhett Butler and Scarlett O'Hara. 'So, he's this height, and she's only up to his chin, that's perfect. Then he takes away one hand and he rubs her hair with it –' Belle placed a flat hand against her own hair, neck and ear, 'and he says, "I love you, Scarlett," and she says to him, turning her face away, "Don't you be holding on to me like that," and he grabs the face on her, and he says, "I love you more than I've ever loved any woman," and she's struggling and she says, "You leave me alone, Rhett Butler," and he says, "Here's a soldier of the American South who loves you, Scarlett O'Hara, who wants to bring the memory of your kisses into battle with him. You're a woman sending a soldier to his death with a beautiful memory – kiss me, Scarlett O'Hara, kiss me just the once." And he bends down and he kisses her, he puts his mouth down sort of sideways across hers –'

Belle tightened the circle of her own arms and drew the arms up towards her own bosom, closed her eyes, and puckered her lips and slowly rotated her head into a wide half-circle. Noreen gazed in the half-light of the little Belfast street and entered the illusion willingly. Belle came up for air, and grinned, 'There y'are. But you'll have to see it yourself.'

Noreen said, 'Oh!' Belle fetched back her handbag and gloves, and waved, a little gay gesture, 'Be seeing you.' They parted.

On Monday, Belle kept looking at the far corner, the door down by Dolly Miller, to see whether he would come and stand in the doorway. He did not, and when she finished her telling for that morning, the women's compliments fell flat upon her. When the dinner klaxon sounded, Belle said to Gloria, 'I think I'll eat my piece out in the open, 'tis lovely and sunny.'

Belle received her reward. As she and Gloria leaned against the street wall, Gloria said to her, 'Eh, there's that fine thing?' and Belle turned in time to see Gene come out of Rufus Street and join some of the lappers leaning against a far wall.

'Big fella,' said Gloria, 'some of them Taigs is big, but.'

Janice watched Belle watching Gene, and said softly, 'Your rescuer, Belle.'

'Aye,' said Belle, not giving anything away.

If Gene saw her, he did not acknowledge her. Belle returned to work.

At leaving time, she hung back slightly as if waiting for the lavatory, and then contrived to leave the building long after any of her usual homegoing companions. Taking her usual route, she turned into Urney Street, minutes from home. Behind her, someone coughed, and she turned.

'Hallo. I followed you. Just to say hallo.'

'Hallo.' Belle half-smiled.

'Are you free tonight?'

'I can't. My mother'd ask.'

'Tomorrow night?'

'Maybe. Where?'

'I don't know,' he said. 'I don't know the place well.'

She looked at the ground.

He pressed. 'I said I would ask you.'

'Ask away,' she half-smiled. She said, 'If you go on past Rufus Street, and don't go over the bridge, only go down to your left, there's a wee piece of ground down there with two trees and a seat before you get to the shipyards. What time?'

He stood there, alert and clean. 'Half-past seven. Tomorrow night, so.'

'Tomorrow night, so.' She smiled and mimicked his accent. 'All right.'

'All right yourself,' he mimicked back.

One Monday years ago, Edith said, 'We forgets the Lord's Day too soon, so we do. 'Twas only yesterday and look at us, carrying on as if it was years ago.'

Ever since, every Monday, Edith took down her Bible after tea and read aloud, as Belle and Lennie sat there in the required attitude of attentiveness. Edith chose – and adjusted – her text to suit her purpose of the moment.

'The Book of Job,' she began, 'Chapter 15. Then Eliphaz the Temanite replied, "Would a wise man answer with empty notions, or fill his belly with the hot east wind? Would he argue with useless words, with speeches that have no value?"'

Edith, stroking the thyroid bulge in her neck, had a way of looking at each of her children as if to signify that the words had been specifically chosen for them. Tonight it was Belle's turn to receive the glances, and once more she sat with her hands folded in her lap and her own glance directed downwards. Edith's meaningful looks fell about her children like silver arrows, but never struck home.

'"But you even undermine piety and hinder devotion to God. And sin prompts your mouth; you adopt the tongue of the crafty. Your own mouth condemns you, not mine; and your own lips testify against you."'

When she had finished, Edith asked, 'Belle, are you still telling them girls at work all about them rubbish pictures?'

'They're harmless enough,' said Belle.

Lennie grinned, and said, 'They all flock to hear them. We're even going up from the lappers' room for our breaks, so we are. To hear *Gone with the Wind*.'

'Shut up you,' said Belle, and took evasive action by finding clothes to iron.

Edith persisted. 'If you took a wee bit more interest in the Holy Bible, there's better stories in there.'

'Nobody minds hearing the pictures so they don't,' Belle protested.

Edith said, 'The Reverend MacCreagh says they rot the soul, so they do.'

'Aye, Belle,' grinned Lennie, 'your soul'll be rotten, so it will.'

'Like your teeth. Sure how would the Reverend MacCreagh know, Mam, if he's never seen a picture?'

'Aye, but he's a well-up man, so he is,' defended Edith. 'He's well up, so he is', and she preened her tall body a little.

Ten streets away, Joe said, 'We've had one great victory. We stopped them conscripting us. Think of that.'

Gene sat with his arms folded.

Joe said, 'And they can go on interning us, and it won't work, because we'll still fight on. My own cousin got TB out on that ship.' On a prison ship anchored in Strangford Lough, four hundred men, IRA or republican and nationalist sympathisers, had been interned without trial since the beginning of the war, with a further four hundred elsewhere in land prisons.

Joe sipped, wiped his mouth. 'What d'you think of this place anyway?'

Gene replied, 'Belfast? There's things I don't understand.'

'Like?'

'Like why there's no blackout at my digs.'

'The Germans,' said Joe, 'is our spiritual allies. The slogans, you should read them. "Join the IRA and serve Ireland."'

Gene said thoughtfully, 'But if you leave the lights on all over the west of Belfast – surely all that will happen is that you make targets for German bombers and the people in the lit houses will get killed and the others that observe the blackout, they'll be all right. So once more, the ordinary people that support the cause suffer and the activists get away.'

Joe changed tack. 'Where do you stand yourself? We were told you were coming.'

'What were you told?'

Joe said, 'We were told, like I said, you were coming.'

Gene, mild and careful, said, 'You make that sound as if I was something important. What you were probably told is there's a new fella coming in to Belfast who has a great interest in the politics of the north, isn't that it?'

Joe looked away. 'And have you?'

Gene replied, 'How could a person not have? Isn't it my own country? I'd want to be deaf and dumb not to be interested.'

Joe asked, 'How interested can we get you to be?'

Gene replied, 'I don't think I'm interested in what you're interested in. [He pronounced it 'inter-*est*-ed'.] What I'm interested in is – how you get used, how both sides get used, how those of us that work, in the mills, like, or the shipyards, how we're kept poor, and kept fighting each other.'

'Aren't you interested in the Struggle? I mean, 'tis a queer Irishman isn't interested in getting England out of the Six Counties?'

'Of course, I'm interested,' replied Gene, 'but not in the way you think. I'm interested because the Partition divided the natural personality of an island unit, but what I'm a lot more interested in is how a small bunch, like the Blackwoods and them, held on to everything by keeping everyone else at each other's throats. And how everything else is arranged down from that, the courts and the jobs and the houses and everything. And even things like not having running water and that, or employers not having to enforce the Employment Acts.'

Joe retorted, mimicking Gene a little, 'And what I'm "inter*est*ed" in is why your long fella De Valera is killing our patriots down where you come from? Answer me that – why is ould Dev executing IRA men? I mean, where does that fucking leave us?'

Gene reddened, and shrugged: 'I don't know. I don't know the intricacies.'

'The intricacies,' mocked Joe. 'The intricacies are that the south doesn't give a tuppenny fuck about the republicans in the north. The whole Catholics here could rot and your fuckers wouldn't lift your ludeens to help us' – he raised his little finger to demonstrate. 'You're all soft down there, soft as fucking butter.'

Gene turned his head away.

Joe asked again, 'Will you come to a meeting so?'

'Athhtth! Meetings?' Gene dismissed. 'Talk.'

'England's difficulty is Ireland's opportunity,' said Joe. 'If you weren't soft you'd, wouldn't you?'

As they left Doogan's pub, two policemen saw them, and knew Joe by sight.

Next evening, Belle said, 'I'm going over to Aunt Sandra.'

'Don't let that fella give you any drink,' said Edith, who had begun her evening rampage around the kitchen. She plastered the pink sperm of 'Windolene' on the glass doors of the crockery cupboard in the scullery.

'I won't,' breathed Belle placatingly.

'You never gave me all last week's money either,' said Edith.

'I gave you most of it. I have to have something for myself.'

'*I* was giving you money for yourself. See your brother Leonard, he does the right thing, he gives me his whole keep every week.'

Belle slipped away.

Rufus Street mill had always paid the wages of unmarried people who lived at home straight to their parents – who could then give back some spending money. Single men did well: mothers gave their sons money to buy cigarettes and feed pigeons; men had pubs and bookies to visit.

Some single women scarcely suffered – the daughters of unenvious mothers, or of women who had been what the men called 'lively in their day'. Such women, racier than Edith, gave their daughters money to buy lipstick, or powder, or such perfume as they could afford. Gloria's mother, for instance, wanted to share cosmetics or clothes.

Edith MacKnight gave Belle money only for planned outings, or some utterly necessary purchases; and Belle had to account for all when she returned: Edith would take the back of an envelope or a smoothed paper bag from the kitchen drawer, and make an inventory of Belle's expenditure.

'Teaching you thrift,' she called it. 'It'll teach you thrift, Belle, against the day you have your own house and children. Although God knows –' and there the sentence hung, with, Edith's particular expertise, the unfinished part ringing more bitterly than the words uttered.

In the winter of 1940, Blackwoods, fearing a wartime drop in their workforce, discreetly changed this controversial policy, and anyone who wished to be paid direct could apply; with Janice's help, Belle began to receive her own wages. Edith, disempowered, had never ceased complaining.

Boys approaching Belle endured similar flintiness from Edith, and so, notwithstanding her prettiness, nobody asked Belle out. Num-Num White (who ate biscuits all the time) spoke for all: 'Who'd brave the mother, though, she's a quare hawk?' – and few did.

In June 1937, when she was eighteen, Walker Spence invited Belle to a dance, 'a bit of a hop'. He worked in the mill: he was born two days before Belle. They went to a hall in Glengall Street, where a small band played from eight till eleven o'clock. Walker Spence spoke very little and every time the dancing stopped, he offered Belle a sweet from a large bag in the pocket of the heavy serge jacket he never once thought of removing. Beads of sweat glistened on his hair-oil.

As they walked home, Walker Spence kicked the lid of a polish tin he found on the street. He kicked it all the way to Belle's front door, and after from indoors she heard him continue to kick, until he faded out of tinny earshot. Edith wished to encourage Walker Spence, liked his mother, knew his aunt. Belle walked out with him on two more occasions: afterwards, he called to play cards with Lennie with the occasional remark in Belle's direction. Walker Spence, early to enlist, died at Dunkirk.

=

125

Gene did not lean against the wall, as other young men did when waiting for their girls; he stood in the middle of the secluded pavement, again the jacket folded over the arm. He said as he walked forward, 'I expected you to come from a different direction.'

'Out of the sky, like?' she asked.

He laughed.

'No. I just thought you were going to come from that way. Don't know why.'

His smile made her smile, and she said, 'You look as tall as my father.'

'How tall is your father?'

'He was six foot four.'

'Was? Isn't he now?'

Belle grimaced. 'No, he's six foot under.'

Gene said nothing, and Belle, ameliorating, said, 'He passed on ages ago.'

'Oh?'

She kept pace with his long stride. They reached the heart of the docks and he stood for a moment to admire the forest of cranes. In the distance, through an open door in the long lines of sheds, some hammering could be heard.

'They're still working?' he asked, as they walked on.

'The war effort,' said Belle.

'Isn't this a big place?'

'This is the world's biggest shipyard,' she said.

'Stop boasting,' he retorted, but she saw him smile.

'There's very few of them gone off in the war,' she said. 'They're all reserved.'

The feathery waves danced in the light. Someone whistled a tune and it carried on the waters of the harbour. Under the iron leg of a crane they stopped, and leaned.

'I don't even know your name?' Belle said.

'Gene. I know yours. Belle.' He held out his hand. 'How do you do?'

She shook it but he held on to it.

'I tricked you', and he smiled again. He looked down at her hand. 'You have nice hands, my mother has nice hands, your hands will be like hers, hers are all marbly now, like ivory.'

Belle stood there simply, her other arm loose by her side. Gene said to her, 'You never held anyone's hand before, did you?'

Belle replied quietly, 'No. Never.'

Gene asked, 'No – fella?'

'No. I mean, not anything. Only Walker Spence and he only kicked things along the road, like if he found a stone or a tin or something. Where are you from?'

'A place called Tipperary.'

'My uncle used to sing it. He learned it in the war before this. What's your other name?'

'Patrick.'

'Gene Patrick. I never heard such a name. Your second name is like a first name?'

He picked up her misunderstanding. 'No, that's my second Christian name, my full name, my surname is Comerford, Gene Patrick Comerford.'

'Gene is like Gene Autry.'

Soon they walked on again, and Gene, still holding Belle's hand, said, 'There's a pub.'

Belle said, 'We can't go in there.'

'Why?'

'That's a shipyard pub, they'd know you for a – I mean, it wouldn't be nice.'

'It's all right.' They strolled on, and Gene whistled a little, then, thinking aloud, said, 'Belle. Belle. "Belle" means "beautiful". Did you know that?'

'It is no such thing. "Belle" is the short of "Isabel".'

''Tis like having a child's hand,' he said, looking down at her hand again.

'Didn't you ever hold somebody's hand before?'

'I did.'

'Was she nice?'

'They were.'

'Oh. They?'

Gene said, 'Well, what would you expect? I'm thirty-four years old, and I'm a man, and one half of the world is made up of men and the other half is women. I worked for a woman for the last ten years.'

'Did you hold her hand?'

'That was one hand,' said Gene, with some emphasis, 'I did not hold.'

'But I s'pose hundreds of other girls?' asked Belle.

'No', and Gene laughed. 'And I have no girl now, I mean at the present.'

Silence. Someone nearby on a ship dropped something with a metallic clang. In the dusk, little could be seen anywhere, just one seabird flapping across the glim over the water.

'Belle. Belle. Belle the beautiful.'

'You said that already,' she remarked.

He asked, 'By the same token, why have you no boy? How come the fellas don't be flocking around?'

'Nobody asks me.'

'Are they mad or something?'

'They're all afraid of my mother.'

'Is that why you go to the pictures so often?'

'Maybe. But I like the pictures, I like sitting there in the dark and watching my own dreams come to life.'

'I know what you mean.' He stopped and turned to look at her.

'What are you looking at?' she asked jovially.

Gene grinned. 'I'm-looking-at-you-your-eyes-are-blue-your-face-is-like-a-kangaroo.'

She laughed.

'You have a grand laugh,' he said.

Belle said, 'Are you a bit of a Fancy Dan?'

'No. I am not.' He said it so gravely that she put her hand to her mouth in apology.

'It's all right,' he said, 'we're strangers to each other. But I'm not a "Fancy Dan", as you call it. And I'll say something now I wasn't going to say, and that I never said this way before. I'm going to like you.'

She tossed the endearment away. 'You'll be the first that does.'

Gene looked alarmed. 'No, that can't be the case.'

Belle replied, 'You don't know my mother.' Then she said, 'You're very nice.'

Gene evaded the compliment. 'The thing I'm noticing up here is. People want you to believe that you are what they think you are.'

128

She looked at him, and then down at her hand in his. 'How do you mean?'

'Well, you say that nobody likes you. They all say to me, "Oh, you're from down south," and so they think I'm one sort of person. As if all people from down home are all exactly the same. Them Blackwoods, if you're any different from what they want you to be, I'd say there could be trouble.'

They walked again, slowly.

'D'you know what time it is?' Belle asked.

He took out a watch. 'Half-nine.'

'I'll have to go soon,' she said, and they turned back. The light on the water had turned dark grey satin.

'Did you hear what I said?' asked Gene.

'Am I deaf?'

'No, Belle. I mean that I think I'll like you?'

'Yes.'

'And what about you?' he asked.

'What about me?'

He said, 'Might you like me?'

She replied, 'How do you know so quick you'll like me?'

He said, 'I like very little and I like very few.'

'Sure how would I know that?' replied Belle wistfully.

'Come over here to me,' he said, reaching for her arm and drawing her near him. He put a hand flat on her cheek and held it there gently. 'I said, and listen to me. I think I'll like you.'

Belle looked away. His hand followed her cheek, stayed there.

'By that I mean – you. Belle. Not anyone else.' And Gene bent and kissed her other cheek.

She stood stock-still. He whispered, 'Is that your first kiss?'

'Apart from your boy, Blackwood,' Belle murmured, 'but that wasn't kissing, that was grabbing.'

'Let me make it a proper one,' he said, and as she raised her face kissed her very softly and quickly on the lips. She took his hand again.

As they drew near Pretoria Street, she let go of his hand.

'Did you go to the pictures wherever you were living before?'

'Oh, 'twas different for me, we didn't have any pictures where I was, we were out in the country.'

'I mean would you go now?'

'Oh, yes, I mean, I have seen pictures. I liked *Ruggles of Red Gap*.'

'I never saw that. What else?'

'Not all that much. There wasn't picture-houses. What we had was the *seanchaí*.'

'The what?'

He spelt out the pronunciation. 'Shan. A. Kee.'

'What's that when it's at home?' Belle widened her eyes.

'The old storyteller. There was this old man used to go round the country telling stories.'

'Telling stories? God!'

'He'd come to a house of an evening, we'd all be sitting down by the fire and you'd hear the knock on the door and the latch'd lift and in he'd come, saying "God save all here" and he'd sit down and warm his hands, and he'd be given a mug of tea and a slice of bread and butter with maybe jam on it, and when that was finished and he'd asked about everyone, he'd start to tell a story.'

'What was he like?'

'Well, the one who came to our house, he was called Johnny Black, we never knew his real name, because he always wore a long black coat and a big black hat summer and winter. And he'd settle back in the chair, light a pipe of tobacco and we all waiting for him to start, and the pipe would take ages to get going, and then he'd throw the other hand out to the fire so that it made a shadow on the wall against the lamp, and he'd start. "Long, long ago, in my father's father's time, there was a man living not a hundred miles from here who had three daughters, every one of them more handsome than the next one."'

Gene stopped, saw Belle's wide eyes.

'And he'd go on, "Now this man, who had more than a shilling or two to his name, he was a very fussy man, and he always made it plain that the local lads needn't think they could go round to his house looking at his daughters. Because he was going to be very particular altogether about the sort of men they were going to marry. In fact, he said, he was going to be the particularest man in all Ireland, or all England or all Europe" – and away he'd go telling the story like that.'

'But hey,' spluttered Belle, 'what about the man and his daughters and getting husbands for them?'

'Oh,' said Gene, 'that story could last two or three nights. He'd stay by the fire until after midnight, then he'd go away, he might sleep in our house if there was room which there never was with twelve of us, or he might sleep in somebody's outhouse or haybarn.'

'And do you know the story of the man and his daughters?' insisted Belle.

'I do, but it would take ages,' said Gene.

'That's very disappointing, that's wicked so it is,' said Belle.

After a moment of silence, she asked, 'Are you going to tell me the story of the man and the daughters looking for husbands?'

He took her hand again and walked on. 'I am,' he said. 'Provided you'll meet me again.' He grinned.

They stood in the twilight at the end of the street next to Belle's.

'When's the next time?' she asked. He looked sideways at her, assessing that she spoke from innocence rather than forwardness.

'Will you come out if Sunday is fine?'

'And if it isn't?'

'We could go to the pictures,' he said. 'They have them on Sundays now, I notice, for the soldiers.'

'Of a Sunday? God help your head. My mother'd kill me dead.'

'Well, a walk or something. So – where?' asked Gene.

'Where what?'

'Where'll we meet?'

'I'll have to think.' Belle looked puzzled. 'The same place is the best.'

'How'll you get away?'

'Next Sunday's easy, she's going off to the hospital to see our neighbour.'

Gene paused a moment, then murmured, 'You're a grown woman.'

Belle did not reply.

Gene pressed. 'I mean, do you think you should be treated like that?'

She replied, 'You've a very soft voice.'

Then she said, 'Same place?'

'Twelve o'clock?'

'That's very early.'

'I just thought of something. I've a surprise in mind.' Gene smiled.

'And that's when you're going to tell me the story of the man and the daughters?'

He laughed. 'If you're good.'

Gene walked with Belle to the corner of Pretoria Street. 'A goodnight kiss?' he asked.

She lifted her face and closed her eyes, very like a child. 'Thanks,' she said, 'thanks very much.'

Returning to his own digs, Gene walked past the front of Rufus Street mill, and stopped in surprise. Some men were standing there with shaded lights.

Gene went forward, 'Hey, what about the blackout?'

'Who're you?' one asked roughly.

'I work here,' said Gene.

'So do I,' said the voice, 'now fuck off with yourself.'

Gene recognised Fergusson, who came over. 'Oh, hallo, lapper.'

'What's up?'

Fergusson took a conciliatory line. 'Nothing. Just a wee late party. You're out late yourself.'

Gene replied, 'It's a fine night.'

'Aye,' said Fergusson. At that moment, Gene heard a commotion inside the open door, the sound of a boy crying.

'What's going on?' he asked. Fergusson looked back over his shoulder, then at Gene, and then back again.

The boy yelped once more, this time in the high pitch of true pain.

'That boy's hurt,' said Gene, 'and why's he out at this hour of the night?' He pressed towards the gate.

Fergusson failed to stop him, turned and shouted, 'Hi! Close that door will youse?' He strode back a pace or two and shouted again. 'Hi! The door. Close the bloody door!'

Gene saw several figures. Two men supported a collapsing boy; a third man, tall and grey-haired, looked directly at Gene, turned his back, then walked swiftly into the deep shadows of the mill's interior. A heavy, soft-fleshed man with white hair and spectacles called, 'Close that door!'

Gene had begun to walk across the forecourt. Fergusson held out his arms wide to stop him. The door clanged shut.

'Out of bounds, sonny boy,' he said.

'I work in there,' protested Gene.

'Not this hour, you don't; that's a private party in there.'

'But,' said Gene, 'there's somebody injured at it. I could go for a doctor.'

The concern in his voice mollified Fergusson, who said, 'No. 'S okay. Best go on home. And say nothing.'

'But I know that man. With the glasses? Don't I?'

'But you don't know this town. Go on home now. You'll do yourself no good by not.'

Gene left reluctantly.

With Edith in bed early, Belle had to contend with Lennie alone.

'Aren't you going on night duty?' she asked.

'Not 'til tomorrow night,' he said. 'Hey, are you after having a scrap with ould Blackwood's cub?'

'Who told you?'

'Oh, a little bird.'

'Where did you hear it?' Belle tried to hide her upset. 'Did you tell Mam?'

'I did not. Not yet.'

Belle said again, 'Who told you?'

'Oh, I hears everything. Part of my job.'

Then softening, 'Ah, who told you, 'tis awful important? Did you hear it at work?'

'Could be.' Lennie smirked.

'Ah, Jesus, Leonard!' When Belle used his full name it signified urgency and 'distress. 'Not at work? No?'

'I didn't say what kind of work, did I? I've more than one kind of work, haven't I?'

Relief lit Belle's face. 'Aw – Malcolm?'

Lennie laughed. 'And he told me what a right puff you were in too.'

'Janice'll kill him.' Belle relaxed. 'Here, I'm making tea.' As she pottered she asked, 'Nobody else said anything?'

Lennie said, 'No, though young Blackwood, he looked very outa-the-way right enough the other morning, and he talking to the

133

new Taig – you know, your friend', and he watched Belle to see where the sting had landed.

'He only helped me out of a fix,' said Belle. 'He's not my "friend".'

Gene Comerford sat in his room, his orderly boots on the floor under the bed. He towelled his face with his hands, and tilted his chair back so that his shoulder-blades touched the wall. For minutes he never moved, staring into the distance. His sincere experiences with women had been as rare as boyfriends in Belle's life. In Sligo, Alicia Black kept him so under her thumb and always within her sight that he never got a fraction of the time off he had been promised. At Fintown, he found the local Catholic girls suspicious or contemptuous, and after two or three unsatisfactory encounters, he withdrew. In any case, he had a substantial long-running difficulty to resolve, one that became plain to him on his first full day's work at Cruisemans.

After their quiet little spat, in which Gene had defended his right to do his work and keep himself to himself, Judy Cruiseman put him to hard labour. Under her gestures and barked instructions, he lifted rocks, shovelled clay, uprooted old plants, hacked out interloping young sycamores. He worked so concentratedly and willingly that Judy's imperiousness began to die on her lips, and her orders mellowed into requests.

'I seem never to have to tell you anything more than once,' she said to him. 'That is unusual in a working man.' He smiled a half-smile. At half-past ten, with the sun climbing, and the crystal cobwebs glistening in the branches, she said, 'You will want a break?'

'My break isn't till half-twelve, ma'am.'

'No, go and get some tea. No. I'll get some tea brought out here. No, you go to the kitchen door and say I want some morning tea for two people brought out here to the kitchen-garden gate.'

Gene moved off and she watched him all the way, saw him disappear into the shadows around the corner of the house, waited, watched him re-emerge and walk briskly towards her. 'They say 'twill be about five or ten minutes, ma'am.'

'Good. I'll sit down.' She arranged herself on a garden seat made

134

of two wooden railway sleepers on the twin carved-stone pediments of an older seat.

'Ma'am, what will I do now?'

'Rest. Stand there and talk to me.' She arranged the long, filmy lavender skirt about her on the wooden spars.

'Now tell me, Mr Comerford – what do you think about?'

Gene looked away. After a pause he said, 'I think about bettering myself.'

'How?'

'About getting a better job, a job that has a way in it of improving all the time.' He looked at her.

'There's something – there's something strange about you, isn't there?' she asked.

'I wouldn't know, ma'am.'

'Maybe I don't mean "strange". Are you very holy?'

'How do you mean, ma'am?'

'Pious. I mean Roman Catholics are meant to be very pious, aren't they?'

'I do my duties, ma'am. No more than that.'

'Do the girls all love you?' Judy Cruiseman asked.

Gene cracked his fullest smile since he had come to Fintown. 'You'll have to ask them, ma'am.'

'I bet they do. I bet they do.' She peered at him, shading her eyes. 'Great big hands you have.'

By five o'clock, Gene had cleared that rockery space completely, dug the earth so deeply that residual moisture had been turned up, even though it dried immediately in the heatwave. Judy Cruiseman stayed near him all day, with occasional forays into the cool of the house, to the lavatory, or to fetch a bonnet, or a gardening book. She took only a brief lunch.

On one of these journeys, she returned by a roundabout way, through the kitchen, then through the kitchen garden, where she could observe Gene for a moment, and from quite nearby, without being seen by him. She leaned against the warm wall as he dug, lifted and shook the clay.

8

In the fourth week of August, Gordon Blackwood 'failed' his medical. The doctor at Musgrave Park, tapping his own heart and pointing to Gordon's, said, 'There is a murmur there.'

'Oh, come on, Doctor,' complained Gordon.

'No. I mean it. In ordinary circumstances it probably would not make a difference to your life – probably. You can appeal, but that will take a few months. By which time the murmur might have gone.'

The doctor telephoned Valerie, and said, 'As you were.'

She rang Rufus Street and said, 'Nesbit, Jack rang, he's seen Gordon. That's fine.'

'Oh, good!' said Nesbit. 'Good!'

Valerie said, 'D'you think Gordon'll be very disappointed?'

'He doesn't have to know,' said Nesbit. 'Jack didn't – mind, did he?'

Valerie said, 'I don't think he liked it too much. I asked them to dinner anyway.'

'Good,' said Nesbit. 'Well done.' In Bangor, looking through the french windows at the sea, Valerie replaced the telephone.

When Gordon reached the mill, Nesbit listened, commiserated and asked, 'Does this mean you can come into the mill a bit more?'

'Love to, Dad.'

They walked into lunch together, and Nesbit opened the boardroom windows. Lunch stood ready, with linen napkins and crystal glass.

Nesbit picked up a napkin. 'These are the new ones.' He tugged the napkin, examined the hem-stitching. 'The new line. *The Balmoral*. The ones I was telling Judy Cruiseman about.' He felt the cloth between his fingers. 'You have to remember, Gordon, that linen is the royal family of cloth. 'Tis as strong as steel and yet 'tis fine enough for any lady or child to have next to their skin.

Now you look at this napkin. You can tug it like a rope. You can pat your face with it as if it was the softest of fleece.'

'Yes, Dad, but you adore linen. It's your god, isn't it?'

'Goddess.' Nesbit held the napkin up to the light. 'I learned to adore it, Gordon. That's what values are. Feel that. Feel it. It might be a blade it's so strong, and you could dry a baby's face with it. What else could you do that with? Go anywhere with it. If you have to go back and you're in the trenches you'll value your linen, I tell you. I did. And when I was at Vimy it was the hallmark of an officer and a gentleman, good linen. And it saved lives.'

'Saved lives? Dad, that's stretching it.' They laughed at the play on words.

'Of course. Strong bandages. Got you there.'

Mrs Innes, in white starched-linen cap and apron, served the soup. The weather remained exceptionally beautiful, the early days of an Indian summer. When coffee came, and Mrs Innes at last had gone out again, and the door closed firmly behind her, Nesbit lit a cigarette, and drew a breath. 'Listen. There is a problem.' He spat and grimaced as if he had bitten a sloe. 'Jesus Christ! This is terrible coffee.'

'Rations, Dad.' Gordon laughed, and then asked, 'Are you serious? Is that the problem?'

'No, no.' Nesbit frowned and waved the cigarette smoke away. 'Odd bloody business. Heckwright.'

'Yes. I saw him this morning. He was arguing with Bingham. Bingham doesn't know his place, Dad, arguing with a Board director.'

'It's not that but this, Gordon. You know that Heckwright's –' Nesbit made a wavering gesture, hoping his hand would say the difficult word. 'He's –' Nesbit funked it again, drew on his cigarette, held it under his nose, picked a nostril with his cigarette thumb.

'I know, Dad.' Gordon smiled impatiently. 'He's a queer.'

'Yes, well, I expect you have it in the army.'

Nesbit fell silent, puffing hard. Gordon nudged, 'What's the problem?'

'Last night. Heckwright was having what he calls one of his parties. He uses the boardroom.'

'For what?'

'God knows. I never ask. So long as 'tis cleaned up in the morning.'

'But who comes to them?'

'Heckwright sends two cars out to a boys' home. At least that's what your Uncle Desmond says.'

'Which one?'

'Doesn't matter, Gordon.'

'Who else goes to these "parties"?' Gordon asked.

'You'd be amazed. But you don't want to know that. Anyway, last night something went wrong. It ended in tears. One of the boys INJURED – ' Nesbit whispered the word in capital letters.

'How old?'

'Ten.'

'Oh, Jesus.' Gordon wrinkled his nose.

'Yes. Quite. Anyway, that part's being dealt with. But the difficulty is – somebody saw, or they think he saw.'

'Who's they?'

'Fergusson was on the door. And that new lapper, the big curly-haired fellow –'

'Comerford. Yes, he's a good bloke,' cut in Gordon.

'He, the luck of it, happened to be walking home. Back from some pub or something.'

'I don't think he drinks. They were talking about him in the Lapping Room.'

'Well, out with some doxy or other – whatever. The thing is – he heard something and may even have seen something. Something damaging. Potentially. How well do you know him?'

'Well, I'm near him every day.'

'What's he like?'

'Fine. No, he's better than fine. I mean, Dad, he's a cut above the others.'

'How would you handle this?'

'In the army he'd be promoted.'

'Can you look after it?'

'I don't know. Let me think about it.'

Nesbit looked at his watch. 'Two o'clock. Merciful Lord, where's the time gone. Not a word to your mother.'

9

On Saturday afternoon, Edith announced that she definitely would accompany the Reverend MacCreagh next day 'to see his poor wife up in Antrim,' at which Lennie looked at Belle and grinned behind Edith's back. Her children knew that Edith would never admit to her friend's having a mad wife, and therefore Edith would never say 'Anniesburn'. Lennie had agreed to do extra roster on Sunday. Belle had the house to herself from half-past ten.

She almost overdid it, polishing two dull buttons on Lennie's uniform, seeing him off from the door: Edith had gone at half-past eight, carrying the shopping bag full of sandwiches she had made at seven o'clock.

Edith justified: 'They're all saying everywhere we should be asking ourselves, "Is your journey really necessary?", but I was saying to poor Mr MacCreagh if this kind of a journey isn't necessary, sure what is?' – and Lennie and Belle agreed.

Belle relished this most delicious of times: the house empty during the weekend; the neighbourhood and the city silent; a seagull cawking somewhere; a door slamming. She talked aloud; she stood in front of the mirror tossing her hair, feeding it through her fingers, holding it out and falling it, folding it; moistening a finger gently over each eyelash; twisting her body in profile to the mirror, smoothing her clothes from her ribs to her hips; or hands palm down on the windowsill, nosing the curtain aside with her head so that its lace framed her face like a veil.

Far away, over the brick terraces, a solitary shipyard crane stood crook-angled like a skeleton's finger. All doors of all houses were closed; all windows myopic and opaque; single plumes of smoke rose vertically, blue prison bars above the roofs.

A child laughed on the street and Belle leaned quickly and eagerly to the window, but the child, having escaped briefly, was hauled back indoors again. The Andersons.

She took out an old schoolbook, with brown paper cover. *Isabel Alexandra MacKnight, aged 10, 11 Pretoria Street, Belfast, Northern Ireland, Great Britain, Europe, The World, The Universe, The Milky Way. The First of September, 1929. Royal Girls' Academy: Headmistress: Ethel F. Simpson.*

Belle stood, stretched, lay down on the small bed, sat up, ran her hands up her bare legs from ankle to knee, caressing the shins.

She lay back again.

'I should have got him to call for me.' She chuckled. 'He could have ridden down the street.' She raised her legs parallel, lowered them; she laughed out loud, then fell silent, then sang a line:

> *'On a hill far away*
> *Stood an old rugged cross,*
> *The emblem of suffering and shame.'*

She stopped, sat up and said, 'I'm putting on lipstick, Sunday or no Sunday.'

Jumping to the mirror, Belle raised her arms and studied her side-view, her shape. 'That fella Gordon,' she said out loud, and said, 'Dth.' She slipped a hand inside either shoulder of her dress and eased her straps, then sang:

> *'You'll easy know a doffer,*
> *When she comes into town,*
> *With her long yellow hair,*
> *And her ringlets hangin' down.'*

Abruptly she sat on the bed and said out loud, 'Jesus, Belle MacKnight. You're going out with a fella? And a Taig into the bargain?'

Blinking in the sunlight, Belle closed the door behind her, dropped the key on the string back in through the letterbox and strode out. She saw one other creature – a dozing cat. Along the deserted docks, she waited in against a warehouse door near a crane; the raincoat Gene had told her to bring lay folded over her arms; a string carrier bag held sandwiches. When she heard the roar of the motorbike she peeped out.

'You look funny,' she laughed; Gene pushed back the big goggles and took off the cap he was wearing with its peak turned back.

'I hope to God this thing doesn't break down,' he said. 'Hop up.'

He parked the bike and showed her how to sit on the pillion. 'You're going to have to put your arms around my waist. Hard luck.'

'I'll pretend 'tis Gary Cooper,' she said. 'Where are we going?'

''Tis a surprise.'

In bright sunshine they rode south through the outskirts of the city and down into the countryside.

'Isn't it lovely?' she shouted in his ear, and he nodded.

After an hour, at the entrance to a village, he drew into the grass verge and cut the engine.

'Do you want to get off and rest?' he asked, hidden behind the goggles.

'Yes.' She slid off backwards, and rubbed her behind. 'I'm stiff. Where'd you get the bike?'

'A friend of mine. His brother has petrol rations he doesn't use. We're nearly there. But we'll walk the rest of the way because there's a lot of old people living here. And the noise, you know.'

'Will we be meeting anyone? My hair.' Belle took a comb out of her pocket and tried to drag it though the curls all tangled by the wind. 'I must look like a sheep.'

Everything sunlit and hushed; lace curtains; few chimneys smoking, owing to the Indian summer warmth; one old lady sat on a kitchen chair in her own doorway, dressed in black, looking out on the world.

'Lovely day,' said motorbike-pushing Gene to the old lady.

'Thank God,' she responded, her hands folded in her lap.

The couple walked on, climbing the hill to the outskirts of the village. Some flowers gleamed in the deep dark-green grass of the cemetery; crows and other birds traded busily in the trees by the church.

'Listen,' said Gene, stopping Belle with a gesture. They listened. 'There isn't a sound,' he said.

'Sunday,' she replied.

'But you'd think there'd be children or something.'

'No. The Sabbath. You don't play on the Sabbath.' Belle spoke seriously.

They panted a little from the climb. Belle asked, 'Did you see your fella Blackwood since?'

'I did,' said Gene, 'I meant to tell you the other night. He apologised to me. He said he did the same to you.'

'He did. I was amazed.'

'Am-aiea-zed,' he mimicked.

She jostled him slightly. 'Go you on.'

'Go-yew-ohnnn.'

Belle restored the seriousness. 'Why d'you think he said he was sorry?'

'Because he did something bad. Or tried to.'

'Tried to. But his sort – they never say they're sorry for anything?'

'Unless they're caught at it.'

'Them Blackwoods can do what they like,' said Belle, 'sure they own the Government.'

'Do they, now?' mused Gene.

Belle asked, 'Did you tell anyone?'

'No. I said I wouldn't. Why?'

'My brother knew.'

'Lennie?'

'How do you know him, oh, aye, sure you work with him.'

'Your brother doesn't know from me.'

'No. He knows from my friend's husband.'

Gene pointed. 'Look.'

Belle saw an old bridge down below them; people had begun to gather beneath the five arches, some broken.

'The viaduct,' said Gene. 'That's where we're going.'

'Where are we?'

He said, 'County Armagh. Near Crossmaglen. Were you ever down here before?'

'God, no.'

They remounted, and with the engine cut, glided down a long slope until they reached the large group of people, mostly men. Gene parked the motorbike.

'What's all this?' Belle asked, as people looked at them.

'Great fun,' Gene replied; a man came over and slapped Gene's arm, 'Ach, the hard and the wild. What about ye?' He turned to Belle. 'How yeh doin'?'

142

Belle smiled.

'You're just in time. Did you bring your money?' he asked Gene.

'You know me, Joey, never bet on myself.'

'Jayzes, I will, then.' Turning to Belle, Joey said, 'This fella's the one to show 'em, so he is.'

Belle smiled again. Gene took off his cap and goggles and stuffed them into the pocket of his coat, which he then threw across the bike.

'Right so. Where are we starting?' They walked with Joey through the crowd and several people said, "Iya, Gene, howya doin' there?' and he returned many greetings.

'Do you know what this is?' he asked Belle as she walked beside him.

'No.'

Gene told her. 'A game. We have to "Loft the Viaduct". Get this ball' – he weighed it in his hand, small, iron, the size of a tennis ball – 'over that bridge. Over the very top. It's not often it's done. And you only get your three chances.'

Ahead of them on the road, the crowd bunched and the arguments raged to and fro. Joey tried to talk down the odds on Gene, saying he had not played at all that year.

'Not since last September, that's a full twelve months,' argued Joey.

'Who's going first?' asked the referee, a tall man with iron-grey hair under a hat.

'Whoever wants to,' said Gene. 'I hate going first.'

A short, burly player with chilblained ears offered; his first throw bounced awkwardly off the russet brick.

'He's in the sheugh,' said Joey.

'In the what?' said Belle.

'In the sheugh,' said Joey, an irritable man.

'What's a shuck?' said Belle.

'If you know how to say it, why don't you know what it means?' He shook his head at the distraction.

'I never heard it before,' said Belle.

'It's the ditch, the drain or stream at the side of the road,' said Gene kindly, 'a trench with a bit of water in it.' And he patted Belle's arm.

Joey said to Belle, 'Jayzes, you must be from the back of beyond?'

'I am not! I'm from Belfast,' she protested.

'Whisht,' he said to her.

All three of the first player's throws had failed. Belle yawned.

The next man, young with a lank lock of hair, picked the ball from the clumpy grass where it had fallen, settled himself down on his hunkers to look up at the viaduct, then stood, ran and threw.

'No, that won't do,' said an older man beside Belle, 'no, thon's a goner.' The ball fell with a clank. Belle looked around behind her for a place to sit, could not find one.

Many more contestants lined up; each had three throws; all failed. Silence fell across the crowd, as a new contestant appeared, a beefy man, whom Belle had not seen before.

In a low tone, Joey said to Gene, as if apologising, 'There isn't anything we can do, you can't bar a man, especially if he's from the locality.'

'What's up?' asked Belle, latching on to anything of interest.

'He's a policeman,' whispered Gene, 'from Newry; his wife is from here.' In reply to Belle's still upraised eyebrow, he continued, 'It's different from where you live. They don't like the police around here. He's a nice man but a bit foolish.'

The policeman's wife watched and cheered as twice he hit the parapet and the third time his ball landed on top of the viaduct.

As a lad ran up to fetch it, Gene said, 'That's him out of it.'

They pressed Gene, who said with a smile, 'No, no, I'll wait,' and all the time he and Joey conferred.

Belle, irritated at the excluding conspiracy, asked, 'What's your hugger-mugger for?' A man beside her drank from a brown bottle. Gene put a finger to his lips, then rubbed together the two fingers of his other hand to indicate cash.

His turn came. Nobody knew how high: local lore said the old plans of the viaduct measured it at a clean hundred feet. The road beneath, now almost grassed over, had been bypassed several years earlier. Joey did a last circuit of the clustered gamblers. Gene abandoned his concentration to attend to the money matters.

'We're getting in big' was his only concessionary remark to Belle: he and Joey gambled an accumulator on, successively, one out of three; two out of three; and, for high stakes, three out of three.

Gene's first throw went clean over. For his second throw, he stood back, and the crowd cleared a corridor among themselves for his run. Just before Gene began, Joey ran down the corridor and pulled out one man, brought him to the back. 'We'll not have a repeat of this fella,' he said to Gene. At an earlier gathering, this man, gambling heavily, had pulled at a contestant's shirt just as the thrower was completing his run.

Gene took off and hurled the ball. It cleared the viaduct, and crashed down the other side, although the 'umpires', watching to ascertain that the viaduct had indeed been lofted, shouted, 'Close thing! It hit, it hit!' and little clouds of brick powder wafted down in the wake of the ball.

'We're in! By Jayzes, we're in. By fuck-and-Dr-Foster,' cried Joey, 'we're in,' and Belle laughed.

As he walked back, Gene said to Belle, 'I think I'm in too far.'

Belle, a look of some alarm on her face, said, 'How much?'

Gene smiled ruefully, 'Five hundred pounds I stand to lose.'

Belle started, but said quickly, 'Och, away to hell, see my Uncle Jed, he'd tell you he'd have that on the toss of a card' – and they both laughed.

As Gene lined himself up, he looked at Belle and winked. She cocked her head and said, in her best Scarlett O'Hara voice, 'Fiddle-de-dee', and Gene giggled. Then he made his face sober and took a few more paces back. Someone in the crowd said something and a few voices uttered sharply, 'Shhhh.'

In all great sporting performance, just as the pinnacle is attempted, the silence in the crowd is ordained by the stillness in the performer. A young bullfighter raising his arm to arrest the raucous brass of the band; a high-jumper, face down, eyes closed, nostrils flaring as he breathes in. The heroism of the moment, even in a village contest, requires, and receives, stillness.

Gene gazed at the ball in his hands as if at a talisman. He looked up at the viaduct. The skill in propelling a ball by hand at any target is first to assess the ball, then view the target, drink it, find your own target point within it, ignore its parameters, then direct all your concentration towards that personal target-within-a-target. Gene, having measured the viaduct as fully as he felt he needed, gazed again at the ball. He might have been alone; he might have

145

been standing on the whitened rock of a Greek island; he might have been a gladiator.

Incongruities occur at such moments. As he ran, his shirt-tail, fallen out on one side of his waistband, flapped behind him. He hurled the shiny little iron ball, he hurled it with all his body behind it and he screamed.

The ball rose in an arc, cleared the viaduct by two feet – 'two full yards', Joey claimed afterwards, and in the following month that went up to 'four fucking yards' – and landed beyond the umpires. Gene laughed and laughed.

As Belle and Gene met on the dockside that day at noon, Nesbit Blackwood and his son Gordon strode along a pathway by the railway line near Holywood. After church and a large breakfast, they told Valerie they would go for a long walk, and expect them back at near two, but no later.

'Are we expected?' Gordon whispered as they left the household.

'No, but I told Fergusson to tell Heckwright we'd call in. Desmond's going to call as well.'

They climbed the steep cinder path that led to the small rich road where Heckwright lived. From the wicket gate, they saw Fergusson standing in the open hall doorway as if awaiting them. He told them he had seen them approaching along the railway line.

Eric Heckwright sat in an armchair by a french window. A precise manservant in a black jacket appeared with a tray and Gordon looked at Nesbit to see whether his father, away from the eagle eye of his mother, would take a drink on a Sunday. Nesbit ordered vodka, smiling that it did not linger on the breath. Gordon ordered the same. Desmond arrived with his usual huffing of breath, and asked for whiskey; 'My house doesn't resound too much to the bells of the Sabbath,' he smiled, and the others chuckled. Heckwright followed his departing manservant, as if attending to some detail of hospitality.

Desmond whispered, 'He looks embarrassed, a bit, or am I imagining it?'

Eric Heckwright came back into the room, his white hair still damp from the morning's bath an hour earlier. As he sat down he rubbed his spectacles heavily without taking them off his nose, and immediately said to Nesbit, 'How is Valerie? Give her my love.'

Nesbit said, 'Well, I'll certainly bring your cordiality home with me, Eric, but it isn't what we came for.' Nesbit cleared his throat. 'Eric, I think we're looking at a wee problem here.'

Heckwright answered abruptly: 'The boy has been seen. I told you yesterday. I've spoken to the doctor myself.' He waved an irritated hand.

'Not what I mean, Eric. I tried to say it to you. Someone else knows.'

At which Eric Heckwright made a sheepish mouth, stuck out his chin. 'You mean Fergusson? I hire him. He's out there. You saw him on the way in.'

'Didn't Fergusson tell you?' asked Nesbit.

'Tell me what?' Eric Heckwright clicked into wariness, adjusted the spectacles.

'The fracas at the door was observed,' said Desmond.

'By one of the men on his way home,' said Nesbit. 'Eric – wake up.'

'Call Fergusson in,' said Desmond.

'No, no. I know,' said Heckwright. 'I know.'

A silence fell. Nesbit and Desmond exchanged glances instructing each other to hold the silence.

Heckwright eventually said, 'Well. What's to be done?'

Nesbit shrugged. 'I do not know' – he spoke deliberately – 'that we can – cover this one – all that well. What do you think, Desmond?'

Heckwright asked, 'Why not?'

'The man who observed.' Desmond blew smoke. 'Not safe.'

'Not safe?' Heckwright wrinkled in enquiry. 'But he's – one of ours. You said. "One of the men".'

'I didn't. You weren't listening.'

Heckwright replied, 'It's impossible to hear someone who's talking *at* you.'

Nesbit clinked his glass with his ring. 'We did not say he was "one of ours". We only said he worked for us. If you came into the mill as often as you should, and if you visited the different areas as often as you should, you would have seen him.'

'You of all people would certainly have seen him, Eric,' said Desmond, 'he's a big, beefy fellow. With auburn curls.'

Heckwright glared.

147

Nesbit said on his fingers, 'A, he's new, Eric. And B, Eric – he's not one of ours.'

'Ohnnn, blast. I get you.' Heckwright dragged his lower teeth on to his upper lip. 'A Roman Catholic.'

'And he's bright, by all accounts.' Nesbit watched Heckwright with dart-sharp eyes.

'Odd thing is,' Desmond said, mildly enough, 'you brought him in. Your niece, wasn't it?'

'Awww, pwwlewwph.' Heckwright clapped his hands behind his neck. 'The new lapper. From Fintown?'

'The very one,' said Nesbit mock-cheerily.

'And you're worried because Judy said he's a stickler?'

'Seems to be,' said Nesbit. 'Seems to be.'

'Oh, shit-and-bricks,' said Desmond suddenly, and jumped from his chair.

They followed the turn of his head and saw Nettie, fur jacket clasped shut, hurrying towards the door.

'Too late,' moaned Desmond, and like a cougar she bounded in the room.

'Here, Des, I'm getting froze. How long more are youse going to be? Eh, what's up, youse all have long faces? What about yeh, Nes? Hallo, Gordon.'

The men rose, and Nettie said to Eric Heckwright, 'Eh, it's yourself and the head on you? You ought to be ashamed of yourself, you ould get.'

She looked at her husband. Desmond blushed and laid a finger on his lips.

'No, Des. I'll not hush.'

Nettie turned back to Heckwright, planked herself on a low ornamental stool in front of him.

'Listen here to me, you. Des told me what about you and the wee boys, sure we all know, we used to call you "Nancy" down in the doffers, so we did. I never liked you.'

'Nettie –' Desmond tried to intervene. In vain.

'I always used to watch and keep the wee boys outa your way, and I seen you coming looking for them. Do you remember the time I told you to fuck off with yourself?'

Heckwright had not yet looked at Nettie. She adjusted her hat with its green feather.

'Well, I'm sorry I told you that,' she said.

Now he did look. Nesbit and Desmond sat down uncertainly; Gordon had not moved. Nettie patted the fur jacket in a soft mould around her bosom.

'Aye, I am, I'm real sorry. I shoulda done what they'd a'done down my street,' she said. 'Nancy fellas like you used to get a hammering, if anyone caught you looking crooked at wee boys.' She straightened her shoulders. 'But since I became a lady, I know different, don't I, Des?' – and she did not wait for an answer.

'I want to know all what's went on,' she said.

Nesbit intervened, 'Nettie, the –'

'No, thanks, Nes. Ould Bollocks-the-Boar here will tell me himself.' She stilled the room with a hand.

'The ah'm, the injured party,' began Heckwright, 'he has a – a sister, and he's gone to her on a holiday from – from –'

'Hold your pony there,' Nettie interrupted him. 'The injured party? Who's the party, like, and what's the injury?'

'A boy.'

'Age?' Her voice had the timbre of a whip.

'Twelve.' Under stress Heckwright pronounced it 'twailve'.

'Twailve?' echoed Nettie, then checked herself. 'And his – "injury"?'

'A bit of bruising.'

'Tell it me' – an order, not a request.

'Dr Pree has seen him.'

'Tell it me.' Heckwright flinched at her velocity.

He twisted his hands about and about. 'Well, it started as a joke. A bottle of champagne put up where it shouldn't be, and the cork popping off.'

'Up his wee arse? Ah, for God's sake! Who did it?'

Heckwright put his hands to his head. 'Well, we all did.'

'This'll make great talk,' said Nettie, turning her head to Nesbit. 'Did you know, Nes?'

'Not the detail.'

She turned back. 'Get that wee boy up to the Royal and get him seen by the best doctor in the country.'

Heckwright made a hopeless gesture.

Nettie closed in. 'I don't mind what you do in your spare time, so long as you don't maim wee boys. Stick to men, would you?'

149

'Nettie,' said Desmond, by now completely accepting of his wife's mastery. 'There's another problem.'

Nettie ignored him. 'Was the wee boy upset? Did he cry?'

'Nettie,' said Desmond.

'I heard you, Des. I'm not ready for you yet. Did there anyone look after him?'

Heckwright gestured towards the hall.

'Fergusson.'

'Fergusson? Sammy Fergusson, standing out there listening?'

They all heard the squeak beyond the door as someone stepped back in the shiny-floored hallway.

'Sammy Fergusson couldn't look after a train leaving the station.' Nettie flicked open her jacket. 'I don't like none of this, so I don't. This is bad.'

'Nettie,' said Desmond for the third time. She turned. 'There's another little problem.'

'What could be worse?'

'Somebody saw. Or at least heard.'

Nettie said, 'I bet there was plenty to hear, I bet that poor wee boy was roaring like a stuck pig.'

'But it was one of the men in the mill who saw,' said Desmond.

'Ach, Des, don't be talking. Sure aren't they after keeping their mouth shut the lot of them for years now?' She turned to Heckwright. 'Who else was there?'

'A friend of mine. A – an important man.'

Nesbit interrupted: 'Eric! Who?'

Desmond interrupted. 'Nettie, this lapper that heard the noise – he's a Roman Catholic.'

Heckwright said, 'Just leave it, Nesbit. I said. An important man. Very important. Is that enough for you?'

Nettie spun around. 'What!?'

Nesbit said softly to Eric Heckwright, 'It was Nicholas Bowling, wasn't it?'

Eric Heckwright replied, 'Do you expect me to answer that?'

Desmond continued, 'And the lapper was concerned enough to make a very particular enquiry of Fergusson the next morning. And he seems like the sort of fellow who wouldn't take "no" for an answer. He asked Fergusson had the competent authorities been informed.'

Nesbit looked at Heckwright: 'Really, Eric! God above!'; then looked at Gordon, pursed his lips and frowned. 'Authorities? Did you know that?'

Gordon shook his head. 'No, Dad.'

Nesbit asked, 'When did you hear that, Desmond?'

'Ask Fergusson,' said Desmond. Nesbit waved away the suggestion.

Nettie surveyed them all. 'Youse men can deal with that. Now,' she addressed Heckwright. 'No more of that stuff – right? I'll ask Des. And he'll tell me. You ought to be ashamed of yourself. Have you a soul to look after you? I mean you may have all your money and all to that. But thon wee man I seen coming in, if he's meant to be looking after you, sure he hasn't a pick of flesh on him. Who cooks your meals? I bet there's nothing wrong with you that a good feed regular wouldn't cure.'

Eric Heckwright waved her away weakly. Nettie stood from the little stool, her back to the others. 'And don't forget, 'cause I'll be asking. Get that wee boy seen by a proper doctor up in the Royal, d'you hear me? C'mon, Des, I'm famished.'

Upon which, nobody else seemed to feel that much remained to be said.

In the conversations after the viaduct, all present accepted Belle carefully, gave her the courtesy due to a friend of Gene. Amid goodbyes, they set out to ride back.

As they climbed on the motorbike, Belle teased him. 'But you're a real hero. You're like a film star, so you are.'

Gene blushed, and Belle pressed her advantage.

'You're like John Wayne. Or Clark Gable.'

Gene laughed and recovered. 'More like Deanna Durbin, I'd say.' They left the village.

After a quarter of an hour or so on side-roads, Gene had stopped the motorbike and said to Belle, 'I'm starving. Come on, we'll take a rest.'

He parked the motorbike under a tree, and they wandered into a quiet field.

'I'm still sweating,' he said.

'Take off your shirt, 'tis warm enough still.'

Belle pegged the shirt out on the branch of a tree, twigs held in her mouth like clothes-pegs.

She opened the carrier bag and began to feed him, waiting, as she had been trained, until he had eaten first.

'Come on,' he said, showering crumbs, 'yourself.'

'No, I'll wait.'

'You'll not!' Gripping his sandwich between his teeth like a dog trained to fetch a newspaper, he took a sandwich from the bag, pressed it into her hand and nodded at her. Belle blushed.

Gene, all food consumed, dusted down his hands.

'How much d'you win?' she asked.

'Count it.' Gene reached into his back pocket, handed her the roll of notes.

Belle looked at it. 'I never seen as much money as that.' She began to spread it out on the grass, and sat beside it. A breeze blew one or two notes a little distance away and she dived on them, to Gene's amusement. Then, all money arranged in notes of different sizes, as absorbed as a child with a painting book, she bent her head, tongue sticking out of her mouth. She counted once, then lifted her head, looked at Gene in disbelief and counted again.

'D'you know how much is here?' she asked.

'To the penny.'

'You do not?'

'I do so.'

'How much?' challenged Belle.

'Five hundred and forty pounds.'

Belle gasped in agreement. 'But that's a fortune!'

'I know.'

'Have you more money made that way?'

'I have.' Belle was silent.

Gene asked, 'Don't you want to know how much?'

Belle said, 'How much?'

'I've nearly two thousand pounds. All in the bank.'

Belle looked flummoxed. 'I never knew. And there's me keeping three shillings a week after paying my mother her share for my keep.'

'Yes, but you're paid a criminal wage. The unions should be doing something to stop that.'

'The Blackwoods won't have the unions, they pay them off.'

'I know.' Gene rolled over to look at her.

'Do you want some?'

Belle indicated the cash. 'This?'

'Yes.'

'No, I can't do that.'

Gene said, 'Here. Gimme.' He took the money and counted out fifty pounds. 'That's for you.'

'No,' said Belle, and recoiled.

Gene said, 'Yes,' firmly and handed it to her. She looked at it askance as if it might burn her.

'To Belle. From Gene.' He winked.

Belle reached out, took the money gingerly and counted it. Gene laughed.

'But this is a fortune,' Belle protested.

'Buy yourself something nice – and keep some for a rainy day,' he said. She looked at him and looked away. He said nothing, merely watched and waited. Eventually she sniffed and laughed.

'Come over here,' Gene asked.

Never looking up into his eyes, head down, she crawled to where he lay, then laid her head upon his bare chest. Silently, he stroked her hair. After several minutes she raised her head and began to inspect him.

'You've hair on your chest.'

'Haven't you?' he asked, making her heave with giggles.

'You've gold hair,' she said in surprised approval.

'Mmm,' he agreed.

'What are these called?' She indicated his right nipple with her thumb, circling it, tweaking softly the hairs that grew from it.

'Same as with you. Nipples.'

'Nipples?' she queried. 'That's something on a baby's bottle.'

'That's what yours are called too,' he said. 'What do you call them?'

'I never called them anything to anyone.'

'What about the women you work with?'

'Tits. Or dugs. One woman says "paps". Nipples?' Belle echoed again. She laid her head on his right nipple, then his left.

'I can hear your heart.'

'Is there music in there?' asked Gene.

'There's a bit of a wheeze.'

'Yes,' he agreed.

'My brother Lennie, he was always wheezing as a child, they thought he had TB, that's why he isn't a soldier.'

Belle hummed a tune for a moment, fiddled with a stem of grass, then raised her head and kissed Gene like a child.

'That's the first time I ever kissed you,' she said. 'You're always doing the kissing.'

'You're getting good at it.'

Belle looked at his chest again. 'Nipples? Two nipples.'

Gene asked, 'How many have you? A half-dozen?'

Belle looked puzzled. 'Why so? Do people . . . ?'

'Oh, they do,' he assured her, 'in decent families the women'll have three or four down their stomachs, you know, like buttons?'

'Really?'

But Gene could not contain himself and burst out laughing and Belle dived on him and pulled his hair. Then she sat up panting. Gene put out a hand and tangled his fingers in her hair.

Belle said, 'I feel funny.'

'Nice. Nice,' said Gene, 'Belle, lovely Belle.'

He sat for a moment and studied her, the way her dark hair fell into the pocket of her shoulders at the front, the chipped front tooth. Then he drew her towards him and, there, sitting together in a field in Armagh, with a wood nearby and small clouds above, he held her close to his chest of golden hair for several minutes.

Kissing her hair he pushed her gently away, rose and fetched his shirt; she watched sweetly and passively.

'Always put back everything as you find it, that's what my grandfather told me,' he joked.

'Kiss me again,' she asked.

'No. I'm not allowed to.'

'Who's stopping you?'

'It could get to be a sin,' he said gravely.

'Oh?' she asked.

He nodded, then knelt in front of her, struggling with the shirt. 'Don't think I wouldn't love to, Belle. Don't think that.'

'You're gone very serious,' she said.

'I know. I know.' He caught her hands. 'Listen. I'm saying this now. To you. Here. There's something awful nice about you.'

Belle shook her head. 'There's not.'

'There is. You don't have to believe anyone else, your mother I mean. You could believe me.'

She escaped and began to gather their debris. Hand in hand they walked to the gate, where they leaned a little apart, for some minutes, in silence.

'You nearly caught me out with that thing about people having half a dozen nipples,' she said.

'Come on, Belle,' he said. 'Did you hear what I was saying to you?'

'I did. But you don't know me.'

Gene rapped the top bar of the gate. 'All right. Tell me what is so terrible about you.'

Belle shook her head. 'My mother says, she says I bend with every breeze that blows, that I believe the very next person I meet.'

Gene asked, 'Did you think about me at all since the other night? The night we went for a walk?'

Belle bit her lower lip. 'I did. I thought about you all the time. But I didn't tell anybody.'

'No. Nor me. And – that's all right. And I couldn't stop thinking about you.'

Belle said, 'What age are you?'

'Thirty-four.'

'You're nine years older than me.'

'But,' said Gene, 'this never happened to me before.' He put an arm around her shoulders and they stood there side by side, leaning against the gate.

Belle and Gene reached Belfast with the last daylight of that golden Sunday. As they rounded the angle of the bridge and went down the steep high-walled slope to where they first met, two policemen, one of whom was Malcolm, watched from the parapet.

The other man, much older, said, 'Isn't that poor MacKnight's young one, you know the sister of that boy in the Specials?'

In her room, Belle looked at herself closely in the mirror to see whether she had altered in any way. She undressed quickly, again slipping the nightdress over her head before removing her underwear. In bed, she lay still, her hands gripping her knees. The blackout curtain made the room entirely dark. For several hours, she hardly changed position, her eyes wide open, with no vestige of sleep. The chimes on all the city's clocks had been silenced by the war: she had no way of telling the time. Once, she raised her hands above her head, but the light chill in the room sent her hands back under the covers. Next, she lay on her stomach, chin on hands on pillow. Finally she turned to the wall, her usual sleeping position, and closed her eyes.

10

When Edith called Belle for work, she rose as freshly as if she had slept all night.

'I never seen you so early of a Monday,' said Edith in the kitchen. Belle shrugged.

At the door, she saw Noreen leaving her aunt's house. They waved.

'You're looking great, Belle.' Noreen picked through her teeth with the edge of an old envelope. 'Do you take porridge, Belle? My aunt makes it with lumps in it, and it only half-baked and the oats sticks in my teeth.'

'Noreen, that's a lovely blouse, you've lovely clothes always.'

Noreen moved to the lower deck of teeth, her mouth open. 'Aahmmm – I makes 'em –'tssss – myself.' She sucked. 'Belle, my aunt is off her head. She takes the cat into the bed with her.'

Belle roared with laughter. 'Noreen, you're always making me laugh.' They moved off together, chattering.

Half an hour later, when Lennie had left the house, Edith entered Belle's bedroom, checking at the window that Belle was under sail. First she advanced upon Belle's raincoat, still thrown on the back of the chair; Belle had not hung it up on the back of the door. Edith searched the pockets and then examined the coat front and back, inside and out; she peered closely at a green stain – paint or grass? – at the hem, then returned the coat to its careless place.

Next, she lifted the end of the mattress, where Belle put her used underwear until she had time to wash it. Edith took out the knickers Belle must have been wearing yesterday and held them up to the light of the window. She ran her fingers all around the elastic at the waist, and then turned them inside out to examine the gusset, which she inspected minutely – even taking her spectacles from her apron pocket – then sniffed the gusset from a distance. She opened out the fabric, and turned the gusset over and back, trying to assess. Returning the knickers to their place beneath the mattress, Edith then turned over the rest of the mattress, found nothing and began her not infrequent comprehensive search of her daughter's room.

The level of face powder in the box had dropped considerably since she had last searched; a new lipstick lay hidden beneath the jumpers; she searched the magazines' pages for any letters or notes, looked at Belle's old school jotters in whose vacant pages Belle sometimes jotted notes resembling diary entries. Edith found nothing.

Next she checked all the pockets in Belle's folded blouses, and the pockets of the other coat on the hanger under the shelf, checked the folds of all the jumpers, poked her fingers into the toes of Belle's two pairs of shoes, took down and turned over all of Belle's meagre supply of underwear. In Belle's other bra she found a sweet paper so carefully folded that it could not have got there by accident; Belle had kept it since her very first walk with Gene by the dockside cranes.

Edith opened the hooks and eyes of the pillowcase and felt the pillow throughout to see whether Belle had buried anything deep within there – no, nothing, no hard objects, no lumps. Likewise, she checked every one of Belle's cushions – 'There's nonsense,' she muttered aloud to herself, 'cushions in a wee house like this.'

Getting down on her hands and knees, Edith finally searched under the bed, and with some effort lifted away the skirting-board to check whether Belle had put anything new in her hiding-place. Tucked on the left-hand side, and tucked back towards the front, all the harder to find, she found the roll of notes, the fifty pounds Gene had given Belle.

Edith knelt upright, and held the cash at arm's length in shock. She peeled the notes from the rubber band, counted the money, held each note to the light, counted it again, put the roll into her apron pocket, dived back in under the bed and patted the length of skirting-board back into place. She checked the room finally to guarantee everything as she found it and went downstairs.

=

Belle quit spinning, and jumped away from her stand.

She called out above the machine roar, 'Right. I'm sick and sore of this. Who wants to hear about Atlanta catching fire and Melanie and Scarlett having to flee for their lives?'

'Me, Belle, me!' roared a nearby chorus.

Belle raced up the Long Room to Janice.

'Shove over, Janice, let's at it,' and made to climb on the high stool. The women began to stop their looms.

'No, Belle, not the day.'

Belle looked at her.

'No, Belle, not the day!' repeated Janice.

'Why?' asked Belle. 'Come on, Janice.'

'Belle, go you back to your stand,' Janice said curtly, and stared Belle in the face and eyes. Alice MacKechnie watched closely. Belle looked from one woman to the other, shrugged, then strolled back to her stand and began to spin on to a new bobbin.

'Wooooo!' A low cry went up from some of the women. All machines had stopped.

'Gloria, what's up with Janice?' asked Belle.

Gloria said in a short tone, 'Don't ask me, Belle, ask Janice.'

The women watched as Belle returned to work.

'Turn back on,' called Janice. 'Mr Bingham says no more pictures for the minute.' The machines came back to life, one by disgruntled one.

Gene, in the Lapping Room, described the game.

Montana Campbell said, 'I had an uncle down in Dungannon, used to go over there and play that.'

Gordon Blackwood said, 'Tell me that again.'

Gene said, 'You have to lift the ball full over, it has to clear all obstacles on the viaduct.'

'Lesson for life,' said Ernest MacCloskey. 'Mmmm? Lesson for life.'

Gene laughed gently in agreement.

The lappers sat at long high tables, the last of their breed. Only a mill as outdated as Blackwoods had lappers working in this way, still examining the cloth against the light, still hand-cutting it into lengths when it came from the weavers' looms, still dictated to by the designers or sample-makers, the absolute elite of the workers.

Occasionally they dealt in special lengths for Noreen and others, who embroidered the patterns, or who made the actual cloths and napkins, the linen product.

Gene and Gordon heaved a wide-width bale, blowing away the dust at the same time.

Lennie watched. 'Where did you learn your trade?' he asked.

'Down the country,' said Gene.

'Fintown, wasn't it?' said Gordon.

'Yes,' said Gene. 'Fintown.'

Lennie said, 'How come you're not enlisted?'

'I wouldn't pass the medical,' said Gene.

'One ball? Is that it?' cracked Montana, and burst into song. 'Hitler had only one big ball.'

'Our friend here, he threw the other one over the viaduct by mistake,' added Archie. Gene laughed.

Lennie pursued. 'And how come a big strong fella like you wouldn't pass a medical?'

Gene stared at him – and made an error. 'Maybe I had a bad chest, too?'

Lennie blazed. 'How did you know that?'

Gene reddened. Lennie jumped.

'How in the fuck did you know that?' Lennie picked up his lapping-stick and advanced on Gene. 'Come on, big fella. Come fuckin' on.'

Gene jumped down from the high stool, and the rest of the lappers scattered.

Archie said, 'Lennie, get you on. Stop that.'

'I'll fucking stop *him*.'

Gene stepped backwards until he stood with his back to the bales of cloth. As Lennie stood before him Gene reached out, almost calmly, and using the stratagem of surprise lightly flicked the lapping-stick from Lennie's hands. In the same fluid movement, he snapped it in two. Lennie looked at him in disbelief. Gene said softly, recovering his lost ground, 'I heard you wheezing. I know what wheezing is.' He tapped his own chest. 'I had a bit of TB. Long time ago.'

Lennie, doubly disarmed, dropped his hands to his sides and turned back. 'I was only greasing him up,' he said sheepishly to the rest of the lappers.

Montana called, 'Big fella, you're going to have that docked, so you are, that stick is, what, three pounds seven and six – and more.'

Gene laughed. 'I'll lick it and stick it back together.'

Gordon said in an amazed tone, 'Jesus, you must be as strong as a horse. Do you know what that is made of?'

'Ebony,' said Gene.

'The hardest wood of all,' said Ernest.

Gene shrugged off the compliment. 'There's a knack to it.'

Belle missed Janice at the end of the day. She called to the house that evening. In Janice's kitchen, Malcolm was mending a cage for the pigeons.

'I hope you're not clipping their wings, Malcolm?'

Malcolm winked at Belle. 'I'll clip your ear, so I will.'

He looked at Janice, rose, fixed the kettle to the range and said, 'Aye. Aye.'

Janice said coolly, 'Hallo, Belle, how are you?' and went upstairs with an armful of clothes.

'Belle,' Malcolm said, 'you'll have to get married.'

Belle said, 'Malcolm, d'you remember Walker Spence?'

Malcolm laughed, and Belle's spirit lifted at his show of affection. 'And the hair-oil and the sweat. It was like a duck, his head was, the oil and the water on it.'

'What kind of man would you like to marry, anyway?' asked Malcolm.

Belle kicked up a leg behind her in fun. 'John Wayne – or Leslie Howard. Or James Stewart, I like him.'

Janice spoke curtly and fast from the stairs.

'Belle MacKnight, are you out of your mind? Twenty-five years old nearly, and you're waiting for John Wayne to come riding up Pretoria Street. God help your brain.'

'What's eating her, Malcolm?'

'Belle, I don't know the mysteries of women, do I? I mean, I'm only a cop walking my beat.'

He shuffled his boots. 'Listen, Belle, go on home. Janice is in bad oul' form. Go you on.'

She peered up the stairs and called out, 'Janice! Janice!'

No reply: Malcolm shrugged, and Belle, a puzzled and troubled look on her face, left.

From the stairs, Janice asked, 'Did you say it to her?'

'No, I did not.'

'You said you were going to.'

Janice came down into the kitchen.

'Janice, this is a sore business, I can't turn around and say to Belle she's not to be walking out with a Catholic.'

'I can!'

'You should not, Janice, that's Belle's business.'

'And if she marries him, what? He might be an IRA fellow. And even if he's not, she has to bring them children up in the Church of Rome, so she has.'

'Janice, she's not married to him, sure, she mightn't even like him, like. You know.'

'Are you blind deaf dumb and stupid you? Belle? Never out with a fella in her life? Belle'll marry the first fella's half-nice to her – to get her away from her mother. And your man? You seen him in this kitchen. He might be a Taig but he looks like a film star. Cop on to yourself, Malcolm!'

The kettle boiled and Malcolm made tea, set the pot carefully on the range to draw, and sighed.

Janice nagged on. 'Never anything but trouble when that happens. She'd be better off not marrying at all. I knew you weren't going to say it to her.'

Malcolm said, 'But if he was a nice fella?'

'Accch, see you, Malcolm Gillespie, you're as watery-headed as your mother! A nice fella? Oh, aye, a gun in one hand and a bomb in the other and a knife up your arse and he smiling to your face!'

'Right enough, Janice, his eyes was awful close together.' He poured tea. 'There y'are, girl.'

Then he sat back in his chair. 'But you're dead right, Janice. See me? I hold no malice against no man. But I seen them boys and they trying to kill one of our fellas. And I seen them above at the jail, and they singing their songs and shouting, "Up the Republic," and I swear to God, Janice, I'm a trusting man but I wouldn't take my eye off of one of them, even and I married to one.'

'Stab you in the back,' said Janice, 'and they'd want our houses for all their children. Why do they have so many children?' Janice's voice rose with the rhetoric in the question. 'So's they'll overtake us altogether, and outnumber us. And then outvote us, that's why.'

'Aye, and they're dirty too, any time we have to go into one of their houses, I hate it, so I do.'

'Malcolm, Belle's marrying no Taig.'

'Janice, all I'm saying is – don't go round it the wrong way.'

Janice looked at him. 'What way, so?'

'How would I know? But leave poor Belle alone.' He paused. 'We can't be telling Belle her own business.'

That same evening, Gordon approached Gene and said, 'My father would like to see you upstairs.'

Gene looked at him apprehensively, and Gordon said, 'I think he wants to give you extra responsibility.'

'Oh?'

'Yes. You've been under observation. Favourably.'

Gene climbed the staircase beside Gordon, who said, ruefully, 'This is where we had our little fracas.'

Gene, suspicious, said forthrightly, 'Is that what this is about?'

'Oh, no, no,' said Gordon: Gene did not seem persuaded.

'Here we are,' said Gordon to his father through the open door of the boardroom.

'Come in. Come in.' Nesbit looked at Gene and said, 'I didn't know you were as big as that. How high are you?'

'Six three the army said.'

'The army?'

'The enlisting office in Enniskillen.'

'I didn't know –' began Nesbit.

'He had TB as a child,' said Gordon. 'He told us today.'

'But whatever about your lungs, your heart was in the right place nevertheless,' said Nesbit, smiling at his own joke. 'Sit down, sit down. Will you take a drop? I've been meaning to talk to you ever since Lady Cruiseman asked us to take you on.'

'I won't, thanks,' said Gene.

'He doesn't drink,' said Gordon.

'A virtuous man?' joked Nesbit. Conciliatorily, he said, 'Do you know, I think you're the first southerner we ever had here.'

Gene, prepared to be pleasant, said, 'There's not much flax, or much linen down south.'

'Yes, that's true, that's true,' said Nesbit, pouring gin. 'Where are you from?'

'County Tipperary.'

'It's a long way,' said Nesbit. 'I suppose everyone says that to you?'

'Now and again.' Gene smiled carefully.

'I was never down that far, that's down very far, isn't it?' said Nesbit. 'My mother used to go and stay at the La Touche Hotel in Greystones, do you know it at all?'

'No, I don't,' said Gene.

'And I have to say, she was always treated very well; of course Greystones has hardly any Roman Catholics. Will you take a mineral water or anything?'

'No, thanks, fine, I'm grand,' said Gene.

Gordon said, 'Dad, this man handled a bit of a bust-up very well today.'

'Oh?' asked Nesbit, sitting down with the siphon cradled awkwardly in the crook of his arm. 'I nearly always wet myself with this thing. A bit of a bust-up? What happened?'

Gordon told the story of the lapping-stick. Nesbit looked at Gene. 'That was well done. Did they tell you the cost of the stick would be docked from your pay?'

Gene said, 'I'd rather pay for it straight out.'

Gordon said, 'I don't think we should. If he hadn't done it, we might have had worse.'

Nesbit pondered aloud. 'And it was the MacKnight boy? Yes, well I can understand that. That's sad, you know that family. But you mustn't take it personally, Comerville.'

'Comerford, Dad.'

Gene said astringently, 'I'd take a clatter from a lapper's broaching-stick very personally.'

'No, what I meant was, you mustn't take his opinion of you personally. Anyone'd feel the same, well they might not, but I can understand.'

Gene looked puzzled. 'Sure he never met me before in his life until I came here? Is he always so headstrong?'

Nesbit said, 'It isn't you, it is what you are. You don't know, do you? Oh, I thought you did. When he was a wee boy, his Dad, who worked here, was a Reserve Police Constable, a very nice man, he was killed by the, you know, the Sinn Feiners, the IRA. Very sad, he was an awful nice man. The girl works here now, of course you know that,' he said to Gene.

'No, I didn't.'

'Of course you do, she's one of the spinning-women. The one who tells the pictures.' Gordon looked over as if Gene had been lying.

'No, I mean I didn't know the father had died like that.'

Nesbit continued, 'Oh, I have a feeling, but it is only hearsay, I have a feeling that to this very day the girl does not know how her father died. The mother, a decent wee woman, very religious – and she had this idea about not breeding hatred, and the girl was only small at the time, and you know – things can go on never being spoken of. Aha, that does it, success –' and Nesbit handed the siphon to Gordon, having squirted a measure into his gin without accident.

'Now,' said Nesbit, 'it's not that but this. How would you like to earn some extra money?'

Gene smiled. 'I never turn down work.'

Nesbit said, 'We need extra care on the doors at night and at weekends, and we work rosters. The men get very well paid for it and now the war, you know.'

Gene sat listening, twisting an end of his lapper's apron in his fingers slowly.

'It would mean probably Friday and Saturday nights in your case, they're the prime shifts, so your work wouldn't be interrupted, and you only work half a day on a Saturday as it is. Being a lapper. Isn't that right?'

'A position of trust,' interjected Gordon.

'Yes, very much,' supported Nesbit.

'If the mill is always closed at weekends and if the last workers leave every night at nine, why do you need nightwatchmen?' asked Gene.

'We don't need them all the time,' said Nesbit quickly, 'just the war. You know.'

'I mean, sometimes,' cut in Gordon, 'Dad and my uncle have meetings here out of hours, emergencies, a shortage of men, that kind of thing, and they need the peace and quiet to discuss things with Bingham or whoever –'

'So how about it?' asked Nesbit.

'Can I think about it?'

'Ah, that's what I like – a reasoned man,' said Nesbit. 'Gordon was right, I should keep a close eye on you, you could be an asset, you could. And you know of course it isn't everyone we could ask, I mean not everybody understands.'

'How do you mean?'

'Well, a position of trust,' concluded Nesbit, 'you'd see confidential meetings, you'd have to take an oath of secrecy and that.'

'A real oath, it is, too,' said Gordon. 'Full-blooded.'

Gene stood. 'Thanks very much. As I said, I'll think about it.'

With polite remarks, thanking him for coming to the meeting, they escorted Gene to the door where they shook hands with him.

Back inside the boardroom, Gordon asked, 'Well, what do you think?'

Nesbit replied, 'I think one thing, I think we're absolutely right to try and keep him quiet. That's no fool.'

'No,' said Gordon, 'and he's not impressed by authority, either.'

'That's what Judy said.'

For three weeks into that first mid-July in Fintown she had worked him in the garden until, as she said, 'The flax will claim you.'

One evening, as they finished, she said to him, 'Mr Duncan told my husband he needs you from tomorrow.'

'Yes, ma'am.'

'I'm going into the house now, and when you have washed your hands could you come and see me; I will be in the Treasury, that's the big door at the top of the stairs.'

'Yes, ma'am.'

'Come through the front of the house, not the kitchen.'

At six o'clock, Gene washed his hands in one of the enamel basins set out for the workmen on the tables at the back of the Big Store, as they called it, and made his way back from the yards to the terrace. Faces watched him from the scullery and the lower kitchen; the girls had been betting on how long it would be before he would be invited indoors by Lady Cruiseman. Nobody speculated to Gene; so far, they hardly knew him, as all his active days had been spent in Lady Cruiseman's company out by the kitchen-garden wall; on her instructions all his tea and his food had been taken out there.

'That one,' said Mrs Ford, 'she hasn't let him out of her

sight since he came here,' but she shut up at the sharpness of Mr Caldwell's glance.

'In here,' called Lady Cruiseman, even though Gene had only ascended one-third of the staircase.

He completed his climb carefully, and notwithstanding her called instruction, knocked at the open door of the Treasury. She waved from the far end of the long, high room; she half-sat, half-lay on a slightly frayed, brocaded chaise-longue, by one of the marbled pillars, able to see through the tall window, but not easily visible from the lawns below.

Gene walked down the room. 'Barry,' she said, indicating the room, 'the architect. He did the Palace of Westminster. This house was his last job before he died. He died before the building of it was finished.' She extended her hands to Gene. 'His son finished it. Help me up.'

He could not avoid taking her hands, and she propelled herself upright by pulling against his grip. Standing before him, but not releasing his hands, she said, 'Goodness, my blasted leg aches,' and said, 'No, I'll have to rest it, here, help me down,' and she lowered herself by using Gene as a steadier.

'I'm a very unsubtle woman, Comerford.'

She stretched on the chaise-longue. 'Look at it.' She pointed to the afflicted ankle and foot. 'What a curse. So as a woman I have two curses, haven't I?' Seeing Gene's uncomprehending expression she said, 'Ooooo, you don't know what I'm talking about, do you?' and then, ruminating aloud, said to the window, 'Yes, ye-es, of course, Catholics and morals, ye-es.'

She snapped, 'Here. Take off that shoe will you.'

Gene walked around to the end of the chaise-longue and leaned down. 'Oh, you'll have to bend. How do you think you're going to undo laces standing up?'

Gene stood.

'No. On your hunkers,' she said irritably.

Gene looked down. 'The shoes look awful tight, ma'am,' he said.

'The foot's swollen with the heat. Look at you,' she said, 'you've found a club-footed Cinderella.'

He looked at her gravely.

'Now,' she snapped. 'Take off my shoe and please rub my foot, it is very sore.'

He shook his head. 'I can't do that, ma'am. I'm a working-man.'

'Oh, you mean this is a job for a girl? Or a cissy?'

Gene shook his head again. 'No, ma'am, 'tis a job for a –' He stopped.

'Stop ma'am-ing me! God in Heaven! And job for a what? A job for a fool? A job for a nincompoop?'

'No, ma'am.' Gene's attitude grew firmer. 'A job for a husband, ma'am, or a doctor, or a nurse.'

Contrary to her usual nature, Judy Cruiseman was nonplussed. She flapped a hand, four fingers closed. 'Go. Bye-bye. Get out. Vanish.' Gene left.

Down in the fields next morning at eight o'clock, Mr Duncan, bald head already gleaming, said to Gene, 'You're going to be pulling lint. Do you know what pulling lint is?'

'No, sir.'

'Go on in there, and you'll learn about pulling lint.'

About thirty men had begun to work in the scrappy field.

'Tack yourself on to them there,' Mr Duncan indicated the nearest group. 'Jimmy, here he is for you,' he called, and a man straightened and accepted Gene dully.

'Get hold of the stem here,' he showed, 'and twist and yank at the same time, and make sure you have enough in your hand to make a beet.'

'What's a "beet"?' asked Gene.

'Were you never in a field before?'

'Flax? No.'

'See that over there?' Jimmy pointed to a bundle tied around the middle with one of its own stalks. 'They're beets.'

'Oh, you mean like a small sheaf?' asked Gene.

'Aye. Watch.' Jimmy bent, pulled, twisted and drew clear of the ground a wide fistful of the waist-high, tough plant, whipped two or three of the outer strands off the edges and wound them swiftly round the middle. 'Like you were making a wee sash for it. Try it.'

Gene eyed the growth in which he stood, took a fistful. 'No. Too big,' counselled Jimmy, and Gene reduced his selection. 'There's the one,' said Jimmy, all of whose advice was delivered in an impersonal tone: after an initial piercing glance, he had never once looked at Gene's face. 'Now. Twist. Aye, far enough. Now. Tug. Straight up, hard. That's your boy, you have her there.' Gene lifted the rough sheaf clear of the ground.

Jimmy inspected it, and said, 'Now your binding. No. Off there, off that end, the straggly bit,' and he directed Gene to the loosest end of the handful. Gene stripped from top to bottom five or six strands of the plant.

'Now hold the beet between your knees and plait the binding.' Jimmy showed him, and then bound Gene's first beet of flax.

'Now, do this one all yourself.' Jimmy watched as Gene whipped the handful out of the ground, stripped the straggly edge much quicker this time and plaited it. Jimmy nodded.

'You're away with the mixture,' he said neutrally. 'Follow them two there. I'll be after you.' He stood and watched Gene through the next three beets.

Mr Duncan came and stood beside Jimmy. 'Will he do?' he asked.

'Do rightly,' said Jimmy. 'How'd we get him?'

'I was telling you,' said Mr Duncan. 'He's a friend of herself's.'

Jimmy shook his head. 'It'll be niggers next,' and the men, old friends, smiled.

11

Three evenings in a row Belle had watched for Gene; likewise, he had been seeking her.

Finally, having avoided Janice and Gloria, both of whom still seemed sharp, she heard his voice behind her.

He smiled. 'I was hoping,' he said, 'that we could meet this week.'

'Aye surely. When?'

'Tomorrow?'

'Great. My mother's always out of a Thursday.'

He said, 'You're looking grand. Did you enjoy yourself Sunday?'

Belle replied, 'I did, it was lovely. But –'

He frowned. 'But what?'

She looked down. 'Two of my friends are after stopping talking to me.'

'Oh,' he said. 'That's a pity. Why so?'

Belle replied, 'I don't know. I can't think of anything I said or did.'

Gene replied, 'Did you ask them?'

Belle shook her head. 'I'd never do that, I couldn't. What'd I do if they told me to shut up?'

Gene shrugged. 'What harm if they did?'

Belle looked away. Gene said quietly, 'You'd be frightened of them, wouldn't you?'

Belle coughed.

He asked, 'Have you any idea at all why they're not talking?'

'No. Not a notion.'

He smiled. 'Well, I'm sure it wasn't anything you said or did. It might be something someone said about you. You know the way people make things up.'

'For what?'

'Well, somebody might be jealous of you going to the pictures and that.'

'Oh, yes?' she wondered, in a light-dawning voice.

Gene said, 'We'll talk about it a bit more Thursday? OK?'

'OK, so.'

'He's a fine thing, isn't he?' Noreen's voice behind her made Belle jump.

'I thought you'd be long gone home?' queried Belle.

'Is he your fella? God, he's lovely,' said Noreen.

Belle blushed. 'Noreen, you won't tell, will you? My mother'd have a fit at me going out with some fella she didn't know.'

'Is that what she'd have the fit at?' asked Noreen. 'I mean. He knows my brother, Joe. They go to meetings and that.'

Belle said, 'Noreen, he's awful nice to talk to. You wouldn't believe how nice he is –' Belle stopped.

'He's lovely-looking,' said Noreen, 'and Joe was saying all the lads like him too. Unnh. But isn't he a Catholic, like? Like me, like?'

'He is. But sure there's no harm in talking to him, is there?'

'God, Belle, I couldn't answer that. Would you look at the state of my fingernails.'

For the next two days, Belle worked harder than ever. Janice prohibited all telling of the pictures. When anyone outside the immediate circle – all of whom had heard of Belle and Gene on the motorbike – asked about Belle and the pictures, Janice said, 'Not for the minute. Ould Blackwood said 'tis to stop for a while.'

Belle watched Janice closely, and in the lavatories walked up behind her and said, 'Janice, come over here for a second.'

Janice replied, 'No.' The word had the shape of a bullet.

Later, when they switched off their machines, Belle turned to Gloria at their stand. 'Gloria, am I after doing something to you?'

'That's for me to know and you to find out,' said Gloria and walked away.

That night, they met at the cranes again.

Belle asked Gene, 'Can we go somewhere else?'

'Why?'

She replied, 'My brother Lennie, he comes down here on patrols. He'll tell my mother.'

Gene frowned, but said, 'I know a place.'

In his own wanderings to discover Belfast, he had found a haven unfamiliar to Belle – within half a mile of her house, behind a derelict factory. The little park, still with some old benches intact, had been created by the factory owners for the use of the workers and their families, all of whom had lived immediately near. Since the decline of the building, the park had fallen into some disrepair, although some of the residents, with no gardens of their own, had made half-hearted efforts to keep the park's vegetation alive. One corner, with a plinth on which some small statue had once lived, provided almost complete seclusion.

Gene found a seat and checked it for dampness before they sat. Two children popped by to peek at the couple holding hands. He shooed them away drumming his heels on the ground in pretended chase: they squealed with delight.

'I like children,' he said. 'Were you a nice child?'

'My father said I was.'

He asked, 'How long is your father dead?'

'Since I was seven.'

'That must have been sad.'

Belle said nothing. Allowing the silence, he next said, 'You must still miss him.'

Belle said quietly, 'Nobody ever before said to me it was sad.'

'Of course 'tis sad.'

'How would you know? Is your father dead?'

'No, he's alive, and so's my mother. But I know what sad is. Anyone knows what sad is.'

Belle shook her head. 'No they don't.'

Gene asked, 'What did he die of?'

'He died of a Tuesday.'

'Seriously?'

'An accident.'

'Where?'

'I don't know.'

'Where were you? At school?'

Belle nodded.

'That must have been very hard.' Neither said a word for a moment, then Gene asked, 'Did you like him?'

'A lot. He was awful nice.' Now Belle stood up and walked away, smoothing her skirt, then rubbing her palms together, her back to Gene.

'What's the nicest thing you remember about him?'

Belle, taken by surprise, said, 'He used to ask me what I thought about everything.'

'Everything?'

'Things in the newspapers, the government, the world, that sort of thing.'

'You mean – your opinion?'

'That's the very word. "Belle, what's your opinion on this?" and he'd show me the newspaper.'

In a tone of closing the subject down, she said, 'He had boots, they were always polished, like yours now. And I often think I still get the smell of his tobacco, and his pipe.'

Belle put her hands to her face and began to cry. Gene made no attempt to stop her. Eventually, he rose and went to stand beside her, his hands behind his back, but he never said a word.

When she raised her face and wiped her eyes, 'I'm a right baby,' she said out loud.

He looked sideways at her. 'Why?'

'Crying like that.'

Gene shook his head. 'You shouldn't be ashamed,' he said.

'Them women at work.'

He accepted her reason for tears and asked, 'You mean they're still not talking to you?'

Belle nodded.

'But did you ask them?' Gene opened his hands.

'I did. I got no soot from them.' Belle sniffed. He put an arm around her shoulders and said nothing. She sat quite straight.

In a while, he began to hum a tune.

'What's that called?' she asked.

'You should know that, 'tis from this part of the world.'

'If I knew it I wouldn't be asking you, would I?'

'An old song, "My Lagan Love". The River Lagan, I suppose.'

Belle sniffed again. 'Do you know the words?'

'Some of them,' and he began. 'This is it:

"Where Lagan's streams sing lullaby.
There blows a lily fair.
The twilight gleam is in her eye.
The night is in her hair."

'That's all I know so far. I have to get the words somewhere.'

'You're not a bad singer. For a crow.'

He laughed. 'How come you don't know it?'

Belle said, 'We'd never have songs like that in our house.'

'Why?'

She fidgeted a little. 'They're – your songs.'

'You mean Catholics?'

'Aye. Taigs.'

'"Taigs"?'

'D'you mean to tell me you don't know what you're called?'

Gene deflected by asking, 'Why is it "Taig"?'

'A name. I don't know. We always call it.'

'I can tell you,' said Gene. 'Catholics call their sons "Tige", or "Taig". It's the Irish for "Timothy". Do you know any Irish?'

'Would you go 'way?' said Belle. 'That'd be nearly treason.'

Gene said, 'Lovely language, though. And you've no songs like that?'

Belle said, 'What we have is hymns.'

'Hymns are only manufactured,' Gene said. 'They don't come from the best parts of us.'

Belle laughed. 'My mother would have your guts for garters if she heard you.'

'What's your mother like?'

Belle said, 'A terror.'

Gene asked, 'A holy terror?' They laughed.

Belle asked, 'Did they call you a Taig down in Fintown?'

Gene replied, 'God knows what they called me behind my back.'

Belle sat closer beside him, her hair touching his shoulder.

'Come here to me,' he said.

'I'm here.'

He turned her face around and kissed her, moving his closed lips laterally, very slowly, from one side of her mouth to the other. Then he pressed her face deep into the folds of his coat. They sat there silently for several seconds, until she said, 'I can't breathe,' and sat back.

Gene sat back too, and asked, 'What's your house like?'

'Very clean. Small, but.'

'And the women in the mill, the spinners and the piecers and doffers and them – the same kind of houses?'

'Of course. Why?'

'Well, I was thinking about that. They're just as – your house is just the same as the houses of the people where I'm staying.'

'On the Falls Road?' asked Belle. 'Why wouldn't they be?'

'What I mean is – that means that the Catholic houses are just the same as the Protestant houses?'

'Course they are. What's up with you?'

'Well, I always thought the Protestants were better off than the Catholics.'

'Course we are. And we've the Government. At Stormont.'

Gene carried on. 'But a lot of you – you've no electricity. Or no running water. And the houses are just as small. And pokey. So – how're you better off?'

Belle snorted. 'We just are. We were always told so. And we are.'

'But how?'

'I don't know. I never seen inside a Catholic house.'

'Well, I bet you my room is exactly the same as yours?'

'But isn't your house awful dirty? We were always told the Taigs were dirty, kept their houses rotten?'

'Who told you that?'

'I don't know. We always knew it.'

Gene said, 'Not at all. The house I'm in is as clean as a new pin.' He stood up. 'D'you know what I'm beginning to think? I think there's a big sham going on. I think you're all told you're better off so's you'll always be at the Catholics' throats.'

Belle said, 'How would I know? And I don't like this talk.'

Gene stood. 'You should think about these things.'

'Look,' said Belle, 'dry up. What we think about is going to the pictures. Or my mother. And her singing hymns. Or Lennie. His pigeons.' She changed the subject and Gene went along with it. 'What kind of things did you do down in Fintown, was it there they made you a lapper?'

'I learned it all.' Gene spread his hands. 'I learned pulling-and-binding, retting, grassing, breaking, scutching, hackling, spinning, weaving, bleaching, beetling, and lapping.'

Belle said, 'All I ever see is the yellow thread and the rove I spin off of it.'

Gene said, 'How d'you think it gets white?'

'Oh, I know that, I'm not a clown. I seen bleaching.'

'Well, I said to myself I would learn the trade from the ground up.'

Mr Duncan always walked ahead of those accompanying him.

'This is where the retting is.'

Three, four, five men stood crotch-deep in a plump, oval pond of greeny, thick water.

'This is where you'll ret. D'you know what retting is? Billy, tell him what retting is.'

A sober young man, with deep black eyebrows and cautious intonation, said, 'You ret the flax, Mr Duncan.'

'Don't tell me, Billy. Tell him.'

Billy turned to Gene without looking at him. 'The boys has been filling the lint in down here on the bottom, and weighing it down with stones, and, c'mere, if you put your hand down there, see, like, they's all in layers, the whole way down, like, d'you see?'

Gene groped. 'Lint?'

'That's the real name for flax,' said Billy.

'They were stacked,' Gene told Belle, sitting in the darkening park, 'upright, so that the roots were down and the heads did not stick out above the water, and they had their weight fixed so's they didn't sink. And the smell would knock you. Stink it was. So in I had to step, into this pond of water, up to my waist nearly. And at the bottom of this pond was all the flax beets, you know, stalks, we had been pulling and binding. Now I was still the new fella, and being from the south, they were all looking at me, but your man Duncan, he was fine, because all he wanted off me was the hard work, and I already gave him that and I pulling and tying the lint. So I had to stand there in the water and hand these beets over to the men retting them, you know hand them down from the men on the bank. And of course they gave more to me than anyone else, and eventually they made me do them all. I didn't mind a bit, I was determined to best them and I won.'

Belle asked, 'Did they say anything?'

'No,' said Gene, 'but I saw them looking at each other.'

Gene did not tell Belle the next part of the story. Lady Cruiseman came by the lint-dam and watched with her husband, then drove away.

'When you're finished,' Mr Duncan said, 'you're to go up to the house. Herself wants you' – and with a glare he silenced the chuckles of the other men.

'Go like this?' asked Gene, indicating the state of his clothing.

'The minute you're finished.'

Gene arrived in the yard and a girl came to meet him.

'You're to go round the front and up to the Treasury,' she said, giggling and running back indoors. Gene walked slowly around, cleaned his boots even more thoroughly on the grass by the terrace and, dank hair, muddy hands and face, dank trousers flecked with green algae, walked gingerly up the stairs.

'I can see you coming,' she called, and she had arranged a mirror by the door that caught every movement on the staircase. 'Echh! You're filthy.'

'But Mr Duncan said I was to come up here straightaway, ma'am.'

'Yes, but go and have a bath.'

'Right, ma'am.' Gene turned to go.

She called out, 'No, you idiot, use my bathroom. Here!' and she gestured.

Gene turned back. 'If 'tis all the same to you, ma'am, I'll go back to my own lodgings. I'll change my clothes and come back again.'

He spoke so firmly that he reduced her to staring at him. When he returned an hour and a half later he was told that Lady Cruiseman was at dinner, was not to be disturbed – and did not need him tonight for the garden.

Gene told Belle, 'There's nothing so hard as retting. It was like the bottom of your back' – he reached behind him to indicate and twisted his body to show her – 'was falling out. Did you ever hear the word "backbreaking"? That's what it was, "backbreaking". I thought I'd never stand up straight again. And I was never so wet and cold in all my life, even though the sun was shining.'

'My mother learned how to do all that,' said Belle. 'She was from down around there. I've an aunt down there. Did you never ever see flax before?'

'No.' Gene stood to stretch his legs.

'How did you get on with them? In Fintown?'

'Oh, great. After a while. But they kept away from me for a long while.'

Belle said, 'We don't like strangers up this side of the world.'

Gene chuckled. 'You'd never think we're all on the same island, would you? Were you ever down south?'

'No, and by the same token, Smartie, were you ever up here before?'

He laughed. 'Fair enough. No.'

They kissed once more while sitting; then they stood and kissed again. Gene said, 'I never talked to anyone as easy before.'

Belle replied, 'I never know what to say to you.'

'You're wrong, you're wrong. You can say what you like to me.'

In the darkness, Belle took Gene's arm as they began to leave the little park. As they turned towards the gate, she jerked.

'Jesus. What was that?' She answered her own question. 'That was a bomb, so it was.' She held her head to listen. 'And no air-raid warning.'

'No, it wasn't,' Gene dismissed it. 'There was no aircraft noise.'

'It was a bomb.'

'Oh, you never know. An old bomb, or a mine or something that didn't go off when it landed, and they're blowing it up.'

They halted at a second report.

'That's a shot,' said Gene quietly, but more alert. 'That came from a rifle.'

'But that's over near where we were walking –'

'Whishhht!' hissed Gene. 'There's someone coming.' He stopped them: they listened. 'I thought I heard a footstep,' he whispered. They listened again: no sound.

In a moment they walked again.

Belle then returned to the earlier subject. 'But if you got on well down at Fintown, how d'you get on with all of them in the Lapping Room? I mean, they're all diehards. They march on the Twelfth and all that.'

'They're all right. Sure I had the Twelfth down the country.'

'What did you make of it?'

'All the fellas went. And for the few days before, and the few days afterwards, for the first couple of years, you always had to be on the watch out. Someone'd say something to try and get you going for a fight, but the best thing to do was to ignore it. One year, I was there about three years, one of the boys came up to me and said, "Do you know what the Twelfth of July is, sonny? I'll tell you what it is."'

Belle interrupted with a chortle. 'Your accent is great.'

Gene continued, '"I'll tell you what the Twelfth of July is, 'tis our HOLY day of obligation."' Gene explained to Belle, 'Catholics have days when you have to go to – to, to the church and that, and they're called holy days of obligation. And this fella, he said, "This is the day we have an obligation for kicking holes in the Taigs, that's what it is. You know – our hole-ey day."'

Belle laughed: Gene waited smiling, then continued. 'I said nothing, but Mr Duncan heard him and nearly sacked him. As a matter of fact, he only didn't sack him because I asked him not to. They never tried it on after that, although after that first summer, especially the retting, they more or less gave over.'

'Did your man Cruiseman, did he march?'

'Oh, sure he did. He marched. Bowler hat and all. He never said anything about it, though.'

He looked at her in the dark. 'I s'pose you know what 'tis all about?'

'Oh, aye,' she said calmly, 'King William and the defeat of the Catholic traitor King James.'

'Is that how they teach it up here?' he said. 'Well, well.'

'What's wrong with it?'

'Well, it wasn't exactly like that.'

'Look, come on, I don't like oul' history.' Belle shook him, knocking him a little off his step.

Gene laughed. 'D'you know what the man in the library said to me? I asked him where's the History Section, and he says to me,

179

"History? That's a dangerous subject up here." He was joking. But now I see what he meant.'

Belle stopped him. 'Listen. Them women I was telling you about. They could be guessing.'

'Guessing what?' asked Gene.

'That I was down in the country with you, or that we met before.'

Gene said, 'Is that a crime?'

'They'd real hate it.'

He said quickly, tightening his arm on her arm, 'I want to see you again.'

Belle sighed. 'Do you?'

'I do. I do.'

'Oh, God. I don't know what to do.'

'Don't you like me, Belle?'

'I do, I do.' She thought for a moment. 'Aye. Sure, where's the crime? All fine for Janice to complain and the grand life she has.'

At the corner of Pretoria Street, they kissed goodnight.

'Tomorrow night again?' Gene asked.

'I don't know.'

'Well – if you can? I mean – would you like to?'

Belle said, 'I'd love to. But we'll have to be not seen, like. For a bit anyway.'

In the silent house, Belle sat quietly, staring into the last embers of the fire in the kitchen range. Lost in thought as she was, the soft rapping at the knocker startled her. She opened the door a notch, to hear Malcolm ask, 'Is that you, Belle? Are you all right?'

'Ach, Malcolm, come on in. Sure why wouldn't I be all right?'

He stepped into the hallway, switched off his hooded torch, took off his badged cap.

'You'll take a cup of tea? Lennie's not here.'

'I know, Belle.'

'Malcolm, what's wrong? Is there anything up with Janice?'

'No, Belle, sure she doesn't even know I'm here, I'm on duty, like, my mate's down the street, so I'll not take the tea, thanks.'

He looked at Belle's coat folded across the chair. 'You're only just in so, Belle?'

'Aye.'

'Well that's why I was worried. There was – an incident.'

'I heard something, right enough.'

'Where'd you hear it from?'

Belle blushed. 'I was up near that wee park behind – what's the name of it?'

'Oh, aye, Madden Park.' Malcolm rubbed his eyes. 'Oh, aye.'

Belle said nothing, looked at him.

'Belle, there was two fellas on a motorbike, they bombed the doorway of a retired army man, you might know his name, that General Knowles. It did an awful lot of damage, and when the old man came out, they fired a shot and injured him. He's bad, too, a bad injury. Belle, I was afraid, when I heard where 'twas, like –'

Belle looked at the floor. 'No, Malcolm,' she said quietly, 'I'm all right, so I am.' She raised her head. 'How d'you know where I was, Malcolm?'

'Look, Belle, the only reason I know, and I didn't tell a soul, not Lennie, nor Janice, nor no one, 'cause I'm fond of you, you know that. But my fellas are watching your big lad.'

Belle raised her head. 'Malcolm, I don't know –'

Malcolm held up his hand. 'Belle, listen, I seen you on the motorbike, last Sunday over near the Albert Bridge.'

Belle, distressed, said, 'Malcolm, he wouldn't hurt a fly. Why are they watching him?'

'We don't know him, Belle. Nor the first thing about him. All we know is he's from down south, and with all that's going on, of course they'll watch him. And now tonight.'

'But Malcolm, he isn't that sorta fella at all. He keeps himself to himself, so he does. And I only seen him three times.'

'I know, Belle, I know that, sure I said to myself, if he has anything to do with Belle, he must be all right. But sure you know the way of it yourself.'

Belle sat again, and Malcolm leaned against the table.

'Does anyone know?'

Belle said, 'No, I told nobody. I just wanted a bit of peace.'

'Are you fond of him, Belle?'

'Malcolm, he's awful nice.'

'Aye, Belle, but this is a tough place. Them boys. I mean they shot poor Constable Murphy just like that. And in front of his wife and kids. And I used to go out on the beat with him when I started and he was nice as your Da.' Malcolm, correcting himself, steered away from the sensitive point. 'What I mean is, your Da was more like my father, if you know what I mean.'

'Malcolm, Gene's not like that.'

'Belle, I have to ask you. Is there any trace of him being involved?'

'Involved?'

'You know. With anything strange?'

'Malcolm, I'd swear not. I mean – he's a fella reads a lot.'

'Aye, you see that's what worries me, and that's what worries my boys, he reads a lot.'

'Och, Malcolm, sure where's the harm in that.'

'Belle, if you saw them boys in court – they spout history out of their ears, so they do.'

'Aye, but maybe they have it to spout.'

'We all have history, so we do.' Malcolm stood to go. 'All right so, Belle?'

'All right, Malcolm. But listen – Janice, she's not talking to me. Is it because – on account of – Him?'

'Och, Belle, you know Janice, she'll blow over that. Sure, she's often that way with me.'

At the door he turned and said, 'If you need help, like – you're OK, you know that, Belle?'

'No, I'm grand thanks, Malcolm.'

12

In June 1933, on the first anniversary of Gene's arrival in Fintown, Mr Duncan approached him one morning as Gene entered the scutching-mill.

'The wheel,' said Mr Duncan, 'don't you bother with that no more.'

Gene looked at him. Mr Duncan said, 'You heard me.'

Inside the mill, the MacArthur twins greeted Gene.

'Ah, then,' said John.

'Ah, then,' said Austin.

Gene grinned.

'He don't say that to many,' said John.

'You're the only one in our time,' said Austin.

The twins, in their fifties, had never married, although Austin, the daring one, had a girl he had been walking out for twenty-two years.

'What's it mean?' asked Gene.

'Atttttsh,' said Austin impatiently, ''tis only the labourers do the wheel forever.'

'Doing the wheel' – a task which, ironically, Gene quite enjoyed – meant removing the weed and the packed algae from the mill-wheel, a job in which being covered with filth and getting soaking wet became inevitable.

Later, as they ate their piece in the open air, Gene asked Austin the crucial question: he had become friendly with the MacArthur twins, friendly enough to tease them and say they were good enough to have come from the south, to ask them things he could ask no other colleague.

'Why did Duncan say that?'

Austin replied, 'Because he sees you working hard. Because he knows he'll not get as good a man as easy in here with a long while, and –' Austin hesitated.

'Yes, Austin?' nudged Gene.

'Your one.' Austin nodded in the general direction of the Cruise-man house.

Gene smiled. 'I see.'

'No, nor you don't,' said John, 'do he, Austy?'

'He do not,' said Austin.

'What don't I see?' asked Gene.

'You don't see 'cause you weren't here. We were all watchin' to see what'd happen. And no one watchin' keener than Duncan.'

Gene looked at them with some surprise. 'So he – doesn't like – Her?' and he cocked a thumb.

'No. Not that. Her oul' capers is what he don't like. And if you'd'a played her game – well, he'd have you be strapped to that fuckin' wheel. Tell him, John – what coulda happened him.'

John settled back to take up the story. 'There was a fella came through here, a weaver from Ardboe, and he was a nice enough fella too, your crowd.' John made a digging motion with his left foot, which always confused Gene.

'In the south,' he told Gene one day, 'the Catholics dig with the right foot, and Protestants with the left, and up here that's reversed.'

Gene grinned at John. 'You mean the wrong way round.'

'Away to fuck,' said Austin genially, 'you and your Pope'll rot in hell, don't we know that for a fact?'

John pressed on: Gene, hunkered down against the whitewashed wall, squinted up at him against the light.

'Anyway, this boy, he was a right good weaver, fast and clean as a whistle, not a bit of rove astray, nothing, and they couldn't keep up with him, except one woman from Castlederg who was here at the time and she a flyer. You could hear her loom down as far as Omagh, the rattle of it, only she used to break it a lot, she was a big, strong woman. But this fellow – not so, he was light with it, so he was, he used to play that loom like 'twas a fuckin' fiddle, and he only coaxing the tunes out of it.'

Austin cut in, 'And he was light on his feet too, he was like a dancer.'

John continued. 'Well, he got a job here, and they was awful glad to have him, and he made a big difference. Only he went down in oul' Duncan's eyes.'

'How d'you mean "he went down"?' asked Gene.

'He failed,' said Austin, and again nodded towards the house. 'Your one.'

'Her Ladyship?' asked Gene.

'The one and only,' said John. 'You see he was a bit of a hopper, like, for all that he was great at his work, and he took to her like a bottle takes to drink, and she lapped him up. And we said nothing, she was only here three year at the time, and we already seen her tricks and we seen fellas falling for them, and she sucking them in and blowing them out in a bubble. You're the only fella so far's got away.'

'And I'm staying that way,' said Gene.

All year Judy had pressured him, invited him, harassed him: sometimes he had to dig the same flower-bed over and over. Patiently, he consistently stepped back from any situation of intimacy she proposed or manipulated.

The twins' story continued: 'Anyways, with your man – for a start-off, oh, it was all great, and he'd tear home from here, and he'd wash himself and he'd dry himself, and he'd put on his new yellow waistcoat –'

Austin said, 'He was like a fuckin' budgie, so he was, in that waistcoat.'

John said, 'And he'd go up there and he'd have to drive her out in the trap, and he'd help her in the garden, and she'd make him do the rockery all over again.'

They looked slyly at Gene, who did not react.

'Only,' said John, 'your man, he took it serious, he thought she was going to run away with him. And man dear, there they were, everywhere, them two, sure if you went down to the river of a summer night, the two of them'd be lying in the long grass and she without hardly the stitch on her.' He grew a little apoplectic. 'Sure, Christ-on-a-bicycle, she had him *readin'* to her. Out loud. Books.'

Austin took over. 'Old Duncan over there, he watches all this, and he hates it, he HATES it, he's watching his own job like, so he has two chances of doing something about it, and them two chances is – none and fuck-all. And all the time, he's straight as a die with your man – what was his name?'

'MacAlinden,' supplied Austin.

'Aye, you're right,' said John. 'MacAlinden. A good-looking fella too. Big head on him. And a'course the day came when she dropped him. Like a rock out of her hand. He goes up one evening and oul' Caldwell and the doctor meets him on the door and tells him to stop tormenting Her Ladyship, he's only a working-man and who the fuck he thinks he is?'

Austin took up. 'Well, he comes into the weavers the following day, don't he, John? Down at Willie Campion's house he was working, there's four looms in there, and he was only shook, shook to the backfuckin'bone. About eleven o'clock in the morning, Duncan comes in to Willie Campion's, and he says to him, Duncan says to him, "Mr MacAlinden" – real polite, like – "Mr MacAlinden, would you ever like a good man go up to the scutch-mill, and do that wheel."'

Austin interrupted, 'And your man says to him, "But sure I'm a weaver, Mr Duncan." "I know you are, Mr MacAlinden," says Duncan, as polite as a parson, "I know you're a weaver, and a bloody good one into the bargain, but if you're going to be working here, you'll work at anything."'

John finished the tale. 'MacAlinden stuck it a week and then he went. In the latter end of it, Duncan had him making tea for the women. He done the wheel three times. In the yellow waistcoat. They even sent him out on the road to block cattle from going in the wrong gates.'

Austin wheezed with a laugh. 'I never seen a thing like it. And one day, he says, "Scutter this for a caper," and he packs his tools and he ups. We all stood to watch him – and away he went.'

'I heard,' said John, 'he took a job up in the Clogher Valley for a while, and then he went off to Scotland and then maybe to Canada.'

'So there you are. Aren't you the lucky man?' concluded Austin to Gene.

'Aye, and for a fuckin' oul' hairy Taig,' said John, and poked Gene's leg with a friendly toe.

Gene found Belle after work in the corridors leading to the door. Most of the women had left.

'I forgot. I can't get out of a meeting I promised to go to,' he said. 'Tomorrow night, instead?'

Belle saw Janice approaching and murmured to Gene, 'No, bother, so?'

'Half-seven tomorrow night? Your own corner?' He had not kept his voice down.

'No,' said Belle, 'meet here.'

Janice swept past so swiftly, and with her departing shoulders so forbiddingly set, that Belle did not chase to catch up, and instead sauntered home to Pretoria Street.

Edith had the iron heating.

'Have you any ironing, Belle?' she asked. 'As I have the iron hot?'

Belle did not let Edith see the look of surprise.

'I've my red blouse, Mam, but I was going to do it myself later on.'

'There's a fry for your tea,' Edith said, and Belle again turned aside to hide the surprise.

'Oh, thanks,' she said.

Edith sorted the clothes. 'I met that Mrs Lyttleton the day,' she said. 'She said she seen you on the way home the other evening, and she was saying you were looking great.'

'She's nice, that woman,' said Belle, 'and all that's after happening to her, two husbands buried.'

'There's war for you,' replied Edith. 'Belle, amn't I glad they turned Leonard down.'

'Yes,' said Belle thoughtfully, waiting to see where the conversation would turn.

'Oh, d'you know who called, your Uncle Jed, and he as mad as a hatter. He gave me soap, so he did, he brought it back with him, and I says to him, "You must think I'm awful dirty or something," but he came in and sat down, so he did, and how long is it since he done that?'

'Ages.'

'He was on again, saying you should be married.'

'Aye, he was saying the same to me the other day,' said Belle.

'He was saying,' cut in Edith, 'he was saying, "Your Belle, she should get a husband so she should, grand girl like that, going wasting," and I says to him, "Belle'll not marry for a while and there's no sign of a fella anywhere."'

'Aye.' Belle stuffed bread into her mouth.

'I mean,' continued Edith with no change in the conversational tone, 'they're all away with soldiers, aren't they, the men?'

'Aye.' Belle glanced at her, puzzled. 'But there's the what-you-may-call-'em, the "Reserved Occupations", isn't there?'

Edith said, 'A woman your age should be married, so she should, all the girls down working with you is. You must be nearly the only one.'

'What's after falling on you?'

Edith flustered a little. 'There's nothing after falling on me. Can't I think about my own children, can't I?'

Belle retreated a pace. 'I don't know, Mam, I might not stay in Belfast.'

'Sure where would you go?'

'Canada, maybe. Or America.'

'Sure what would you do for the fare? And you no money saved, Belle?'

'Mam, don't you know well you can't save money on what oul' Blackwood pays.'

In the house on the Antrim Road, his host smiled when Gene commented on the blackout curtains.

'All Catholic houses don't have them.'

'No. Part of the whole thing. But they have their uses. The Germans aren't the only ones can't see us,' he said, and Gene grinned at him wryly. This, Gene's fourth meeting, each time a different venue, made him feel no more relaxed than he had been at the first.

'But I don't want to speak Irish,' he told Joe. 'I learned a bit of Irish at school, not a lot, maybe, it was only starting, but enough. I'm not that keen on it.'

Michael O'Neill reassured him: 'It is not against the law any more to speak your native language.'

'No, but you know well, Michael. Anything in the province of Gaelic or spoken Irish is equated with the IRA. The Republican movement.'

MacBride mimicked: '"Equated with the IRA." We *are* the Republican movement. Only we're the cultural end of it.' He grinned sardonically. MacBride never succeeded in shaving the little crop of hair from his Adam's apple.

'But if they are watching us – ?'

MacBride grinned again. 'The polis is always watching us. If you're born a Catholic up here they're watching you from the day you're born.'

'I will always be uneasy about this,' said Gene.

'Well, be "uneasy" so,' said MacBride. 'All we're saying is – what we asked you to do was come and help us broaden the dialect we're learning. You have southern Irish, we don't know what it sounds like and we should know if we're to be full Irishmen; we should know all the dialects in the country. Anyway, you haven't been stopped yet, have you? By the police.'

'No,' said Gene, 'but that's only because of where I'm working.'

'You mean they think you're a Prod?' asked Michael O'Neill with scorn. 'Ah, will you go 'way and look at yourself in the mirror. They know what you are, they knew what you were the minute they clapped eyes on you.'

'Well, why don't they stop me, then?'

'The war, maybe,' Michael O'Neill said. 'But you can bet they know all about you. By the way, how did you get on down at the viaduct?'

Gene smiled. 'Great. I won a few bob.'

'Did the bike hold out?'

'Not a thing wrong with it.'

Joe came forward, arm extended to introduce the man by his side. 'You know each other, I believe.'

Gene looked at him. 'Ye-es?'

The newcomer answered the query in Gene's voice. 'I'll remind you. You were at Fivemilecross one evening.'

Joe said to Gene, 'This is the man knows it all.'

'I don't remember your name,' said Gene.

'Dermot Donaghy.'

'Ah, yes,' said Gene pleasantly but cautiously. 'Ah, yes.' They shook hands. 'And are you working up here in Belfast now?'

'In a manner of speaking,' replied Dermot Donaghy.

An hour after the MacArthur twins had told the MacAlinden story, Mr Duncan said to Gene, 'You know why you're not doing the wheel?'

'I never minded doing it, sir.'

'I know that, I know that, and I never said you did. You find me a straight man, I take it?'

'I do, sir.'

'Straight is straight, so, am I right in saying that you're taking care how you're getting on with Herself?'

Gene replied, in the confidentiality of employee to his immediate superior, 'I keep my distance, sir.'

'And that's why you're not doing the wheel. A working-man's a working-man,' affirmed Mr Duncan, 'and neither pet nor puppet.' He frowned. 'And I don't like scheming, and I admire a man who won't have it near him.'

Gene murmured, 'None of my doing.'

Mr Duncan looked at him. 'Did I say it was?'

Mr Caldwell strode into the scutch-mill, stooping under the door lintel.

'What time's he finished?' he asked Mr Duncan, indicating Gene.

'Same as always. Six.'

'He's to drive Milady to Fivemilecross.'

Mr Duncan asked incredulously, 'He can't drive a motor-car?'

Mr Caldwell said, 'She wants to go in the trap. The fine weather. He can drive a pony and trap, can't he?'

Gene nodded.

'He's to be in the yard in his best at seven.'

Mr Duncan said to Mr Caldwell, 'A queer caper that she never asks Hoppy Halloran to drive the trap' – the simpleton who, dribble-mouthed, cleaned up around the yard: the men laughed.

Gene, on the stroke of the hour, stood by the tackled pony and trap, face shining, shirt fresh, boots gleaming, jacket over his arm. Lady Cruiseman appeared, limping over the cobblestones. Nin stumbled along with her, carrying shawl and bag; wide tears stained Lady Cruiseman's face. Gene held the door of the trap open for her, and looking at him as fiercely as if he had slapped her, she climbed in. Gene followed her and, having fastened the door of the trap behind him, took his place on the seat opposite, and grasped the reins.

As they left the yard, Lady Cruiseman, raising the heels of her

190

hands to mop her eyes, snuffled, 'How do you know where I'm going?'

'I heard Mr Caldwell say Fivemilecross, ma'am.'

'And how do you know where Fivemilecross is?'

'I was over there once, ma'am, by chance. One Sunday.'

'Is that what you do on Sundays?' Lady Cruiseman sniffed between her tears.

'I like to get to know the countryside, ma'am.'

She said, 'You haven't asked me why I'm weeping.'

'I didn't like to, ma'am.'

'My foot hurts, that's why. I like pretty shoes and pretty boots and every time I put something nice on this foot it hurts.'

Gene said quietly, 'Can't you get something special made, ma'am, a good cobbler, or something'd fix you up.'

'I was top of my class at school. And I got a First. And look at me.'

Gene misinterpreted the rhetorical question and turned to look. She faced him. 'I am pretty, am I not? And look at me stuck out here in this place. Married to a silent man who never speaks to me except to say at breakfast [she mimicked aggressively], "M'mm, clouds, it might rain," or, "M'm, clear skies, fine again," and clears his throat and leaves the room every time I'm upset, who looks away – and walks away, actually walks out of the bloody bedroom – when I'm undressing. And you, bloody Comerford, you behave as I have leprosy. With your big bloody hands.'

Gene turned away.

'Look at me again,' she commanded. Gene looked.

'Since you came here – what, oh my God, it is a year ago today. Our first anniversary. You bloody Catholic. Since you came here [she sang] "a year ago today" – I have been nice to you, haven't I?'

Gene nodded slowly.

'My husband can't shit, Mr Comerford, can't do his number ones or is it number twos Catholics call it? A shit who can't shit. Oh, Jesus!'

She calmed down, dropped her voice. 'All I want is your comfort, Mr Comfort.' She smiled a thin, sad smile. 'Your comfort, Mr Comfort. Do you hear me?' Her pointed nose twitched.

Gene looked, nodded firmly, then attended to the pony again.

'What do you have to say to that, Mr Comfort? On this lovely evening. This lovely summer evening.' She threw out a gloved hand dramatically. 'Well?' she asked aggressively. 'I'm waiting for an answer!'

The pony and trap now set on a straight stretch of road and clicking along briskly, the yellow wheels shirring, Gene said without looking at her, 'Ma'am. I come from nowhere. I come from nothing. Poor people. As poor as you'd get. I want to get on in the world. And I can make myself get on in the world. Other people who came from places and families as bad off as myself got on. But I want to get on the way that won't harm me. I want to get on so's I can always say to myself I didn't do anything I disagree with.'

'Well, Oracle,' she said. Her tears had stopped. 'What does all that mean?'

'Ma'am, if I want to put it the hardest way possible, I'd only get into trouble for being' – Gene hesitated, then continued – 'for being friends with you.'

'Nonsense. I'd see to it that you didn't.'

'Ma'am, but you don't come down retting or scutching where the men is, where my work is. You're not working down there. And I am. And I an outsider already.'

'But that's part of your attraction to me, you – you Darwinian!'

'Ma'am, I don't care what names you call me, that's no good to me.'

Judy Cruiseman said, 'But I was depending on you. For some friendship.'

'Ma'am, I'll work like a Trojan for you. That's what I'm here for. To work.'

She asked, 'But what am I to do?'

'About what, ma'am?'

She sighed. 'About life, I suppose.'

Gene said nothing for a moment, then, 'There's a lot of things in the world to learn.'

'You mean – I could study? Read?'

'Yes, ma'am.'

'Will you be friendly towards me, though – under your rules?'

'I will, of course, ma'am.'

=

192

They passed nobody on the way to Fivemilecross, not another soul. At one cottage children came out to look; at another a man leaned over a wall, smoking his pipe after his evening meal. Beyond the village, she directed him through limping gates, up a long avenue, to the gravel forecourt of a limestone mansion with a portico.

'If you think I'm troubled, you should meet this bunch,' she murmured, as Gene helped her down from the trap. 'Every one of them is as mad as a hare.'

He could not help smiling. 'I will be exactly three hours. You are expected to go round the back to the kitchen and ask for a cup of tea. But be right here in three hours, that will be' – she wore a large gold wrist watch – 'at half-past ten. There's a full moon so they'll be truly crazy tonight.'

The housekeeper, who had a swollen earlobe, gave Gene a mug of tea and some bread and ham.

'How're you getting on with Herself?'

'Very well, thanks,' Gene answered.

'Busy over there?'

'Very.'

'Is Himself around these days?'

'Yes.'

Gene's monosyllabic answers to several more questions made her give up and leave the kitchen. At half-past nine he strolled into the yard, found a bucket, filled it with pewter-coloured cold water from the pump and held it for the pony to drink. Returning the bucket, he checked the kitchen clock. He strolled to the front of the house and waited. In the twilight he heard footsteps on the gravel.

'Hallo.' A man with a cap walked by, paused. 'How're you doing?'

'Hallo,' said Gene.

'Whose is that?' asked the man, pointing to the pony.

'I'm from over at Cruisemans.'

'Fintown? Bad fuckers them.' He approached Gene. 'How'd they come to hire a Catholic?'

Gene said rather stiffly, 'I had good references. How'd you know I'm a Catholic?'

'Aw, for Jayzes' sake, cop on to yourself. And I have good references too, but I can't get a job offa that crowd.'

'But you're working here?'

'No, I'm not, I'm out for a walk.' He smiled, so winningly that Gene smiled too.

Lady Cruiseman emerged. Nobody appeared behind her at the great front door, which she drew closed. Waving her wrist, she indicated the time: 'See! On the dot!' She halted when she saw the stranger.

He looked coolly at her, then said to Gene, 'See you around, so,' and walked on, into the stableyard.

'Comerford, how do you know that man?'

'I never saw him before in my life, ma'am.'

'Keep away from him. Keep away from him. His name is Donaghy. He's been in jail. He has served ten years, that man. He makes bombs.'

Lady Cruiseman climbed into the trap, indicating the house with a backward head motion. 'Mad. Crazy. You'd know the moon had risen. They sang for me.' She laughed. 'If you heard them. It was like – it was like rubbing a piece of glass across a piece of tin.'

Gene's tongue touched his teeth.

She laughed again. 'Melly. The oldest one. Do you know what she's just done? She has moved her bed into the lavatory on the ground floor. The big downstairs lavatory. I asked her why and she said she couldn't be bothered walking across the landing when she woke up during the night to "U-ryne-eight", as she called it. "U-ryne-eight." Three words she makes of it. Wait 'til I tell Richard.' She paused. 'Not that he'll give a damn. But you find it amusing, don't you?'

Gene said, 'It is droll, ma'am. There's no doubt about that.'

Not a word was said for some minutes. The trees on the avenue stalked past in the opposite direction; long shadows fell from them in the light of the moon; the wheels crushed the gravel.

'Oh, blast,' she said, with the mild inflection of someone who had forgotten something unimportant.

'Did you forget something, ma'am, d'you want me to turn back?'

'No, Mr Comfort. I was just thinking – about things.'

'Right, so, ma'am.'

'No, not "right so". All bloody wrong.'

=

194

Dermot Donaghy held on to Gene's hand long after their handshake at the Irish Club meeting.

'I knew you were a kindred spirit when I met you that night. But I went down south after that. To get some peace.' He winked. 'How did you get on with them? They say the Cruiseman one is a right rattler, is she?'

Gene replied, 'I just worked, I needed the job. But it was very quiet down there. I never read so much in my life. I used to clean the town library in Omagh out of books.'

The meeting came to order. Dermot Donaghy said, as he searched for a chair, 'We must talk. I think we'll have a lot in common. I believe you're staying at Mrs MacCartan's, is that right?'

'How did you know that?' asked Gene.

As he sat, and paid attention to the Chairman, Gene froze. Michael O'Neill had placed a guitar-case on the top table, and from it he drew a rifle with a highly polished butt. Gene rose to leave the room. Dermot Donaghy grabbed his jumper and pulled him back down.

'Sit. Sit. No cause for alarm.'

'No,' said Gene, troubled. 'I don't want anything to do with this. Not at all. Not at all.' He pressed on. Donaghy rose, grasped him, hauled.

'If you leave now,' whispered Donaghy, 'they will surely compromise you. They will. That is certain. Stick here, and you may be able to cover your tracks.'

'But –' protested Gene.

'You're compromised as it is, merely by seeing the thing,' persisted Donaghy. Gene sat slowly.

The Chairman called for order. 'The debate,' he said, 'could be endless. How much political action can we take that has any value? You know what Michael Collins said. "England never listened to anything except the words that came from the barrel of a gun." We now have the opportunity at this meeting to feel what Collins meant.'

A voice called, 'Take the minutes of the last meeting, Chairman.'

'How can I take them when I haven't them?' responded the Chairman. 'Nobody took them down.'

'Jimmy Hagan took them down,' said the same voice.

'But he's not here, is he?' replied the Chairman.

'Are we going to send a letter of protest to De Valera, or aren't we,' asked another voice, 'to tell him to stop imprisoning patriots?'

'Imprisoning? To tell him to stop killing the IRA,' called Donaghy. 'He's executing the sons of the men he fought with.'

The room muttered, 'Hear, hear.'

Mr Chairman handed the gun to a man sitting near him.

'I am passing this "noble liberator" around the room,' he said, 'I want each and every one of you to handle it, and I want you to tell me whether you think, when you have felt the power of this – of this engine, whether Michael Collins was right.'

The gun came to Gene and he raised his hands in a gesture with two meanings – they meant 'warding off' and 'not touching'.

'No,' said Dermot Donaghy, 'not good enough. Take it.'

He laid the gun, as though a silk scarf, across Gene's lap. To get rid of it, Gene had to pick it up. He caught it gingerly by the stock and the blue-grey barrel.

'Tighten your grip. Feel it.' Donaghy looked at him, his long neck angled. 'That is our future. Aim it. Put it on your shoulder. Look along the barrel.' Gene did so half-heartedly. 'No. Like this.' Donaghy manipulated the gun more firmly into Gene's hands and helped him raise it to the right shoulder. 'Curl your fingers along the barrel, but not in a way that impedes the sights.' He helped Gene to his feet. 'Snuck it into your shoulder. Tight, that's it. Get your cheek to it, to the stock, along here.' He placed a hand in the middle of Gene's curly hair and pressed Gene to the gun. Gene set his cheek to the bright wooden stock, and then disengaged, handed the gun forward to the man in front of him. He sat down.

'I wish you hadn't made me do that. I don't want that sort of thing.'

'It's the gun that's supposed to recoil,' said Dermot Donaghy. 'Anyway – how can you understand the first thing about revolution if you don't handle the hardware?' he asked in a reasonable way.

'But I was asked here to talk about the Irish language,' Gene whispered back.

'All revolution begins in language and ends in gunfire,' murmured Donaghy. 'That is a universal truth – as accurate as prayer itself.'

The meeting never discussed the Irish language after that. As they broke up, Gene said to Joe, 'I'm not coming to another of these.'

'Are you not interested?'

'Oh, sure I'm interested in politics, but I am not coming here again.'

'You'll take a drink?' Joe slid away from the point. 'There's a girl I want you to meet.'

The gathering drifted apart and into the night. In the pub Joe reappeared pulling someone by the hand.

'Gene, this is my sister, Noreen, she's working at the same place as you.'

Noreen smiled at him and said, 'I know you well to see.'

'And I you. I didn't know you were his sister, I saw you today, eating your "piece", as they call it up here. Where are you from?'

'We're from near Newry.' She smiled up at Gene. 'And yourself – where are you from?'

Gene asked, 'Where did you get your green ribbon? Is that left over since Patrick's Day?'

'I wear it to work to spite them,' she said.

'You've to be careful. They're spiteful enough as it is.'

'And they get away with it. What got done about the wee boy that got hurt?'

Gene looked at Noreen in surprise. 'How did you know about that?'

'There's nothing in that place a secret. I heard you put the fear of God in them, they're afraid you'll tell the cops.'

Gene asked, 'Are we the only two Catholics?'

'No, there's two others in my end, over in the warehouse, and there's three women down in the wet hackling. Oh – and a cleaner.' Noreen hopped about as she talked, moving from one foot to the other, like someone always jigging to music in her head. 'And then in the spinners there's three or four women, but they're given the worst of it, like, down at the end of the Long Room where there's draughts from the windows and the doors, and their machines is the worst and they're always complaining and nobody ever listens to them.'

'So we're the only two in any kind of "clean" jobs?'

'And the two others in the warehouse. I'd say so.'

'Out of what, nearly seven hundred all told? Is it the same everywhere up here?'

Noreen nodded. 'All over the Six Counties. Houses is the same. If you get married up here and you're a Catholic, you have to go on living with your father and mother, there's no houses for Catholics.'

Gene shook his head. 'I thought 'twas bad down where I was before.'

Gene and the MacAuleys in Fintown had debated, night in, night out, the jobs position for Catholics in the county. For several years, Michael MacAuley kept cuttings from *The Sentinel* of official functions, dances, photographs of parties, annual awards ceremonies, works dances and dinners, outings, shows, trade and official events and celebrations. He had kept them carefully in large brown paper bags, each year marked clearly on the outside. Through the years, as he pointed out to Gene, very few Catholic names or faces appeared at official functions. Prizes won at an Agricultural Show, or certificates handed out at a company dinner-dance, or advertisements for official employees in the county – all of these names came from the Protestant community. Michael had even worked out, knowing he was entitled to an answer, that of five thousand public employees in the counties Fermanagh and Tyrone, fewer than eighty were Catholics. In other public employment, nobody expected Catholics to join the RUC, nor were they welcome in the B Specials. 'Although, God knows,' he said in his ironic way, 'the RUC could do with the pretence. But look at that –' – he showed a series of advertisements – 'drivers, road-sweepers, office cleaners, they all go to Protestants.'

Gene outlined to them his experience, utterly opposite. From the south, after the founding of the Irish Free State, thousands of Protestants emigrated – to Scotland, or England, or up here to the north, knowing the balance of their power had changed forever.

'They even went to Wales,' he said.

'To Wales?' echoed the MacAuleys in wonder.

As he painted it to them, it seemed Utopian, that a Catholic could get a job or a house.

'So,' asked Michael MacAuley, 'never would a Catholic in the south have to go and be interviewed and at the same time have the despair and insult of them pretending to consider you?'

When Gene nodded, 'Yes, that's exactly it,' Mrs MacAuley said, 'That's what I call fat.'

Gene asked them how to defeat the system; the MacAuleys said, 'There's only one way, and that's not guaranteed – but you have some sort of chance if you get so skilled they can't turn you down.'

Michael held out his palms.

'See them hands,' he said to Gene. 'I've no gift in them hands, I can't do nothing with them hands – only dig or hoe, or something. I can't make things, I'm not knacky or nothing. Now there's a lot of people like me, and most of them is Protestants up here, 'cause they're in the majority, so they'll always get the jobs for the people's not knacky.'

'Tell me, then,' asked Gene, 'how all this works out. I mean – are you saying the IRA represent people who can't get jobs? Or are you saying the IRA represent people who want a united Ireland?'

Michael MacAuley had fuelled his permanent indignation by steeping himself in everything he could read about the politics of Northern Ireland. He summarised.

At the time of the Anglo-Irish Treaty, effective from 1922, the Catholics in the Six Counties, being partitioned off from the rest of the island, knew they would be isolated. All the indications told them that a majority Protestant population would dig in, would tighten its grip on Northern Ireland, and would protect the wealth resources with Protestant labour. Anyone who aspired, or was thought to aspire – by thought, word, deed or even family name – to an all-Ireland, thirty-two-county state, independent of the Crown, became a natural enemy. In the south, political lines divided between those who wanted the Treaty and those who did not, and therefore they fought a civil war, and when this was over the emerged political parties drew up their policies and nailed their electoral appeal to the same pro- and anti-Treaty colours.

The Catholics of the north began to feel that now the south had got largely its own way, they would be left to the mercy of the Protestants. From that moment they began to suspect that they were on their own, that the south, having numerically over-whelmed the Protestants, having reduced them to a tenth or less of the population, and eventually taken their lands one way or the other, would get plump and forget the north.

Michael MacAuley then outlined to Gene – 'no offence, like' – how Gene would be seen by both factions in Ulster.

'Even that name, "Ulster", I mean, that's real offensive,' he pointed out. 'The name belongs to the old kings' province of nine counties. I mean the Six Counties is only Antrim, Armagh, Fermanagh, Tyrone, Down and Derry. And there's a real insult for you. Everyone who lives there, Catholic, Protestant, Dissenter, they calls it "Derry", but them fuckin' Unionists, they calls it "Londonderry". I mean there's even a "Lady Londonderry", for fuck's sake. So whenever I hears "Ulster", I says to myself, "And don't forget Cavan, Monaghan and Donegal."'

Gene asked him, 'So where would I fit in?'

They told him, in direct fashion. The Protestants would suspect him from the moment they set eyes on him. First of all, why had he not stayed in the south where the Catholics had all the jobs? Secondly, any big, fit Catholic man coming north almost certainly had an ulterior motive – namely, to blow up people and things, to fire bullets at policemen and soldiers. Thirdly, unless he had considerable acumen, if he did get a job he ran the risk of being seen as a slave.

'I mean,' said Michael MacAuley, 'no offence, Eugene, but you'd be the same as a big black fella with them American houses, or in Africa, a servant, they'd nearly expect to pay you no wages.'

At this Gene raised an eyebrow, and Mrs MacAuley modified.

'Not as bad as that,' she said, 'but very insulting all the same.'

'But,' said Gene, 'if the population is sixty per cent Protestant and forty per cent Catholic, then surely the Catholics have to get some work? I mean – what about teachers, and convent schools and that?'

'Ah, yeh, ah, yeh, but there's only a few of them.' Michael MacAuley reached into one of his paper bags and produced a long typewritten document. A report, commissioned by the Nationalist Party, on discrimination against Catholics in jobs, stated that from a series of researches it had been established that eighty-eight per cent of the male workforce in Derry city had been unemployed on a long-term basis, and that in some families male unemployment now seemed certain to go into the next generation. 'There's men in Derry,' he said, 'never worked, and never will work.'

'And that's most men,' his wife interpolated.

'So how come,' said Gene, 'I get a job with the Cruisemans?'

'Because you were recommended by a Protestant, and 'tis ideal, and the Cruisemans can then say to everyone, "Look how fair we are, we have Catholics working for us." And then they'll say with their eyebrows raised, "And they're actually very good, you know, most surprising." That's where you're fitting in.'

'Go back to my original question,' asked Gene. 'Are you saying this is what the IRA are, well – fighting – for?'

'Yes and no. If there was a united Ireland the Protestants couldn't do this to us, could they?'

'Right,' asked Gene, 'if the Protestants think I'm some kind of bomber or gunman – how do the Catholics look on me, coming up here from down south?'

'A bit suspicious too. Unless you're "one of the boys". I mean – if it gets known that you're not "one of the boys" they'll be asking what are you doing here, so?'

To Noreen, Gene said, 'The thing that fascinates me is the way the Unionists have fixed the pecking order.'

Noreen looked over at her brother, deep in conversation with Dermot Donaghy. 'You're beginning to sound like Joe.'

Gene laughed. 'No, I don't mean to.' He corrected himself. 'I mean I'm not saying there's anything wrong in sounding like your brother, what I'm saying is – the thing I notice is this. The Protestants who work in Blackwoods are just as poor and just as badly off as the Catholics. But they've been given the impression that they're somehow a cut above the Catholics. Clever, that is. Clever.'

Noreen asked slyly, 'How do you get on with Belle? She's a Protestant, isn't she?'

Gene blushed. 'She's a very nice girl, but I don't know her very well. And I could never talk to her like this.'

Judy Cruiseman tried one last time. On an October morning, when her husband was performing one of his six public duties a year, sitting as a magistrate at the assizes in Enniskillen, she sent for Gene through Mr Caldwell and Mr Duncan. Gene, relieved that he had received the message before he began to work, and could therefore climb the stairs in clean clothes and boots, stopped at the ajar door of the Treasury and knocked. Her voice called from along the corridor, 'I'm not there, I'm here,' and he found another door ajar. 'In here,' she called again from the bedroom.

The light from the east streamed into the long windows, one of which she had opened; she stood on the little wrought-iron balcony, her smallness emphasised by the size of the huge stone flower-urn.

Looking over her shoulder at Gene, she said, 'Are you free later to do some gardening for me?'

'I'll have to ask, ma'am.'

She reversed into the room, closing the tall windows, and when she turned to face him, she had already tied her gown tightly enough to be sheer across her body; she folded a hand inside the gown and rubbed her shoulder. Gene looked away.

'I haven't decided, yet. I may need you.'

'All right, ma'am.'

'I wish you weren't so stubborn,' she said.

'Ma'am, I said I'd be a good friend to you, if that's what you wanted. And I said I'd always work like a horse for you. That's what I'm here for.'

She sat on the edge of her bed, and as if suddenly cold, wrapped her arms around herself.

'Where did you get that formidable maturity?' she asked.

'I only want to do the right thing,' said Gene.

She said suddenly, 'I've been thinking. I give in. No more. You will be my friend and I will make sure everyone knows that's all you are.'

He left. She moved from the bed and sat in front of her own mirror. She spoke to her reflection.

'Judy Heckwright, you have done it again.' She held her fingers as pointed as a tent to her forehead, and then each hand tapered upwards to her cheekbones, and then rang her bell.

'Ally, I want Porteous. Only if he's sober.'

'He will be this hour, ma'am.'

'Get him.'

Within the hour, Dr Porteous arrived, bag in hand.

'I've not had a bath,' she said, 'but I want you to examine me, I don't feel well.'

'How are you complaining?'

'The usual. Every bloody month.'

Dr Porteous rolled the sheet back over her, 'Fine, fine, everything fine, I'd say.'

'You never say anything else, do you?'

'What else could I say?'

She looked at him, her mood growing ever more foul.

'But you know I am not well?'

'Why do you say that?'

'None of your business,' she snapped.

'You're my patient.'

'So?'

'You should have children.'

'By whom? Tell me that. By whom?'

'By your husband, of course.'

She dismissed the doctor. 'Have you told him that? He married me for my money, not my –' She stopped herself. 'In any case, that is quite enough from you.'

Dr Porteous left as she settled herself on the pillows.

At lunch, when her husband came to her room, Judy Cruiseman began her long, quiet vilification of Gene Comerford, a ferocious and unrelenting campaign.

'How would we know,' she asked her husband, 'whether we had hired an IRA man? We wouldn't know, would we?'

He nodded ruminatively.

She continued, 'One thing I'm certain about – Comerford, he's not an IRA man. That's for sure, isn't it? Or can we be sure?'

At dinner next week she said to her husband, 'Richard, do you know whether Alicia Black is well?'

'Oh?' Richard Cruiseman, during any meal, used his napkin more than his knife or fork, wiping, dabbing, folding, unfolding, dusting the tablecloth. 'Why?' he asked.

'Just wondered. Our new man. Comerford.' That became another part of the strategy – the care to get Gene's name right in all circumstances. 'He said something. I think I'll write to her.'

No more, that was all: just a little sting of enquiry.

One late afternoon of the following month, she went down to the mill with Mr Caldwell, ostensibly to see Mr Duncan.

'Mr Duncan, what is our very best?'

'I'd say, Milady, the straightforward, the full strong sheet.'

'And our damask?'

'No. I've never liked ours, you know that, Sir Richard knows that.'

'H'mmmm.' She fingered the bale. 'This?'

'Yes.'

'Good for a silver wedding anniversary?'

'The best.'

Again she pondered, and Duncan, although pretending not to look, never took his eyes off her.

'Ye-es,' she said. 'Ye-es.'

She turned and left the office, walked down the wooden steps outside the building. Through the window she had seen Gene leave the building below and stand in the open air. He turned at the sound of the footsteps on the stairs.

Lady Cruiseman beamed at him. 'Mr Comerford! Just the man I wanted to see. How are you?'

'Grand, thanks, ma'am.'

'I wanted to say "thank you". Now that it has settled, I can see that you made the most marvellous job of that rockery for me. I did not fully appreciate how good a job it was but now that it has settled and had its first rain and that it seems marvellous. I hadn't appreciated what a naturally good gardener you are. Thank you. And Mr Duncan will not let me steal you away any more.'

She walked close to Gene and smiled at him warmly and whispered, 'No hard feelings? Good friends?' and he nodded.

She left with Mr Caldwell – and wondered aloud but for Mr Caldwell's ears, 'Interesting past, I believe. Ye-es. Did you know he knew that Donaghy fellow, the bomber?'

Not another querying word did Mr Caldwell ever hear from her on the subject. For some time, Judy Cruiseman's unhappiness seemed to abate; she grew quieter, more contained, and within six months Nin had begun to comment that 'Herself hasn't screamed at us in an age, has she?' For months at a time Gene never caught sight of her, and within two years she had faded considerably from the daily gossip of the Cruiseman employees. In the spring of 1937, and again in 1938, she went away, some said to London, some to

Switzerland; when she came home after each three-to-four-month interval, her robustness returned; but she and Gene had no further encounters.

In the pub, Gene and Noreen moved on to discuss books.

'Did you ever read *Knocknagow*?' he asked her.

'No.' She knuckled the band of freckles across her nose. 'Who wrote it?'

'By Charles Kickham.'

'Who's he?' Noreen's enquiry never got a reply. Dermot Donaghy strode into their group.

'We need a volunteer.'

Gene recoiled at the word.

'No,' said Donaghy irritably. 'We need someone who'll volunteer to take the "guitar" home. I can't do it, they're watching me.'

Noreen said, 'I'll do it.'

'You will not,' said Donaghy, 'it is too big for you.'

'Listen to him and the head on him.' Noreen rolled her eyes.

Donaghy looked at Gene, who shook his head. 'Under – no – circumstances.'

Donaghy said, 'I knew you were going to say that.'

'Listen,' said Gene. 'I should never have been walked into that – at that meeting tonight. I should not.'

'What happened?' asked Noreen.

Donaghy said quickly, 'None of your business,' and looked warningly at Gene. 'Don't tell her.'

'I will tell her. They made me handle a gun.'

Noreen laughed. 'Is that all? Jesus, I had a parcel of stuff I told the polis was bacon from my mother for my aunt the last time I come up from home.'

Gene shook a head disapprovingly. 'I don't want that sort of thing at all.'

'Ah, grow up,' said Donaghy. 'Easy known you have it all your own way down south. You'd not care if we rotted.' He turned away impatiently. 'Come on, who's taking it?'

Michael O'Neill said, 'I will. I brung it.'

They dispersed. At the pub's back door Gene and Noreen smiled goodnight and parted; Gene walked away as Noreen and Joe said goodnight to Michael O'Neill.

PART TWO

13

Next morning it might have been flaming June, as the Indian summer of mid-September came into its own. Janice mystified Belle by beckoning smilingly at her.

'Are you feeling a wee bit better now, Janice?' Belle asked with an expression somewhere between mischievous and tentative. Janice smiled again.

'Up there with you,' she said, indicating the table. 'The Blackwoods can go to hell.'

Belle pranced. 'Hey up!' she told the women in the room. 'I have a real treat for you today.'

Anne Acheson shouted out, 'A fella with a big knob, is it?' They roared.

'He has to have a uniform on him,' called Anne Byers.

Belle clapped her hands. 'Miscellaneous Facts. Are you going to shut up, are aren't you? 'Cause if you don't I'm not going to tell you what Anna Neagle showed *Photoplay* she carries in her handbag.' They fell silent instantly.

Except Gloria. 'Oy! Fuck you off outa here, you.' Everyone turned. 'Warehouse doll!'

Noreen had slipped in through the door behind Janice and stood to listen to Belle. Noreen stuck her tongue out at Gloria.

'Go on. Out!' yelled Gloria. 'Enid, shift that young one, willya?'

Noreen replied, 'I work in this mill, too, so I do.'

'Yer arse! Work?' said Enid. 'You wouldn't know what work was if you found it in your porridge.'

Janice said, 'She's all right. Dry up everyone.' Janice turned to Noreen. 'Don't mind them. Come on in over here.'

Belle clapped her hands again. 'Ladies! Pull-eeeze!' and she made them laugh, defusing.

'Now. Anna Neagle, she carries a small, pearl-embroidered bag.'

'Oh, same as meself,' came an anonymous voice from far down the room. More laughter.

'And this,' said Belle, preparing to tick off her fingers, 'is what she has in it.'

'Her drawers,' shouted another voice.

Belle rose above it and quoted exaggeratedly. 'The first thing that fell out on the table was her work permit in her real name of Florence Marjorie Robertson. 'Cause Anna Neagle is only her stage name, like.'

'Aye,' shouted Edith, 'Edith Millar is only my stage name, my real name is "Virginia". They call me "Virgin" for short.'

Several women groaned at the old joke and called out in unison, 'Oh, aye, "but not for long".'

'If you think I'm going to stand here all day –' Belle threatened unseriously. Janice called them to order. Belle ticked her next finger.

'And a compact with her name, "Anna", engraved on it. And three wee jars, with cleansing cream, powder, and rouge. She has a locket with two pictures of her Ma and Da, and for luck she has the signet ring her Da gave her Ma. What else?' Belle paused and pondered. 'Oh, yes. She has her lipstick, her bobby pins for her hair, and her barrette of course' – Belle turned the back of her head towards her audience – 'and she always wears the barrette across here': she indicated a point halfway down the back of her head. 'And she has a handkerchief with her name on it. And a wee calendar. And her comb. Oh, and her key for the front door. Did I leave out anything?'

'Perfume?' asked Janice.

'Oh, right enough she has a wee sachet.' Belle pronounced it 'sachette'.

Noreen called in a helpful tone, 'Sashay. 'Tis called a "sashay".' Belle waved a friendly thank you to her and turned to the front once more.

'Shut up!' called Gloria to Noreen, who blushed a little. 'Aren't you going back to your work – this isn't the warehouse.'

Noreen moved to the door.

Janice called her back. 'No, no. You're all right.' Janice turned back again to face the room and winked soberly at a puzzled Gloria.

'Where are we up to?' Belle cried. 'I know. We're up as far as the war is over and Ashley coming home, and every place in flitters. Right.'

Belle wore a cream turban-headscarf today, and had put on lipstick in the lavatories. She needed no rouge, and her hair had stayed in that Madeleine Carroll style now for some weeks. These mornings, she rose a little slower, then rushed – and tried to time the last few hundred yards to Rufus Street very slowly, in case Gene appeared from the tangential streets. Twice in the last twenty-four hours they had seen each other in the mill; twice he had winked, and the second time, in the crush in the hall, she whispered to him, 'You're a great winker, aren't you?' He winked again.

This morning she whispered gravely as she pressed past his shoulder, 'I've something to tell you.'

'Oh, what? What?'

'Janice's husband came in the other night. He warned me off you. I haven't time now. See you.'

Astride Janice's high chair, Belle rubbed her hands. In her 'the story-so-far' voice she announced, 'So. Atlanta's burnt to a cinder and all the explosives is blown sky high.'

'Like Belfast,' said Alice MacKechnie.

'And Rhett has taken Scarlett and Melanie and the baby and Prissy back towards Tara and halfway there he's left them and he's gone off to join the army. Right? And after a fierce hard journey, Scarlett gets back to Tara. On the way she passes Twelve Oaks, the Wilkes's home place, d'you remember where they had the barbecue, and d'you remember – the place is in ruins, now, and d'you remember what I said about the very stairs where she seen Clark Gable for the first time?'

'A skeleton, Belle.'

'That's what I said, like an oul' skeleton there that stairs, the banisters standing up on their own in the moonlight.'

Belle folded her arms, and now not a sound could be heard in the room, except the ticking of the halted machines and distant noises from other parts of the mill. The women leaned on their benches and listened.

'Well, just as Vivien Leigh gets near to Tara, doesn't the pony die. Right there between the shafts. And the night is pitch black

211

and she can't see a thing, and she don't know whether her own house is still standing. At that very minute' – Belle raised her eyes skyward and tilted her head and pointed a finger upward at the end of an outflung arm – 'at that very minute, who sails out like a big coin from behind the clouds only the moon. And there in the light of the moon she sees Tara. And it still there.'

The women made a low 'oooooo!' sound.

'Scarlett runs up to the door and she beats on it.' Belle hammered the air, her little fists like ivory trip-hammers. 'And the door creaks open as slow as a ghost story. And who's standing there only her oul' fella, Gerald O'Hara. But sure he's gone off his head. His eyes is red. He's shambling like oul' Jimmy Rafferty down our street.'

The women's faces moved with the story.

'Then Mammy, the big fat Negress, she comes over, like, and she tells Scarlett that her two sisters has the typhoid. But they're all right. I mean they're as weak as water, but they're getting better. And then – Scarlett asks after her mother. The big fat one, Mammy, she starts to tell her – but Scarlett, she knows, like. She knows.'

Belle's head dipped in the sad affirmative. Far off, somewhere in the mill, a door banged.

'Scarlett goes over to a door and she opens it. And she stands in the doorway and she goes "Nehnh?"' Belle did an intake of breath full of the sound of tears.

'There lying on a black bed is the corpse of her own mother.'

'Awwwhhh!' sighed the room.

'Scarlett walks over, and she looks down and her face is plastered with dread, and then – and then –' Belle turned the suspense up to the scream. 'She screams – "Aaeeeeuyiah!" and she drops on the floor like a stone.' Belle let her head and shoulders plunge into a sag as dramatic as a dying swan.

All that morning she told them *Gone with the Wind*. When they had first discussed the film's arrival in Belfast, Belle assured them she'd make it last for weeks, and she kept her promise. She had rationed them, and today she gave them the biggest instalment so far. On and on, through Tara's dilapidation, the Yankees' scorched-earth depredations, Gerald O'Hara's decline into sad drunkenness and derangement – up to the moment of Scarlett's smudge-faced, wild vow, oathed against the red sky: it thrilled them.

'As God is my witness.' Belle, too, shook her fist pugnaciously at the rafters. 'As God is my witness. If I have to rob – or murder – or tell lies – I'm never going to go hungry again. As God is my witness.'

They cheered – and jumped to the klaxon.

Noreen had stayed throughout, and she said at Belle's elbow, 'Belle, there's no two ways about it, I'm going to have to see that picture. I'm going to borrow the ticket money off my brother.'

'That cardigan's lovely, Noreen, did you knit that yourself?'

'I did.'

'Fair Isle's awful hard,' said Belle. 'Listen. We could try and get in one night. I know one of the men on the door.'

'*Wuthering Heights* was great, Belle. But this'll be – it'll be –'

'Magnificent?' finished Belle.

'And more than that,' said Noreen. 'I'll be asking you out to dance with me, Belle.' Noreen trailed her arms wickedly and Belle laughed.

In the Lapping Room after lunch, Gordon approached Gene. Lennie watched, but could not overhear.

'Anything to report?' asked Gordon in a smiling, mock-military fashion. Gene stood, uncomprehending.

'I mean – have you given it further thought?'

'Ah.' Light dawning, Gene said, 'I have.'

'And? Have we reached a verdict?'

'Do you mean,' asked Gene, intent on his measuring, 'will or won't I?'

'Yes.' Gordon stuck his hands down into his apron pockets, flapped them tightly within.

'I don't think I'll accept.'

Gordon sucked his teeth. 'Oooh, really?'

'No. I mean – yes, really.'

Gordon walked a little closer, but stood sideways to Gene. 'How could I persuade you?'

'I don't think you could.'

'We could make the money – bigger.' Gordon withdrew one hand, and rubbed imaginary cash in his fingers.

'Tis not a business of money, or that,' said Gene.

'What is it a "business of"?' asked Gordon.

'Well, I like to be independent. To be able to speak my mind, have my own thoughts.'

Gordon looked alarmed. 'Speak your mind?'

'I mean – I'll do an honest day's work for an honest day's wages, when I'm hired for what I do. But you're not offering to hire me for what I do. You're offering to hire me for something else.'

Gordon misunderstood – and that night would misconstrue to his father, would misinterpret Gene's remark as, 'He obviously wants to keep himself in a position where he can talk about what he saw. I mean, look, Dad: he said to me, "You're offering to hire me for something else" – meaning, "You have another reason altogether for hiring me," meaning, "I know that by making me this offer you want to buy my silence about that boy and Mr Heckwright."'

'Yes, Gordon. Yes.'

'I said he was no fool.'

Nesbit shook his head irritatedly. 'You don't have to dot every "i" and cross every "t".' He paused. 'Trouble is we don't know enough about this fellow. Typical Judy Cruiseman. She sends this fellow up to us, says keep an eye on him, report back and won't fully say why. Do you know if the telephones down to Fintown are still working?'

'Yes, they are, they go through the Republic and back up again.'

After Gene turned down Gordon's offer, Montana found a way of sitting beside Gene for a moment.

'I heard all that. You're an ape. A big ape.'

Gene looked at him. 'Why am I an ape?' he asked, smiling.

'Only an ape refuses anything from the Blackwoods. They'll nail you for it. You'll be out on your ear here.'

'They need the manpower, though,' said Gene. 'I thought about that beforehand.'

'You're a fuckin' ape. They'll nail you. I'm telling you. There's only one thing worse – and that's a Taig riding one of our women.'

Gene blushed deeply and Montana poked him, saying, 'Ah-hah? Giddyap? Fuck me, fuckface, you'll be hoppin' up and down soon if you're not careful. They'll be firing at your feet, and saying "Dance, friend," they will.'

214

He made imaginary Colt .45 noises with his thumbs and forefingers and galloped away.

Unlike Montana, Lennie had misinterpreted. 'You're very friendly with the bosses already, aren't you?'

'No,' said Gene. 'The opposite.'

Lennie scoffed. '"The opposite"? I'm not blind.'

Gene quickened the last few steps towards Belle and grinned.

'Do you wear red a lot?' he asked.

'You always should if you've black hair.'

He bent to her face. 'Can I have a kiss?'

'Course you can.'

She put her arm around his waist and they went into the little park.

'You said you had to tell me something?' he asked as they sat. 'Here, give me another kiss, first.' When their faces parted, he said, 'God, Belle, I can't get you out of my head, so I can't.'

She said, 'I keep trying to remember your face exactly, and I can't.'

He put his face to her hair. 'God, this is all lovely. Lovely.' He laid his head on her shoulder for a minute. 'I love this, sitting here beside you.' She reached up and stroked his hair.

He sat up. 'Now. What were you going to tell me?'

'They're all warning me.' She told Gene about Malcolm's late-night visit, told him every detail and looked at him expecting an answer.

Gene merely said, 'Yes, they were watching me down in Fintown too.'

'What did they want to know?'

'You know what they wanted to know. Did I carry a gun?' Gene laughed.

Belle asked, 'But d'you know what happened? D'you remember when I said to you – when I said to you was that a bomb? And you said nothing.'

'Belle, I do know what happened, and I know there's an elderly man badly hurt, and I hate thinking about such things, much less being near them. That's why I said nothing.'

'But you know a lot about politics? And history?'

'And you know a lot about the pictures,' he retorted, 'but you're not a film star?' He retreated a little and smiled. 'Not yet anyway?'

She smiled too, relieved.

Gene said, 'I bet that policeman friend of yours told his wife.'

'No, he wouldn't.'

'I bet he did. And besides, isn't she the doffing-mistress?'

'Janice?'

'Why was she so cool with you lately, you said it yourself? And I saw her giving me a strange look today.'

'No. Malcolm wouldn't tell. And anyway she's all right with me again.'

'I don't know. Men will tell everything to their wives. I would if I had a wife.'

They said nothing for a while. Belle broke the silence. 'I love watching it get dark.'

'Give us another kiss.'

Belle kissed him, her nose bumping his.

'We should have noses we could take off – just for kissing,' she said.

'How do you, how do you – think – about me?' Gene asked.

Belle smiled in the dark. 'I'm getting in a state. I don't know what's going on in my head. My head's spinning, like.'

Gene asked, 'Did something like this not ever happen before?'

'No. Sure I hardly ever spoke to a boy. I mean, my stomach was sick coming out tonight.'

'Mine, too,' he said.

They turned on the old rickety park seat and embraced tight, tight.

Gene said, 'I never have anyone to talk to, I mean close.'

'I haven't neither. A man, like. I've the girls and that, Janice, and Gloria. But that's no excitement, like this.'

'Belle, you're so innocent.'

'Aye, that's what they all say to me, but I don't even know what that means.'

Gene traced her eyebrows with his finger: she blinked. 'It means,' he said, 'or what they mean is – you've no badness in you.'

Belle said, 'Ooh, I'd say I have, I'd say if I had to, I'd be real bad. I keep it inside me, but I often feel real bad. You're the one with no real bad in you.'

Gene drew her head down on to his neck, and for several minutes pressed small kisses on her hair.

'This is what they call in the books a "whirlwind romance", isn't it?' Gene said.

'How d'you know about that?' asked Belle.

'I know about a lot of things.' He grinned and they kissed and kissed and kissed.

Belle and Noreen went to *Gone with the Wind* the next night. Noreen sat when they played 'God Save the King' at the end of the film – even though a man behind them whispered loudly, 'Get up, you ignorant strap!'

In the aisle she whispered, 'Belle, I hope I didn't embarrass you, but I could not stand up for that, I never can.'

Belle, magnanimous, said, 'Noreen, live and let live, isn't that what we all have to do?'

Side by side, Noreen again linking Belle's arm, they walked to Pretoria Street.

'D'you know, Belle, you're every bit as good as Vivien Leigh. How could I ever get that good? I'm not going to bother.'

'No, no. 'Tisn't hard. Come on. You could practise your telling on me.'

'Now?'

'This minute. No one'll see us in the dark.'

'I don't even know how to start, Belle.'

'Well, pick a thing that happened, that you'll always remember.'

Noreen made them stop while she paused for thought. 'The thing that got me was the time Scarlett killed the soldier on the stairs. You know. Just pointed the gun at him, and he thinking she had something valuable hidden in her hand.'

'Now,' said Belle, 'this is how you begin.'

She showed Noreen how to create context: 'Don't jump straight in, tell a wee bit of what's went on before.' And without ever having known that such formal principles existed, Belle related the ancient rules of storytelling. She summarised the importance of outcome: 'You have to make them want to know what's going to happen'; colour – 'Only ever say a thing is grey or black if there's sadness going on, I mean if there's a dance there'll be someone wearing green, won't there?'; mood – 'They want to cry as well as laugh, don't they, and they want to catch their breath. I do watch Alice MacKechnie, she's my measurement, like, of if the picture is going well when I'm telling it, and if her mouth isn't open, or if she's looking down at her hands, I'm not doing it right, and Alice loves a great cry. She had tears in her eyes today when Scarlett's mother was dead.'

And above all action: 'Noreen, the thing is, nobody be's something, everybody has to do something, if a person be's something, I mean, they could be just standing, just to be. But if they're doing something, then something else is going to happen. Now, away you go.'

Noreen began haltingly, her voice a deeper timbre than Belle's, her accent broader.

'They come back to Tara, and there isn't a juge to drink nor a bit to eat. And Scarlett, she says, she don't care, she's not going to starve and she starts them all working, picking cotton and that.'

'And what?' asked Belle.

'Well – picking cotton.'

'What about it?'

'Well, their fingers was sore, and their backs was sore?'

'Aye, so tell that, 'cause every one of the women listening knows what that's like, sore hands. The more they know other people is sometimes like them, the more they'll listen.'

Noreen continued. 'And one day she looks outa the door –'

Belle interrupted again. 'Where's she standing?'

Noreen said, 'She's standing on the stairs.'

'That's right. Tell them that – tell them she's standing on the stairs looking outa the door and she's just after sending Melanie back to bed 'cause she's not fully better yet. Noreen, you're going to be real good at this.'

Noreen nodded. 'And in comes this soldier and he gets offa his horse and he comes into the house and Scarlett, she tiptoes back upstairs to get a gun, and she takes off her shoes to slip back down the stairs real quiet, and she sees him going through her jewellery –'

'Her mother's jewellery,' cut in Belle.

'How d'you know that?'

'Her mother's initials was on the box, and that's an awful lot better 'cause we all know Scarlett's mother isn't cold in her grave and here's this hobo of a soldier robbing her jewels.'

'Oh,' said Noreen in wonder. 'So you have to stare hard at everything.' She pondered for a moment, then continued. 'So the soldier looks up the stairs and he sees Scarlett.'

'What's she doing?' asked Belle.

'She's standing with her back pressed real hard up against the wall on the side of the stairs and she's looking at him and he starts coming up towards her. And his face is real ugly.'

Belle asked, 'What's it like?'

'How d'you mean?'

'What does his face remind you of? I mean, is it like porridge? Or a pig? Make it like something or someone they know.'

'Well, 'tis like the face of a fella in the Lapping Room, I don't know his name, but if he had whiskers, 'twould be the spit of him, a pudgy fellow. With a cow's lick to his hair.'

Belle roared with laughter, and could hardly stop. 'And a blink to his eyes?'

'Aye.'

'That's my brother, Lennie!' She laughed again and Noreen, after initial embarrassment, joined in, then said, 'Oh, Belle, I'm awful sorry.'

'Oh, no, sure I thought the very same the first time I seen the soldier.'

They had reached Pretoria Street.

'Belle, I'm terrible sorry,' said Noreen again. 'And them tickets, thanks very much. I mean, you're great, you are.'

'The first picture I ever went to,' said Belle, 'was *Anna Karenina* with Greta Garbo, and I thought I was going to die with the excitement –' and began to re-create for Noreen that first night's luminous thrill. 'She was standing up by herself, looking out along –' Belle stopped suddenly. 'Is that heels?' she asked, an ear cocked. Lowering her voice to a whisper, Belle said, 'Hang on here a few minutes, Noreen, that's my Ma, let her go in home first.'

While Belle and Noreen watched Atlanta burning, Malcolm and Lennie had been patrolling along the Shore Road again. Lennie cleared his throat.

'Are you starting a cold, Lennie?' asked Malcolm.

'No. I was going to ask you something.'

'Oh, right?'

'That new fella, Malcolm, Comerford. He told me the other day he knew I had asthma. How would he know that? He said he heard me wheezing, but I wasn't wheezing this year back.'

'Aye,' said Malcolm, 'aye.'

'And I'm very doubtful about him, Malcolm. I mean – he gives an answer for everything. I mean, he's not quick on the tongue, or that, but there's no one ever catches him out.'

'He's a big lad, isn't he, though?' said Malcolm.

'He is, but I was thinking that a few of the boys might sort him out with a bit of a hammering, I mean, no violence, like, but a bit of a hammering, like. You know, just to remind him, to keep him tame.'

'I wouldn't agree with that, Lennie. That's breaking the law.' Malcolm reflected, then said, 'If I tell you something, can you keep it a secret?'

'Of course I can.'

'Now, Lennie, I'll measure you by this. I'll know if you're a grown man if you can keep this a secret. This is like police work, confidential. You know?'

'Yeh, of course.'

'I know how your man, the lapper, how he knew about your wheezing.'

'How so?'

'Your wee sister.'

'Belle?'

'Aye, Lennie, Belle. Work it out.'

'How?'

'You know what I'm saying, Lennie.'

'I don't, Malcolm.'

'Go you on outa that. You do a'course.'

'Are you saying Belle's – that Belle knows him or something?'

'Oh, aye and a wee bit more than that?' Malcolm walked with his hands behind his back.

'A wee bit more than that?'

'Where was she the other Sunday?'

'The other Sunday? I don't know, she was off out the day, but so was I, she never said, she coulda been at home all day and I'da never known and my mother, she was off out the day too.'

'Well, I'll tell you where she was, she was down in Armagh on the back of a motorbike. I mean she was on the back of his motorbike.'

Lennie stopped. 'Malcolm, you're telling the truth, so you are, he was telling us about him playing. And he won money off it.'

'Now, Lennie, how're you going to keep that a secret?'

'My sister, Belle, see her?' Lennie boiled. 'She needs a good hiding.'

'Lennie, this is police work, you can't tell on her. 'Tis her business. Janice'll talk to her.'

'But how does our Belle know that fella at all?'

Malcolm replied, 'D'you remember I told you about her and young Blackwood?'

'Aye.'

'Well, d'you remember? 'Twas your man caught young Blackwood at Belle.'

The Reverend MacCreagh told Edith again that he would go much oftener to visit his 'poorly wife' if buses had not proven so awkward, especially now in the war and all that.

Edith said to him, as she always did, 'I understand. Of course, you mean to – and that is the thing that matters.'

At first he did not use the word 'Anniesburn' with all its connotations of lunacy, nor would he use anything but the word 'poorly'. Once or twice he let himself slip, and then corrected himself and said 'up in County Antrim', or if he said 'my poor wife's mind' he corrected himself and said 'my poor wife's spirits'. They had had no children, and he said, 'Wasn't it a blessing?'

Edith stood on the chair and the Reverend MacCreagh handed up the large safety pins. He called her 'Edith' when they were alone; she called him 'Samuel'; in the presence of anyone else it was 'Mr MacCreagh' and 'Mrs MacKnight', and he looked at her legs as she stood on the chair and said to her, 'Yes, yes,' as she pinned the new curtain cloth with her whisking vigour.

When she stepped down he helped, by holding out his hand and arm, and she coiled her fingers round the bare skin of the wrist, and the black hairs on it, and lowered herself carefully. They looked at the curtains together.

'Not a chink of light will get out there,' she said with some satisfaction.

'Nor can anyone see in,' he murmured with his little cough. He sat down on the frayed couch, and she stood fixing the curtain here and there.

'It'll make the room warmer you'll find. It did to us.' She gazed up at the curtain rail, and he stroked his chin and looked at the empty fireplace.

'This room could do with that. And I expect yours too,' he replied.

'I dread the winter,' said Edith. She looked at him, without him noticing.

'How tall are you, Edith?' he asked unexpectedly.

'I don't know. They said in the hospital once I was nearly six feet. Why?'

'I saw a woman today who reminded me of you. Only she was wearing a hat.'

Two years ago he had asked her to sit opposite him in a chair much higher than his position on the couch. With small commands, he had directed her into a sitting position, and she, who challenged everything, had not questioned.

'You have to sit down very firmly,' he had said, 'it is a chair with a hard seat and you have to sit on it very firmly for your own safety, and you have to sit with your back hollowed forward so that you are sitting hard down. Posture. You know.' Then he indicated, by sitting upright and opening his thighs. 'Like this,' and that was how she always sat in this room and did so again tonight. 'That's how you'll never get yourself a bad back. Posture.'

Little cough. 'Edith, I was just thinking the other night, do you remember, the very warm night, what was it, Sunday, and I was thinking if we were like the well-off people and had the telephone.'

Edith looked and listened, then asked, 'Do you pray when you can't sleep, Samuel? I worry about Lennie. If he's all right, when he's out with the Specials.' She added. 'And Belle, of course.'

'Sometimes I read the Bible.'

'Oh, there you are, isn't that funny, that night you were talking about wasn't I reading the Bible myself, so I was. And I was reading

222

Samuel.' When Edith smiled girlishly she half-closed her eyes.

'Well, I don't believe this!' He looked at her in pleased alarm. 'I was reading Samuel. Let me get the passage.' He leaned his long, angular body over to the table within reach, and fetched the Bible. 'Here it is, I always have it marked.'

Edith sat. He read; he was not an unobvious man; he had a geometrical jaw. '"One evening David got up from his bed and from the roof of his palace he saw a woman bathing . . ."' He read so softly that had snoopers been leaning on the very windowsill of Capetown Street, they could have heard not a sound from inside, so heavy were the Reverend MacCreagh's new blackout curtains. The pair sat peacefully when the reading ended, and looked into the empty fireplace. The Reverend MacCreagh, an innocent man, coughed and murmured, 'I am blessed with good friends.'

Edith replied, 'That's because you're such a good man.'

Lennie was standing, no room to pace, when Edith walked into the kitchen.

'What are you doing up?' she asked irritatedly. 'I was fine getting home by myself.' Usually she liked to fix the kitchen quietly for the breakfast, and check that neither Belle nor Leonard had left the teatowel soaked wet. She looked closer. 'What's chewing you, Leonard? You look like a man caught something off a dog?'

He said with more aggression than she had ever heard him use, 'I have bad news for this house. For this whole house.' He beat the air. 'Bad news.'

Edith put down the breadboard and breadknife quickly. 'Leonard, what's up with you?'

He struck a fist into a hand. 'Bad news.'

'Leonard! What's at you? Are we to lose the house or what? Your work? Have you it still?'

'No. I have. We're worse.'

Edith went to him, restrained his sleeve emphatically. 'Stoppit here. What is it at you?'

He faced her. 'D'you know what I'm after hearing? D'you know? Do you?' His face lunged at her.

'How could I and you not telling me?'

'Our Belle!' Fury pinked his eyes.

'What about her?'

'She's being walked out by a Taig. And what's more there's people think he's a Fenian.'

Edith recoiled and sat down. 'No. She'd not do that. But she would. She wouldn't have enough sense. How do you know?'

'Malcolm seen 'em. Her on the back of his motorbike. And she's going out to meet him in the evenings and she saying she's at Janice's or Uncle Jed's.'

'Who is he? How d'you know he's an IRA fella?'

'Isn't he working alongside me? Isn't he the new lapper?'

'Oh, God in his Heaven,' said Edith. 'God above.' She looked at Leonard, he red in the face, she white. 'Is it serious?'

'You know them fellas, there's nothing they'd like more than destroying the character of a decent girl.'

Edith looked around the kitchen in the dim light of the low-wattage bulb.

'Leonard, what's going to happen to this house? What's going to happen? And there bombs falling, and people getting shot too, that poor man, that General Knowles, he died. Did you know that? He's dead. Every night you go out there I think of your poor father and what them animals did to him. And will it happen to you? And we're always the ones getting shot, you don't see ould Blackwood getting shot, and we're praying for our lives and no one to do a thing to protect us. I mean, 'tisn't that often one of their own gets shot, is it? And look at us and this house blighted all its life nearly. And now Belle and this – this – man. And she'll be in any minute on top of us. I wish the Reverend MacCreagh was here.'

Edith, more distressed than Lennie had seen her for years, clasped her long knees and quoted, '"These are they which came out of great tribulation, and have washed their robes, and rendered them white in the blood of the Lamb."'

The door clicked merrily, and Belle hummed in. She stopped feet away from the tableau of her mother and brother.

'Where were you?' Lennie asked in a dead, seething calm.

'I was out,' Belle arched back. 'What's up?'

'Where were you?' Lennie repeated.

'Mind your business. Anyway, where's the ghost you two are after seeing?'

Edith pointed to the chair at Belle's table place.

'Sit down, Belle.' Her mouth half-open in an expression of

caution, Belle went to the chair with some hesitation. 'And you, Leonard –' Edith indicated his place: 'sit.' Edith swung around to put her elbows on the table.

'Belle,' she began. 'You know nothing. You know next to nothing. About anything.' As Belle opened her mouth, Edith held up a hand and rasped, 'You'll not interrupt me at my own table until I give you leave to.'

Belle rose, and Edith said, 'And if you get up from this table now, you'll never sit down at it again.'

Belle sat slowly. 'Eh, whose circus is this when it's in town?'

Lennie cut across. 'You'll get circus across your face and eyes if I get over there to you.'

'You will not!' she rejoined. 'You touch me and I'll go to your Superintendent, so I will.'

Edith took final command. 'Belle, I've had two bad pieces of news in my life. One was the day John Robinson came to this door to tell me my husband, your father, was dead, and the other was tonight.' Edith lowered her head and closed her eyes.

'Would somebody tell me,' said Belle, her voice grown small, 'what this is?'

Edith raised her head and looked into the neutral distance. 'I'm after hearing you're walking out with a Roman Catholic.'

Belle said, 'Who told you that?'

'Malcolm. He told your brother Leonard. Belle, what would your father say?'

Belle replied, 'My father would ask me if I liked him. My father liked me.'

Edith put out her left hand softly and took Belle's hands. She placed one upon the other, and her own hand on top. With Belle's hands thus held to the table, Edith's right hand whipped Belle a stinging blow across the cheek beneath the eye. Belle attempted to rise and retreat. The hand flashed out but did not connect, as Belle swayed her head back. With both hands Edith pinned Belle's forearms to the table.

Belle began to cry, and wailed, 'What are youse doing to me?'

Lennie said, 'I haven't started yet.'

Edith, still looking straight ahead into the distance, asked in a voice of metal, 'Belle, what colour was your father's eyes?'

Belle replied, 'Brown.'

'Aye,' said Edith. 'Brown. Like your own eyes. Well, I'll tell you now something you don't know. And like I said, you know nothing, Belle. One of them eyes ended up rolling into the gutter because a Catholic like your fancy man shot your father from behind. He shot him in the back of the head and he held the gun so close the bullet went through his head and drove out one of his eyes.' Belle gulped.

Edith continued, 'I told you you know nothing, Belle. And the fella that did that, he's still walking around below in the south. A hundred mile from here.'

'Where your fella is from,' added Lennie.

'And you carrying on with one of his sort.' Edith squeezed Belle's forearm. 'And he's treating you like the wee whore you are, is it he gave you the money, is it?'

'What money?' Leonard looked incredulous.

Edith tried to hit again and when she failed grabbed the forearms again. She and Belle wrestled in their chairs. 'Ask her. She's the one did the whoring for it.'

As Edith aimed again, Belle wrenched free and raced across the tiny kitchen before Lennie could stop her. He caught her at the door, but Belle screamed so spectacularly he let her go. She stumbled backwards on to the street and shouted, 'If you come after me, Leonard MacKnight, I'm going to go for the polis!' She ran. A door opened nearby and Lennie stepped backwards into his own home, confused and denied.

At the corner Belle leaned her face into the comfort of a silent and dark lamp-standard. She could hardly catch her breath, and her nose bled slightly: Edith's single successful blow had been ferocious. Sniffing, trembling, she leaned back against the wall, gulped air. It had begun to rain slightly. The air-raid siren wailed – at which she sat on the street in slumped helplessness and did not move until, with no raid, no searchlights, no anti-aircraft fire, the all-clear sounded an hour later.

Jed called, 'Whoever you are, you shouldn't be out in the black-out.'

Then, in the dark of the open doorway, he saw and asked, 'Belle, Belle, who's ringing our bell?'

She shook her head.

'Belle, Belle. Come in, come in. Coming for more brandy?' He cackled and led the way. 'I knew you'd get the taste for it.'

'Uncle Jed –'

'Will we cut the cards? Quick game of twenty-one? Or Beggar-my-Neighbour?'

'Auntie Sandra? Is she awake?' He looked at her and swayed a little. Sandra appeared on the stairs, peering without spectacles through her dim kitchen. Immediately she grasped. 'Oh, Belle, pet. Oh, Belle, what's up there? Oh, Belle. Pet. What's up?' She ran down the last few steps and folded Belle in her arms. Steering her to a chair, she knelt and rocked her, and glared drunken Jed to bed.

On the stairs he said, 'Belle, so long as he's a – as he's a nice fella itself?'

'Och, you!' Sandra glared again. 'Go to bed.'

'Hee-hee, I knew I was right, nothing wrong with my nose for a'sniffing out things. Belle, you're not to hide him from us. Unless – unless – has he a hump or something?' Jed slipped heavily, recovered and thumped up on the landing.

'Shhhhh, shhhhh. All right, pet, all right, easy, easy.' Sandra did not get Belle into their spare bed until six o'clock in the morning.

14

During the Second World War, the IRA attempted to mount a conflict within a conflict in Belfast. They received assistance from one of their greatest allies – suspicion. Many people believed the rumours that the Germans dropped secret agents every day on the wild Atlantic coast of the west. Some even parachuted into Northern Ireland; two landed, it was said, in a field near Fintown. People 'actually' saw them, as they had 'actually' seen Martians, described the men as vital and energetic, tall, aristocratic and Prussian in their bearing, brilliant in their capacity, imaginative in their subversive espionage, commanding in their presence. They wore moustaches, leather coats and monocles, hid themselves amid the people (notwithstanding, obviously, dense German accents), rented quiet apartments; eavesdropped on conversations, watched troop movements, radioed back to Germany.

In Dublin, Eamon De Valera, the Prime Minister of the Republic, displayed his usual sharp-edged ambivalence. On the one hand he renounced Britain and all her war efforts, and rebuffed every attempt by Churchill to use Irish ports for British shipping; nor did he declare hostility to Hitler. On the other hand, he executed IRA men for the same kind of guerrilladom he had practised twenty years earlier. He railed against Belfast's policies towards Catholics and Republicans – and then sent ambulances and aid north from Dublin on the night Belfast was blitzed.

In the early days of the war, IRA supporters thrilled to the possibilities of a German-assisted revolution. Aircraft with black markings were seen overhead, flying low over Belfast Lough – so low and so identifiable that Royal Navy ships riding at anchor fired at them. In anticipation of a German ground force, Republicans burnt gas-masks in the streets, shouted pro-German slogans and painted them on the walls of Catholic west Belfast. 'Join the IRA and serve Ireland'; 'Up Hitler'; and 'Remember 1916'. When they flouted the blackout, they also lit bonfires in the streets off the Falls Road.

Counter-rumours flew. Who was the IRA agent, up from Dublin, using the name of Maguire, asking the locals to collect knowledge about army personnel? Was he in fact a British agent? Was he a German agent, who had landed in a rubber boat off County Clare? Did a flying-boat land on the River Foyle near Derry to take him away one night? He had mustered all IRA active members and supporters to write down the details of every defensive gun emplacement in Belfast. Or was he in reality a British agent who used the cover of German sympathies to unveil all the IRA cells in the city?

Next, the IRA became convinced that as a pre-emptive measure, Churchill intended to invade the south. A Luftwaffe squadron mistakenly dropped a stick of bombs on Dublin's North Strand area, and Dublin Republicans ascribed it to the misleading propaganda of British agents who wanted to foment anti-German feelings in Ireland.

Amid all this, the Protestant ruling classes regrouped their defences, and as a primary measure restructured the Ulster Special Constabulary. Derived from the Ulster Volunteers, self-formed at the beginning of the century to combat the notion of Home Rule, this armed reserve force, composed entirely of working-class Protestant men, saw as their enemies, first, the IRA; second, the Republic in the south and all that issued from it; and third, Adolf Hitler, against whom they were to be mobilised in the event of an invasion. Lennie MacKnight had joined the Specials as soon as they would have him; his recruitment was hastened as a mark of respect to his late father; 'A motivated Special is a good Special,' the Superintendent told Edith.

The army agreed with the B Specials in seeing the internal defence of Ulster against the IRA as their priority. A leading article in the *Belfast Telegraph* in October 1940 echoed the confidential report of a senior British general. 'Those of us who know Ulster, and who would defend our union with the Crown to the death, expect more danger from within the island of Ireland, than from all of Hitler's jackbooted divisions.'

Protestant observers in workplaces all over Belfast knew to report to the B Specials, and the Royal Ulster Constabulary, and

to anyone in authority, every suspicious Catholic, every movement, hint or suggestion of IRA action. Stormont Castle, the head-
quarters of the Northern Ireland administration, had been warned
over and over to expect a new and vigorous wave of IRA violent
deeds. Another confidential 'Situation Report' counselled that in
this dangerous eventuality, 'any moves by the IRA will immediately create a very dangerous situation which, if not quickly con-
trolled, may well necessitate the use of troops'. Members of the
B Specials were told that the IRA's most dangerous tactic was
infiltration. 'They will get into our workplaces – some of them are
very skilled. They will get into our homes as lodgers; they will be
very plausible. And they will even try to marry our sisters and
daughters.'

Anonymous men in moustaches and leather coats told Specials'
briefings, in clipped English accents, that 'IRA men are creeping
into Belfast in droves. They have hiding-places in houses that have
tunnels between them, and when they're finished what they came
to do up here, they get back into the countryside and hide like
foxes up in the Mourne and Sperrin mountains.'

A little learning had stimulated all security antennae: the IRA
heightened matters by burning down a huge food depot in 1940.
Stormont made loud appeals for the complete sealing-off of the
border with the Republic and began to intern known Republicans
as they interned Czechs, Slavs and all other suspect European
aliens living in Ulster.

Nesbit Blackwood moved around within the circumference of
all such anxiety and suspicion. He served on a Police Advisory
Committee; Blackwoods also gave a challenge cup for the Northern
Ireland Civil Service Golfing Society and Nesbit presented it to
the winner every year at Royal County Down golf club.

'Influence is more interesting than power,' he told Gordon, 'and
more powerful in a funny way. The main thing you have to find
out in life is how to get things done the way you want them.'

'What are you going to do about Mr Heckwright?' asked Gordon.

Nesbit smiled. 'Knowledge first,' he said. 'You can do nothing
without knowledge. I have ascertained that there has been no
report of any kind to the RUC. Therefore, secondly, I am going
to find a way of praising Eric publicly. Give him something new
and big to do. And make sure that we tell everyone.'

'How does that sort out the problem of the lapper?'

Nesbit smiled again. 'Gordon, we have to sort that out. You wanted it sorted out too. No, no, it's all right, it's all right, boys will be boys,' he said when he saw Gordon blushing. 'I won't tell you the trouble I was in with the girls here when I was your age.'

Gordon coughed helplessly in a fit of embarrassment.

Nesbit patted him on the back, 'Cough it up, it's only a brick. Anyway, there's a third problem with Mr Lapper. Yes, we'll call him that. He's stiffing up to that girl. And you know what that means.'

'No,' said Gordon.

'It means fights in the mill. The last time a Catholic man was interfering with a Protestant girl, we had a knifing on our hands.'

'Oh, my God!'

'Exactly, oh your God. So – something has to be done. But I'm doing something.' Nesbit lit a new cigarette off the old one. 'I rang Judy Cruiseman.' He puffed to get the cigarette going. 'And she said – the key to the whole thing is this fellow Donaghy.'

'But why did she keep this fellow working down there? The lapper I mean. So long down there?'

Nesbit shook his head. 'Obvious. So they could keep him under control, keep a tighter eye on him in a small place. The foreman she has, Duncan, splendid man, I tried to hire him from her several times. He kept Mr Lapper so tight that he never made a move. But then she decided she'd send him up here to me to finish off the job. Thanks very much, Judy, I said to myself. And to her.'

One morning six months earlier, in March 1942, Judy Cruiseman had looked at her husband across the dining-room table. The rain lashed outside and he took longer than usual to read the paper.

'Richard.'

'Oh?'

'I have been making enquiries.'

'Oh?'

'I always know when something is bothering me.'

'What is that?'

'Our Mr Comerford. He is a man with a past.'

'Oh?'

'We should have checked his references.'

'Dear, he's been here nearly ten years. He has turned out excellently. Don't be ridiculous. And all that time you've been quietly calumniating him. The man keeps himself to himself. He's never even seen anywhere. He's as quiet as a mouse.'

'That must be the longest speech you've made to me in years.'

'Look.' Richard Cruiseman joined his hands. 'I was a magistrate, remember? We heard everything and we saw everything. This man has not a blemish attached to him. And I do not want to come home on a hard-won and hard-travelled leave from this bloody war to hear you playing the same ancient tune.'

'Do you remember the letter he showed Caldwell and me?'

'Judy. Stop! He's been here nearly ten years.'

'You said that, Richard. Do you not even remember what you said now one minute to the next?' Richard turned the page.

'He had a letter of reference, given to him by his schoolmaster.'

'People often do.'

'But this was written by a notorious gunman called Thomas Kane. A Sinn Feiner.'

'It is too long ago for me to recall the exact details.'

'I said. A notorious gunman.'

'What are you trying to say?'

'I'm saying if you don't know what we might have in our midst, and a war on.'

'Oh?'

'He could be a trained agent. The Germans have been training IRA men. And there is one patch in his life where he was missing for over a year. From seventeen to eighteen and a half.'

'But – didn't he have TB or something? And anyway, he was only a boy?'

'Oh, Richard,' she said with scorn. 'You know how young they recruit them. And as for TB? Those sanatoria they have, it is a well-known fact that they are actually – in reality – training-camps for the IRA. Now. What are you going to do about it?'

'Nothing. And not now. He's due here in five or ten minutes.'

'Why?'

'Duncan is sending him up with something to show me, a catalogue of a new machine he knows about. Duncan swears by him.'

'Really! You might have told me. I have to go and get dressed.'

When Gene arrived and waited in the hall, Judy Cruiseman

called down the stairs to him, 'Good morning, Mr Comerford, how are you this morning?'

'Very well, thanks, ma'am.'

She came slowly down, her new walking-stick held like a sword.

'I haven't seen you for, what? Nearly a year now it must be. And now – my husband – tells me' – she pointed accusingly at Gene – 'that you continue to be – a great success. That Mr Duncan thinks the world of you.'

Gene inclined his head in a gesture that indicated some acceptance of the praise. Judy Cruiseman stood on the bottom step and tapped his shoulder lightly. 'This is what the King would do if he were making you a knight. "Arise, Sire Comerford," he would say. I am – very proud of you, Mr Comerford, and they tell me that everybody likes you. How lucky we were to get you here,' and she swept on hobblingly. Gene gazed suspiciously in her wake. She walked across the hall and sat in a wicker chair, gazing out through the porch on to the lawns.

At lunch she said to her husband, 'I wonder how we are going to deal with this?'

'There is, I am certain, Judy, no need to deal with it. If there was anything wrong about the man, Duncan would have found out, and so would Caldwell. And the man is invaluable.'

Judy Cruiseman stabbed her cane on the floor. 'I don't care,' she said. 'The man who will sort him out, is Nesbit.'

Gordon stirred and stirred his coffee. 'So now what?'

'I'm going to take expert advice, Gordon.' Nesbit Blackwood, in response to a timid request from the staff, had once refurbished all the managerial and secretarial offices – new furniture, fittings, everything: everyone commented that now, when refurbished, he had made them look exactly as before.

Gordon sipped. 'What did Judy say?'

Nesbit warned, 'You're going to have to be confidential about this, Gordon.'

'Dad, I'm an officer. In the army.'

'She said – she said she was well wise to him, and she said a peculiar thing, she said that's why she recommended him to us, because she thought he'd be found out in Belfast.'

'What did she mean by that?'

233

'You know what Judy is like. She often talks in riddles. But what I think she meant is that our friend was more likely to take the chance of coming to the surface so to speak here in Belfast, than down there where he'd be seen quicker. But she wasn't in any doubt about him.'

'What did you say to her about her Uncle Eric?'

'Nothing. I'll wait 'til I see her. But I know what she'll say, and she will want that hushed.'

At a quarter to one, as Gordon Blackwood went upstairs to that lunch with his father, Lennie left the Lapping Room and travelled the mill. He returned fifteen minutes later, accompanied by four men. Each one carried a tool of his trade – spanner, hammer, shovel; one, Jim Cardew, a dray handler, brought a whip.

'Stand there behind me,' Lennie said to them. Across the lappers' table he faced Gene, who sat at his table: he had just opened his sandwiches.

Lennie addressed him. 'Taig!'

Gene looked up and alerted.

'Are you listening to me, Taig?'

Gene rubbed the crumbs off his mouth.

'If you know what's good for you, Taig, you'll leave decent women alone.'

He motioned to the men. Each rested an implement on the table opposite Gene. 'There's no place in this place for scum.'

Gene looked at him, looked at each of the men. Ernest, Archie, Montana and all the other lappers watched in silence, retreating gently to the back of the powse-dusty room.

'I spoke to you, scum. Didn't you hear me?'

Gene looked all around, then back at Lennie, who picked up his own lapping-stick and began to walk around the table. 'Go you ever near a decent woman again in this town, Fenian, and this is what you'll get.'

Jim Cardew, his tattoo gleaming, said, 'No, Leonard, not here. Best for him never to know when.' Cardew flicked the whip across the table, and Gene recoiled, his open hands held out in defence of his face like a southpaw boxer. The whip caught the sandwich packet, and scattered Gene's lunch to the filthy floor.

Lennie said, 'Aye, you'll never know the minute, Taig.'

Gene, watching them all the time, backed down out of his high chair. His foot trod a sandwich. He backed out of the lappers' room, and walked briskly downstairs and then ran out into the open air of the yard below.

While Nesbit and Gordon Blackwood lunched, and Lennie Mac-Knight and friends menaced Gene Comerford, the elders of the women's tribe, Janice, Gloria, Alice, Enid, Edith and the three Annes, stayed together in the lavatories during that lunchtime. They had been conferring thus for many days, unknown to Belle, who had not come back to work, recovering at her Auntie Sandra's. As yet the women had not heard of the fracas with Edith. They even speculated that Belle had run away, but Gloria had seen Gene that morning.

In the combination of fascination and concern that ravished them, they agreed on Gene's physical handsomeness; on the very attractiveness of his Catholicism as forbidden fruit; on the vulnerability of Belle to such a man; they even refused to condemn him as a human being – they only wished to observe tribal rites.

Janice, her capacity for taking offence now hugely stimulated, said, 'I'd sooner see her dead than marrying a Catholic.'

Gloria, always whetted by the gruesome, seconded. 'When you start to count,' she said, 'and you list out the things his crowd done, I mean – terrible.'

She summarised some of their awful lore: Belle's father – they all knew the tale of 'the eye blown out of the poor man's head'; a Special Constable held down and shot in the face, and the widow wasn't allowed to see the body, the damage was that bad; a bomb that took the two legs off a lovely girl from Lepper Street, one leg gone from below the knee, the other halfway at the shin and the bone sticking out like a white knife when they found her; and the wee boy who lost his eye; and that soldier in Banbridge home on leave, and he and his wife shot through the window, the bullet goes through his throat and into his wife's head and they sitting having their tea and they both killed and their married daughter sitting looking at them and the grandchild on her lap.

'But Belle, and that stubborn streak in her,' said Enid Mulcaghey, 'and if she thinks she's in love with him . . . ?'

Edith Millar said, 'She could be doing it to spite her Ma.'

'No,' squinted Alice MacKechnie, 'I know what 'tis.' They turned to look at her. Alice, as they all said of her, 'was in the habit of being right'.

'No, I bet 'tis that she thinks he looks like a film star, I mean you have to give it to the bugger, he looks like a film star, don't he, all that curly hair?'

They chorused agreement in murmurs.

'The thing is,' said Anne Acheson, 'how would we persuade Belle to leave your man alone? I mean on account of the war there's not that many other men around.'

'Or tell him to leave her alone,' said Enid.

'Belle'd never talk to us again if we did that,' said Gloria.

'What about this for a trick?' asked Janice. 'I was thinking this. See Belle? She doesn't know men at all. I mean she's nearly fool enough to ask that fella to marry her.'

'Where are you driving?' asked Alice, amid all the murmurs of assent.

'So she'd be easy put out, wouldn't she?' asked Janice.

Their faces agreed.

Janice played her trump. 'Put some other young one his way? One of his own?'

'That wee warehouse doll?' twigged Gloria. 'And she's a Taig.'

'They breed like fuckin' rabbits,' said Enid.

'Well – she's friends with Belle,' said Janice.

'Aye, but sure everybody's friends with Belle.' Anne Byers looked doubtful.

Janice said, 'But Belle's teaching her telling the pictures, and isn't that how your man the lapper saw Belle first day?'

They looked at Janice expectantly.

'Supposing she, that young one, started telling the pictures? I mean – Belle's not here, is she?'

The women reflected.

'What this needs,' says Janice, 'is a messenger.'

'A messenger?'

This time, Alice twigged. 'Someone to carry a letter? Get one of the wee boys.'

Belle did not appear inside Rufus Street for the next two days. She stayed at Auntie Sandra's, spent much of the time weeping.

236

There came a moment when Sandra wondered whether Belle had begun to slip her moorings; from the table she heard Belle, sitting by the fire, murmur, 'Solomon! Where is thy throne? It is gone in the wind.'

'Are you all right, Belle?' Auntie Sandra asked, with all the tenderness of the world.

Belle answered back, 'Babylon! Where is thy might? It is gone in the wind.'

And then, 'What's that you're saying there, Belle?'

'I'm only saying a wee poem, Auntie Sandra.'

'Yes, pet.'

When Jed awoke at eleven o'clock, hung over but sober, with Belle still in the other room, Sandra explained. They took time to think. Jed asked the same question Edith had asked of Lennie.

'Is it serious?'

'She's never before had a man friend,' answered Sandra.

'What's to be done now?' Jed put on the other sock.

'Well, someone's going to have to talk to Edith. And Lennie.'

Jed said, 'That wee one shouldn't go back to work for a few days. That's a terrible thing to happen to her.'

Jed and Sandra went together to see Edith. She told them it was none of their business. They disagreed, and pointed out that it had become their business, as Belle was now lodging in their house and refused to go home.

Edith said, 'I'll come and get her myself.'

Sandra replied very simply, 'No, Edith, you'll not do that,' at which Edith blushed.

'You don't know her like me and Leonard do.' When anyone sought to praise or defend Belle, Edith wagged her finger. 'Belle only looks after herself, she never thinks of another soul. You don't know her 'cause you don't live with her.'

Uncle Jed took Edith on. 'Aye, but she's not an animal, is she? You're making her sound like as if she was a – a – a hyena or something? You can't sit here in this room and tell me that wee girl, and that grand big laugh she has, has badness in her.'

Edith lashed back. 'Nor can you talk outa your own mouth, you that's off gambling and drinking. You never seen Belle stubborn, she'd seem grand to the likes of you who only thinks of himself

237

too, but I know Belle. And ask her brother Leonard, he seen her selfish – selfish past what you'd think someone could ever be. And he seen her sulking too, d'you ever ask Belle to do something she don't want? And ask them women she works with?'

Jed says, 'They all like her.'

'They do not. I heard Malcolm Gillespie's wife, and this is years ago, the one with no children, and she was saying things about Belle I wouldn't repeat.'

'And you stood listening to her giving out the pay about your own daughter?' said Jed, with incredulity.

'And you gave her drink, us that has a house of temperance always,' retorted Edith.

Sandra took over. 'This isn't getting us Belle sorted out, is it?'

Edith said, 'There's only one sorting out.'

Sandra said, 'She'll not do it, Edith. She's fond of him, and he's fond of her.'

Edith replied, 'What has fond to do with it? Belle don't know her own mind – and his crowd, they don't know what fond is, don't talk about fond in this house that his crowd destroyed the life in. That shot the eye outa my poor husband's head. And Belle's knocking around with folk that did that?' Edith had retreated slowly across the kitchen until she stood with her back to the scullery wall. 'I'm going to have to talk to the Reverend MacCreagh about this, I need advice.'

'That's a good idea,' said Jed, 'he is a Christian man.'

'What would you know about a Christian man?' snapped Edith.

Sandra took over again. 'And in the meantime, Belle is going to need her clothes, Edith.'

'Is she staying with you forever? You'll soon enough get sick of her.'

Jed replied, 'She is thinking of going abroad. And by the way she wants her money.'

'What money?' asked Edith, who had not asked them to sit down. 'I've no money of Belle's. Belle doesn't even give me her wages any more, that's what she's turned out like. That's what you don't know about her.'

As Jed looked puzzled, Sandra stuck to their main point. 'Money or no money, she'll want her clothes, and she's not my size, Edith.'

Edith fished out the worst and oldest of Belle's clothes she could find; she included no bra and the shabbiest underwear.

Jed said, 'I've an idea, Edith. Why don't you go down to our Maisie for a few days, let this blow out?'

Edith replied, 'I'm going anyway. Leonard wants me to make some enquiries down in Fintown for him.'

On Thursday afternoon, Belle said to Aunt Sandra, 'I need a wee walk.'

'Aye, away out for a dander.' Sandra then called after her, 'But come back to here, mind.' Belle nodded.

She hung around near Rufus Street, in the direction Gene habitually took. He duly arrived, registered shock at her appearance.

'I was wondering if there was something up.' He steered her down the street and away from the expected hordes of departing millworkers. 'In fact I was going to try and get a message to you.'

'How did you guess?'

Gene made a face. 'Your brother. He warned me, no, I'll tell you the truth, he threatened me.'

Belle's shoulders sagged.

When Gene finished describing the incident with Lennie, he said, 'And ever since then I'm watching myself like a hawk. So I have the police watching me, your brother's cronies are watching me, and I'm watching me. What happened to you?'

Belle told him and finished, 'Now I don't know, I mean – what'll we do?'

'Oh.' He shook his head in despair. 'But – I have to be with you?'

Belle grabbed his sleeve. 'And me, too. I've nobody else to talk to.'

'Nor me. I never met anybody like you.'

Belle said, 'I mean only my Da . . .' She stopped in mid-pace. 'And I didn't even tell you that awful bit of the story.' She burst into tears. Afraid to put his arms around her in the open street, Gene stroked her upper arm over and over and over. 'I know. I know. I know.'

'How d'you know?'

'I don't know the whole story. The Blackwoods told me a bit of it. Just that your father was – you know, that he died like that.' He stopped, realising something afresh. 'Listen! Belle! That must be it! They must have known, everyone must have known all along that you and I were – friends.'

Belle implored, 'But we're more than friends, aren't we? Aren't we more than friends? I mean – a lot more than friends?' She plucked at his coat in a feverish way. 'More than friends.'

'Oh, more, more. Easy, easy. Easy. Poor Belle. Go easy on yourself. Look, we need time to think. Time to take it calmly. Can you get out easy?'

'Yes, no bother.'

'Tomorrow night?'

'Will we go back to that wee park?' Belle asked. 'Our own wee corner?'

'We can't. The police watch that now. Everywhere I go I seem to see one of them. And if they see us together – your brother'll hear.'

'The first place we went to, down by the cranes? The shipyards?'

'All right. Eight o'clock, it'll be well dark.'

'C'mere.' She led him by the sleeve, aside into an alley entry and they kissed. 'Again.' Gene kissed her on the lips once more and when their soft mouths parted, she held on to his lapels with the ferocity of a missing child found. He rocked her a little in his arms.

Gene did not tell Belle of a further exchange he had had the previous evening. Dermot Donaghy 'happened to be walking' outside Gene's lodgings and asked, 'Here, what did you do to the B Specials?'

'How do you mean?'

'There's some of them Specials talking about you as if they hate you?'

Gene said, 'I made the mistake of getting friendly with one of their sisters.'

Donaghy raised his eyebrows. 'God, that's what they get real vicious about. You'd be safer if you were throwing bombs.'

'I know, but – I got carried away.'

'Aye, and carried away you'll get, unless you get away out of that. Stick with our own crowd. Find one of our own now, that'll send out the right message.'

'How'd you mean?'

'If you were known to be, say – serious – with a Catholic girl – you'd be in the clear, wouldn't you? Stands to reason. I mean, if you don't do something, the least they'll do is tar-and-feather you – or your woman.'

Gene said as Belle walked up to him, 'We have to get outa here, there were two fellas in uniform walked past over there.'

'Where'll we go?'

'The Botanic Gardens.' The giant cranes stood over them like patient, hooked predators.

'At this hour of the night?' Belle asked. 'Why don't we go to Madden Park?'

'I said. They're bound to be watching it. Besides, I know a broken part of the railings.'

As they walked, he said, 'Any news?'

Belle replied, 'My uncle and aunt went to see my Mam. They got no soot from her.'

'How do you mean, "no soot"?'

'I mean, she gave as good as she got. I didn't tell you, she took that money you gave me. I had it hidden.'

Gene shook his head.

Belle asked, 'Do you ever go back down to Fintown now?'

Gene replied, 'No. Why do you ask?'

'My mother is going down there. Her sister, my Auntie Maisie, lives in Fivemilecross. Auntie Sandra and Uncle Jed said she threw my clothes at them.'

'I know Fivemilecross well. What's the woman's name?'

'And she gave them all the worst clothes I had. A funny name. Pederson. She was married to a Denmark man.'

'No. Never came across them.' Gene stopped at the railings of the Botanic Gardens: by a loose spar they slid in. In the lee of a building they found a garden bench. Belle snuggled up to him.

She said, 'Were you thinking about me at all? I was thinking about you a lot.'

'Yes,' said Gene. 'What were you thinking?'

Belle replied flippantly, 'We should go to Australia?'

He said quietly, 'That'd be lovely.'

She asked, 'You'n me – can? Can we go on? No matter what?'

'How d'you mean – "no matter what"?'

'No matter what anyone says.'

'Without doubt. Without doubt.' He sighed. 'I find myself – confused.' He shook his shoulders, dislodging Belle's head. 'I'll have to stop letting it get me down. I think you're right about Australia.'

'I've a stone in my shoe,' she said.

'And a stone and a half in the other one?' he asked.

'God, you're full of old jokes,' she said, 'd'you ever get pains from it?'

'Twice a week and once a fortnight,' he said.

'Ach. You!' Belle bent, kicked off the shoe, picked it up, foraged through it as if searching for something in a drawer, raised a pebble and pitched it away.

'A brick,' he said, at which she laughed.

No word was said between them for several minutes. Then, 'Hornet's nest,' said Gene aloud.

'What?'

'I said – hornet's nest.'

'What's a hornet?'

'Very like a wasp. They sting and when the nest is disturbed they all sting together.'

'You know everything, so you do.' She burrowed into his coat. 'We should tell people about us, I mean out in the open, then my mother'd have to leave me alone?'

'Whisht,' hissed Gene, 'there's someone coming.' He stopped them: they listened. 'I thought I heard a footstep,' he whispered. They listened again: no sound.

Belle leaned over. 'I want a kiss.'

He turned and kissed her harder than ever before. 'God, you nearly winded me,' she said, 'that was lovely.'

Gene stood up, ran his hands through his hair; Belle could not see him a few feet away in the darkness.

'What are we going to do?' he asked, more of himself than of her.

'I love you,' the whisper burst forth from her, words rehearsed for days and hours on end, her mouth forming the shapes and

circles in front of the mirror, feeling them on her tongue, wishing
to make them familiar to her lips, words practised for years against
this moment, words prepared as diligently as she had been taught
to pray when a child, words without which her mouth, she sometimes felt, would never work. Now she had the opportunity to say
them. 'I love you.'

He turned towards her. 'Ah, Belle. Ah, Belle.'

'I'd give you my very heart.' She had heard the words so often,
in the dark of the cinema.

'And me the same.' Gene locked his two hands behind his head
and said over and over, 'And me the same. And me the same. And
me the same.'

'Come over here to me, and I'll give you my heart,' she said.

He stood before her, placed his hands on her shoulders, raised
his face to the night sky in desperation. Softly, Belle clawed open
her coat, and slipped apart the buttons of her blouse. Underneath
she wore an old woollen vest she had owned since she was seventeen. This she raised and she sat back, arms slightly raised, eyeing
as a child watches a doctor or a nurse in examination. Gene held
the blouse gently at her waist where it hung like a fallen sail.

'That colour vest is called "Peach". You can't see it fully in the
dark,' she said.

They might have been in a forest, a pair of children. He kissed
the top of her head.

'Will you look after me?' she asked. 'I never had anyone to look
after me since my Da died.'

'Belle, Belle.' She watched as he hunkered down before her,
and traced both fat olive nipples with his tongue. He pressed his
face to her breastbone. Then he raised his head again, drew her
towards him and held her bare breasts close to his old coat. Kissing
her hair again he pushed her gently away, and drew her clothing
back on; she watched passively, a sweet and nervous smile on her
face.

He patted everything into place, and stood above her, with one
hand resting lightly on her hair. 'I have to go,' he said.

'But we're only after getting here.'

He said, 'I'm getting very nervous. I mean. About all this. You'll
understand, you'll understand soon.'

'Understand what?'

243

'I'll explain.' He grabbed her head and held it to his chest. 'If we can get away – will you come?'

'I don't care where it is,' she said.

In the last pool of darkness before their exit from the Botanic Gardens, he suddenly turned and kissed her and held her. His head deep in her hair, he said, 'Belle, Belle, Belle.' He moved his mouth down to her neck and pursed his lips there, as if drinking.

'You won't let me down, will you?' she asked in sudden panic. 'You won't let me down? Ah, Jesus in Heaven, you won't let me down? Gene? Gene?'

'No, no. Oh, no, no, no. I'll never let you down. But I have to go,' and he vanished into the blackout.

Belle returned to work. Edith sent a note with Lennie to the mill.

> I will be away until Saturday and when I come back I hope
> you will have everything soarted [*sic*] out. I am praying for you,
> and so is the Revd MacCreagh.
>
> Your loving mother, Edith.

No 'Dear Belle', no form of address.

In the Long Room, Lennie stood a little awkward in his white apron and Union Jack armbands. Belle took the note coolly from his hand.

'How are you?' he asked.

'I'm fine, why wouldn't I be?'

'Mam's gone to Auntie Maisie,' he said, reddening. 'Will you be getting my tea for me?'

'I may be going away myself,' she said archly, and returned to her place.

The women, all of whom knew by now what had happened, gave Belle a relaxed welcome back. Janice had counselled them, 'The more ordinary all this looks, the better it'll work.'

Alice MacKechnie said warmly, 'Belle, you know what I'm talking about and we all love you, but what you're doing isn't right. There's other grand fellas around. But 'tis your business, and we should help you.'

'Thanks, Alice,' said Belle.

Later, she walked to the far side of the mill to find Noreen, who from the end of the warehouse shook her head emphatically indicating that she could not at that moment talk to Belle.

At homegoing time, Janice took her arm firmly and said, 'Come on, Belle, I'll walk you home.'

When Belle protested, 'No, Janice, I have to see someone,' Janice wagged a finger.

'Belle, no, I want to hand you into your own house and warn Leonard he's not to say one word to you. Malcolm is waiting for us there.'

Malcolm stood as the women entered.

'Ah, Belle, there you are, and isn't it fresh and well you're looking. Welcome home. I mean – to your own house.' He sat again; Lennie, in uniform already, fiddled with his cap.

'Now, Belle,' said Malcolm, 'your Mam is away, and Lennie and me've been talking, and what Lennie wants to say is he has no row with you, but he don't want you having any truck with that man.'

Janice piped up, 'And you know that all we want is the best for you.'

Belle replied, 'But Janice, the best for me is my own feelings.'

'But sure, Belle,' said Lennie, 'until the other day you didn't know what your true feelings about anything was, 'cause you didn't know what happened to your own father.'

Belle, nonplussed, began to cry again. Lennie blushed, and Janice put an arm around Belle's shoulder. Malcolm walked forward and patted Belle on the arm repeatedly.

'Belle, sure you're all our favourite, sure you know that, I mean we know Edith's a bit hard, but sure she's had her burden to bear. And I loved your Da, I mean, Jesus, Belle, he used to play marbles with me down on his knees out there in the road, and he a grown man in his uniform, and no tribe that'd do to him what was done to him could ever have your eyes taken off them so they couldn't.'

Belle shook her head repeatedly, an action that also distanced her from Janice. Still shaking her head, she climbed to her room and, resisting all calls from the bottom of the stairs, did not emerge until all three had left the house. She spent the entire weekend alone, retreating to her room every time Leonard re-entered the house. Silent behind her locked door, she gave no indication to him whether she lived or breathed.

—

On Monday morning, Edith MacKnight, her mouth a rigid purse, stood on the polished landing by the Treasury in Judy Cruiseman's house. Behind the closed door, she heard the hum of talk. Soon, the big, black-suited man opened the door again.

'Her Ladyship will see you now.'

Edith, taking care not to slip on the highly polished wood, walked the length of the room to where Judy Cruiseman was sitting upright on her chaise-longue facing the window. She rested her good leg on the ground beside her, the club foot stretched ahead of her; she reached a hand out awkwardly across her body to shake Edith's hand. Bringing up the rear, Mr Caldwell arranged a chair for Edith.

'Would you like me to stay or go?' he asked.

'We'll be all right. But you could ask Nin to bring us some tea, maybe?'

Edith shook her head. 'No tea for me, thank you very much,' she said firmly.

Judy Cruiseman raised an eyebrow in surprise, but said, 'That will be fine, Mr Caldwell. Won't you take off your hat, Mrs Mac – ? And am I to assume that since you said it was an urgent personal matter and confidential you are looking for a job for yourself?'

'I believe you know my sister, Your Ladyship, Mrs Maisie Pederson?'

'I do. I do. Best ironer in the county, they tell me.' Judy Cruiseman turned the lap of her blouse. 'Look. And look at this cuff.'

Edith glanced and then returned to her own business: arranging the hatpin in the lapel of her coat; resting the hat in her grey lap.

'We have no jobs, Mrs Mac – ?'

'Knight.'

'I suppose you know that. Business is not that good, although we personally are all right, you understand. My husband is a prudent man – although not prudent enough to stop himself getting posted to France,' Judy added tartly. 'Have you got menfolk enlisted?'

'My husband is dead, Your Ladyship.'

'In action? A hero?'

'He was killed by the IRA, he was a polisman. And my son Leonard, he has a bit of a noise on his chest' – Edith tapped her own hard, bony sternum – 'and the army wouldn't take him.'

'But he's a Special, I hope?' asked Lady Cruiseman sharply.

'Oh, he is, Your Ladyship, and he'd be in it twenty-four hours a day, seven days a week, if Mr Blackwood'd only let him.'

Judy Cruiseman perked up. 'Oh, he's at Rufus Street, is he?'

'He's a lapper. And they have my daughter Isabel as well, Your Ladyship, and that's what I want to talk to you about.'

'But I said we have no jobs?'

Nevertheless, the natural alliance waiting to be engendered between the two women had begun to form, the one deprived of a husband by an atrocity, the other denied her husband's attentions because of his disgust with her deformity.

'Your Ladyship, I know that, and that wasn't what I was most of all looking for although 'twould have been very handy if you had. But I was wanting to know something from you, because, like, I have a real problem with my daughter on account of the fact that she's walking out with a fella used to work for you down here, a Roman Catholic, Your Ladyship.'

'Comerford,' said Lady Cruiseman. A more perceptive watcher than Edith might have thought her tone unsurprised. Judy sat up and swung her other leg to the floor. 'Comerford,' she repeated thoughtfully. 'A big honey-coloured man?'

'I never seen him myself. But, ma'am, I want my daughter away from him, and me and my son we were wondering if you knew anything about him that'd get Mr Blackwood to get rid of him?'

'And he told me,' said Judy Cruiseman, thinking aloud, 'that he was unprepared as yet for any kind of relationship until he had bettered his life.'

She stood. 'My stick.'

Edith jumped and fetched the silver-topped swordstick.

'I will see what I can do to get your daughter a job here. As to the man himself – what did you have in mind?'

'Well, Your Ladyship,' said Edith, walking in pace down the room, 'if Mr Blackwood ever thought the man had ever been involved, like –'

'Mr Blackwood, you will be pleased to know, telephoned me last week, with similar questions. I believe the fellow may have come under suspicion at last.'

They stood at the door. 'Give me about a week, Mrs Mac –?'

'Knight.'

247

'I mean to find out about a job for your daughter, yes, she should not be near a man like that.' Judy opened the door. 'Now, how long will you be here? You must bring your sister to the kitchen for tea one day and then come and say hallo to me. If you see Mr Caldwell will you tell him to come and see me.' She turned her back abruptly: Edith had not even put on her hat.

When Mr Caldwell walked up the staircase he saw Judy beckon to him from the open doorway of the Treasury.

'What is your wife's brother called?'

'Edward. Eddie.'

'No, I mean his rank?'

'Oh, he's a Superintendent. He has charge of a lot of the Specials.'

'We may need him. If Nesbit Blackwood does not have the influence he says he has –'

Mr Caldwell smacked his hands together once. 'Nesbit Blackwood *has* the influence he says he has.'

'All right, all right.' Turning, she led him into the room. 'Lock the door. We have something to celebrate.' She walked to the chaise-longue and lay down, eyeing backwards to survey his progress towards her. As he rounded the end of the chaise-longue, she said, 'Stand there, we're still only at the looking stage, you know,' and slowly she began to raise her long skirt to a point just above her gnarled instep. Mr Caldwell stood, his hands clasped behind his back as she had first taught him to do, and gazed at the foot. When he eventually left the room, having stood for the allotted three minutes, gazing as instructed, Judy did not, for the first time, shed tears.

15

Nesbit looked at his watch.

The waiter said, 'Another one, Mr Blackwood?'

'I will, thanks, Robert.'

'He's never this late, sir?'

'Did you hear any sirens, Robert?'

'No, sir, I did not. Oh, here he is, sir.'

Ernest Larkwood surged through the doorway, arms out in supplication. 'Nesbit. What can I say?'

Nesbit rose. 'No, no. Don't apologise. As long as you're here.'

'It was the bloody petrol rations. I had the wrong book with me, just picked up next month's off the hall table without thinking.'

They sat and drank a whiskey each before ordering lunch. Once Robert had taken the order, and ensuring that no other members sat within earshot, Nesbit began.

'I need your advice, informally certainly – but it may become formal.' As he told Gordon over and over, 'Real power never speaks in a loud voice. Nor does it whisper. It murmurs, Gordon, it murmurs.'

To Ernest Larkwood he now outlined the problem as he saw it. At Rufus Street he had employed this Catholic in a responsible position – but not too responsible; 'A good man as it turned out, but that's neither here nor there.'

A number of things had come to light. First of all, Judy Cruiseman, who had recommended him, did it so that he, Nesbit, would flush out the fellow's IRA credentials – 'But damn it, typical Judy, she never made it clear at the time.'

'Isn't Richard Cruiseman a magistrate, though?' asked Ernest Larkwood.

'That pair don't speak to each other any more. Or scarcely.'

Secondly, the man had caught young Gordon *in flagrante delicto* with one of the mill-girls; there had been a row, young Gordon had torn the girl's dress or something. 'You know how these things are, Ernest – Gordon had only just come back from France on leave, and dammit all, what do you think, the lapper is now walking the doxy out himself?'

Thirdly the man had witnessed, had overheard, a most difficult and embarrassing incident, one with potentially criminal repercussions for that bloody fool Eric Heckwright. And there's no guarantee that the lapper – who suspected that a wee lad had been assaulted during one of Heckwright's 'evenings' – would keep his mouth shut. And fourthly, the fellow's impervious – *im*pervious – to all blandishments.

'Yes, I can see your problems,' said Ernest Larkwood.

'Not to mention the war,' said Nesbit.

'Mmmmmm.' And Ernest Larkwood and his host went on to talk of other things. At the end of lunch, he said to Nesbit, 'If it was me, forgive my grammar – I'd have him brought in for questioning.'

'But if he hasn't done anything wrong?'

'Soften him up,' said Ernest Larkwood, 'and perhaps get him out of here. He might just go back where he came from if he was leaned on a bit.'

Nesbit signed the bill. 'Academic question, Ernest. If you were cross-examining a chap like that, if he was up before you on a charge, and you were prosecuting – what'd the chances be?'

'Hundred per cent. You can always get the Catholics on circumstantial evidence.'

Next day, Janice walked down the Long Room and back to the top again, then down the room once more. Stopping at the end where Mary Harney, Josie Burke and Anne MacElhatton worked, she said, 'Girls, I've a bit of bad news for you.'

'What's that, Janice?' asked Mary Harney.

'Bingham's after asking me can the three of youse be shifted.'

'To where?'

'I don't know. He never said.'

'Janice, the last time he did that, he wanted us out in the yard nearly?'

'I know, I know,' said Janice sympathetically. 'I'll ask him again.'

'But sure he won't agree,' said Josie Burke who had hair as

straight as black straw, 'he'll only shove us out the harder. What's it about anyway?'

Janice looked away then back again. 'If I tell you, will you say nothing?'

The Catholic women, who liked Janice, and considered that she behaved justly towards them, nodded.

'It's a bit awkward, and she doesn't know yet, but Bingham's keen on Belle.' The other women looked puzzled. 'As a matter of fact,' continued Janice, 'I wish there was a way to knock the shine offa Belle, she'd never be able for Bingham.'

'Aye, sure look at what happened her with young Blackwood,' said Mary Harney.

'I'm trying to quieten her down so's he'd stop noticing her,' said Janice. 'You see the way he's always here when she's telling the pictures in the mornings.'

The women nodded in agreement – although had they been discussing it among themselves they would have realised it had little truth; Bingham had appeared once or twice and had smiled ingratiatingly at Belle, but it never went farther – and in any case he always eyed everybody who did not look, as they put it, 'like a yard-brush'.

'So,' mused Janice, 'I just don't know.'

'And we love Belle's stories,' Josie said.

'And there's no way of stopping her telling them anyway,' laughed Janice affectionately. 'You know Belle.'

They did not, but nobody said so.

'And of course Bingham'd let her do what she likes,' said Janice as if thinking aloud. 'That's what's wrong with it. I mean if Belle was working down this end, there'd be no question of youse ever being shifted anywhere.'

'Why so?' asked Mary.

'Because Bingham knows full well the stories keeps us all quiet,' replied Janice. 'Yourselves in particular.'

She had to say no more. As the morning ended, the women had grasped among themselves that to avoid being sent to the large sheds along the lower yard, they somehow had to make themselves attractive to the room.

They reasoned it out among themselves. If they reduced the concentration on Belle they would please Janice; she and Belle's other friends would support any move they made to stop Bingham slinging them out – people got tuberculosis in those sheds. And were they to do something that would give them a prominent contribution in the eyes of the Long Room and the overseers, they would have further protected themselves. In effect, they calculated along the exact lines Janice had hoped. Janice also knew that Mary Harney had been instrumental in getting her cousin, Noreen O'Connor, into Blackwoods.

Next, Janice caught young Cooper. She handed him the letter.

'Go down the lappers. D'you know the big new fella? You're to watch and watch and when you see him on his own give this him – ask if there's an answer but don't say who sent you. Bring the answer back to me.'

The boy, terrified of Janice anyway, ran.

Gene took the letter to the window.

Whenever I see you in the distance, I like you more and more.
Can we meet again – soon.

He wrote an immediate, unsigned reply.

Every time I see you anywhere, I like you more and more. I'll meet you any place any time.

The Cooper boy brought the letter back to Janice who pocketed it.

'Belle, go you on home early. You look tired. Is your Mam still away?'

'Aye, Janice.'

Janice strolled to the warehouse.

'Noreen, don't go home without telling me.'

Janice made Noreen wait. As they stood at the front door when all the others had gone, Janice said, 'We're going to need someone telling the pictures. I s'pose you know about Belle's bit of trouble?'

'No?'

'There's a bad fight in her house and we're afraid the Blackwoods is going to ask her to go.'

'Why so?' Noreen stared.

'On account of your man Belle's chasing. That new fella. He's after coming to me and saying Belle won't leave him alone. And he doesn't want trouble, like. He's a real nice fella too. No, I mean it,' she added. 'So would you come and start telling us the pictures?'

Noreen wrinkled her nose.

That evening, Gloria called to Belle's house. They talked; they looked at magazines; they fiddled through old dress patterns; they drank tea.

On the doorstep, Gloria said, 'Belle, none of my business, but that wee Taig one, I seen her talking to your fella. Twice.'

Next morning, Janice again called the Cooper boy and told him to deliver Gene's letter – she had put it in an envelope – to Noreen. 'Just hand it her and run. Don't say a word or I'll skin you.'

16

A silent week passed. Each afternoon, Monday, Tuesday, Wednesday, Janice sent Belle home early, saying that Bingham had ordered it. In the Lapping Room, Ernest MacCloskey, asked for advice by his cousin, Janice Gillespie, piled 'emergency work' on Gene, delaying his departure. Thus, the lovers were manipulated apart.

On Thursday afternoon, Belle waited an hour in an alleyway, and then followed Gene at a distance along the street after work. She ran on tippytoes up behind him and playfully tugged the back of his hair. He jumped and turned, a fist raised.

'Aw, Jesus, Belle! I nearly hit you!'

She grinned. 'Did I frighten you?'

'You shouldn't do that. Where were you?' He threw out his hands in supplication. 'Where *were* you? I was looking for you all the time, I nearly called to your house.'

'Och, don't be cross.' She made a face at him. 'I was only tricking. Anyway you're in an awful hurry so you are, I had to run to catch up with you.'

He said, 'I can't stop and talk, I've to go to the doctor.' He indicated his chest. 'This asthma.'

'Aw, c'mere. Sure I only wanted to see the cut of you. I was sent home early every day. My Ma is away and my brother's out more than ever, he's after taking up air-raid duty and they're even giving him time off. And I was wondering – what you were doing tonight?'

Gene said eagerly, 'Can I call around?'

'What time?' asked Belle, standing right in front of him.

'When I'm finished up at the hospital –' Gene made a gesture of unknowingness with his shoulders.

Belle said to Gene, 'I don't know where Lennie'll be. Could I be somewhere to meet you?'

'Very hard to say,' said Gene. He coughed, and, to cover his mouth, had to withdraw his arm from Belle's grasp. 'I mean I don't know how long I'll be.'

'Jesus, that's bad.'

'No, it isn't, it goes away quickly,' protested Gene. 'You're looking lovely. God, Belle, I think about you.'

Belle, looking over Gene's shoulder, grew agitated.

'Oh, God,' she said. 'Oh, God.'

'What's up?' He turned.

'They're friends of my brothers.'

In the dusk, two policemen stood watching them from down the other side of the street.

She turned back to Gene. 'Couldn't you go to the doctor another time?' she pleaded.

Gene frowned sadly. 'The trouble is, I'm getting no sleep – and if I don't look after this, I could end up staying in the hospital . . .' he ended lamely.

'But what'd be the difference if you went in the morning? Oh, God, I'd better go. They're coming over to us.'

Exhaling in a mixture of exasperation and sadness, and wheezing again, Gene said, 'Belle, I – I don't know. I'm awful caught up with this. If we could – if we could leave it, just for the minute like.'

Belle put her hands to her forehead in desperation.

'But you touched me. I mean you're after seeing and touching my – my skin. I mean like you're not supposed to do unless we were engaged or something.'

Gene put a hand out towards her. 'I don't mean that, I mean my own chest.' He smiled but Belle did not laugh. 'I mean – I'll be right by tomorrow. I know I will.'

'Tomorrow's Friday!' She grabbed his sleeve. 'I know. You're scared. I don't blame you. You're frightened. You're fucking frightened, I don't blame you. Now I'm frightened and I'm using bad language and I don't fucking know what to do.' Belle's lip curled down in a wide, fat welt, a prelude to tears.

'Oh, listen, listen, Belle, everyone's telling me, they're all telling me, that you and me shouldn't, that I should stick to – that we shouldn't –' He stopped in hopelessness. 'And they're wrong. I want to be with you. Talking to you.'

The policemen crossed the street. Belle and Gene began to back away from each other.

'What d'you think they're telling me, Gene? What d'you think they're telling me? What d'you think they're telling me? Every day they're saying something to me, sly, like, and they think I don't notice. But I notice all right.'

Belle slumped back against the wall, and pressed her hands flat to the bricks behind her hips.

'Couldn't we go 'way somewhere, Gene, I mean couldn't we go down to where you come from, wouldn't we be all right there?'

Gene tugged at the shoulders of his coat. 'Belle, I have to go.'

She said, 'I'll follow you. Gene, I'll follow you. I will.'

'Please, Belle. Please.' They stood facing each other, full of pain.

Gene coughed again and said, 'I can't tell you how bad this is.'

Belle, prodding her own heart, said, 'You don't know how bad this is.'

Gene moved as the policemen, who had not seemed urgent, drew within five yards. They watched him go, and said, 'What about ye, Belle? Howya doing? How's Lennie?'

Next morning, Friday, Janice, to Belle's surprise, knocked at the breakfast-time door in Pretoria Street.

'You were on my mind,' she explained. 'None of us was that good to you lately.' She and Belle had tea, and Lennie, sitting opposite, behaved in the presence of Janice.

'Your sister is precious to us,' said Janice. 'We have to mind her.'

Lennie softened and muttered, 'And she's after having a bad shock, aren't you, Belle? About our Da and that,' he explained to Janice.

With Edith away, and in Janice's presence, the siblings lightened and spoke more warmly towards each other.

'Why was I never told about our Da?'

Lennie, polishing his own boots this morning, said, 'I said to Ma once that if I knew, you should know too, and she said you were too hysterical.' He pronounced it 'high-sterical'.

'I'm not, am I, Janice?'

Lennie said, 'She only said it because she said anyone going to the pictures the way you were wasn't able to face anything.'

256

'But everyone else, I mean the whole city of Belfast, they knew,' said Belle.

'I thought about telling you, Belle, but you know Mam, she'd kill me.'

Janice asked, 'Did you two talk at all about – your man at work?'

Lennie said, in some embarrassment, 'I don't want to talk about that, and Belle knows that.'

'All you are,' said Belle not unkindly, 'is against him anyway.'

'The thing is, Belle, I'm after having a good look at him, and to tell you the truth – I mean for what he is he's not bad. He's great at his job, for one thing. But what would we do if he turned out to be an IRA fella, eh?'

Belle said, 'And what would you do if I married him?'

Janice and Lennie looked at her in amazement. She continued, 'I might, too.'

Lennie said, 'Is it that serious? I mean – is he after asking you?'

'No. He's not. But he might. And if he does – what am I going to say?'

Janice said, 'Anyway, Lennie, you promised Malcolm that after the last night you'd keep outa this.'

Lennie blushed. 'I did, and I'll keep my promise, I wasn't very good at keeping it before, but I promised Malcolm. But God, Janice. Marrying?'

'Leave it be, Lennie. Or – why don't you and Belle come over one evening and the four of us, Malcolm and me with you, we'll talk it out.'

As the two women walked to work, Janice said, 'Belle, the sooner you get back into your stride the better, I want you up there this morning telling us the rest of *Gone with the Wind*.'

Belle giggled. 'I'll never get it finished in a morning. Or a day, Janice.'

They turned simultaneously at the 'yoo-hoo' behind them. Noreen waved and trotted up. 'What about yeh, Belle?' she greeted. To Janice, from whom Belle expected a tart response, she said, 'Hallo.'

Janice smiled, 'Hallo, Noreen. I thought youse warehouse girls didn't go to work until later?'

Noreen, out of breath, said, 'We do, but I've to go in that early 'cause I want to get out early.'

'That's fair enough,' said Janice. 'Belle's back on her form today,' she added jauntily. 'I can't wait to hear what happens between Clark Gable and Vivien Leigh.'

Noreen said, 'She was born in India so she was, Vivien Leigh, and they even started making the picture before they found out she was going to be Scarlett.'

Janice looked from Noreen to Belle to Noreen, who continued. 'And she was picked because she had the dark hair and green eyes same as in the book. I'm reading it at the minute, I got it out of the library.'

The women reached Rufus Street. Belle went on ahead and Janice said to Noreen, 'Don't say a word, but I think your man is after dropping her.'

Inside, Janice told Alice and Gloria, 'All nearly settled.' She counted out in whispers. 'I did the letters. I got Ernest to keep your man back. I got that young one in here this morning, and by Monday she's going to be going against Belle with the pictures. What about you?'

Gloria replied, 'She didn't believe me. I said it to her, and she didn't believe me.'

Janice saw Belle approaching and said quickly, 'I'm after telling the young one your man's dropped Belle. I'll give her a message to take to the lappers today.'

At twenty past seven Janice clapped her hands. 'C'mon, Belle.' Several of the other women, primed to the occasion, cheered and echoed: 'C'mon, Belle.'

A lot like her former self, Belle ran up to the top of the room. Outside the sun shone as brilliantly as if November had been spring. Excitement ran rife around the mill, and Belle caught it too; people stopped and talked about the news on the wireless, quoting the man on the BBC: 'Out of the desert there has come tonight the news for which we have always been waiting, the news that all the world that has been fighting for freedom has been wanting to hear. The Axis forces in the desert are in full retreat. There's no shadow of doubt about it – the enemy are on the run and we after them.'

Joanie Wilkinson came in late, ran to Janice in tears and hugged her, and shouted to everyone, 'Didja hear, didja hear? My Alec, my Alec, he's after pasting oul' Rommel,' and everyone went 'Aaaaahh!', recalling that Alec Wilkinson had been posted to the Eighth Army in North Africa.

In this mood, Belle did not sit on Janice's chair, but stood on the table. Bingham had not left the room, but stayed to talk to Joanie Wilkinson. From the bottom corner, Mary Harney and her colleagues watched closely as Belle began. They saw Bingham fold his arms, eye Belle's legs and buttocks, and lean back against the wall contentedly. 'Celebration,' he reassured Janice's raised eyebrow. 'All right for one bit of a morning. Now and again.'

Today, Belle wore lipstick; she had put it on at home in Edith's absence; she had pinned her hair high; briskly she eschewed her usual preliminaries.

'The story so far,' she said, 'General Sherman won. He hammered Atlanta and he beat all before him. Just like General Montgomery.'

A huge cheer went up. At the back of the room Noreen slipped in and stood beside Mary Harney.

'Did you see it, yet?'

'No.'

'Oh, 'tis massive. You should see Clark Gable. I'm going again.'

Belle said, 'And they all know at Tara they're beaten – and that's the end of the war, and they're all asking what in the name of God were they fighting for?'

'Where's Ashley?' called Gloria. 'Where's Leslie Howard, we didn't see him with ages?'

'Gloria, you know very well what I'm going to say,' retorted Belle, but with less than her usual spark. 'Are you sure you weren't there?' The room laughed. 'I mean at the pictures, not in Tara,' and the room hooted. Gloria pouted merrily and Janice watched carefully.

Belle spoke with increasing difficulty. 'All the men – comes drifting back to Tara, and their uniforms – only stinking the place out, and the big fat Negress one, Mammy, she makes them take off all the trousers and she piles them into a big steaming bath – the trousers not the men.'

'Wooooooo!' went the women, and Bingham laughed.

'Olivia de Havilland, she says to Scarlett with tears in her eyes, "If the war's over, that means Ashley's going to be home." Then one day, they're all standing at the front door and they're only sick and tired of feeding every old broken-down soldier who limps past the house and –' Belle did one of her hunched hushes, a dramatic pause, one hand held out, the other hand on her hip. As usual she got the complete attention of the room immediately.

'They see a fella walking up the road, up the avenue.' Silence. 'They turn to look at him, Scarlett and Melanie.'

From the back of the room a voice cut in – Noreen: she shouted, 'Belle, you forgot about the jail.'

'Ah, fuck it. Shut up!' shouted a woman's irritated voice; several others echoed.

Belle's spell of the moment collapsed. Nevertheless her voice contained no rebuke as she asked, 'What jail?'

'D'you remember,' said Noreen, 'Melanie's after hearing that Ashley's in jail?'

'Oh, you're dead right, Noreen, so he is. I forgot that bit.'

Noreen came forward a little. 'And the colour of the clay, d'you remember we were saying how unusual it was.'

'Didn't I say that?' asked Belle.

'No, you didn't.'

Bingham stood on his toes to look the length of the room and called, 'Hoy, come up here.' Noreen walked forward.

'Who're you when you're at home?'

'Noreen O'Connor.'

'But you're from the warehouse?'

'I know, but I do come over here sometimes, when we're waiting for new cloth to come in, they're my friends.' She indicated Mary Harney and the others.

'Go you on back to your warehouse,' Bingham said. Noreen left the room to mutterings.

The mood had been dislodged, and Bingham sensed it.

'Mrs Gillespie, 'twould be as well for them all to work a bit harder the day now,' he said.

'All right, Mr Bingham.'

Belle clambered down, and Bingham approached her.

'Show me where you're working,' he said. They walked down the room. He inspected her machine.

'That's one of them Belgian jobs, they're good and old by now.'

'They're always breaking down,' said Belle. He and she stood engaged in conversation. Behind them, several feet away, Mary Harney and friends observed the special attention.

Eventually Bingham left, by which time the room had started humming again with work.

In the entrance hall, beneath the feet of the supervisors on their platforms, Noreen said to Belle, 'There's going to be frost the night and I've no gloves, Belle.'

'I've several pairs, see my Mam? She's always knitting.'

'I missed you, Belle, last week; were you all right? Nobody was saying anything. I didn't like to ask, and I didn't get the chance, like.'

'Noreen, I had terrible troubles, so I had. And the trouble is, I can't tell anyone a thing. I mean a real thing.'

'God, what's up?'

Belle shivered as they came out into the night air. She stood there, watching over Noreen's shoulder all the time. Suddenly she saw Gene leave the mill furtively, and she said, 'Hold on a minute, Noreen, no, don't wait for me,' and she began to move. Gene moved too quickly. Belle ran a little, then stopped, crestfallen. She returned to Noreen, who stood there waiting, holding Belle's gloves.

'Noreen, can you keep a secret?' she asked, and as they walked, she confided everything: the motorbike trip to Armagh; the walks, talks and kisses; the row with her mother and Lennie; the death of her father. In one of her worst coynesses, she even conveyed the impression that the occasion Gene touched her breasts had been more intimate and involved.

'And then last week, one night in the Botanic Gardens, I mean – we were, we were lovers – real lovers, Noreen. We were. I mean, you know him, he's from the same religion as yourself and you seen him, and you have to admit, you won't often see a finer man, will you? And he's Mr Right, Noreen, he's the man I was waiting for when I used to daydream that John Wayne or some-one'd ride up our street.'

'I'd settle for a fella on a bicycle,' interjected Noreen.

Belle grew more and more agitated, and her hands flapped.

'I know I'm in love with him, 'cause I never had feelings like that before, and he loves me too, I know by the way he talks to me, but my brother who's all right but he's very hotheaded, he's after threatening him, and –'

Belle unburdened relentlessly.

'Noreen, when I read in them magazines that Gary Cooper is six feet two and has brown hair and blue eyes and a scar on his chin, this is what 'tis like, or when I see in *Screen Romances* that my cousin sends me that Pepsodent with Irium will remove that filmy coating that clings to your teeth and bars the way to romance – this is the moment I've been waiting for, as they say.'

Noreen took her arm. 'Belle, sure, look, life is what you make it. My aunt, she was in love with a fella for fourteen years and she got him, and the minute she did – she didn't want him. All my family knows that, and when he proposed to her, do you know what she said to him? She said to him, "Thanks very much all the same, but there's other fish in the sea," the whole town of Newry knows that story.'

Belle said with energetic and grave emphasis, 'But that's it, Noreen. There isn't other fish in the sea. Not for me.'

Outside her own door, Belle turned. 'Noreen, you're my friend. And you're the same religion as the man I love. You could tell him I love him, couldn't you, and that there's nothing to be afraid of, I mean him and me – we could go off somewhere.'

'Belle,' said Noreen in the dark November night, 'there'sn't anything I can do.'

Valerie Blackwood had taken some trouble to arrange the table; she knew Nesbit wanted to talk to Judy, and she knew Nesbit wanted to talk to Ernest. At the same time, Judy would want to talk to Ernest but she did not want Nettie near Ernest. Nor did she want Nettie near her, nor did she want Nettie near Gordon. Yet how could she bring all of that off?

'Not enough buffers,' she murmured a week earlier. 'Nesbit?'

He peeked out of the dressing-room.

'This dinner?' she asked. 'So far, we have us three, that's you, me and Gordon; we have Desmond and the "bride". That's five. [Valerie still could not bring herself to use Nettie's name.] We have Judy, and I presume she will bring Dr Porteous.'

'Not necessarily. But yes, somebody will have to be driving her.'

'That's seven. We have Ernest and Audrey. That's nine.'

'And that's enough,' said Nesbit. 'Remember what it's for.'

'Yes, but it's all out of balance,' said Valerie, 'I'd ideally like to have three more. Oh – I said I'd ask Jack and Denise?'

'Provided she doesn't drink too much.'

'No,' corrected Valerie, 'provided she does drink too much. Because then she'll not remember a thing that was said. And that leaves us one man too much. Does Gordon have to be here?'

'Absolutely.'

'H'm.' Valerie chewed her lip. 'I'll ask Clarrie Orr, I think.'

'Oh, good idea.'

'If it gets too – spicy – well, can't you and Judy and Ernest repair to the study or something?'

'Yes, sure.' He slipped his hand under Valerie's hair at the back of her neck and massaged.

All who lived near arrived on time; Judy, this time driven by Mr Caldwell, came at half-past four and decided she would lie down, then have a bath. Valerie told Mr Caldwell, yes, of course he was invited, and he, observing the protocol, said he understood Lady Cruiseman wished him to join in some of the conversation. He thanked Valerie for her hospitality.

'Now you know, Mrs Blackwood, don't you, that I have a sister living near here, and I'm going to stay the night there?'

Valerie, in the hallway, replied, 'Oh, I didn't know – and we had provided for whoever it was, it's usually Sir Richard or Dr Porteous, but that's fine – of course we understand. I'll explain to my husband.'

Mr Caldwell returned in a very dark suit, introduced himself to Desmond and Nettie on the doorstep.

Nettie said, 'You must be the tallest man I ever seen, isn't he, Des?'

The three large couches around the drawing-room fire accommodated them all easily. Gordon sat beside Judy.

Nesbit asked everyone, 'Isn't that terrific about Alamein and that? I mean, Rommel, he's supposed to be a military genius? And there he is – beaten to the ropes.'

Ernest Larkwood pointed to his wife sitting across the room from him and said, 'Tell them, Audrey. Go on, tell them.'

'Tell us what?' asked Valerie. Earlier she had put on a slip never before worn; she had bought it in Paris in 1936, kept it in the box since then. Nesbit stood behind her, kissed her shoulders. Smiling at him in the mirror, she said, 'You always glint a bit when there's something tough in the wind,' and held his hand tight.

Audrey Larkwood had one of those faces on permanent apologetic-smile duty, and began every sentence with, 'I'm afraid' – but then trumped everyone.

'Audrey,' commanded Ernest again.

'Well, I'm afraid, it's not very interesting,' she began.

Nesbit said, 'Let us be the judges of that.'

'Well, I'm afraid my brother is one of Montgomery's adjutants.'

'Oh, bravo!' said Desmond.

'What's he called,' said Judy Cruiseman, 'because I think my husband is about to become a colonel?'

'He's my oldest brother, I'm afraid, John – John Easton.'

Mr Caldwell asked, 'Do you mean – Brigadier Easton?'

'Yes, I'm afraid he is a brigadier, rather.'

'Oh, I know him well,' said Mr Caldwell, not a man who exaggerated. 'He has that big farm of land over near Limavady, hasn't he?'

'Yes, I'm afraid it is rather big.'

Judy Cruiseman said, 'Oh, you know him, Mr Caldwell, I wonder does he know Richard?' She turned to Audrey Larkwood and said, 'That's my husband, Sir Richard Cruiseman.'

Audrey blushed a deep red.

'I know Richard – I know your husband. Actually.'

'Oh?'

'Well, I'm afraid we used to dance together years ago,' said Audrey.

'There y'are now, Judy,' cut in Nettie, 'you never know where you're going until you get there.' To Audrey she said, 'Was he a good dancer itself. I love the rumba. Don't I, Des?' Then she turned from Audrey's shining eyes, to Judy. 'You must have had great dancing so, Judy.'

'I have a club foot,' said Judy acidly, 'as if you didn't know.'

'You should use it to play golf,' retorted Nettie sharply, who had fought too many battles with Bingham and others on the floor of Rufus Street to be intimidated by Judy Cruiseman.

Valerie intervened with a chirrup. 'Yes, it is great news about Rommel and all that, and maybe now we'll be able to get nylons again.'

'The Americans have plenty of them,' said Nettie, 'I've about four dozen pairs that I have since before I met Des, Des loves to see me putting on my nylons, don't you, Des? He sits there watching me,' and she grinned at everyone.

'He's a very good farmer,' said Mr Caldwell to Audrey. 'Your brother.'

The door opened. 'Dr and Mrs Haig,' said the voice. All the men stood: kisses and handshakes and exclamations.

'What's going on?' asked Dr Haig. 'I have never seen so many patrols? Ernest, is that because you're out for the evening?'

The great prosecutor laughed. 'No, they've stepped up. Poor General Knowles's death. The Chief Constable has drafted in what men he can get.'

'Poor General Knowles,' said Clarrie Orr. 'I'm still shocked. Nesbit, did you know he was at school with my father?'

'No,' said Nesbit. 'Funny thing, we approached him about ten years ago to see would he sit on our board, but he said no. I mean, he said it very politely, and then I went around to see him and try to persuade him and he said the nicest thing, he said he had discovered solitude. His wife had died, and although he missed her, he had discovered the joys of being alone, and he had believe it or not learned to play the piano. And he said, now that he had discovered what a pleasure it was to be alone he didn't want to clutter it up.' Nesbit grimaced.

Clarrie Orr said, 'He married when he was twenty, and there was some story that he and my father were rivals for my mother.'

'Are you married yourself?' asked Nettie.

Clarrie said, 'No,' quietly, and again Valerie intervened.

'Does anyone know exactly what happened at poor General Knowles's?'

Clarrie had famously given 'the best years of her life' to a judge who had married another, and it was now rumoured at the golf club that she had become his mistress. Certainly it was true that at times when he was supposed to have gone to Manchester, she went to London – twice within the past year, not easy in wartime.

Jack Haig said, 'I can tell you exactly what happened, I have it from one of my housemen who does his bit by going up to Musgrave Park in his off-duty. He was saying the general refused to go to a hospital that wasn't a military hospital.'

'Oh?' said Nesbit. 'So he was lucid.'

'Only for a while, only for a while. But sure the poor man –' Jack Haig rubbed a finger hard behind his ear. 'There was only the one shot, and the funny thing is it wasn't that that killed him, I mean direct, it didn't go into the heart or anything, but he was too old to take the trauma of it, and the tissue is thin at that age and he began to bleed internally.' He threw out his hands. 'And that was it.'

'Bastards,' said Nesbit. 'Excuse my French.'

'Well, we're all here,' said Valerie, 'shall we go in?'

As she sat, she said, 'Now you'll have to forgive my making-do. I mean, Denise, wouldn't you think carrots wouldn't be affected by the war, and I wanted to do my carrot soup?'

'Och,' said Mr Caldwell, 'if we'd only known. We'd an acre under carrots . . .'

'Mr Caldwell, you're there, and Gordon, you're there opposite Mr Caldwell, and' – Valerie smiled at Nettie – 'I'll put you here beside Mr Caldwell.'

Nettie grinned and said, 'Aye, we're the workers,' an observation unendearing to Valerie.

'Judy, can you sit beside Nesbit, and Clarrie, no, I mean Audrey, you go on the other side. No, that's not right, yes, it is, yes, that's right; Jack, you're up here beside me, and Clarrie, sit here beside Desmond; Desmond, you're here on the other side of me . . .'

Valerie worked it out so that Clarrie, relatively loose in her opinion, would sit far away from Nesbit but close to Desmond, whose marriage perhaps should not last, better for all concerned; and as Nettie had perceived, the tradesman connection led Valerie to seat Caldwell and Nettie side by side.

The opening dish of smoked fish produced the usual questions and answers, and Valerie once again told them of the little man up in Antrim who did his own smoking, and again they praised her initiative in finding him.

Judy Cruiseman dominated the table. 'To all intents and purposes we have no war down in Fintown. And the funny thing is – Richard hasn't either, back from France, by the way, Nesbit,

266

and not a bit pleased about it, he says that apart from the blitz and the rubble they all have to climb over the following morning – he feels he has no war in London. It is a little bit more exciting than usual – but they are having wonderful parties and he won't tell me one word of his working day. We are short of men at the mill, though, and that is getting difficult. Getting difficult.'

Nettie looked at her plate. 'Des, what's that thing there?'

'An artichoke,' he said across the table, and he did not try to conceal the fact that Nettie had never seen one. 'They grow them out on the farm at Crawfordsburn.'

'They seem to be everywhere at this time of the year,' remarked Valerie.

'Tell 'em that up the Shankill Road,' said Nettie with spirit.

'Girlfriend yet, Gordon?' asked Judy Cruiseman, who kept loosening the feathers at her collar. 'Or should I say – girlfriends?'

'Neither in the singular nor in the plural,' he smiled.

'Now are you telling me that you are not your father's son?' persisted Judy Cruiseman.

'Hoi hoi!' said Nesbit.

'But, Nesbit, you were a famous Don Juan' – Lady Cruiseman pronounced it 'Don Whon'.

'They used to say a Blackwood would tip a cat going out a skylight and the kittens on the way back in,' said Nettie, 'that the only time 'twas inside their trousers was in the frosty weather. And 'tis the last thing to get frostbite anyway.' She compounded the remark by saying, 'Isn't that right, Valerie?'

Valerie rang the small but loud bell at her side, and asked for more gravy, even though the table did not need it.

'Anthropology,' said Dr Haig. 'Studies in anthropology of an old Belfast linen family.'

As the main course ended, Judy Cruiseman came straight to the point. 'I don't know whether Nesbit has told you,' she said to the table, 'but we're all here on a matter of conscience. At least most of us are.'

Valerie raised an eyebrow, and Nesbit, making a helpless response, let Judy continue.

'What would you do if you felt morally sure that somebody you knew was a bad egg – but you had no proof?'

'Don't tell me, Judy, that you have uncovered a German agent down there in the wilds?' Desmond laughed.

Judy held up her cautionary finger. 'Nesbit and I are here because we both know of somebody – and so do you, Gordon, I believe, and Mr Caldwell and I have already discussed it – who is certainly worthy of grave suspicion.'

Jack Haig said, 'We're all worth a suspicion or two, I suspect.'

Nesbit whispered down the table, 'Different, Jack. This one.'

Judy continued, 'This is a serious question. We're in a position where we have been watching someone. Now we know what his politics are, I mean, he is a Roman Catholic. But what we don't know for certain is what he has been up to.'

'Meaning you can't report him?' asked Dr Haig.

Judy said, 'Precisely.'

Dr Haig said, 'Tell us a little about him.'

Judy put down her knife and fork. 'He came to us with very good references. He's from down south. And he is very presentable, and when Mr Caldwell here brought him to me for interview, I mean he was so plausible, wasn't he, Mr Caldwell? And he proved so capable. And then I noticed that after a few days he was, I don't want to use the word "insolent", but he was looking at me in a way that would, well, have made our great-grandfathers fight duels. Richard even noticed it and God knows Richard doesn't notice a lot in that department.'

'But, Judy,' protested Jack Haig, 'that may only make him a man of very good taste?' They laughed.

Nettie said, ''Tis when they stop looking that you're in right trouble.'

'Thank you all, thank you all,' said Judy. 'What I really mean is, I'd go into the kitchen garden – he helped out around the house and garden before it was time for the flax to come in – and there he would be. I would turn another corner and there he would be.'

'You mean he had a crush on you?' asked Denise Haig.

'No, that's too strong. It was as if – as if – as if he believed, and wanted me to observe it, that he felt no barriers between me and him socially, that he was entitled to look at me as he might look at, say, one of the maids. I challenged him one day, and we got to talking, and you would not believe the views this man had. He

268

really did believe that we were all wrong, that we had deliberate policies of trampling on our workers, and we have had, as I pointed out to him, the same people working for us in Fintown for over five generations.'

Mr Caldwell said one of his few words of the evening. 'My great-grandfather came there as the land agent. Same job as me now, different title, maybe.'

Dr Haig said, 'That still does not make this chap a – dangerous man.'

'Well, there's something about him,' insisted Judy. 'I can't put my finger on it.'

'I bet she can't,' murmured Nettie to Jack Haig who laughed.

Nesbit heard. 'We took him on. He's a lapper. And excellent at his job, isn't he, Gordon? Gordon's working with him.' Gordon nodded with his eyebrows.

Nesbit continued, 'And we've noticed a funny thing about him. Two funny things. First thing is, he acquainted himself with every corner of Rufus Street, he stayed back in the evenings and prowled all over the building.'

Gordon chimed in, 'You'd come down the stairs after working late, if I was in the boardroom or something, and there he would be.'

Nesbit pressed on, 'And secondly, the security men have found him outside the building late at night. D'you recall, Ernest, I was telling you the other day?'

'He was asking all kinds of questions,' added Gordon.

'Has my Uncle Eric been up to his little-boy tricks again?' asked Judy.

Nesbit pressed on past her remark. 'I know it's terrible in this day and age,' he concluded, 'to be suspicious of another human being – but I look at the world and I think – that was the last straw for me, that decent poor man General Knowles. I mean that grand man – for goodness' sake, he had a stamp collection.'

Dr Haig asked up the table with a smile, 'Why don't we take Counsel's opinion?'

Ernest Larkwood laughed. 'Clearly it's a long time since you consulted a barrister, Jack, you've no idea of our fees.' All laughed.

'What does he look like?' asked Clarrie.

'He's big, he's handsome, he's curly-haired, he's the colour of honey,' said Judy Cruiseman, wine-flakes at the corner of her mouth.

'But seriously,' the prosecutor went on, 'we're asked to report every suspicion these days. You know what the army think, they think the greatest danger to Northern Ireland still comes from within. And that's even after our own dreadful blitz. And the number of cases I've seen that have come to light by the merest thread of thought.'

Ernest Larkwood stopped, having captured his audience. 'How about this for a solution? I said it to Nesbit at lunch. At least have him brought in for questioning, at least have him fingerprinted, it might even be a deterrent.'

'We'd all like his fingerprints by the sound of him,' said Nettie, and this time they all did laugh at her joke, Valerie included, but that may have been relief that the issue felt somehow resolved.

'I already had a word with someone,' said Nesbit, 'but I told him to hold back until I'd thought about it, and that's why you're here, to help me think about it.'

In Pretoria Street, Belle sat at home, warming her legs by the heat of the range in the kitchen, yet trying to sit sufficiently far back to keep 'diamonds' from forming on her shins. The weekend was passing quietly. Edith did not return. Lennie spoke to her with friendliness; they raised no difficult subjects between them. With Lennie long gone to attend his pigeons, Belle answered the knock at the door. Outside stood Alice MacKechnie.

'Gloria said to me this morning your Mam wasn't back yet, so I just called and I passing the door.'

They sat facing each other.

'None of my business, Belle, but men is often more trouble than they're worth.'

Belle said nothing, did not smile.

'The thing about them is, you don't know what they're thinking about you.'

Belle looked at her carefully. 'Alice, I know nothing about men, but I know about my own feelings.'

An observer crouched on the small staircase of Belle's house, looking down at the two women, would have concentrated on the extraordinary physical difference between them. For all her recent difficulty, Belle seemed to have grown in attractiveness, the hair shining. How she had made them laugh when she discovered (in *Photoplay*, another Joan Crawford tip) and first tried out the virtues of an egg to make a shampoo: 'And when I woke up the next morning, I was looking around to see was there a chicken in my hair.'

Alice MacKechnie, on the other hand, seemed to have lost most of her blood somewhere on the way through life; she had sunken cheeks and grey eyes, and one wisp of iron hair always escaped her control. Her speech suffered similar enervation. Sometimes you had to stoop to hear what she said, but then when she raised her voice, as she did on the mill floor, she could take a slate off the roof.

In Rufus Street, people held together for survival rather than from mutual liking. If fond of each other, that proved a bonus – but any woman going under, failing to survive, threatened them all; the humiliation of one, by whatever force – employer or domestic – undermined all.

Several of their men still suffered the hangover of the last war with its fantastic brutalisations; many ordinary men, formerly given to a pint and pipe of tobacco, and no greater excess than that, came back from the battlefields of France sad monsters, unable to respond to a civil question except by snapping or barking, and then weeping at their own defects. On top of that, unable to allow their women to observe their distress, or comfort their tears, they had no way of handling it except by lashing out physically.

All near them suffered. Not a few, alienated by their own behaviour towards their wives, entered upon incestuous relationships with their daughters. Alice's father was one of those – but Alice, fifteen at the time, refused to fight him, to resist him, and instead treated him covertly as if she were the wife. In this way, she reduced the ardour of his furtive attentions, and by welcoming him to her bed reckoned she saved his life. Bertie Gallagher two streets away – he blew his brains out with his brother's police revolver.

In time Alice's father went back to his own bed and his own wife, and over ten years the family's surface healed over, settled down again, and Alice married.

'Feelings, Belle? I know.' Alice paused. 'Look, I'll be straight

271

with you. If you haven't much experience of men, your first feelings is very confusing. And men's very exciting. And them feelings – they're all about finding the kind of man you can have your children for. But Belle, that's where the confusion is. You can meet a man and he can make you very excited, but 'tisn't the right kind of excitement. I mean, there's two kinds. There's the kind that makes you want to dance with a fella, and kiss him and that. And there's the kind that makes you want to have his children for him.'

Belle asked, 'But if the two is the same?'

Alice replied, 'It nearly never happens like that, at least not to our kind anyway. We're too poor. I mean lookit my sister Jeannie, she met a fella and she couldn't eat thinking of him. And we all told her he was a dipper, so he was, like he'd be dipping his wick everywhere he could.'

Alice watched Belle carefully to see whether she understood the term; Belle did not react.

'I says to Jeannie what my mother said to me, "Never marry a man who pulls your knickers over your eyes." And why, "I'll tell you why, Jeannie," says I, "'cos there's no pockets in a pair of knickers." But she married him none the same, and there she was, three children in three years. And the next thing, there he was, up and gone. Big good-looking fella, his brother married a Taig, and that came to no good either.'

On the way home Alice called to Janice's house.

'At the same time, she's no fool. D'you know what she said to me? She said, "Alice, did you come here to tell me something?" I said nothing.'

'It needs one more lift,' said Janice.

Out in Bangor, Valerie, to Nesbit's continuing irritation, insisted that at her dinner-parties the women withdraw 'for the men to tell their stories': no use his pointing out, 'Valerie, I'm not my own grandfather.'

Nettie 'planked herself down', as Valerie called it afterwards, beside Judy Cruiseman.

'C'mere, I want to ask you a wee question or two? This big buck – did he say "no" to you by any chance? And has he now a girl that's putting your nose out of joint?'

Judy, accepting a cigarette, asked, 'Where d'you get these?'

'Dez knows somebody out in the Officers' Mess in Lisburn.'

Judy dragged, exhaled, and said, 'The answer to the first question removes the need to answer the second.'

Nettie interrupted, 'You must do crosswords or something.'

'What I'm trying to say,' said Judy, shuttling her jaw as if testing its muscles, 'is, there is no need for my nose to be "put out of joint", since the possibility of jealousy never arose, since I am a happily married woman.'

'Your arse you are,' said Nettie. 'You have the kind of lonesomeness in your eyes I'd never want to have in mine. That husband of yours, I bet he's sleepy enough when he's at home.'

Nettie lit up, inspected the lipstick on her cigarette-tip. 'At the same time, that other fella – if he's on your mind?'

Judy's turn now came to size up her opponent accurately. 'If you must know, the mother of a mill-girl came to see me the other day, a Mrs Mac-something, with a daughter called "Belle", and this man you say I fancy is trying to seduce the girl.'

Nettie straightened up. 'Belle? I know Belle, I know Belle well, she's only a child.'

'Exactly.'

Upon which Nettie expanded, and gave Judy Cruiseman the sad salient details of Belle's life.

The men returned. Judy beckoned to Jack Haig. When he stooped over the back of the couch, she said, 'Could you give me five minutes?'

'Now?'

'Yes.' Leaning over Nettie's head, he helped Judy to her feet.

Valerie, the perfect hostess, called, 'Nesbit's study, Jack.' All knew that Judy asked every doctor she met to examine her.

Jack Haig closed the door and smiled at Judy. 'Well?'

'Look, Jack, I never said this to you or anyone before. But because Richard is away, I have had time to think.' She sat heavily. 'Why do I want him dead?'

'Who, Judy?' She did not answer.

Jack drew up Nesbit's swivel chair and sat in front of her. 'Let's see that foot.' He unbuttoned her shoe and took it off. She waggled the toe a little.

'I don't know, Judy, why do you want who dead?'

'Well, I'll put it another way. I had a bad row several years ago with Dr Porteous, you know that. I tried to tell him what I felt. About all kinds of things. I couldn't.'

'Judy, he was old even then, the older men don't necessarily understand women's feelings –'

'He's ancient now, and I can get no sense from him at all.'

'Is there something – new? Is there something new the matter?'

Judy sighed. 'No. I just – I just have this –' She banged the arm of the chair. 'I just have this bloody feeling of, I don't know. Uselessness. I'm horrible to everyone. I seem to spend my time thinking up ways of hurting people. And I feel. Well, useless. I look horrible.'

'That can't be true. Look at you.'

She turned on him. 'Oh, for Christ's sake, Jack. Don't. Just – bloody – don't. I know what it's like. I go out somewhere. A new man comes into the room. I'm sitting down. He shines on me, he thinks, "Oy, oy, here's a piece," and then I stand up to go into dinner or something and I see his face. Look. It even happens on a night like tonight, where chaps like you forget for a moment about my foot. And then you see the old slot being opened – if you'll forgive my mis-association of words, Jack. And out pop the words, "Oh yes, Judy Cruiseman, Judy Heckwright that was, pretty face, but a gammy leg." I see your faces, Jack. I've always seen Richard's face. That's why I feel so desperate.'

He said carefully, 'I think – I think it's probably – more in your mind than in ours.'

'Jack, look.' She glared at him like a stone mask. 'I see Clarrie tonight and the wives on edge when she comes into the room. You might think it base of me, but I'd love to have that effect – even once.'

'I could suggest an old-fashioned remedy.'

She yelled in a whisper. 'I warn you. If you suggest prayer, I will brain you.'

A short silence fell between them while Jack Haig inspected Judy's foot again. Then he asked – and she did not answer – 'Who do you want to see dead?'

She shook her head.

=

Mr Caldwell and Lady Cruiseman returned to Fintown on Sunday evening; a leak in the car window made her knees wet, and she complained. Nevertheless she applauded Mr Caldwell's prescience and sense of good arrangement to have had two stops planned where he could fill up with petrol, and not too many questions regarding rations. Anyway, as a magistrate, Richard's allocation had never been questioned, notwithstanding his absence at war.

On Monday at twelve, Mr Caldwell knocked at the Treasury door. 'Here we are, my Lady.' He accompanied Edith down the room, and pointed quickly to the edge of the large rug lest she trip.

'This time you cannot refuse,' said Judy, and Edith melted in the warmth of that smile. 'I had the tray brought up just before you arrived.'

Edith, as suggested, took off her coat and draped it carefully on another chair; Mr Caldwell left; Edith did not take off her hat.

'Easier if you pour, I suppose,' and again Edith did the bidding.

'Nice holiday?'

'Yes, thank you, my Lady.'

'When are you going back?'

'Today, my Lady.'

'Sister well?' Edith nodded.

The women settled their tea and seedcake.

'I want to ask you something, Mrs Mac*Knight*.' Judy stressed the surname as if to prove she had either learned it, or memorised it; she had taken the trouble to write it down with Nettie. 'How do you get on with your daughter?'

Edith looked up, measuring. 'Not that well, if the truth be told.'

'How "not that well" is "not that well"?' asked Judy, and then put it less confusingly. 'I mean – what do you mean? Exactly?'

'Well, I can't understand her. She spends all her time in her bedroom, or out at the pictures, and she reads all them rubbishy books about film stars.'

Judy asked, 'What was she like as a child?'

'She was her father's pet. Climbing all over him, and he singing to her, she was never out of his arms when he was in the house. She was born just before the last war ended and he just home, and he nearly didn't go out to work looking at her. Then he joined the polis so's that he'd have odd times off, so's he could work when she was asleep and then he'd be home when she was awake.'

'Did you resent that?' asked Judy, wiping the palms of her hands with a napkin.

'Rez. Rz?' Edith had difficulty.

'Did you "Resent", did you – dislike – that about him – and her?'

'I thought it wasn't fully right, I thought it wasn't good for her.'

'How do you and she speak to each other now?'

Edith became embarrassed. Judy pressed home an advantage, 'You see, I was up in Belfast at the weekend –' and then, as Judy always did, she preferred the little sadism of not pressing home the advantage fully, of leaving the other person guessing. Edith was allowed to imagine that Lady Cruiseman might have been asking questions in Belfast about herself and Belle, whose mutual acrimony was famous among the mill-women.

'We have bad times,' Edith confessed.

'Are you hard on her?'

'I am. Because – she don't live a right life, she's no sense.'

'I could find a job down here as a maid for her. But it's not a nice job, there's outside work as well. And it's lonely.'

Edith said, 'But that'd be great. I don't know if she'd be any good, but she'd try probably.'

'No chance of her getting married much, I'm afraid,' said Judy as if thinking aloud. 'No men around here.'

'Sure Belle hasn't the sense to marry –'

'But you did say she was pretty?'

'She's all right looking.'

Judy pounced. 'Mrs MacKnight, looking at it from all sides – I would say you are jealous of your daughter, aren't you?'

Edith fiddled vigorously with the plate on her lap, scooping, scooping, crumbs into a little pile. Judy did not hold back, did not spare her.

'By all accounts she is very pretty indeed, they tell me she's like a bowl of cream. Not only that, she is very popular, and I mean very, very popular – with all the women she works with, which, God knows, is rare for a pretty woman – to be popular with other women. And in many ways she is rather exceptional, by which I mean she is seen as good, she is liked, she is kind, very, very kind, by all accounts, they speak well of her. And yet you haven't a good word to say for her and she is your own daughter? I have no children, Mrs MacKnight, but if I had a daughter like the girl you have – I would not speak to her the way they tell me you speak to your daughter.'

Edith, whose slightly goitred neck had begun to glow red, looked at Judy Cruiseman as if to contradict or interrupt. Adolf Hitler would not have confronted Judy Cruiseman, and so Edith desisted. Judy finished.

'I know jealousy when I see it. Do you know how it is? Envy is something that happens between unrelated people. Jealousy is a family matter. You are jealous of your only daughter. It happens. Your daughter was more loved – you thought – by your husband than you were. She is obviously lovely, I can't wait to see her. And she must have a notable personality if she can entertain all those women so wonderfully every day. Even Mr Blackwood was singing her praises. So everybody likes her – except her own mother.'

Judy's natural force, and the class distance between the two of them, quenched most of the fire in Edith; yet she managed to hurl one last stone at the citadel.

'And you'd have the girl you say she is – marry a Catholic?'

'That,' said Judy, 'will not happen. That is in good hands. What I would like you to do, though, is go home and take another look at that daughter of yours. I will want her down here in about a fortnight.'

On that same Monday morning, Belle came in and went straight to her workplace; no hanging around chatting, and no sign, as usual, of Gloria. Anne Byers said, 'Howya, Belle? God, see my children? They's driving me outa my mind, wouldya ever come over one evening and tell them a story, Belle?'

'I will so, Anne.'

'Listen, Belle, your friend, Noreen. I'd keep an eye out for her, so I would.'

'No, Anne, Noreen's the best.'

Anne looked – a long furtive look. 'I'll tell you again, Belle, when I've more knowledge. But I'll tell you one thing, them Taigs they stick to their own, so watch yourself.'

Suddenly Belle spat at her. 'Shut your mouth, Anne Byers, you

277

that has scabs from going with a sailor from Newtownards and you hoping your husband won't catch it.'

Anne Byers recoiled. 'What are you saying, Belle MacKnight?'

Gloria arrived with the silence of an angel and smoothed Belle away.

'Over here, Belle, over here.'

'Gloria, d'you know what she said?'

Gloria soothed and soothed. 'I know, Belle, they're all saying it, but you must follow your own heart.' Belle vanished to the lavatories where Janice found her and did some more soothing.

At three o'clock, Gene, standing with his back to the table and trying to clear a space wide enough for an incoming bundle, heard Archie at the door say, 'Sure we're not strangers, come in.'

Gene turned around and saw Noreen. 'Who do you know here?' asked Archie.

Gordon said with enthusiasm, 'Hallo. Who are you?'

Lennie looked up.

Gordon said, 'This place could do with a bit of a brighten-up today.'

Noreen handed over her parcel to grave Ernest. 'I'm from the warehouse. Moll says this is faulty.'

'I like your hairdo,' said Gordon.

'I copied it offa Loretta Young,' said Noreen. 'That's the way she had it in *The Lady from Cheyenne*.'

'Hah! Another picturegoer. Do you tell the pictures too?' asked Gordon.

'A bit,' said Noreen, looking at Gene for approval. He smiled broadly but kept out of the conversation.

'Here you are, then,' said Gordon, pulling out a high stool, 'up you get and off you go.'

'Howya?' said Noreen to Gene.

'Fresh and well you're looking,' he replied.

'Ach, so you remembered! I'm trying to teach him how we talk up here,' said Noreen to the assembled room.

She began to leave, but Gordon took her arm gently.

'Here, here, here! Hold hard. You're not getting out of here without telling us a story?'

'What story?' Noreen's black eyebrows arched up to meet under the red hair.

'What about a picture? A good one, you know, a love story or something?'

Even in the late afternoon, when Gloria said, 'He's very big, that fella of yours, isn't he? And all that curly hair?', Belle said nothing.

'Have you a headache or something, Belle?'

'I'm off the wall a bit, Gloria.'

'Well,' said Gloria, 'the course of true love never runs smooth, Belle.'

Belle did not seem to hear.

Gloria said to Janice at mirror-time, 'Well. You're working something. I never seen her so quiet.'

Janice replied, 'I never seen her go home so quick either.'

At the gate, Gene waited.

'Did you ever get my message?'

Belle smiled her first smile of the day, and said, 'No. What message?'

'After your message. I wrote a note to that wee boy. What happened to it?'

'I don't know. I never saw him. What was in the note?'

He looked at her curiously.

'Well, here I am anyway.' She fell dull again.

'Have you time to go for a walk?' Gene asked.

Belle nodded. A cold rain fell as they reached the bridge. He led her down to the shelter of the arch beneath. They leaned against the wall. Belle took his sleeve in her hand.

'Belle, listen.'

'I was missing you, Gene. I wished I could have got hold of you yesterday.'

'Why yesterday?'

'Oh, it was a lonesome old day. What did you do?'

'Not much.' He fidgeted.

'What did you do Saturday night?'

'Listen, Belle.'

'I mean, Saturday night, it would have been great if we went to the pictures or something.'

'Belle, listen, I wanted to see you.'

'Where were you yesterday and Saturday night, Gene?'

'Belle, listen to me. I'm desperate for you. Listen to me.'

'Gene, what is it that's going on?'

'Belle, I'm going to Mass every morning to pray for us. I am. I mean it.'

'Gene, there's something going on.'

'Belle, listen, listen. As a matter of honour, it seemed only fair to say to you.' He stopped.

'No, I'm not listening to this. I'm not, Gene, I'm not going to listen. I told my mother and my brother that I would walk out with who I liked.'

'Belle, it's not that but this.' Gene disentangled Belle's hands from his coat.

'Gene, I love you and you know it, and there's something going on, they're all saying it to me. If there wasn't you'd be calling for me. Why can't we go out in the open? We're grown people. That's what you said I was. A grown woman. Why can't we go away somewhere?'

'Belle, I was laid up all weekend, the doctor said to stay in bed.'

'Can we go to the pictures tonight? Now? Gene? Can we?'

'Come on, Belle, I can't.'

'Why can't you?'

'I'm not supposed to be out.'

'You were at your work, Gene.' Her voice was rising.

'That's 'cause I don't want to give the Blackwoods an excuse to sack me.'

He backed away from her, his hands held in front of him. 'Belle, I have to go. I really have.'

She stood. 'Gene, don't leave me, Jesus, don't. Don't leave me. I'll be on my own if you leave me.' She stood, supplicating desperately. 'Ah, Jesus, don't leave me. Gene? Gene?'

Still he backed away. 'Belle, I have to go. I have to.'

He left, taken to safety by the darkness. Belle stood there; in the outside world, rain dripped from the parapet of the echoing arch.

'Gene! Gene!'

=

Belle left the archway, and walked to Alice MacKechnie's house.

'You're drenched with the rain,' said Alice. 'Were you home yet?'

'No,' said Belle. She sat down on the chair immediately inside the door, her hair dripping like a black duck. 'Alice, what do you think of me?'

Alice assessed. 'Belle, we think you're lovely. You know that. We're your friends.' Alice took the leap Janice had suggested. 'Belle, if there's something up. Go and see him, maybe,' she said, 'face him, Belle. Or face her. Face that one. That Noreen.'

Next, Belle called to Janice's house.

'We're just going over to my sister's, d'you want to come?' said Janice.

'No, I won't, thanks,' said Belle, and she walked with them to the corner.

Belle asked, 'Am I all right, Janice?' and Malcolm replied, 'Course you are, Belle, you're a lot more than all right.' Janice hugged her.

On her way home, Belle called to Anne Acheson's house. The small boy who answered the door received a rebuke from within for opening the door too wide in the blackout. Belle slipped inside past him.

'Belle, where are you off to, look at you, you're soaked.'

'Anne, I was only passing and I thought I'd say hallo.'

'Were you talking to Janice?'

'I was, just now.'

'Ah,' said Anne Acheson, and slipped into her role. 'Look, Belle, 's'only fair a body should know what's being done to them. Wee bitch, and her red hair down to her waist, I'd like to cut it off, so I would.'

Belle asked, a little angrily, 'What are you saying, Anne?'

Anne flustered beautifully. 'I know, Belle, you're friendly with her and I shouldn't say that about her.'

Belle turned and walked briskly out. Anne called after her, 'Honest, Belle, I never meant offence –'

By the time Belle reached home, tears had begun to stream down her face, and she had no control over them, not even when she reached her own door.

'Your hair's leaking on to your face,' said Lennie. 'I thought I wasn't getting any tea. Mam's not home yet.'

Belle took off her coat, draped it over a chair near the range and reached for the kettle. She set about the evening round of domesticity, tears pouring simply down her face.

Lennie prattled on. 'You should dry your hair first, it must be raining awful hard. Do you know what's after happening? Ernest's nephew is after getting mentioned in dispatches, in the desert.'

He grunted as he laced his boots. 'Archie's trying to sell me two pigeons and pretending they're his best and I knowing full well he's trying to load them off. D'you know, Belle, I can get a licence for a gun of my own next month and I twenty-one.'

Next he fixed the stud on the shirt collar. 'Hey, we had someone telling us the pictures in the lappers' room the day, the wee red-headed one outa the warehouse.'

Belle had her back to him; she froze in mid-step.

'And she was right good at it too, she did it for nearly an hour. I seen your boy Gordon eyeing her real close, I'd say he's going to have an oul' cut at her. We're going on a new patrol, Malcolm and me. Is it raining that hard? And she's teaching your fancy lad, the big Taig, how to say, "Isn't it fresh and well you're looking?" And – "You'll do bravely." Oh, aye.'

Lennie opened the back door a chink and peered out. A chill breeze blew through the house and the newspaper lying on the table shuffled; the suddenly-opening front door had created a through draught with the open back door. Edith came in.

'You're right in time,' said Lennie, 'the tea's just wetted.'

'Hallo the two of youse,' said Edith. 'I'm going up the stairs this minute for I'm soaking.'

Belle arranged matters so that she did not sit with Lennie after she had served his tea, nor was she in the kitchen when Edith came down.

'Aye, Belle's soaking too,' said Lennie. He finished and left. Belle, changed and dry, came slowly out of her room. From the landing she could see Edith's jaw from behind, chewing. Down the stairs she stepped, a towel at her hair, rubbing. Edith turned when Belle had reached halfway.

'Lennie said you were wet as well, come over here and warm

yourself. And you had nothing yet. I'll make fresh tea. And you have to have an egg.'

Belle sat, uncomprehending.

'What's up with you?' she asked quietly.

Edith blushed. 'Nothing. There's nothing up with me.' She rubbed the heel of her palm on her thigh. 'How did you get on in the week?'

'Fine.' Belle's tears began again.

Edith gulped and said, 'Belle, don't cry again. A woman like me, I haven't a lot to say that's any good, only my prayers and that.'

A tear sprinkled on to the platform of yellow butter on Belle's slice of white soda bread.

'And since your Dada died, I was always afraid. And that Leonard'd be killed, or that you'd go wrong or something. Afraid of my shadow.'

Belle never looked at her.

'A queer thing,' said Edith, her voice less firm. 'I know how to ask the Lord for forgiveness. Asking the Lord's easy.'

Edith folded her arms tight and sat back in her chair, at an angle away from Belle. 'Me'n' you, we know, Belle, we know 'cause women you know's said it to me, we're not great with each other are we? And I know I'm hard on you, and I know, they say to me, Janice often said it, and Alice, though I never liked her, they say to me, I shouldn't be so hard on Belle. And I always tells them look out for their own and leave the rest of us to live our life.'

Belle, tears drying suddenly, said like an arrow, 'I don't like you.'

Edith stopped, turned around astonished. Her voice faded.

Belle said, 'I don't like you. You never told me about my father.'

'What we have to do, Belle, what I have to do, is be – a bit better –'

'Shut up!' Belle hammered the table with the handle of the breadknife.

'Be a bit, a bit better to you. The nights I wished –'

Belle looked at her mother, whose eyes had now filled with tears.

'No. I'll not listen,' said Belle.

=

283

Next morning, Tuesday, Gene and Noreen met coming out of six o'clock Mass. At the same moment each said to the other, 'Aren't you the holy one?'

Noreen laughed. 'I'm not. I only go if I can't sleep. Here. Can you hold this 'til I fix my coat?' She handed him her bag.

'God, what's in it? Rocks?' he mock-gasped.

'I've to take home samples to do 'em again sometimes,' she explained, 'but you'll do bravely, a big strong fella like you.' He laughed.

'Say after me,' she commanded. 'Again.'

'You'll do bravely,' he repeated, and she smiled.

'I've a toothache,' she said, 'and I couldn't sleep.'

'I got in the habit of this years ago,' he inclined a head towards the church interior, 'and I an altar-boy. Are you going straight to work?' he asked. She nodded.

'But what about your breakfast?'

Noreen replied, 'I have a piece with me to eat early.'

'Will I walk with you, so?' The pair strolled, avoiding the puddles of last night; dawn reached the city, and the first trams clanked by.

Belle had slept badly, rose at six, sat quietly at the kitchen table. As Edith came downstairs, Belle hurried to finish breakfast. The women looked awkwardly at each other.

Edith began. 'I was down in Fintown to see –'

Belle rose abruptly and without comment gathered her coat from the chair and left the house, a quarter of an hour earlier than usual.

As she turned the corner of Pretoria Street into the Ormeau Road, she saw ahead of her in the brightening air the couple on their way to work. Belle looked, checked, stopped – then began to walk more slowly. Neither Gene nor Noreen looked back; Belle watched as Gene looked down at Noreen many times, and Noreen gazed up at Gene; they made each other laugh; he was carrying what looked like her sample bag.

So intently did Belle watch them that she missed her footing on a number of occasions and stumbled heavily. Yet neither person ahead thought to turn. As the pedestrians accumulated towards Rufus Street, Belle walked close enough to hear the hum of their words and the couple's laughter, but not the content of their conversation. At the mill gates, Belle diverted, walked down a sidestreet, leaned her arm and forehead against a wall. In this position Gloria found her, linked her, led her to the mill.

Inside, Gloria found Belle's apron, and helped her with it, then rallied Janice, Enid, Alice.

Belle kept saying, 'It's true, isn't it, Gloria? It's true?'

Janice replied, 'It isn't the end of the world, Belle.'

Gloria walked white-faced Belle to their joint workplace; by now all the others had come in.

Looking back, several people agreed that an atmosphere descended on Rufus Street that Tuesday – a sullen mood not unlike that dark stillness that came just before the sky unleashed its foulest rain on the galvanised iron roof. Others said afterwards they felt the same as they did the minute they heard the first solid deep drone of the innumerable aircraft the night eighteen months earlier, 15 April 1941, when the Germans blitzed Belfast, killing seven hundred and seventy-five relatives, neighbours and friends.

Not that anyone could say precisely, could say, 'Yes, at ten o'clock in the morning I noticed such-and-such,' or that someone else could chime in, 'That's right, at half-past ten I saw so-and-so, and they were doing this-or-that.' Nothing so clear: just a general feeling: women found their arms cold, or were snappier than usual; a sour quiet hung over the room. No machines had yet been turned on: the mechanics had begun one of their maintenance sweeps, a fact which heightened the unusualness of the dour air: machine inspections had a holiday feeling, with much banter, and baiting of the men.

Winter sunlight tipped the rafters of the room and began to tilt down towards the floor. The overseers, having noted the extent of the maintenance required, and the mechanics' likely finishing time, departed, and somewhere a woman called, 'Hey, Belle, where are you?'

Janice shushed the woman with a wave of her hand, but another woman took up the call, 'C'mon, Belle, wake us up.' A third echoed. Janice called for quiet.

Mary Harney slipped away, returned. Five minutes later Noreen appeared at the bottom door, skipping into the room. She sat herself on the edge of their tables, and began to talk to them in low tones. The three Catholic women stopped work, and were seen to focus on Noreen. Others nearby stopped work too; the pool began to widen as women on the outer fringes overheard and drew nearer. Janice stood up in her chair to try and figure out what was happening, but could not see over the heads of the growing knot of women around Noreen.

Gloria, working alongside Belle, heard a loud 'Aaahh!' and turned.

'Listen!' she said to Belle.

They listened, and heard Noreen saying, 'And at that very minute, Melanie puts her hand to her throat, and she looks real hard down the avenue. The clay is all red, 'cause that's what the clay of Georgia is like – and Melanie gasps. She recognises the man stumbling slowly up along the avenue.'

Gloria said, 'The bitch! The bitch, Belle! D'you know what that bitch is doing? She's taking over your job.'

Belle did not move. Gloria nudged her.

'Belle! Look at her! Look at the bitch.'

Belle rose to her feet, glanced quickly backwards, then looked straight ahead. She slipped into the aisle, walked very deliberately to the top of the room, moving away from Noreen and her group. Belle, white-eyed, stared into Janice's face, then matter-of-factly climbed on the table that ran the width of the room. The women working there, including the three Annes and Alice, cleared a space for Belle's feet.

'That wee bitch,' said Janice up to Belle, 'I knew she was up to nothing.'

Belle turned. None of the women in Noreen's group had seen her. Belle surveyed them for a moment, hand held to her eyes as if gazing a great distance. She took a deep breath, then screamed.

'AAAAAAAGGGH!'

Everybody turned to look. Noreen stopped and looked.

Belle pointed to her, and screamed again. 'YOOOOUUUU!'

Noreen raised an unconcerned eyebrow, turned her back, tossed her hair, and with gestures indicated that she had resumed her telling. A few women turned with her.

Belle screamed again. 'Stop. You bitch!'

Now she had their attention: nobody had ever heard Belle utter a wrong word.

'STOP!'

All heads turned slowly.

Belle, astride the table, pointed her tented fingers towards her breast.

'Listen to me. I've a different picture to tell.'

Even Noreen stopped.

Belle began haltingly. 'I don't have a name for this picture yet. But I'll get one. I was going to call it *The Great Lie*. But there is a picture called *The Great Lie*. Starring Bette Davis. And George Brent. The poster says, "Sometimes there's a terrible penalty for telling the truth." But I'll tell this picture ANYWAY!' Her voice rose to a wild scream on the final word. A machine began whirring, but its operator stopped it immediately.

'Belle!' called Janice, not too loudly but imploringly.

'FUCK. OFF. JANICE!' shouted Belle. 'AND. LISTEN!'

She composed herself and began.

'There was this girl. A working-girl. A nice girl. She never did no harm to anyone.'

All the room turned to face the figure on the table, her cream face now dead white, lipstick a red scar. The women nearest the long table fell back a little distance, the women behind Belle came to the front to look.

'This girl's name was "Isabel". But when she was a wee girl her father called her "Belle" – because it means "beautiful". And her other name was MacKnight, because her family was once noble. A long time ago. They were knights. On horseback.'

Belle clasped her hands. 'She had good friends. People were fond of her. She was fond of people. She went to work every day. In a dirty oul' hard job.' Belle held up her hands, and displayed them back and front to the audience.

'"Overworked, roughened hands can cause as much annoyance as anything you can think of,"' she quoted, her voice vicious and hissing. '"And it's no secret that this condition is aggravated by a halfway laundry soap. It's a sensible idea to change to Sweet Nature soap." And Belle changed to Sweet Nature soap for the sake of her hands, and "the richer golden soap fairly floats dirt away". And she got her cousin in America to send her Hampden's powder base because it's "as soft as a butterfly's wing". And she made sure her lipstick was as "red as the velvet of a queen and as daring as the spirit of YOUTH"!'

Each time she screamed, Belle seemed to have a greater effort in controlling herself for the next piece of her story. She gulped for air.

'And every day, at work, she entertained her friends at work. By telling them stories. Stories of the stars. "Could you tame Stirling Hayden?" "How Linda Darnell lives." And stories of adventure. An' handsome men. "It takes a man like Randolph Scott to know that what seems like a detour at first is sometimes the shortest road to happiness." Nice stories. Big stories. Lovely clothes. An' sailing ships. The stories she saw in the pictures. Shiny cars. Stories of love. "She hated him and feared him. Yet she wanted to protect him. Could that be love?" LOVE!'

Belle stepped gingerly to the edge of the table and leaned out over the first bank of machines, as if across footlights.

'And her friends all liked Belle for tellin' them these stories. They took up collections so she could have the best seats at the pictures. And secretly all Belle ever wanted was a man of her own, who would give her a life away from the hard work, give her a house like the ones in the pictures. And a baby maybe. And she met the man.'

The group near Noreen widened to look towards Belle; as they parted, Noreen was left standing alone, facing her friend.

'He was a big man and the path of true love was never going to run smooth. But that did not matter. Because this man liked Belle. He was good to her. He listened to her. He gave her presents. Money. Because he liked her for the way she told stories. And then one day, with the sun shining, he kissed her.'

She quoted again. '"Sometimes a kiss can change the course of a woman's life. Sometimes it can even change the course of history." This man, this lovely man kissed the girl. And she fell in love with him.'

Belle jumped from the table. The women immediately in front fell aside to make way for her.

'But another girl comes along, and she befriends this girl, Belle, in order to be as good as her, to learn how to tell stories, too. Belle teaches her. Belle befriends her. Belle even takes her to the pictures, shows her all the tricks of the trade. Then Belle tells this girl her troubles and asks for her help as a friend. The girl agrees.'

The room moaned at the revelations. Belle advanced down the room. Noreen, anxious, stared at Belle.

'But why did this girl agree? She agreed so's she could get Belle's man. And she DID!'

Noreen, worried now, shifted, then moved back a foot or two.

Belle stood within feet of Noreen; a space had opened up between them as with two gunfighters.

'And then one day the story ends. Belle finally sees what's happening. The man won't marry her. He says he can't see her any more, will never kiss her again. Belle's friends tell her he's always talking to the other girl. Belle sees him, sure enough. He's carrying the other girl's sample bag. They're laughing. An' then the girl, her own friend – she steals Belle's place at tellin' the pictures.'

At the top of the room the door opened and in walked Nesbit Blackwood and Bingham. They stood, assessing; only Bingham, seeing the 'pickers' hanging from Belle's waist, understood what was about to happen, but he moved too late, the distance too far.

'Belle decides she'll KILL herself!'

Janice, too, tried to get through the crowd, but as she later described it, all she saw was the upraised hand. Belle held the 'pickers' at an angle as if to describe a downward arc towards her own stomach. Then suddenly she switched direction.

'No! Instead – she kills the girl, the betrayer. Belle wanted REVENGE!' she screamed.

Those nearer remembered it as more of a scuffle. All agreed only two blows were struck. Belle grabbed Noreen's hair, and forced her head back, then raised her pickers, sharp and deadly, half-knife, half-scissors, high and struck Noreen in the front of the neck, in the hollow place beside the Adam's apple.

'Belle stabs her enemy first in the NECK!'

Belle withdrew the pickers, feeling the squelch, twisting it a little to get it out.

'And then Belle stabs her again – UPWARDS! Because she knew from Errol Flynn that you can't get to a person's heart by striking downward, you have to stab UP!'

With Noreen's body leaning back, her mouth gurgling, hack-gasping for air, Belle drove the pickers with great force through

Noreen's white starched apron into the gap beneath the rib-cage, below the left breast. She pulled the pickers from Noreen and let the girl slump to the floor.

For, it seemed several seconds, nobody moved. Bingham got there first. Belle stood shaking, staring at the body on the floor in front of her, making its last sucking noises; Belle never heard the screams all around. Nor did she hear Mary Harney say over and over again, 'She'll swing, she'll swing.'

By eleven o'clock Belle sat in a cell at Donegall Pass RUC station. The Blackwoods closed the Long Room immediately, and sent all the women home for the day. Alice and Janice called to Belle's mother. Bingham sent for Lennie to break the news. As he left the lappers' room, Lennie met three policemen walking urgently down the passageway, accompanied by Fergusson, limping faster than ever to keep ahead of them.

At a quarter past eleven, Belle was charged with the murder of Noreen O'Connor. Fifteen minutes later, Gene Comerford was brought in past the cell where Belle sat: she never saw him. He was searched, fingerprinted and lodged for questioning in a cell at the other end of the corridor. By nightfall, he was charged with the murder of General Henry Knowles.

PART THREE

17

Nesbit Blackwood ignited. He – and he believed himself alone in this – foresaw all the implications, and listed them to the Civil Servant.

'Look, we have two capital charges. They both affect Blackwoods, and outside of the shipyards we're the biggest employers in the province. So you can't mind, Kenneth, if I take an especial interest.'

The Civil Servant said, 'But there is a course of law, Nesbit?'

'I know, I know. All I'm saying is we must give the law every help to come to the right conclusions. We must be diligent. We must be more than diligent.' He smiled. 'Remember your Proverbs, Kenneth. "Seest thou a man diligent in his business? He shall stand before kings," Kenneth.' Nesbit smiled again; senior civil servants sent to Belfast by Whitehall could, if uncomplaining, expect a knighthood on retirement.

Next, Nesbit sent for Eric Heckwright, and at a lunch attended by Gordon, said, 'Eric. Two things. First, we have to change everything from top to bottom. New machinery, a building scheme, the lot. You are to do it. You are to announce it. The *Telegraph* will have it on their front page if Mr Hitler hasn't been up too early that morning. Say it will make a thousand more jobs, war or no war.'

Heckwright blinked and opened his mouth to ask.

'Second thing,' said Nesbit. 'No more parties, Eric. From now on if you want to enjoy yourself' – his cigarette glowed – 'do it over in London.'

Eric Heckwright cleared his throat.

Nesbit twisted this two-edged blade. 'We're not out in the clear yet,' he said. 'Supposing Comerford talks?'

Finally, Nesbit telephoned Ernest Larkwood.

'Of course I'm a worried man, Ernest, have you understood the implications? There is only one ideal outcome we can have here, and you know what that is.'

Ernest Larkwood, KC, too shrewd to ask what Nesbit meant, said, 'I suppose it had better be handled at the top?'

'The very top. That's all there's to it. Every loose end has to be tied tight. I don't want Blackwoods burnt to the ground. Can we meet?' and Nesbit replaced the telephone.

Sensation had attended immediately, as the implications stabilised. In July, the hanging of the nineteen-year-old IRA volunteer, Thomas Williams, for the murder of Constable Murphy, had caused more unrest in the Catholic community than Stormont had expected. Even Protestants, notwithstanding their view of Republican activists, had flinched. Now, Belle had complicated matters irretrievably: a Catholic girl had been killed by a Protestant. All Protestant conversation focused upon one question: 'Can they hang him and not her?' The Catholics asked, 'If they hang him, what about her?'

Complications proliferated. A Protestant hanging would appease the Catholics, allay a little their complaints that they always suffered injustice. This would enable the murderer of General Knowles to be hanged without outcry. In Thomas Williams's case, unease had spread, as it appeared more and more certain that, of the six accused, he was the least guilty and had certainly not fired the fatal shot.

'And look at this,' said the Chief Constable. 'Comerford's chief witness, his alibi, is the girl charged with the murder of a Catholic girl.'

'A mess, actually,' said Ernest Larkwood to the Chief Constable. 'That part of it?'

'A mess.'

'And she swears she was with him at the time, even heard the explosive going off, and the gunshot?'

'Yes, but his fingerprints are on the gun. And he knew O'Neill, the man seen dumping the gun.'

'How in God's name did O'Neill get away?' Larkwood said accusingly to the Chief Constable.

'Broke from the van – at the door, just as they were loading him.'

'What else?'

'When Constable Murphy's murderer was hanged, a Special Constable and a civilian – Protestant, needless to say – were killed down in Tyrone. We know our man was in the clear at the time – but there is good circumstantial evidence to suggest he may have had a lot to do with the IRA down there. He knew, was seen talking to, a known IRA man down there, called Donaghy.'

'Where is Donaghy?'

'We can't find him, we think he's gone down south again.'

'Bloody Free State! It might as well be Germany.' Ernest Larkwood shook his head. He looked out of the Chief Constable's window. 'Well, I can't do both trials, so which do you want me to do?'

'Both.'

'I can't. They'll overlap.'

The Chief Constable said, 'No, they won't. We can get the Comerford case mounted straight after Christmas, and I can't see it lasting more than, what, two weeks? And her, the girl – straight afterwards?'

Larkwood looked at him intently. 'Just to go for a minute, back, to this question that has nothing, I may say' – he bridled – 'to do with the law. On the one hand, hanging her would appease the Catholics, and you say that is not beyond the bounds of a judge to do, and I agree with you.'

The Chief said with equal force, 'That is why both trials have to be dealt with at the top.'

'Not my decision.'

The Chief Constable cocked his head in wryness. 'Oh yes?'

Ernest Larkwood ignored it. 'On the other hand, what about Protestant riots?'

'Do I look like a man who sleeps well?' asked the Chief Constable tartly.

'So – there's only one result possible?' Ernest Larkwood gazed out of the window. 'Do you really want two hangings?'

'I want no hangings. I never want hangings,' said the Chief Constable, and he jerked a thumb in the direction of the window and therefore Stormont. 'They do.'

'Even a Protestant? Even a girl?'

'Don't talk to me. I'm a policeman thirty-three years and I think I still don't fully know how twisted people are.'

'Look at another possibility. He gets off. We do her for man-slaughter.' Larkwood drummed his fingers.

'I'm not putting money on it. I'm not putting money on anything.'

The confluence of events had produced three main reactions – excited newspapers, a confused republican movement and worried outrage in the Protestant community. Both arrests, fully reported in all newspapers north and south of the border, were linked as if the crimes of which both were charged had a connection. The relationship between Gene and Belle generated predictable com-ment – although only the London newspapers used the phrase 'Romeo and Juliet'. A Rufus Street outing, and a Linen Princess contest for which she had been an entrant two years earlier, yielded photographs of Belle; none could be found of Gene.

In the Belfast IRA, they argued whether a statement should be released disowning Gene, saying he had never been a member. A harder line carried the day, claiming that Gene's arrest took the heat off Dermot Donaghy and Michael O'Neill, still being sought: Joe O'Connor had also gone missing. The Belfast Command reasoned that after the backlash to July's hanging, Gene would receive a commuted death penalty; or a life sentence, therefore out after seven years; or, if he could convince them of his genuine innocence, he would get off.

Gene had not believed the arresting officers.

He turned to Gordon Blackwood and asked, 'Is this a bit of a cod, or something?'

Gordon, humanely enough, having seen Gene's shock, held up an authoritative hand: the constables had first asked for him by name, and Fergusson introduced him with due obeisance, and Gordon had turned and pointed: 'That is Gene Comerford.'

To Gene, 'No, it's no joke, but if you think there is some – misunderstanding, the best thing to do is not make it worse. Just do as they ask.'

'But what am I supposed to have done?'

Gordon replied, 'I don't know. But I'm sure they have orders based on something or other.'

Gordon prevented the police from handcuffing Gene, who walked steadily out of the room, having hung his apron on its hook and collected his jacket and coat. As Gordon gazed after the departing group, behind his back, Montana, catching Archie's eye, drew a large frame in the air. Across the lapping-table, Ernest glared at Gordon.

'Mr Blackwood,' he said, 'whatever a man's religion – and if he worships God, he's all right with me – no man should be exposed to injustice for motives other than fairness and principle.'

Gordon blushed a deep red, and within minutes left the room. On the staircase to report to his father, he heard aghast the news of Belle's frenzy, of which Gene knew nothing, and would know nothing for several days.

In the van, the police behaved calmly. And in the police station, the police behaved calmly. Gene's belongings were noted, he was asked to agree the list and sign it, and he was placed in a comfortable cell, given a cup of tea, then taken to an interview room. Throughout it all, he walked slowly, at his full height, and answered all questions courteously. When being fingerprinted, they did not even need to press his fingers to the ink – he did so himself with the required pressure.

As they sat him in the interview room many hours later, he was asked if he wanted anything.

He smiled. 'Two things. I want a ticket that'll get me out of here, and something to read. But I realise I might have to settle for the second one.'

The elderly sergeant brought him yesterday's newspaper. Soon afterwards, Detective-Constable Buckle, the arresting officer, reappeared, and stood in front of Gene.

'Stand up.'

Gene rose, half-smiling, in enquiry.

'Eugene Patrick Comerford, I am arresting you for the murder of Brigadier-General Henry Masterson Knowles. You are not obliged to say anything, but I must advise you that anything you say may be taken down and used against you in court evidence.'

Statements gathered throughout the twentieth century from people who have been wrongly accused, or convicted by a grave injustice, report a pattern: disbelief; amusement; laughter; disbelief again; anger; fury; frustration; despair and, if their rationale can reach it, some degree of resignation. Gene Comerford, an uneducated man, who had walked carefully all his life, who had evaded many snares, sat down abruptly, rose again, stumbled – and vomited on the table and floor of the interview room.

Detective-Constable Buckle went to the door and called for a policeman; Gene was escorted to a cell and from that moment was watched by two policemen until next day, when he was lodged in Crumlin Road prison. Admitting him, warders spoke nothing other than commands; they strip-searched him, made him lean over a table, his hands outspread; one held a torch, another pulled his naked buttocks apart, then poked around underneath his scrotum. They accompanied him to a large, empty bathing area, where he washed alone, then was instructed to dress in grey prison clothing, none of which fitted comfortably. His cell, a long walk away, and down three steps at the end of the corridor, contained a table, chair, narrow bed and sanitary bucket. The cells nearby had no inmates, nobody within speaking distance.

A solitary hour later, he was taken to see the Governor.

'Do you understand your status?'

Gene, blinking, wheezing, replied, 'I don't know.'

The Governor had watery eyes. 'Your status is – you are on remand, and that will be your status until your trial is over.'

'My trial?'

'Yes. Has nobody explained to you?'

Gene said, 'Nobody.'

The Governor said, 'You are entitled to see a solicitor. Has anyone got you one?'

Gene said, 'I don't know anyone.'

The Governor made a note in the little notebook he held tightly in his hand. 'I'll do something about that.' He looked up at Gene. 'You're very pale. Are you all right physically? No ill-health? We have a doctor.'

Gene said, 'I don't know what's after happening to me.'

The Governor said as patiently as if to a child, 'You have been arrested and charged with murder. There will be a trial at which the police will present their evidence against you, and you will be given the chance to defend yourself. A jury will assess all the evidence they hear and they will decide whether or not you committed the murder of which you are charged.'

Gene said, 'And what will happen then?' During all of this he had looked everywhere but at the Governor.

'If you are found not guilty, you will walk out of that court with your head high. If the police are thought to have acted in any negligent fashion, you may have a claim for compensation.'

Gene said, 'And if I am found guilty?'

The Governor replied, 'Why don't we cross that bridge when we come to it?'

They took Belle to Armagh prison. Within hours of arrival, she was visited by an off-duty wardress who introduced herself and said, 'Do you remember me at all?'

Belle looked at her and said, 'No.'

'Jeannie. Alice's sister.'

Belle perked up. 'She was only talking about you on Sunday.'

'I work here, I've been here eleven years, it isn't so bad.'

Belle plucked at the skirt of her prison overall. 'These clothes are awful.'

'I know. I'm wondering whether we could get you wearing your own clothes. Anyway I'm after asking can I be assigned to you. They do that with special cases.'

Belle asked, 'Am I a special case?'

'You are, pet, but we won't talk about that now, the first thing is, do you want anything, is there anything you're needing?'

Belle replied, 'I'd like to write to my mother. And to Alice and Janice and them.'

Jeannie said, 'What about your solicitor, did you see him yet?'

'No, but he's coming in.'

As they led her back from Noreen's body, Belle stared and stared. Her right hand had blood on it and she wiped it on her apron as absently as if cooking. Bingham held back the group of women around Belle, and said to Janice, 'Them pickers, take them off that string.'

Belle watched as they detached the pickers from her, and then removed her bloodstained hessian apron and her overall. Slowly they walked her to the top of the room. Nesbit had gone to telephone the police. As Belle sat, Janice stood by, her hand on Belle's hair, smoothing, caressing, saying, 'Now, Belle, now, love.'

Belle said, 'Janice, I meant to kill her. I did. I know it.'

Gloria and Alice MacKechnie formed a team of women to support Belle in prison, to arrange transport for Edith and for any other mill-girls who wanted to visit her or whom she consented to see.

Within days, their arrangements became unnecessary; a bomb blew a hole in the side of the women's prison in Armagh. The explosion occurred away from the cell blocks, but the authorities believed it was intended to warn them that harm might come to Belle. They moved her to a specially prepared small wing of Crumlin Road in Belfast, the prison in which Gene had been placed in solitary confinement: 'For your own good,' he was told.

The Civil Servant telephoned the Governor.

'I presume they cannot in any circumstances meet? Or even see each other across a yard? Or otherwise know the other is there?'

'Is that an observation or an order?' asked the Governor, whose quiet tone permitted him an unnoticed subversiveness.

The Civil Servant said, 'There is one danger area – their weekly remand appearance in court, but I will be switching the dates. No newspapers, I take it?'

'Prisoners no longer get them. I even have to buy my own,' said the Governor.

'And you cleared the cells either side of him?'

The Governor said, 'Notwithstanding the difficulties of accommodation, there are no occupied cells anywhere near the prisoner.'

Noreen O'Connor's funeral took place in Newry. Police turned out as controllers of traffic, and as observers; at the request of Canon McAree, they did not patrol. Initially, the local Superintendent protested, but the Canon's fiery strength of personality overcame even their claim that they still needed to question Joe O'Connor. Canon McAree told them that if they as much as spoke to a human being they would start a riot. Joe, in any case, did not appear.

In slow steps the coffin was borne from the house to the main road; the undertaker, a cautious man, feared his hearse wheels might sink in the soft earth leading to the front door. The black-and-white sheepdog raced and whinged like a mad thing at the edge of the great crowd. Once or twice, sleet hissed and spat, but eventually the wintry sun took over. Noreen's other six brothers, with help, stumbled the coffin down from their shoulders and slid it into the hearse drawn by one horse, with one black plume. All the priests in Armagh archdiocese attended, and stood in black-and-white soutane-and-surplice on the steps of St Malachy's.

The congregation stood; younger folk, and the inquisitive, and those knowing no better, turned to gaze as the procession began from the rear of the church. Noreen's parents, as small, grief-stricken and black-and-grey as South American peasants, walked first behind the coffin up the aisle. Noreen's youngest brother, Shane, seven years old, blond and quick, watched everything, wept only when he saw his brothers' tears. The plainchant rose, an untuneful, argumentative sound, as thirty unmelodious priests sang from their hymnals the great black notes of the Requiem Mass. All three celebrants moved with great slowness at the altar, the black brocade of their vestments stiff with silver trims. Throughout, the high candles flickered in the breeze from the door held open to permit the participation of the hundreds forced to stand outside.

As Canon McAree climbed, exhaling, to the pulpit, a young man slipped into the aisle, walked forward and draped a green, white and orange tricolour on Noreen's coffin, whose grained wood glimmered like satin in the candlelight.

'Dearly beloved brethren. Once again our community is visited by terribleness. Once again, we lose a young person to death. Once again, our parents weep, our neighbours mourn, as a loved one is taken from us before her fulfilment. Noreen O'Connor grew up in this parish. She went to school here, she learned her history here. With that brightness of spirit and that intelligence all her teachers had remarked upon, she got herself full and distinctive employment where it was not easy to do so. And now she returns to us for the full rites of departure to God who loves us all. A life gone by needlessly soon. A young woman taken before she could contribute to our community the children she would like to have had.

'She was a lively girl. Many of you here heard her play the fiddle in your own kitchens. She loved dancing and she was a good dancer, she was a champion dancer. She won a medal in Dublin for unaccompanied singing. And she was a great joker, she had a joke for everything and everyone. Her dear mother said to me once, that every time Noreen came into the house, she brightened the whole place up. I remember her at school, she was always one of the first to put her hand up to answer a question when I called to examine the children on their catechism.

'It is not for me, dear brethren, to comment on the manner of Noreen's dying, except to observe its tragic nature. The law will – and must – take its course. What I may say, on this sad occasion, as sad as it has ever been my pastoral duty to oversee, is this.

'Whatever the legal outcome, we all know that the foul power of prejudice contributed to this terrible moment in the life of this parish. We cannot escape that fact. We must not ignore it. But we must avoid being provoked by it. I have spoken from this pulpit before about prejudice. I have quoted to you the words of one of the politicians in Belfast, Basil Brooke. Nine years ago he said, "Many people in this province employ Catholics, but I have not one about my place . . ." The following year he said in a debate at Stormont, "We are carrying on a Protestant Parliament for a Protestant people."

'Such remarks, appealing as they are to certain factions within our society, do no long-term good. They foment injustice, bitterness, and eventually, as we see here today, tragedy. I must ask you, as your parish priest, to try and put aside any bitterness you feel. I must ask you not to retaliate in any way. I share your sadness. I am hurt with you. My heart cracks too. But what we must do is show that fairness is our goal, fairness and justice. Fairness and decency. Fairness and toleration. I therefore put everyone here, every man, woman and child, I put you all on your honour, in the name of Noreen O'Connor, to take no step, utter no word, perform no deed that will further the tainted cause of prejudice, that will swell the vile tide of discrimination we, as Catholics, know as our daily lot.

'If you can do that, Noreen O'Connor's death will not have been in vain. If you can hold your tongue where you are tempted to cry out, if you can offer peace where you are inclined to brandish retaliation, if you can do as Christ urged and turn the other cheek, then by persuasion and example and moderation, we shall all achieve days of harmony and justice.

'Let us pray now for the dear departed soul of our beloved sister Noreen, taken from us at the age of twenty-one and now in the sight of God and in the Communion of the Saints.'

The crowd at the door formed an avenue of shoulders for the coffin, from which the tricolour was discreetly removed lest the police move in. Nobody had thought to open the cemetery gate, which stuck: the hinges had rusted in recent rain; eventually, it was forced with a metallic screech. Gravediggers had cast down clumps of grass, to pad and conceal the waterlogged clay at the bottom of the deep, narrow slot. Canon McAree motioned Noreen's parents to the head of the grave; the family, all eleven present, followed. Taut, herringboned canvas straps lowered the coffin and the murmur of prayers meandered like a flux of sound through the crowd, out as far as the street. At the last moments of blessing four young men stepped forward and held the tricolour low over the grave, covering the mouth for exactly one minute. When they took it away, Canon McAree shook the small orbed silver rod of holy water over the coffin far below, with its winking plate that said, 'Noreen Mary O'Connor, born 1921, died 1942. RIP.'

'For dust thou art, and to dust thou shalt return. In the name of Our Lord Jesus Christ. Who livest and reignest. World without end. Amen.'

And the crowd replied, 'Amen.'

In early November, when it became clear that neither trial would reach the courts before Christmas, Nesbit Blackwood drove to Fintown and sat with Judy Cruiseman at the far end of the long table. The rain washed the terrace, highlighting the lichen badges on the limestone steps. Every time the dining-room door opened, a breeze rustled the dried beech-leaves in the tall crystal vase.

'You can't get good vegetables in Belfast at the moment,' he said.

'The hair in your nostrils is precisely the same colour as the grey in your hair, Nesbit,' said Judy.

'I'm getting old,' he said, 'and this blasted business isn't making things easier.'

'Come along, come along. You're not your father's son when you speak like this,' Judy said. 'It will all work. Click-click. You'll see. Don't brood.'

Nesbit sliced the roast parsnip, held it up to appreciate it, then bit into it. 'Wuhw!' he said. 'Sslrrlsupp! Gorgeous, this.' He swallowed. 'Straight question, Judy. In the interests of "It will all work". All right?'

'Yep.'

'Do you want hangings?'

She looked at him; she wore a sapphire butterfly on her pointed breast; against the black silk it winked like a come-hither. 'I want one person hanged.'

'Him, I take it?'

'If I could, Nesbit, he would be up there' – she raised her fork and pointed at the ceiling – 'instead of the chandelier, and he would rotate as slowly in the breeze as a fan in Calcutta. Much more *sat*isfying to look at than the chandelier.'

Nesbit winced. 'That's a bit on the tough side, Judy.'

'Unlike the beef, I hope?' she replied.

'You might not get that. Him hanged, I mean.'

'Nesbit, I expect you to know how these things are arranged.'

'But if they hang him, I mean – the girl was actually seen doing the thing.'

'Finish those parsnips, I won't.'

'Second straight question. Will You-Know-Who preside?'

'Nesbit, Valerie's doing you no good, you're getting to be as namby-pamby as she is. Shall I rephrase for you? What you want to ask me is – "Judy, dear, will you please make sure that the Lord Chief Justice of Northern Ireland, bless him, in whom our hopes repose, tries this case himself?" Isn't that what you want to say?'

'Both cases?'

'Nesbit, in which case, and forgive the pun. Please make sure that you get the name and address of every juryman in each trial. That is your punishment.' Judy raised her glass of beer. 'See it as a little victory for my Uncle Eric. He rang. Hm-hm, he rang, and he told me about your little two-edged ploy. Extra responsibility. Public statement of how important he is. Very good, Nesbit. So, say – here's to you, Uncle Eric.'

Nesbit laughed, a little unwillingly, and raised his glass: 'Here's to you, Uncle Eric.'

Judy wiped her mouth. 'I was adding up last night, Nesbit. All you had to lose. Gordon's little fracas. Uncle Eric. The mixed-marriage possibility – in Blackwoods', my dear, oooh, oooh, oooh!? The riots. And then you get your chappie taken in, and his one witness gets herself discredited – discredited a touch dramatically, it has to be said? How did you manage all that, Nesbit?'

'Judy, it ran itself, I only suggested to You-Know-Who –'

She interrupted: 'How many You-Know-Whos do you have, Nesbit?'

He laughed and continued, 'I suggested they, well, have a look at him, and then they found his fingerprints on the gun. *Quod erat demonstrandum.*'

'Ooh, Nesbit, we're getting very sophisssttttt! Did he do it?'

'Judy, that's none of my business.'

A week after his arrest, Gene's asthma returned in force – on the day that his solicitor told him of Belle and Noreen. He asked, 'Why? What happened?'

The solicitor could enlighten him little.

'My interest is the bearing it has for you. Will she testify on your behalf, will she support your story?'

Gene replied, 'It is not a story, it is the truth. And anyway, why shouldn't she testify, she was with me?'

'Well, we'll approach her; you can be sure of that.'

Once the dates had been set for the trials, the case faded from the newspapers. Christmas came and went, cold and wet. Gene, in his cell with nothing to read, nothing to do and not even a departure from the usual fare – even though the warders let him know the others were receiving turkey and ham – wept until he fell asleep. He had seen his lawyers six times, once every fortnight; their conversations confirmed what Gene feared most – he had only one witness who could disconnect him from the murder for which he was charged, and there was no guarantee that she would testify on his behalf. And even if served with a subpoena, could she be relied upon to tell the truth, to swear she had been with him at the time – given why she was in prison too?

Mr MacMahon, whose upper teeth rested on his lower lip, said, 'We can only try.'

Mr O'Connor, the briefing solicitor for the Defence, and always in a hurry, 'No answer from her yet. And, look, even if she does come forward, even then, you can be quite sure they'll make the most of the charge she's on. In the meantime, I said to you – we have to approach anyone you think'll testify for you.'

'Yes.'

'But – you didn't give me any names?'

Gene replied, 'Well, I don't know anyone well enough.'

The lawyers looked at each other. Mr O'Connor said, 'Can you write letters? I mean – to anyone who knew you and who would speak for you?'

c/o The Governor, Crumlin Road Prison, Belfast
29 December 1942

Dear Master Kane,

I had a letter from my mother and she said you were over to see them. Thanks for that, it was a great comfort to them. As you probably know, I am completely innocent, and I am writing to you because my mother's letter said you offered to do anything you could. My lawyers have asked me if I can find character witnesses, but I only came to live in Belfast last summer and I know hardly anyone here. I still have that great reference you wrote for me, and I wonder if you could write at all to the court a similar letter.

Kindest wishes to you and Mrs Kane.

Thanking you,

Your obedient former pupil,

Eugene P. Comerford

c/o The Governor, Crumlin Road Prison, Belfast
29 December 1942

Dear Mr Duncan,

As you probably know, I have hit a bit of troubled water, through no fault of my own. Things were going well up here until this happened, even though I still missed a lot about

Fintown. As you probably know, I am completely innocent, but to prove it I need character witnesses, people who know I could not possibly have done such a dreadful thing as they accuse me of. So I am writing to you because I know hardly anyone up here, and if you could write a letter to the court, I think it would be a great help to me.

Kindest wishes to you and Mrs Duncan and I hope 'the twins' are still working hard.

Thanking you,

Your former workman,

Eugene P. Comerford

c/o The Governor, Crumlin Road Prison, Belfast
29 December 1942

Dear Mrs Black,

As you will know from the newspapers, I have had a bit of misfortune, as you will also notice from the above address. As you probably know, I am completely innocent, and I am writing to you because my solicitors have asked me if I can find character witnesses. I know you wrote a very good reference for me ten years ago when I left Sligo and went to work in County Tyrone and I wonder if you could do the same for me again. Forgive this asking, but I know very few people up here.

Kindest wishes, and wondering if Piper is still alive, he must be a great age by now and probably too old to be saddled up.

Thanking you,

Your obedient former servant,

Eugene P. Comerford

When the worst of that asthma attack had passed, Gene began to take exercise in his cell.

'Callisthenics,' said the doctor. 'Did you ever hear the word?'

'No.'

'Greek. It comes from words meaning "beauty" and "strength".'

'I don't feel much of either,' said Gene, 'if I ever did.'

'There's a leaflet, all prisoners can have it, I'll get you one. Are you sleeping well?'

'No, I'm not, I'm waking up a lot.' Gene held his arms wrapped around him as if permanently cold.

'At what time d'you wake?'

'I don't know, they took my watch, I'd say the early hours of the morning.'

The doctor said, 'I'm not allowed to give you anything for it, unfortunately.'

Gene said, 'I try to pray. But.'

'But what?' asked the doctor, packing his bag.

'I don't know. I suppose because all prayer is about – about eventually seeing God.' Gene drew his arms tighter about his chest.

After four mornings he gave up the callisthenics and again took to lying down most of the day.

The week before the trial opened, Judy Cruiseman telephoned Nesbit.

'We should have spoken sooner, but I had this dreadful flu, and Richard was home and he caught it.'

'Have you all recovered?'

'Yes. Anyway, that's not what I phoned you for. Have you done everything?'

'Yes.'

'Ooh, Nesbit, I've never heard you sound so discommoded.' After a pause, Judy asked, 'What news of chappie?'

'Judy, how could I know?'

'Nesbit, testy, testy, testicle! It's only me, Judy.'

'Well, I have no news of "chappie", as you call him.'

'Mr Caldwell, my steward, has been saying that people may not believe that he did it. Can you nip that in the bud, please, Nesbit?'

'Well, I have to say it is not by any means watertight, and there's a real feeling running for him. I mean from the most surprising people, including our bloody bishop.'

'MacKendrick?'

'No less.'

'Always a loose mouth,' Judy said. ' "Loose lips sink ships." Well, Nesbit, I'm going to do my bit.'

'How do you mean?'

She cooed a little. 'I'm going to testify. But not what you might think. I'm going to testify for chappie.'

'For the Defence? You're going to be a witness for the Defence? Are you going dotty?'

'No, dear. I know what I'm doing. I spoke to Ernest Larkwood. He knows – even if the Defence don't know yet. Ernest is a good strategist. Despite that brainbatty wife of his. And he loved the dialogue I suggested.'

'Judy, be careful.'

'No, Nesbit, you be careful. "A shut mouth catcheth no flies."'

When he came in from the telephone in the hallway and repeated the conversation's gist to Valerie, she said, 'She knows what she's doing. But –'

'But what? For God's sake don't hit me with one of your buts now, Valerie. Not now, no, not now.'

He spun on his heels, agitated.

Valerie said, 'What I meant is. I meant – "But" we must never tell Desmond's wife that we know anything of what's going on. That mouth of hers.'

Nesbit replied, 'No, you're too prejudiced. She won't say a word.'

'Well,' said Valerie in her 'I-know-better' voice, 'she asked to see me. She rang. I put her off until next week.'

18

The *Belfast Telegraph*, which appeared as usual at noon, abandoned its customary headline layout on the first day of Gene's trial, and ran a copy of the *Court Notice*, with some embellishments, notably the names of expected witnesses.

> *Rex versus Eugene Patrick Comerford*, at the Belfast Assizes, Monday, 18 January 1943.
>
> Before the Lord Chief Justice: For the Prosecution, Ernest Larkwood, KC; For the Defence, Adrian MacMahon, KC, instructed by O'Connor and Mehigan, Solicitors, Bank Buildings, Castle Junction, Belfast.
>
> *Notified to be called for the Prosecution:* Constable Derwent; Constable Joyce; Detective-Constable Buckle; Dr Douglas Winston; Edward Wheaton; Special Constable Leonard MacKnight.
>
> *Notified to be called for the Defence:* Lady Cruiseman; Norman McCullough; Thomas Kane; Isabel MacKnight.

For this detail of witnesses, the Lord Chief Justice, when the proceedings resumed after lunch, delivered a rebuke to the newspaper, but stopped short of a summons for contempt of court. Had he but known, one excitable sub-editor had suggested procuring and publishing the names of the jurors sworn in – *in camera* – during the morning. That procedure itself had caused some acrimony, with the Lord Chief Justice forbidding Mr MacMahon to question any jurors as to their religious affiliations.

MR LARKWOOD: M'Lord, this trial depends upon evidence, not upon where people pray.

MR MACMAHON: M'Lord, I wish to cast no aspersions upon anyone, but –

LORD CHIEF JUSTICE: Then don't, Mr MacMahon.

MR MACMAHON: But, m'Lord, we cannot ignore the fact that hostilities exist between the two main religious communities in this province.

LORD CHIEF JUSTICE: Not in my court, Mr MacMahon.

MR MACMAHON: But, m'Lord, my client is a Roman Catholic, and the names of the empanelled jurors –

LORD CHIEF JUSTICE: What about them, Mr MacMahon?

MR MACMAHON: Let me read them to you, m'Lord. Agnew, Cresswell, Harris, Hastings, Livermore, Luckman, Medcalf, Orpen, Pattison, Rees, West and Wraight. These, I suggest, are Protestant names. My contention is – how can my client get a fair trial? These are not the names, one would suggest, of a jury of his peers.

LORD CHIEF JUSTICE: Mr MacMahon, this is the thinnest ice I ever recall you treading. Do you wish to persist in impugning the potential of this court to see that justice is done?

MR MACMAHON: No, m'Lord.

LORD CHIEF JUSTICE: Then can we get on, please?

CONSTABLE DERWENT: We were on foot patrol, by Harkin Street and the junction of Madden Park.

MR LARKWOOD: 'We', Constable? It is important to give the court all the details. Who was with you?

CONSTABLE DERWENT: Me and Constable Joyce, sir. M'Lord.

MR LARKWOOD: What time was this?

CONSTABLE DERWENT: It was a quarter to nine in the evening, sir. M'Lord.

MR LARKWOOD: Bright or dark?

CONSTABLE DERWENT: Just gone dark, m'Lord.

MR LARKWOOD: And – Constable?

CONSTABLE DERWENT: We heard noises, sir, there was three of them in a row. The first was a motorbike, revving and stopping. Not far away, m'Lord. About five hundred yards from where we was – were. Then there was a kind of a bang, big enough. And then there was a sharper bang, more like a report, m'Lord.

MR LARKWOOD: Constable, what is your hobby?

CONSTABLE DERWENT: Motorbikes, sir, although I've no petrol at the minute.

MR LARKWOOD: Are you expert enough to recognise the sound of a motorbike, the engine, I mean?

CONSTABLE DERWENT: Oh, I am, sir, I go to Dundrod for the races every time.

MR LARKWOOD: So you know your bikes?

CONSTABLE DERWENT: Oh, I do, sir.

MR LARKWOOD: What was this bike you heard, in your opinion?

CONSTABLE DERWENT: Sir, it was a fair bike, it was a Norton, and five hundred c.c. and more, sir, more seven-fifty, I'd say.

MR MACMAHON: M'Lord, this is opinion, and the Constable is giving evidence on account of his supposed facts.

LORD CHIEF JUSTICE: A good enough point, Mr MacMahon, but it may become relevant, we shall see.

MR LARKWOOD: Constable, the second noise? What was it?

CONSTABLE DERWENT: The motorbike, sir, stopped, it cut out, there was a small bang and then breaking glass.

MR LARKWOOD: A small bang? How small?

CONSTABLE DERWENT: Well, big enough, sir. Sir, it had an echo.

MR LARKWOOD: What did you do?

CONSTABLE DERWENT: I said to my fellow officer, sir, I said, that's a bomb.

MR LARKWOOD: How did you know?

CONSTABLE DERWENT: I heard bombs before, sir, even before the war. And the noise went up in the air, then flat out across. And we started to run.

MR LARKWOOD: And then what happened?

CONSTABLE DERWENT: Then we heard the third noise, and that was a gunshot, sir, off of a rifle. I heard them before, too, sir. And then, m'Lord, the motorbike, we heard that, it started up and revved off.

MR LARKWOOD: To where did you run?

CONSTABLE DERWENT: To Madden Parade, sir, just off the back end of Harkin Street.

MR LARKWOOD: And what did you find?

CONSTABLE DERWENT: We got to a house, sir, and there was an old man in a kind of a dressing-gown and trousers and he lying in the door, and the door open, and I was worried on account of the blackout because there was light coming out the door and he was lying there.

MR LARKWOOD: And what did you do, Constable?

CONSTABLE DERWENT: Sir, I went down on one knee and he was talking, he said [consulting his notebook], he said, 'I'm Brigadier-General Knowles and some' – I don't know if I should say the word, sir – 'is after shooting me.'

LORD CHIEF JUSTICE: It is all right to say the word, Constable, this court has heard and will no doubt hear many such words.

CONSTABLE DERWENT: 'Some bugger', sir, 'is after shooting me.' He then said, 'Constable, I'm an old soldier but I'm still capable of fear. Can you telephone my daughter, please, she's Mrs Hamill?'

Gene watched from the dock, a prison warder either side, two policemen standing behind. When the Lord Chief Justice entered, Gene stared at him, puzzled, as if he had seen him before. Mr MacMahon's line of questioning dwelt upon the Constable's powers of hearing and the darkness of the night, but he failed to extract any advantage from Constable Derwent's or, after that, from Constable Joyce's evidence.

In the van on the way back to Crumlin Road, nobody spoke to Gene; the warders and police observed the same silence as they had on the way to court that morning, and as they would throughout the trial.

And so, for the months of January, February and March 1943, the war took second place in the conversation of Northern Ireland. The *Belfast Telegraph*, echoing the great trials of the eighteenth and nineteenth centuries, printed a special edition which went on sale every afternoon within an hour of the court's rising. All the newspaper's best shorthand note-takers – including some secretaries – took down every word, and all proceedings were published: the transcript form had proven popular, and each afternoon the newspaper set out the running order for the next day like a concert programme.

Witnesses became celebrities; for a brief time Constable Derwent became affectionately known among his colleagues and friends as 'Bugger' Derwent, which made him smile. Queues formed in the early morning for admission to the public gallery. The barristers rose to the occasion, becoming ever more theatrical in their demeanour; the Lord Chief Justice discreetly brought out a new wig he had taken delivery of from Ede's in Chancery Lane.

Two factors heightened the drama. Inexorably, and undefined, the early belief in Gene's possible innocence had begun to spread. His conduct since his arrest, ever polite, ever composed, had impressed all in contact with him. Prison warders, predisposed to treat him harshly, had slowly retreated, and most ceased referring to him gibingly. His command of himself moved the Governor, who made a point of seeing him once a week, and commented more than once upon the man's disposition, and reported to his Deputy Governor the good manners and warmth with which Gene greeted his visitors – the prison doctor, who said Gene's asthma had probably been exacerbated by the powse dust from the Lapping Room; the Roman Catholic chaplain, Father Egan, who found Gene, he said, 'devout without being pious'; the lawyers, who, during the trial, consulted with their client every day, sometimes until seven, eight and nine in the evening, and who said, 'He's a quiet sort of man, and he makes the little education he has go a long way'; and the few visitors – Ernest MacCloskey, who asked Gene whether, though not of the same faith, he might pray with him, to which Gene agreed; Mrs MacCartan, who brought a cake of soda bread, and the Governor permitted it; and, the surprise, Norman McCullough from the library: he brought Gene a collection of poems and ballads from Australia, called *Around the Boree Log*, and a copy of *Anna Karenina*; two weeks later, he brought *The Citadel* by A. J. Cronin, and James Stephens's *Irish Fairy Stories*, illustrated by Arthur Rackham.

In general, therefore, the view taken of Gene, and the opinion to which his behaviour obliged people, brought a small transformation to the life of the Governor of Crumlin Road prison, who now had within his care a man out of the ordinary, but one who might yet suffer a miscarriage of justice. Gene's stock rose further upon confirmation that a former employer, the well-known Lady Judith Cruiseman, herself the wife of a magistrate, would testify on his behalf.

His cause widened in popularity owing to the observations of the women in the public gallery, who exclaimed so approvingly when Gene appeared each morning, that the Clerk of the Court had to remonstrate. Many wives went home from the day's hearings and told their husbands the man was innocent, you could see from his face. Few Protestant husbands agreed – nor did the women in Rufus Street mill, whose condemnation of Gene remained as adamant as granite. He had ruined their Belle; he had betrayed her on every level; the motorbike on which he had taken her to Armagh was undoubtedly the same from which he had fired the bullet into General Knowles; no doubt about his guilt; 'a bad bastard,' they chimed. 'And where did he get all that money the police found in his room – except from the IRA who got it from America to buy guns.'

Yet – even they could not hide their fascinated curiosity when it came to the great talking-point. WILL SHE, WON'T SHE? The *Belfast Telegraph* even hired a London-based 'psychological writer' to assess what the effect on Belle MacKnight might be, were she to testify against her former lover.

'In these circumstances, even though they are, thank Heaven, rare,' wrote Angela Brooke-Gill, 'we must try and imagine the misery of the witness. As she stands in the witness box, gripping the rail until her knuckles turn white, dare she as much as glance at the man into whose eyes she once gazed with such soft and inexperienced love? One thing is certain: she will not emerge from the fray without deeper scores alongside those scars of betrayed love she already bears.'

Janice read this out at work next day; they spoke of little else these days in the Long Room; two of them, Enid and Alice, had received permission to visit Belle, and had begun knitting, as Belle had complained of the cold. Janice said she did not wish to visit Belle in prison, on account of the sensitivities associated with Malcolm's job and his friendship with Lennie, but she arranged that, by rotation, she, or Gloria, or Anne Byers, or any one among them, tried to visit Edith every day. All reported, not entirely unamusedly, that every time they called, the Reverend MacCreagh answered the door.

'Youse are disrespectable shites,' said Enid. 'I'm sure he's a great comfort to the poor woman.'

Their information systems went full steam ahead, and they soon could ascertain every twist and turn in Belle's life. When she had to be moved from Armagh, even though they declared their outrage at the bombing incident which caused her move, they welcomed her back to the city as if she had walked into their midst at Rufus Street that morning. A massive greetings-card was constructed, and every employee in the mill was asked to sign it, except the handful of Catholic workers. The day after the killing of Noreen, Janice had approached Bingham and suggested to him that the room be reorganised, and that Mary Harney and her two colleagues be moved to another room for their own safety. Bingham duly took them to the place Janice suggested, the new location in the yard the three women had so feared; within a month all three had left.

Nesbit Blackwood, although taken aback by 'The Long Room Incident', as he would thereafter call it, had the capacity to apply the rigid disciplines necessary. Next morning he visited the room and stood at Janice's chair.

'I sympathise with you all on the loss of not only one colleague, but of two. I know that Miss O'Connor did not work directly with you here, but Belle MacKnight was a great favourite among you, and I know we all wish for as good an outcome to this appalling matter as the law can make available to us. My son tells me that you have formed a fund, to collect money for the legal defence of Miss MacKnight. Obviously none of us must take sides in any of these matters, but a mill-girl, by the very nature and shape of her life, does not expect to have to defend herself in court, and I am therefore pleased to announce that Blackwoods Mills Ltd will feel able to make a contribution. Mr Bingham will arrange it with Mrs Gillespie here.'

MR MACMAHON: Did you yourself clean the wound, Dr Judd?

DR HILARY JUDD: That is correct.

MR MACMAHON: He was a slender man, the General?

DR HILARY JUDD: Yes. A light frame, is how I would describe him.

MR MACMAHON: Dr Judd, what procedures do you follow in the event of such an admission?

DR HILARY JUDD: You mean where the nature of the injury suggests a possible police interest?

MR MACMAHON: Exactly so.

DR HILARY JUDD: I know I don't have to, m'Lord, but I always

316

take the fundamental measurements: height, weight. If possible, general medical condition. We do it because Musgrave Park is a military hospital.

MR MACMAHON: Did you in this case?

DR HILARY JUDD: Yes.

MR MACMAHON: What height was General Knowles?

DR HILARY JUDD: He had probably been five eight in his normal life, but with age, he was now about five feet six.

MR MACMAHON: You're sure?

DR HILARY JUDD: Not to the millimetre. He was lying down.

MR MACMAHON: Of course. Of course. Now you say the bullet passed into his sternum? At what angle?

DR HILARY JUDD: There wasn't one.

MR MACMAHON: What do you mean?

DR HILARY JUDD: I mean – it went straight in.

MR MACMAHON: You're sure?

DR HILARY JUDD: Yes, that's the point. We thought he would live because the bullet went straight out the other side. If it had gone in at an angle it might not have come out, and he would not have found an operation to remove it easy to survive – at his age and frailty.

MR MACMAHON: Dr Judd, it is important that we are all clear on this. You say the bullet went straight through. How straight?

DR HILARY JUDD: I'm sure the post-mortem will make this clearer, but I would say it was the only time I have ever seen a bullet go straight through a body. You could poke a rod – I don't wish to be crude, my Lord –

LORD CHIEF JUSTICE: No, no, carry on, Dr Judd.

DR HILARY JUDD: The channel of the bullet was so straight you could poke a rod straight through.

MR MACMAHON: Now, Dr Judd, where exactly is the sternum? Could you be so good as to demonstrate?

DR HILARY JUDD: Here. Just below the breastbone.

MR MACMAHON: And therefore about, what, four feet or so above the ground in the General's case?

DR HILARY JUDD: Ye-es, that's about right.

MR MACMAHON: The accused is six feet three inches tall, Dr Judd, and therefore would have towered above the General?

DR HILARY JUDD: Ye-es.

MR MACMAHON: To create with a bullet a channel so straight, no angle whatsoever, as that you found in General Knowles, a wound you yourself cleaned, inspected, investigated – a six-foot-three man could not have done that, could he?

MR LARKWOOD: M'Lord, Dr Judd is not here as an expert witness in ballistics?

MR MACMAHON: M'Lord, it would take a doctor to describe the bullet's trajectory and Dr Judd was the first to see the wound in detail.

LORD CHIEF JUSTICE: Mr Larkwood, I see the point you raise, but I think Mr MacMahon's questioning is helping to clarify something.

MR MACMAHON: Thank you, m'Lord. Dr Judd, one last question, as his Lordship has permitted it. A wound such as the one you described – it would have to be created by a weapon absolutely level with the point of entry – and exit. Wouldn't it?

DR HILARY JUDD: Yes.

MR MACMAHON: Undoubtedly?

DR HILARY JUDD: Undoubtedly. It could not in my opinion happen otherwise.

She stepped down, and left the court. The pathologist, Dr Douglas Winston, was called. Mr MacMahon pursued precisely the same line of questioning. Dr Douglas Winston gave almost identical evidence, with no material disagreement. So ended day four of the trial; all the explosives experts and ballistics people had been heard; next day, Friday, Edward Wheaton, the police fingerprints expert, would be called.

'And then, next week, the fun starts,' said Mr MacMahon to Gene in the holding cell downstairs.

'The fun?'

'Next week it starts getting personal. Which means that we had better do some more preparation. Saturday, Sunday, all right? You're not going anywhere special, are you?'

Gene laughed more easily than he had recently been able to do.

Nettie rapped hard a second time. Inside, Valerie called the house-keeper, then realised she had gone home, and went to the door.

'Oh, hallo,' she said in the tone Nesbit called her 'pretty voice', and she smiled.

'There you are, Valerie,' said Nettie, hoarser than ever. 'Jesus, but it's cold.'

She bounced into the hallway past Valerie, who looked down the drive, and then asked disingenuously, 'Where's Desmond?'

'I'm on my own. Is Nesbit or Gordon here?'

'No, they're not home yet.'

'That's good, for it's you I want, Valerie.' Nettie went straight into the drawing-room, and sat as close to the fire as she could get. 'I see you're reading it up, Valerie,' indicating the 'TRIAL: FIRST WEEK ENDS' headline on the strewn newspaper.

'Isn't everyone? Can I get you tea or – anything?'

'No, this'll not take long.'

Valerie sat, and, as she always did, smoothed her skirt underneath her.

Nettie said, 'There's something went on, isn't there? In this trial, some old thing, Nesbit and that?'

'Nesbit and that? Some old thing?'

'No guff, Valerie, Nesbit knows something. That boy, that Catholic, he didn't do it, did he? And we know it, don't we?'

Valerie said, 'I don't ever – ask – about Nesbit's business.'

Nettie said, 'Valerie, see me? I did sums at school too, I can add up. We was all here that night, and we was here to discuss a wee problem, and this was the wee problem. Your boy, he seen too much. 'Cause you don't know it but I was out with Dezzie at oul' Heckwright's when that all happened. So there's fish for sale, Valerie, isn't there?'

Valerie appeared bewildered. 'Fish for sale?'

'Aye. It stinks.'

'What is it you're trying to say?'

'I'm trying to say that Nesbit and the rest of youse fixed it so's that boy was taken in. Now maybe it's went too far, and maybe it wasn't meant to be that he was charged with murder, but youse all have your hands in it.'

'Where did you get this idea?'

'Dezzie was in his cups big last night. He said a lot. And I think youse should all stop it.'

Valerie made a gesture of protest. 'But how could we – I mean, what would we do?'

'Just undo it, I'd say. And if you don't, someone's going to have to, Valerie.'

'And you say Desmond told you?'

'He did. He told me Nesbit's awful busy behind closed doors.'

Valerie gazed tranquilly into the fire. She created a silence. After several seconds, she spoke, in the same 'pretty voice'.

'I wonder if you weren't mistaken about Desmond. What you don't know, my dear, is that we have a great difficulty in our family. We have this family trust. Do you know what I mean?'

'Oh, aye, that we're all supposed to trust each other. But since you'd trust me not as far as you'd throw me, where's the sense?'

'No. No.' Valerie fluttered in a gentle protest. 'A different kind of "trust",' she explained, as to a child. 'The Blackwood Trust. I'm sure Desmond has told you a little about it. It's all about money. It's – it's where our money comes from. I mean our real money, not salaries and that. The rules of it are very strict. We have, for instance, always to go to the same church on Sundays, and we can't sell our shares to anyone outside the family. Of course, you're family now, dear, and that sort of thing. That is why I wonder whether some kind of – mistake has arisen over Desmond saying funny things to you. I know they say money is the root of all evil, but in a funny way the demands Nesbit's grandfather made of his family – it really has, it really truly has, kept the family together.'

Valerie rose to fix curtains that needed no fixing.

'So that if one member of the family has outreached himself – or herself – all the rest of us, well, we simply have, we simply have – to stay in line behind him. Or her. Or if we don't – the trust fund dries up in that direction.' Valerie now straightened the other curtain.

Nettie began, 'Trust, or no trust, there's something being done behind people's backs here, and I'm told that wee girl Belle was fooled into thinking that Taig was two-timing her and he wasn't, and them two were fond of each other, and I don't like to see working-people being made fools of –'

Valerie turned like a velvet-clad cobra. 'What is your married surname?'

'You know well what it is, this isn't the moon we're on. You know what it is.'

'Yes. I do know what your married surname is. Blackwood. How good is your memory?' Valerie looked with open hostility at Nettie. 'By which I mean – will you be able to remember when you open your eyes in the morning what your married surname is?'

'I will, so.'

'Good. Then do. Do remember. Blackwood. Of the Blackwood Trust. Fur coats. Holidays.' She walked to the door. 'By the way, my dear, did you ever get me the name of that woman in the Antrim Road who can get oranges? Oh, and I have the name of that man who smokes the fish, Desmond wanted it.'

Since his elevation, the Lord Chief Justice had trained himself to keep all equine references from his courtroom observations. As a barrister, colleagues had teased him for his 'bit between the teeth' remarks, or 'closing the stable door after the horse has bolted'; or 'looking a gift horse in the mouth'. These epithets (he kept hunters, rode at gymkhanas) persisted somewhat when he became a judge, and 'Bowling-watchers', as some barristers called themselves, collected them with glee. Nicholas Bowling knew this and began to deny them. Yet the 'Bowling-watchers' had established one fact, and the knowledge that they were right about it irritated him: when engrossed in a trial, his passion for horses still slipped out. On that Friday afternoon, Mr MacMahon cross-examined Edward Wheaton, the leaning-forward fingerprints expert.

MR MACMAHON: You said in your evidence this morning, Mr Wheaton, that you found the accused's fingerprints on the barrel of the gun?

MR WHEATON: [pause] Correct.

MR MACMAHON: Only on the barrel?

MR WHEATON: [pause] Correct. [pause] Only clearly on the barrel.

MR MACMAHON: Only clearly on the barrel?

MR WHEATON: [pause] Correct.

MR MACMAHON: Would you define 'clearly'?

MR WHEATON: [long pause] Plainly.

MR MACMAHON: I would be most grateful, Mr Wheaton, if you

would answer a little more speedily. There will be other witnesses, you know.

MR WHEATON: [pause] I need time to think.

MR MACMAHON: M'Lord, could I prevail upon you to ask the witness if he might be a little brisker in his answers. I know that this is the well-known ploy of the trained witness, but we should press on.

LORD CHIEF JUSTICE: Mr MacMahon, the witness has said, quite reasonably in my view, that he needs time to think, so I'm afraid you've had a refusal at the first fence.

MR MACMAHON: Thank you, m'Lord. You don't mind if I apply the whip a little? [smiles in court] Mr Wheaton, let us deal with the gun barrel first. The prints you found that you say were those of the accused. In what position would his fingers have had to be to make these prints?

MR WHEATON: [pause] Please clarify.

MR MACMAHON: Would his fingers have been pressed down on the barrel as if he had tapped it, or, say, examined it out of curiosity?

MR WHEATON: [pause] No. M'Lord.

MR MACMAHON: Then would the prints have been consistent with his fingers curled around the barrel tight?

MR WHEATON: [pause] Possibly.

MR MACMAHON: You are aware, Mr Wheaton, from your long, your very long, experience in courtrooms that you ought to answer 'yes' or 'no'?

MR WHEATON: [pause] Correct.

MR MACMAHON: Then how can you say 'possibly'?

MR WHEATON: [long pause] There is a difficulty.

MR MACMAHON: A 'difficulty'? I recall no difficulty in your evidence to Mr Larkwood this morning.

MR WHEATON: There is a difficulty.

MR MACMAHON: What 'difficulty'?

MR WHEATON: [longest pause yet] There were other prints.

MR MACMAHON: 'Other prints'? You mean there were – on the barrel of this gun – the fingerprints of people other than the accused?

MR WHEATON: [pause] Correct.

MR MACMAHON: You did not say that this morning, did you, Mr Wheaton?

MR WHEATON: I was not asked.

MR MACMAHON: How many 'other prints'?

MR WHEATON: [long pause] Again, there is a difficulty.

MR MACMAHON: Another 'difficulty'? What is it this time?

MR WHEATON: [pause] There were many prints.

MR MACMAHON: How many prints?

MR WHEATON: [pause] Several.

MR MACMAHON: Of two persons? Of more than two?

MR WHEATON: [pause] Of more than two.

MR MACMAHON: Let us pick a number. More than, say, five?

MR WHEATON: [pause] Ye-es.

MR MACMAHON: More than – ten?

MR WHEATON: [pause] Perhaps.

MR MACMAHON: And yet you picked out the accused's fingerprints from this multitude of pawmarks?

MR WHEATON: [silence]

MR MACMAHON: You said in your evidence this morning that you found the accused's prints nowhere else on the rifle?

MR WHEATON: [pause] Correct.

MR MACMAHON: Did you find any of this multitude of prints?

MR WHEATON: [pause] Perhaps.

MR MACMAHON: 'Perhaps'? Did you or didn't you?

MR WHEATON: [pause] There was a problem.

MR MACMAHON: A 'problem'? Following all of these 'difficulties'. You have a hard life, Mr Wheaton. What was the 'problem'?

MR WHEATON: The butt of the gun, the stock, is of very smooth wood and prints get easily obliterated.

MR MACMAHON: So – we're back to the prints on the barrel of the gun? Remind me – did you tell us how those prints might have been made?

MR WHEATON: [pause] No.

MR MACMAHON: I thought you hadn't. Would you tell us now? Please?

MR WHEATON: They were consistent with fingers curled around the barrel.

MR MACMAHON: Leading to nice fat burns, I should say, if a gun were fired while held like that.

LORD CHIEF JUSTICE: Mr MacMahon, please confine yourself to fact. Resist the attractions of speculation.

MR MACMAHON: M'Lord. Mr Wheaton – this multitude of fingerprints, this plethora of 'dabs', as I believe they're called in your trade – is it possible to tell – and here we really do need your expertise – is it possible to tell if many of those 'dabs' were of the same age?

MR WHEATON: Yes.

MR MACMAHON: Yes, it is possible, or yes, they were of the same age?

MR WHEATON: It is possible.

MR MACMAHON: And?

MR WHEATON: And what?

MR MACMAHON: Were they of the same age?

MR WHEATON: [pause] Many were.

MR MACMAHON: Could this have come about if a lot of people had handled the gun at the same time – as if inspecting something new for instance?

MR WHEATON: [pause] It might.

In number 11, Pretoria Street, the gloom had not lifted. Edith, whose thyroid would not let her rest, did the same tasks over and over. And over and over she asked, 'What'll happen to Belle?'

The Reverend MacCreagh read to her, thanked her for the hot shaving water and the privacy of her scullery; he praised her breakfast. Leonard moved about the house like a man who would remain forever subdued. He made little comment; once he said with sad eyes, 'We'll have to go out of this country after all this. We'll have to go to Canada or someplace.'

MR LARKWOOD: Just as a last clarification. All that was said that day was said in – joking? Right? But your colleague, the accused – he did not see it like that? Right? So that there may be no doubt whatsoever in the jury's minds – take us through, once more, what exactly happened.

SPECIAL CONSTABLE MACKNIGHT: As I walked towards him, he backed off. Then he grabbed the stick from my hand, I mean I had to let it go, he grabbed so hard. And he held it up, and broke it over my head.

MR LARKWOOD: Did he break it easily?

SPECIAL CONSTABLE MACKNIGHT: Like 'twas a matchstick, sir.

MR LARKWOOD: What is the stick made of, Special Constable?

SPECIAL CONSTABLE MACKNIGHT: Ebony, sir.

MR LARKWOOD: The hardest of woods?

SPECIAL CONSTABLE MACKNIGHT: Yes, sir.

MR LARKWOOD: Special Constable, a man meeting you in the street might ask why are you not fighting for King and Country? Especially as lapping is not a 'reserved job'.

SPECIAL CONSTABLE MACKNIGHT: I failed the medical, sir.

MR LARKWOOD: On what grounds?

SPECIAL CONSTABLE MACKNIGHT: What, sir?

MR LARKWOOD: Why did you fail the medical?

SPECIAL CONSTABLE MACKNIGHT: I have a touch of asthma, sir.

MR LARKWOOD: How did you get your asthma, Special Constable?

SPECIAL CONSTABLE MACKNIGHT: They say I might have got it from the powse, sir, the dust, offa the cloth.

MR LARKWOOD: Any other reasons?

SPECIAL CONSTABLE MACKNIGHT: Sir, my mother said I never had it until my father died.

MR LARKWOOD: Did he die suddenly, Special Constable? I mean asthma can be brought on by a shock.

SPECIAL CONSTABLE MACKNIGHT: He did, sir.

MR LARKWOOD: What was it, heart attack?

SPECIAL CONSTABLE MACKNIGHT: He was shot, sir.

MR LARKWOOD: Oh – was he a soldier?

SPECIAL CONSTABLE MACKNIGHT: No, sir, he was a policeman in the RUC.

MR LARKWOOD: And what age were you at the time?

SPECIAL CONSTABLE MACKNIGHT: Three, sir.

MR LARKWOOD: Thank you, Special Constable. M'Lord, I have no further questions for the witness.

MR MACMAHON: Mr MacKnight, when did you find out about the relationship between Mr Comerford, the accused here, and your sister, Belle?

MR LARKWOOD: [intervenes] M'Lord, the witness is here to testify to his experience of the accused's tendencies towards violence, not to discuss affairs of the heart.

325

MR MACMAHON: M'Lord, the witness may have ulterior motives which could conceivably have distorted his evidence.

MR LARKWOOD: But, m'Lord, my learned friend must surely know by now in his career that his job is to challenge the evidence as presented.

MR MACMAHON: M'Lord, astonishingly, I have managed my career so far without the explicit, though no doubt well-meant, help of my learned friend. The witness is unsound if he has direct personal interest in seeing the accused found guilty.

LORD CHIEF JUSTICE: Mr MacMahon, I fear you will have to prove that through the evidence – or else you will have to call the evidence you need from your own witnesses when your turn comes for the Defence. And indeed, if you prove to my satisfaction that the witness ought to be recalled then I will do so. But for now, you must cross-examine on the evidence.

MR MACMAHON: Very well, m'Lord. Mr MacKnight – did the accused ever show any further aggression to you after that incident?

SPECIAL CONSTABLE MACKNIGHT: I'm not sure.

MR MACMAHON: Please use the correct form of address, Mr MacKnight, address your evidence to his Lordship and address the bench as 'm'Lord'. My learned friend should have told you that. Now – you say you're 'not sure'. Did he or did he not ever make a threat towards you, strike you, move aggressively towards you after that incident you allege took place?

SPECIAL CONSTABLE MACKNIGHT: It did take place. I'm not alleging.

MR MACMAHON: 'M'Lord'? Remember?

SPECIAL CONSTABLE MACKNIGHT: My Lord.

MR MACMAHON: Did he?

SPECIAL CONSTABLE MACKNIGHT: He might have done.

MR MACMAHON: 'He might have done.' Do you mean you didn't notice?

SPECIAL CONSTABLE MACKNIGHT: He might have done it behind my back. My Lord.

MR MACMAHON: But how would you know? If he did it behind your back? [laughter in court]

SPECIAL CONSTABLE MACKNIGHT: I'm not sure.

MR MACMAHON: You're not sure of very much, are you?

SPECIAL CONSTABLE MACKNIGHT: [silence]

MR MACMAHON: Did you ever threaten the accused?

SPECIAL CONSTABLE MACKNIGHT: No, my Lord.

MR MACMAHON: Never?

SPECIAL CONSTABLE MACKNIGHT: Never – my Lord.

MR MACMAHON: Did you not bring four cronies of yours to the Lapping Room one day and warn him to keep away from your sister? And didn't one of them threaten the accused with a whip?

MR LARKWOOD: [intervenes] M'Lord, here we go again. What on earth is my learned friend trying to do?

MR MACMAHON: His learned friend, m'Lord, is engaged – and rather successfully – upon the well-known technique of discrediting the witness. I would have thought my learned friend would have heard of that procedure by now.

LORD CHIEF JUSTICE: Gentlemen. Halt your gallop, please. You are not comedians in the music-hall – not yet, anyway. Mr MacMahon, why do I have to remind you that you may only discredit the witness on the grounds of the evidence he has given in examination? You may dislike his tie, or the quiff in his hair, or the way he laces his boots, but you are only allowed to pursue the material evidence. [laughter in court]

MR MACMAHON: Thank you, m'Lord. Mr MacKnight – what is your relationship with your mother?

LORD CHIEF JUSTICE: Mr MacMahon, what are you up to now? Where has the witness's relationship with his mother appeared in the evidence he has given?

MR MACMAHON: Very well, m'Lord. I have no further questions – but I should be most grateful if the witness were put on notice that he might have to be recalled.

MR LARKWOOD: [intervenes] We do not see the need for that, m'Lord.

LORD CHIEF JUSTICE: Mr Larkwood, please – do not make things any more complicated than they are. Let us see what transpires. Thank you, Special Constable, you may step down, but please inform the Clerk of the Court – and your

Superintendent – as to your whereabouts for the next week to ten days.

SPECIAL CONSTABLE MACKNIGHT: Yes, my Lordship.

The Governor stood with his back to the door of Gene's cell, his shoulders blocking the observation flap from any outside eyes. Years of dealing with the Northern Ireland Home Office had taught him to frame questions – always short ones – in a way that released information far beyond that which he was permitted to seek.

'How is everything going?'

'Well, it seems to be going very well, sir. The barrister is pleased.'

'Feeling all right?'

'I'm often very nervous, and I don't like the way it is a bit of a circus at times. 'Tis very difficult to sit there and hear people telling lies about me.'

'Enough of everything?'

'I don't know whether we can get the witnesses we want. The trouble is, I have no evidence to offer, except the one witness. And we don't know if she'll agree.'

The Governor handed Gene a letter. 'This came.'

He looked at the postmark; 'Master Kane,' he exclaimed, and took it out of the already opened envelope.

'You know we have to do that,' said the Governor apologetically, 'like reading the letters going out.'

Gene, engrossed, did not hear him. 'That's very good news. Master Kane is coming up. He's driving my father and mother.' Gene sat on his bed. 'That's very good news.'

The Governor said, 'You're well under your quota of visitors.'

'But he's driving. The whole way to here?'

'Father Egan speaks well of you. He was up to me for a cup of tea this morning. He always calls in on Sunday.'

'And,' said Gene, 'they were to leave home yesterday. They'll stay somewhere tonight. They expect to be here tomorrow. I wonder where he got the petrol rations?'

'Father Egan asked me if it was all right for you to meet other witnesses here, if they were coming up from the country.'

'There's only one other coming from the country, and that's

Lady Cruiseman,' said Gene, switching back to the Governor's conversation. 'And – I don't want to see her.'

'Have you enough exercise?' asked the Governor. 'I mean – are you able to exercise enough on your own?'

'I jump up and down a bit in here too,' smiled Gene. 'I don't want to be any trouble.'

'And the warders, all all right?'

'They're very nice to me, sir.'

'I'm bringing a new man in tomorrow, you'll like him, very decent man, Mr Gilbert. He has a young family.'

The Governor did not tell Gene that he had removed a warder from the corridor, after reports from others on the floor that the man had spat in Gene's soup, and mixed mucus from his own nose in with Gene's mashed potato.

Two floors up, and five minutes' walk away, the Governor next addressed the wardress sitting outside Belle's cell.

'How are her spirits?'

'Quite good, sir. She doesn't say a lot.'

'Visitors?'

'Her mother and another friend are coming in this afternoon.'

'Even though I can't give instructions, she is to have more or less no restrictions on visitors.'

'Thank you, sir, I'll see that she knows.'

'No, don't do that, I don't want her to think she's getting special treatment. But I don't want her in bad order. Tomorrow morning, at ten o'clock, would you bring the prisoner to my office, please?'

'I will, indeed, sir.'

19

The second week began. Dressed in black, and at her throat a heliotrope chiffon scarf, Lady Cruiseman took the stand on Monday morning as the first witness for the Defence. Mr MacMahon led her through the history of Gene's period of employment at Fintown.

LADY CRUISEMAN: He arrived on a summer day. I had had a letter of introduction from a friend I knew and trusted.

MR MACMAHON: You interviewed him?

LADY CRUISEMAN: I did, my Lord.

MR MACMAHON: And how did he impress you, Lady Cruiseman?

LADY CRUISEMAN: Very highly, my Lord. He seemed self-contained, and willing.

MR MACMAHON: Did you find anything sinister in him?

LADY CRUISEMAN: Not at all.

MR MACMAHON: How closely did you observe him?

LADY CRUISEMAN: It fell out, my Lord, that he arrived before the flax harvest, and I was rebuilding my garden at the time.

MR MACMAHON: Lady Cruiseman, did you have opportunities to have conversation with the accused?

LADY CRUISEMAN: Several, my Lord.

MR MACMAHON: Did they have any typical threads?

LADY CRUISEMAN: I don't quite understand.

MR MACMAHON: Did you find that themes recurred?

LADY CRUISEMAN: Oh, yes, my Lord, he was very interesting to talk to, especially for a workman.

MR MACMAHON: In what way?

LADY CRUISEMAN: Well, we talked about many things. He has a great interest in history.

MR MACMAHON: Can you give us an example?

LADY CRUISEMAN: He had read about Napoleon. He knew

about the Boer War. He was most interested in the history of
Ireland.

MR MACMAHON: But he's not an educated man, is he?

LADY CRUISEMAN: No, but he is perfectly capable of being
educated.

MR MACMAHON: Did you talk about nationalism and Irish
republican politics?

LADY CRUISEMAN: Many times.

MR MACMAHON: Did you, from an old Unionist family, object to
discussing these topics?

LADY CRUISEMAN: No. To the contrary. I raised them.

MR MACMAHON: How did you find his views, Lady Cruiseman?

LADY CRUISEMAN: Well, of course he believes in a united Ireland.
[murmurs in court]

MR MACMAHON: And how did you respond to that?

LADY CRUISEMAN: I told him that in my view the holding of such
views was no crime, but that in this society he had better keep
them to himself.

MR MACMAHON: And his response?

LADY CRUISEMAN: Oh, he was very clear, he already knew that
he should be discreet.

MR MACMAHON: Did you find anything vehement about him?

LADY CRUISEMAN: No-o, my Lord. I can't say that I did.

MR MACMAHON: You have offered your testimony as a character
witness: was he a good worker?

LADY CRUISEMAN: Excellent. No fault there.

MR MACMAHON: Was he well liked by the others on your estate?

LADY CRUISEMAN: Oh, yes, insofar as he mixed with them. This
is a quiet man, you understand. He kept himself to himself.

MR MACMAHON: Did his superiors in the mill ever complain of
him?

LADY CRUISEMAN: The contrary again, my Lord. Mr Duncan,
my foreman, a man not easily pleased, commented upon the
man's strength and his commitment.

MR MACMAHON: How would you describe his time at Fintown,
in terms of his character and his capacity, Lady Cruiseman?

LADY CRUISEMAN: He worked hard, stayed out of sight, did not
force his republicanism upon anyone.

MR MACMAHON: Lady Cruiseman, your former workman is here

on a charge of murder. Did you see or find in him any characteristic that would suggest he was capable of murdering a frail old man?

LADY CRUISEMAN: Well, of course, I'm not trained in character judgement, so I can only say that as far as he worked for me he was a marvellous, and I mean a marvellous, worker. [murmurs in court] Very strong, physically.

LORD CHIEF JUSTICE: Mr Larkwood, I had expected an intervention from you on Mr MacMahon's introduction of speculation?

MR LARKWOOD: I thought it better not, m'Lord. Lady Cruiseman is here as a character witness, so perhaps a little more leeway . . . ?

LORD CHIEF JUSTICE: Yes, that's what I thought, too. Do you have further questions, Mr MacMahon? I'm looking at the clock.

MR MACMAHON: Just one, m'Lord. Lady Cruiseman, Eugene Patrick Comerford is on trial here for his life. What do you have to say that would persuade this court he could not have possibly committed the crime of which he is accused?

MR LARKWOOD: [intervenes] Oh, now, m'Lord, I really do object.

LORD CHIEF JUSTICE: Well, yes and no, Mr Larkwood, yes, because you are substantively right, but no, because I believe Lady Cruiseman can deal with any questions – as no doubt you'll discover after lunch. [to witness] You may answer.

LADY CRUISEMAN: How can I say? I'd never met a republican before.

At lunch, Ernest Larkwood said, 'I have to say, Adrian, nobody examines his own witnesses better than you do.'

Adrian MacMahon laughed a little bitterly. 'I'm not sure that's a great compliment, Ernest, I mean – doing well with your own witnesses is the least we're supposed to be able to do.'

'No, you misread me. The art form with your own witnesses is to close off every chink from the cross-examination. That's what I meant.'

'Ernest, I'm always worried when you start paying me compliments. The last time you paid me a compliment, you won on the eighteenth green.' The men laughed. Mr MacMahon then said, 'In any case, I'm not sure I'm certain whose witness she really is.'

=

During the morning appearance of Judy Cruiseman, Belle walked from her cell in the wettest part of the prison, walls green with condensation, to the office of the Governor.

'Everything going all right?' asked the Governor.

'Yes, thank you.'

'Any special difficulties?' he asked.

'No, thank you.'

'This is my wife.'

Belle said, 'Hallo,' and the woman smiled again.

'I believe you know my brother?' said the Governor's wife.

'I don't know,' said Belle. 'Who is your brother?'

'The Reverend MacCreagh.'

'My mother knows him,' said Belle.

The Governor said, 'Sit, won't you?'

Belle, hands in her lap, sat and looked at him calmly.

'My job here often goes beyond that of keeper. It's a very interesting job.'

'Yes.'

'I often get a chance to help.'

'Yes,' said Belle.

'People get very lonely in here and I often find a way of helping them.'

'Yes.'

'It's amazing what people can do for other people,' said the Governor.

'My husband's trying to tell you something,' said the Governor's wife; he looked across at her with a frown, and tried to speak again, but his wife, who always spoke unnecessarily loudly, continued.

'He's trying to tell you that if you give evidence in this trial on at the minute, when your own turn comes people won't forget that you helped the law take its course.'

'And,' said the Governor, 'there is also –'

'What my husband was going to say is there's also the matter of conscience. If any of us knows something that affects the way the law is handed down to us, we should speak up.'

'The truth is the thing,' said the Governor.

'Yes, he's right there,' said his wife.

Belle shook her head. 'I haven't made up my mind.'

The Governor stood up behind his desk. 'I have to go. Stay here, please, and talk to my wife.' He nodded.

Belle sat quite still. Her hair, now without evident lustre, had been brushed back from her forehead, and she wore no lipstick. The prison overall and dress concealed her body; the shoes she wore had extensive scuffing at the toes; nothing could suggest that she had once voraciously devoured the glamour of the cinema. Anything singular about her had fallen away – no sign here of the thrilling girl astride the table telling pictures; she had bitten some of her fingernails. The hands were red, the spinner's welt exaggerated. On her face, now blotchy, a spot had erupted in the middle of her forehead, and she had squeezed it, leaving pinch-marks in its vicinity. Her eyes had grown hooded, and in this reduced state a droop at the corners of the mouth became noticeable.

'Before you say whether you'll be a witness,' asked the Governor's wife, 'will you answer me a thing or two?'

Belle looked at her suspiciously.

'Say yes or no, I can't be doing with people who don't know their minds.'

Belle said, 'Yes – I s'pose.' The woman looking at her had features usually denigrated as 'horse-faced'.

The Governor's wife asked, 'Who is the person who knows you best? Now,' she said quickly, 'don't answer immediately, you're not in a hurry.'

Belle appeared to think and said, 'Janice, I think. Janice Gillespie.'

The Governor's wife had clumsy darns in the sleeve of her blue cardigan. 'What's the thing about you that Janice knows best, would you say?'

This time Belle did appear to think hard, and answered, 'I don't know.'

'But she's your friend? Your best friend?'

'I think so.'

'Right. Your best friend. Let me try another tack. What is the thing that you know best about yourself?' Though an abrupt woman, her questions came out kindly. She clawed the hollow of her throat while she talked.

Belle answered, 'It isn't something Janice knows.'

'What is it?'

'I'm always afraid.'

The Governor's wife asked, 'You mean inside your stomach and chest?'

'Yes. All around there.'

'Show me.'

Belle drew a circle with her finger – around her abdomen, up to her rib-cage.

From across the office the Governor's wife watched, then asked, 'Always?'

'Always.'

'Did you ever tell anyone that?'

Belle replied, 'There was nobody to tell.'

'Nobody to tell that you were frightened a lot of the time.'

'Not a lot of the time. All the time.' Belle spoke hesitantly and quietly; had there been a window open the Governor's wife would not have been able to hear her.

'What did it do to you?'

Belle, still motionless, said, 'It made me be nice to everyone even if I didn't like them.'

'And now, Belle, you're more frightened than you know how to say?'

Belle nodded once and did not lift her head back up from the nod. 'I was always frightened. Every day at work. My stomach.'

The Governor's wife asked, 'If I promise to ask you all about it and to listen to you, will you promise me something?'

'I will.' No hesitation.

'Will you help someone else who must be really frightened?'

'I will.' Again, no hesitation.

'Can I tell my husband you've agreed?'

'Yes.'

The Governor's wife said, 'I shouldn't be telling you this, but your young man, he never was unfaithful to you, he did never go out with that girl. Did you know that?'

'No. Because – they all said.'

'They were – they were wrong.'

Belle asked, 'Do you ever get afraid?'

'Often.'

'Often?'

'Very often,' and she led Belle from the office to the door and

walked with Belle and the wardress along the corridor to Belle's
cell.

The Governor's wife said as they parted, 'I'm also hard as nails,
Belle, and I'm an unpleasant woman by my own standards. But
you don't have to be nice to me. I like you already, but my husband told me I would. And he could get sacked for the things I'm
saying to you.' She embraced Belle, while the wardress looked
away.

MR LARKWOOD: Lady Cruiseman, that is a glowing picture you
   paint of the accused. You must have observed him closely.

LADY CRUISEMAN: My Lord, I did. We are a small community,
   and one of the ways in which it works is by observing those
   who work for me closely. I call it 'taking an interest'.

MR LARKWOOD: In this case you took a close interest, is that a
   fair observation?

LADY CRUISEMAN: It is, my Lord.

MR LARKWOOD: An unusually close interest?

LADY CRUISEMAN: 'Unusually?' I need an explanation.

MR LARKWOOD: By unusually I mean this – the accused is, I
   should think, not an unattractive man physically?

LADY CRUISEMAN: As the eye can see, my Lord.

MR LARKWOOD: And your eye, Lady Cruiseman?

LADY CRUISEMAN: The eye of the beholder, my Lord, but in
   answer to the question – yes, of course he is an attractive man.

MR LARKWOOD: Is that why you're here?

LADY CRUISEMAN: I beg your pardon?

MR LARKWOOD: Is that why you're here, Lady Cruiseman? If he
   had been a gap-toothed hunchback, would you have driven
   all the way up from Tyrone, using up precious petrol rations
   to appear as a character witness for a workman?

LADY CRUISEMAN: I like to think I would, if asked, my Lord, and
   if it were appropriate.

MR LARKWOOD: Lady Cruiseman, it seems I must be much more
   blunt with you. Did you 'fancy' the accused?

LADY CRUISEMAN: What?! Really, my Lord.

MR LARKWOOD: Answer the question, please. Were you
   physically attracted to the accused? The kind of praise you gave
   him in your evidence was rare indeed.

LADY CRUISEMAN: I do not make a practice of 'fancying', if you must be vulgar, my workmen.

MR LARKWOOD: Oh? [pause] Well, then – did he fancy you?

LADY CRUISEMAN: [stammers] I – I can't say.

MR LARKWOOD: 'Can't say.' Is it that you won't say?

LADY CRUISEMAN: No. Yes. No.

MR LARKWOOD: It is a lady's privilege to change her mind, but Lady Cruiseman, which of them is it – no, yes or no?

LADY CRUISEMAN: I don't know.

MR LARKWOOD: I'll put it to you another way, then. Help you get clearer in your mind. I put it to you that the accused here paid you attention – which from a man of his looks and presence cannot have been anything other than flattering? Did he?

LADY CRUISEMAN: He has very good manners for a workman.

MR LARKWOOD: Hoh! The Workman with Good Manners. Well, well! How far did these good manners extend? Did he pursue you in any way?

LADY CRUISEMAN: If ever I needed anything doing, he was very willing. [sniggers in court]

MR LARKWOOD: We must not dwell on the implications of that remark, must we, Lady Cruiseman?

LADY CRUISEMAN: [silence]

MR LARKWOOD: Must we, Lady Cruiseman?

LADY CRUISEMAN: You're trying to twist my words.

MR LARKWOOD: They're your words, not mine. Shall we call a spade a spade, Lady Cruiseman – your husband was frequently away from Fintown. In his absence, did the accused ever – kiss you?

LADY CRUISEMAN: No! Of course not!

MR LARKWOOD: Did he ever try?

LADY CRUISEMAN: [silence]

MR LARKWOOD: Answer the question, please!

LADY CRUISEMAN: [silence]

MR LARKWOOD: M'Lord, would you direct the witness –

LADY CRUISEMAN: It wasn't like that.

MR LARKWOOD: Oh, so he did try to kiss you?

LADY CRUISEMAN: I may have been mistaken.

MR LARKWOOD: Mistaken? Can a lady really be mistaken about whether a gentleman – or a workman – is trying to kiss her?

LADY CRUISEMAN: I said. It wasn't like that.

MR LARKWOOD: Well, what was it like?

MR MACMAHON: [interrupts] M'Lord – when I attempted the same type of questioning with an earlier witness, I was forbidden. I suggest my learned friend is doing exactly the same as you disallowed with me.

LORD CHIEF JUSTICE: Mr MacMahon, if there was a relationship that we do not know about between the witness and the accused, then it disqualifies her as a character witness. I mean, if they were on intimate acquaintance, he might as well have a wife, if he had one, testifying as to his good character. I'm sorry, Mr MacMahon.

MR LARKWOOD: Thank you, m'Lord. Lady Cruiseman – you were about I believe to describe to us this kiss.

LADY CRUISEMAN: There was no kiss.

MR LARKWOOD: Very well, then – describe this 'no kiss'. [sniggers in court]

LADY CRUISEMAN: We were driving home from a visit I made to some friends.

MR LARKWOOD: 'We?'

LADY CRUISEMAN: Comerford and I.

MR LARKWOOD: Oh, he was your chauffeur, was he?

LADY CRUISEMAN: No, he can't drive a car. It was a pony and trap.

MR LARKWOOD: How romantic! But did you not catch your death of cold?

LADY CRUISEMAN: It was a summer night.

MR LARKWOOD: Ah, even more romantic! And was there a moon?

LADY CRUISEMAN: I believe there was, my Lord.

MR LARKWOOD: Aaahhh! Do go on, Lady Cruiseman, this is better than *Gone with the Wind*.

LORD CHIEF JUSTICE: Mr Larkwood?

MR LARKWOOD: I beg your pardon, my Lord.

LADY CRUISEMAN: On the way back we stopped, to look at the river, and I stepped down to walk down to the water's edge.

MR LARKWOOD: And under the leafy trees, in the moonlight, by the tinkling silver stream, he kissed you?

LADY CRUISEMAN: No, my Lord. He took my hand, to help me step down out of the pony and trap. And he did not let go of it.

338

MR LARKWOOD: Your hand or the pony and trap? [laughter in court] Were there other such contacts?

LADY CRUISEMAN: I did not allow any.

MR LARKWOOD: Did you get the impression you could have had them had you wished?

LADY CRUISEMAN: I did not allow any.

MR LARKWOOD: You already said that. But could you have had them?

LADY CRUISEMAN: [silence]

MR LARKWOOD: Lady Cruiseman, were there other such contacts?

LADY CRUISEMAN: He was very attentive – until.

MR LARKWOOD: Until what? Until you stopped him?

LADY CRUISEMAN: I did not need his help as much, and he spent more time down at the mill.

MR LARKWOOD: Come now, Lady Cruiseman – you mean you got worried about his would-be amorous pursuits of you, and therefore you made sure he was fully occupied as far away from the house as possible?

LADY CRUISEMAN: If you say so.

MR LARKWOOD: I'm sorry. Could you speak up – I didn't hear that, my Lord.

LADY CRUISEMAN: If you say so.

MR LARKWOOD: So you have come here to testify as to the good character of a man whom you found undoubtedly attractive – no harm in that, we're all human – but who showed no respect either for your marriage, or for the rightful distance between a workman and his employer's wife. Some character, some witness, if I may say so. Now, during his employment at Fintown, did you ever see the accused associate with known undesirables?

LADY CRUISEMAN: Not 'associate' exactly.

MR LARKWOOD: Well – how 'exactly', if we want to use the word 'exactly'?

LADY CRUISEMAN: I did see him once, talking to someone.

MR LARKWOOD: To whom?

LADY CRUISEMAN: To a local man. I warned him.

MR LARKWOOD: Who was this 'local man'?

LADY CRUISEMAN: He was someone who had been in jail.

MR LARKWOOD: For what – burglary?

LADY CRUISEMAN: No. For guns offences.

MR LARKWOOD: You mean – he was an IRA man?

LADY CRUISEMAN: I believe so, my Lord.

MR LARKWOOD: What was this IRA man's name?

LADY CRUISEMAN: Donaghy.

MR LARKWOOD: Do you know whether his full name was Dermot Donaghy?

LADY CRUISEMAN: I believe it was, my Lord.

MR LARKWOOD: Do you know whether this is the same man that the police want to question in connection with the killing of Brigadier-General Knowles?

LADY CRUISEMAN: Perhaps, my Lord.

MR LARKWOOD: And who is also sought in connection with two other murder enquiries in Tyrone – the murders the IRA called 'reprisals' following the hanging of an IRA man last July? And who comes from down south, from the same region as the accused? Thank you, Lady Cruiseman, there is no need to answer, you can't be expected to know everything.

LORD CHIEF JUSTICE: Mr Larkwood, from now on would you please limit your remarks to the case in hand.

MR LARKWOOD: Of course, m'Lord.

Gene, red with embarrassment, shook his head in the cells below, as his lawyers made consoling remarks. When he reached the prison that Monday afternoon, he was not returned to his cell, but taken straight to a meeting-room beside the Governor's office.

The warder said, 'Wait there,' and stood Gene in the corridor. In a moment he opened the door and beckoned him in. All three people rose to greet him – his father, mother and former schoolmaster. One by one they shook hands. His mother gave him a brown-paper parcel, from which the string had been untied and loosely re-tied.

'They had to open this at the gate,' she said. 'I'd say,' she whispered, 'they'd love some for theirselves.'

'We were searched inside out,' said his father accusingly. 'The Master here was taken away and searched.'

Gene said, 'I have your book in my cell, Master Kane, the

warders all want to borrow it.' He looked at the tall teacher. 'I didn't know your hair was gone so white.'

'Old age. Old age, Eugene. Now are you all right?' asked Thomas Kane. 'My wife sent you this gooseberry jam of hers, they poked into it with a knife to see were we hiding something in it?' and he smiled.

Gene said, 'It was very good of you to come.'

Thomas Kane replied, 'You know that we know you're innocent, don't you?' Gene's breath caught, and tears hit the backs of his eyes.

'Easy, easy,' said Thomas Kane. 'Easy. Are you holding yourself together?'

'I think so.'

His mother said, 'We're all distracted. And everyone at home is asking for you and praying for you.'

His father said, 'And when you get out of here you're to come straight home, do you hear. This place isn't safe at all, God, if it isn't Hitler 'tis someone else causing trouble.'

The schoolmaster sat down. 'Now what's the best help we can be to you? I suppose for a start we need to know the whole story. What happened to you at all?'

Gene told them. They interrupted from time to time: his mother asked, 'Was she a nice girl itself?' His father asked, 'And were you the only Catholic man in the whole place?' His former school-teacher asked, 'And your barrister, what other cases did he appear in?' His mother asked, 'Are they letting you get Confession and Holy Communion here?'

After the hour's visit had passed, the trio from the south left the prison, having been searched again on the way out. As they climbed in the car and set off to find the bed-and-breakfast Thomas Kane had booked, Gene's mother asked, 'Master, d'you think he'll be all right?'

Mr Kane said in his kindest tone, 'You'd have to be a lawyer yourself to work that one out.'

MR LARKWOOD: Well, Mr McCullough, this is very interesting. How many times did you say?

NORMAN MCCULLOUGH: Five. I checked, your Lordship.

MR LARKWOOD: Five? I see. And how long would the longest

conversation of that five times have been? An hour? Two hours?

NORMAN MCCULLOUGH: Heavens, no. Ten minutes, at most. I'm a public employee.

MR LARKWOOD: So even if you had five conversations of ten minutes each, that's at most fifty minutes. And you can say after that what kind of man the accused is?

NORMAN MCCULLOUGH: I know he's not an evil man. My Lord. Your Lordship.

MR LARKWOOD: And how do you know that, Mr McCullough?

NORMAN MCCULLOUGH: There are other ways of judging a man's character. Even on short acquaintance.

MR LARKWOOD: Oh, this is very interesting. You and I have only had a short acquaintance, and perhaps you can tell me something about me?

NORMAN MCCULLOUGH: I came here to give evidence on behalf of Mr Comerford, your Lordship.

MR LARKWOOD: Oh, but go on, prove your point. What can you tell about me?

NORMAN MCCULLOUGH: We-ell, I can tell you're very vain.

MR LARKWOOD: Vain? Goodness, this is revelatory. How are you afforded this brilliant vision of other people's souls, Mr Public Employee?

NORMAN MCCULLOUGH: You're wearing cream-coloured socks. [laughter in court] With black trousers. [more laughter]

LORD CHIEF JUSTICE: Do you really want to continue this line of questioning, Mr Larkwood? I shouldn't if I were in your shoes. Or socks. [laughter in court]

MR LARKWOOD: Thank you, m'Lord. Mr McCullough, I believe you are wasting the court's critical time. You come here to give character evidence for a man you've met five times, and even on those occasions fleetingly at most. Do you mean to be serious?

NORMAN MCCULLOUGH: Your Lordship, Mr Comerford's lawyers wrote to me and pointed out that I was one of the few people Mr Comerford had met more than once, since he came to Belfast. As a librarian you get to judge people from what they read. Nothing in Mr Comerford's choice of books suggests that there is anything bad about him.

MR LARKWOOD: So you believe that what a man reads can tell you whether he is a criminal?

NORMAN MCCULLOUGH: I believe it can tell me whether he has a tendency towards good or evil.

MR LARKWOOD: And supposing, shall we say, Mr Comerford was a man who also wrote books?

NORMAN MCCULLOUGH: Your Lordship, we do have people who write books coming into the library, and they do not seem like criminals.

MR LARKWOOD: I presume you are aware that Adolf Hitler also writes books?

NORMAN MCCULLOUGH: So does Mr Churchill.

MR LARKWOOD: Ah, now we see your sympathies and psychological abilities very clearly, Mr McCullough. If you are prepared to mention Winston Churchill in the same breath as Hitler, you can't really tell good from evil, can you? No further questions, m'Lord.

NORMAN MCCULLOUGH: Your Lordship, what I was trying to say was that –

MR LARKWOOD: No further questions, m'Lord.

As they adjourned for lunch, Ernest Larkwood said to Adrian Mac-Mahon, 'Really, Adrian? Is that the best you can do? Bottom of the barrel there.'

'We saw who was doing the scraping,' replied Mr MacMahon.

The Clerk of the Court approached.

'Mr MacMahon, could I have a word with you, or Mr O'Connor?'

They stopped in the corridor beneath the courtroom.

The Clerk said, 'We've had word from the police. Your witness for this afternoon. That man, Kane.'

'What about him?'

'He's been detained.'

'But he's in Belfast, he's already here, he arrived yesterday.'

The Clerk said, 'No, no, I know, he's been detained by the police.'

'For goodness' sake, why?'

'"Questioning" is all they'll say.'

Mr MacMahon asked, 'Have you told the judge?'

'Not yet.'

'This is ridiculous. I'd better go with you. Ask Mr Larkwood does he want to come.'

By the fire in his robing-room, the Lord Chief Justice sat unfolding his napkin.

'Nicholas, I'm sorry to barge in on your lunch.'

'Not at all. I just wish I could invite you and Ernest to join me. We should be more like the American courts and not have all this wretched formality.'

'Nicholas, my witness for this afternoon, one of my key witnesses, has been detained by the police for questioning.'

The Lord Chief Justice looked over his spectacles.

'Oh?'

'And for no reason that I can think of, other than that he has driven up from the south, from the far south at that. He brought Comerford's parents with him.'

'I don't seriously want to adjourn, Adrian. I really don't. This case is causing too much publicity. I said from the beginning I want no legalistics.'

Mr MacMahon said, 'But this is manifest interference with a witness!'

Nicholas Bowling said, 'Adrian, you know as well as I do – you won't even get that one into the starting-gates.'

'Nicholas, please. It is complex.'

Ernest Larkwood walked in behind Adrian MacMahon and said, 'Nicholas, I'm not bothered. If Adrian wants an adjournment until tomorrow.'

'Yes, but I don't. I don't want any adjournments.'

'Can I put it to you another way?' Ernest Larkwood took off his wig. 'The publicity on this is not going to be good.'

'That is exactly why I don't want an adjournment,' said the Lord Chief Justice.

'But,' said Ernest Larkwood, 'if you grant an adjournment, then perhaps Adrian can get the whole thing sorted out this afternoon.'

'On what grounds can I grant an adjournment? What can I say that won't cause a storm?'

'Anything. Let us prepare something,' said Mr Larkwood.

Nicholas Bowling said, 'Why was he arrested anyway?'

'I don't know and I haven't been told,' said Adrian MacMahon. 'I expect it's because he was a hero down there in the old days.'

'You mean a gunman?'

'Yes.'

'And you called him as a witness?' Nicholas Bowling looked at Adrian MacMahon.

Ernest Larkwood cut in. 'There is another problem that has just struck me. If this man does not appear – then who are you going to call next, Adrian?'

'I haven't got another witness – yet.'

Mr Larkwood asked, 'What about the girl?'

'She hasn't agreed – so far.'

'And the accused himself?' asked the Lord Chief Justice.

'You know I'm not putting him on the stand, Nicholas.'

'High-risk strategy, eh, Adrian?' asked the Lord Chief Justice.

'A southern accent in front of that jury? You must be joking. There's five shipyard workers there.'

Nicholas Bowling looked from one advocate to the other, from the florid Mr MacMahon to the keen-haired Mr Larkwood.

'Court adjourned for legal argument. All right? And no more adjournments.'

'Yes. Thanks, Nicholas.'

Not that it made a difference: any effectiveness Thomas Kane might afterwards have had as a witness was pre-empted that night. An *Irish Times* reporter, with good contacts in the RUC, received a tip-off. He verified the story and told the news desk in Dublin, where the News Editor sought a comment from political quarters. When the statement came back, it was attributed to Eamon De Valera directly.

'We are watching the progress of this trial with interest. In July last year, a miscarriage of justice clearly took place with the hanging of a nineteen-year-old Irish boy of nationalist sympathies, Thomas Williams. Now the Royal Ulster Constabulary has sought to interfere in the Comerford trial by arresting groundlessly a key witness. I would expect the Northern Ireland Home Secretary either to order the release of this witness immediately – who, incidentally, has travelled a long way to testify – or to call a mis-trial and release Mr Comerford.' Once again in the *Belfast Telegraph*, the war with Hitler became relegated to the inside pages.

=

All the women who visited Belle agreed on one thing.

'There's a big difference in her,' said Alice. 'She's quieter.'

'But,' said Janice, 'you know what Belle's like – always something to say. And is that not the case now so much?'

'I don't mean she's silent or anything,' said Gloria, 'but more – more, I don't know what you'd call it.'

'Has she lost her looks?' Janice asked.

'Ah, shite's sake, Janice,' said Enid, 'she's only there five weeks.'

Alice said, 'If anything she's better-looking –'

'Composed!' blurted Gloria. 'That's the word.'

Belle interviewed each woman who visited, firing a list of questions. She sat across the table in a room newly thrown together with partitions to accommodate visitors for the few Protestant women who had been moved from Armagh. What were the papers saying? Had anyone of the spinners left at Christmas, a typical departure time? Any new romances? What was the news of the war? Did the Blackwoods do anything about heating the Long Room? Was there a sale on in Anderson and MacAuley's?

'The thing I noticed,' said Janice, 'was – she never once asked what was on at the pictures. Is her mother going in often?'

Edith's first visit to Belle had been to Armagh two afternoons after the fatal day; Bingham, with Nesbit's permission, arranged for Fergusson to drive. The Reverend MacCreagh went along.

'Remember, Edith, this may well be one of the most difficult trials she will have to face. Her own dear mother. She may be feeling a sense of shame.'

'I'll never be able to thank you enough for the help you're being to me,' replied Edith.

Belle entered the room behind Edith. She stood for a moment, watching her mother from behind, watching her fidget with her fingers. Edith finished blowing her nose and turned in her chair.

'Hallo, Belle.' Belle half-smiled.

'Come over here to me, girl.' Edith sat, and Belle walked a circle to take her around to the other side of the table from Edith.

'Belle, how are you?'

The two sat there, Edith looking down into her busy white handkerchief, Belle looking at Edith who stood and reached out her arms. The two women stood there, tall and all awkward angles, trying to embrace across the narrow table – which at least kept their breasts from touching. Belle broke first, but Edith caught her again and, sidling along the table to get it out of the way, held on to Belle, a more organised hug this time. They stood in each other's arms calmly, patting each other all the time. Eventually they released each other; Belle sat.

'Well, Belle, here we are. I brought you this.' Edith opened her handbag and handed Belle the squeezed roll of money she had taken from Belle's hiding-place in the skirting-board of her bedroom.

'Oh, Mam, I don't need that – not here, anyhow.'

'But 'tis yours, Belle.' Edith sat.

'You mind it for me, Mam.' The daughter had become the mother and vice versa. 'Or buy yourself something with it.'

'Belle, I'd never spend all that.'

Belle pressed her mother's hand back towards her handbag. 'No, 'tis all right.' She smiled.

Edith made herself busy returning the money to the handbag and then she had no more to do. She looked up at Belle and said, 'Well, here we are, Belle.'

'Here we are, Mam.' Both women made slow, intense washing motions with their hands.

'How's Lennie?'

'He's grand, Belle.' Edith paused and surveyed Belle's prison clothing. 'That grey they give you to wear.'

'I know, Mam,' Belle said. 'Not the best, is it, but if we saw it in the shops and bought it ourselves, we'd say it was lovely.'

'We would. We would.'

'How's the Reverend MacCreagh?'

'He's grand, he came down with me. He's awful good to me, so he is.'

'That's good. You're looking well, Mam. I thought you might be –'

'Belle, you look more and more like your father,' and Edith, the floodgate open at last, began to babble. Incessantly, her hands soothed down her own bosom.

'Belle, if I only known that that man, your fella, was – I mean, like your feelings for him – sure I never met a man like your father, and never would – and I understand them feelings – maybe I understand them all the more since I don't ever talk about them

347

– but that's only because I don't have the gift of words, like you do – your father, he did all the talking for the two of us, I used to say to him I don't know how he ever saw me at all when we met, 'cause he was the talker, that's where you get it from. Belle – I blame myself, because if you and me had been close, I would have known your feelings for the man and I'd never have interfered – and Belle, my hand itself is sorry for the way it hit you –'

'Mam. Mam. Whisht. There's no need.' Belle took her mother's hands.

'There is need for me, Belle. There is need for me to talk.'

'There isn't, Mam, 'tis only a short visiting time.'

'There is, Belle, there's need for me to say you're my flesh and blood – and I'm here for you, no matter what, and I don't think anything but the best of you – and I'll scratch at anyone who ever said otherwise – although God knows nobody ever says a thing but the nicest for you – and they're all asking after you – and they want to send you parcels, only I said I'd have to find out first – and Jed and Sandra want to come down – he says he'll show you a few card tricks and you can make a few bob in here in this place –'

At which Edith began to wail aloud, then sank into snuffles. Belle watched her closely and dispassionately, and held Edith's hands.

No other conversation of moment took place, apart from enquiries by Edith as to the general conditions at Armagh, followed by Belle's calm questions about the war, and the house, and the people along Pretoria Street. When visiting time ended, the two tall women walked arm-in-arm to the door of the room and embraced easily.

In the car on the way back to Belfast, Edith whispered to the Reverend MacCreagh, 'Even though she never mentioned him, not even when I did, she's still in love with that man.'

Watching the rain absently, he replied with a quotation, 'Many waters cannot quench love, neither can the floods drown it . . .'

LORD CHIEF JUSTICE: I am sorry to have to interrupt you, Mr MacMahon.

MR MACMAHON: Not at all, m'Lord.

LORD CHIEF JUSTICE: Mr Higgins, what is the noise?

CLERK OF THE COURT: M'Lord, there is apparently a substantial crowd on the street outside. A lot of people who got into the building still have the impression the public gallery has spaces.

LORD CHIEF JUSTICE: Why has somebody not put up a notice? Or else closed and locked these doors?

CLERK OF THE COURT: M'Lord, we are now subject to fire regulations, but we can put up a notice straightaway.

LORD CHIEF JUSTICE: Five minutes' adjournment.

LORD CHIEF JUSTICE: Now, Mr MacMahon, if you please.

MR MACMAHON: M'Lord, I have one last witness to call. As you are aware, there has been a difficulty.

LORD CHIEF JUSTICE: The witness – Thomas Kane? Has that been resolved?

MR MACMAHON: We are to receive a written testimonial.

LORD CHIEF JUSTICE: Mr Larkwood, you can't be too pleased about that?

MR LARKWOOD: I'm afraid not, M'Lord, it means I can't challenge the witness.

LORD CHIEF JUSTICE: Nevertheless, in the circumstances, I believe I should allow the letter when it comes.

MR LARKWOOD: M'Lord, my instructions are not to raise an objection.

LORD CHIEF JUSTICE: Very well. Proceed, if you would, Mr MacMahon.

MR MACMAHON: M'Lord, I propose to call Isabel or Belle MacKnight. [noise in court]

LORD CHIEF JUSTICE: Silence! I have a preference for cleared courtrooms.

BELLE MACKNIGHT: I swear by Almighty God that the evidence I shall give shall be the truth, the whole truth and nothing but the truth. So help me God.

CLERK OF THE COURT: What is your name, please?

BELLE MACKNIGHT: Isabel MacKnight.

CLERK OF THE COURT: And what is your address, please?

BELLE MACKNIGHT: Eleven Pretoria Street, Belfast.

CLERK OF THE COURT: Your present address, please?

LORD CHIEF JUSTICE: No, that's all right. [to witness] You may sit down, if you wish.

MR MACMAHON: Miss MacKnight – Belle – I have very few

questions to ask you. Do you remember where you were on the night of September the eighth last year?

BELLE MACKNIGHT: I do.

MR MACMAHON: Will you tell the court, please.

BELLE MACKNIGHT: I was out. I was in Madden Park, 'tis called. I was sitting talking.

MR MACMAHON: Who was with you?

BELLE MACKNIGHT: Gene Comerford.

MR MACMAHON: Do you see the man who was with you in this courtroom?

BELLE MACKNIGHT: I do – that's him there. [points]

MR MACMAHON: Was he with you all the time?

BELLE MACKNIGHT: He was.

MR MACMAHON: From what time to what time?

BELLE MACKNIGHT: From half-past seven 'til about nine o'clock.

MR MACMAHON: All the time?

BELLE MACKNIGHT: The whole time.

MR MACMAHON: No question about that?

BELLE MACKNIGHT: No.

MR MACMAHON: Did he go away and leave you for a few minutes?

BELLE MACKNIGHT: No.

MR MACMAHON: How can you be so sure?

BELLE MACKNIGHT: We had our arms around each other all the time, he couldn't go away without taking me with him. [murmurs in court]

MR MACMAHON: You're sure?

BELLE MACKNIGHT: Positive.

MR MACMAHON: Did anything unusual happen?

BELLE MACKNIGHT: It did.

MR MACMAHON: What?

BELLE MACKNIGHT: Just as we were leaving, 'cause 'twas getting cold, I heard a bang.

MR MACMAHON: What kind of a bang?

BELLE MACKNIGHT: A real bang.

MR MACMAHON: Did you say anything?

BELLE MACKNIGHT: I did. I said, 'Jesus. What was that?' And then I said, 'That was a bomb, and there was no air-raid warning.'

MR MACMAHON: Did Mr Comerford – did he say anything?

BELLE MACKNIGHT: He did. He said, 'No, there was no aircraft noise.' And then he thought and he said, 'Oh, maybe there's some old bomb or a mine or something that didn't go off when it landed and they're blowing it up.'

MR MACMAHON: What happened next?

BELLE MACKNIGHT: There was a second noise.

MR MACMAHON: Another bomb?

BELLE MACKNIGHT: No. A gunshot.

MR MACMAHON: How do you know it was a gunshot?

BELLE MACKNIGHT: I hear them in the pictures.

MR MACMAHON: Did Mr Comerford say anything?

BELLE MACKNIGHT: He did. He said, 'That's a gunshot,' and then he said, 'That's a rifle.' And then we stopped, we were walking and he said, 'There's someone coming.' But there wasn't.

MR MACMAHON: Then what happened?

BELLE MACKNIGHT: Nothing. He walked me home to the corner of my street.

MR MACMAHON: And at no time since you met for your evening's appointment was he ever out of your sight?

BELLE MACKNIGHT: No.

MR MACMAHON: You're certain of that?

BELLE MACKNIGHT: I'm on my oath.

MR MACMAHON: Thank you, Miss MacKnight.

LORD CHIEF JUSTICE: Ah – no, Miss MacKnight, please stay where you are, Mr Larkwood wants to ask you some questions.

MR LARKWOOD: How did you meet the accused?

BELLE MACKNIGHT: Who?

MR LARKWOOD: The accused. The prisoner. The man sitting over there who is accused of murder?

BELLE MACKNIGHT: I met him at work.

MR LARKWOOD: At work?

BELLE MACKNIGHT: Yes. He works in the same mill as me.

MR LARKWOOD: How did you meet him? Do you work side by side?

BELLE MACKNIGHT: I saw him at work one morning.

MR LARKWOOD: Have you no manners? [mutters in court]

BELLE MACKNIGHT: I've plenty of manners.

MR LARKWOOD: Why don't you address the court properly?

BELLE MACKNIGHT: How do – how do you mean?

MR LARKWOOD: You are supposed to address your answers to the judge, and you are supposed to call him 'my Lord'.

BELLE MACKNIGHT: Well, I'm sorry, I didn't know. [applause in court]

MR LARKWOOD: To repeat my question – how did you meet him?

BELLE MACKNIGHT: He was standing in a doorway.

MR LARKWOOD: Standing in a doorway?

BELLE MACKNIGHT: Yes.

MR LARKWOOD: Why was he standing in a doorway?

BELLE MACKNIGHT: He was listening.

MR LARKWOOD: What was he listening to?

BELLE MACKNIGHT: He was listening to me.

MR LARKWOOD: What were you saying?

MR MACMAHON: [interrupts] M'Lord, where is this going? My learned friend has heard the evidence the witness has given.

LORD CHIEF JUSTICE: No, Mr MacMahon. This is material. You may answer, Miss MacKnight.

BELLE MACKNIGHT: I've forgot what he asked.

MR LARKWOOD: I asked you – 'What was the accused listening to?' You said, 'He was listening to me.' I asked you, 'What were you saying?'

BELLE MACKNIGHT: I was telling something.

MR LARKWOOD: Telling something. Telling what and to whom?

BELLE MACKNIGHT: I was telling my workmates a story.

MR LARKWOOD: A story? How nice. Was this a fairy story? Was it a bedtime story? Was it – forgive my leap of the imagination – a true story?

BELLE MACKNIGHT: It was a picture.

MR LARKWOOD: A picture? You mean something that hangs in a frame?

BELLE MACKNIGHT: No, a picture – at the pictures.

MR LARKWOOD: The cinema?

BELLE MACKNIGHT: Yes.

MR LARKWOOD: What cinema?

BELLE MACKNIGHT: The Ritz.

MR LARKWOOD: Oh, I see. Not any old cinema. Mmmmmm. Now, Miss Mac, Miss Mac –? Oh, yes, MacKnight. Now,

Miss MacKnight. This man standing in the doorway – Oh, what was the picture, by the way?

BELLE MACKNIGHT: *Gone with the Wind*.

MR LARKWOOD: Oh, I haven't seen it myself, is it good?

BELLE MACKNIGHT: It is, it's very good.

MR LARKWOOD: Good. Good. Sorry, m'Lord, I've distracted myself. I was going to ask, the doorway, yes. One second, *Gone with the Wind*? That's Clark Gable, isn't it?

BELLE MACKNIGHT: And Vivien Leigh. And Olivia de Havilland. Leslie Howard's in it too.

MR LARKWOOD: Oh, my goodness, thank you. You know them all, don't you? This is very interesting. Please forgive me, Miss MacKnight, Belle, isn't it?

BELLE MACKNIGHT: Yes, sir.

MR LARKWOOD: Please forgive me, Belle, I'm a great film fan myself, but I've been so busy. So you were telling all the folk at the mill about *Gone with the Wind*?

BELLE MACKNIGHT: I was.

MR LARKWOOD: Do they enjoy it?

BELLE MACKNIGHT: Yes, they love it.

MR LARKWOOD: As a matter of interest, what does it sound like, when you tell them?

BELLE MACKNIGHT: I just tell them the story, sir.

MR LARKWOOD: Mmmmmm. Yessss. I gathered that. Could you give us a taste of it?

MR MACMAHON: [interrupts] M'Lord, where is –

LORD CHIEF JUSTICE: It will become clear, I feel sure, Mr MacMahon. Indeed, Mr Larkwood, it had better.

MR LARKWOOD: Go ahead, Belle.

BELLE MACKNIGHT: It isn't easy. Here.

MR LARKWOOD: Take your time.

BELLE MACKNIGHT: Well, I'll only do a part of it. The whole thing, like, 'tis four hours long.

MR LARKWOOD: Of course. Of course. Would you like to stand up?

BELLE MACKNIGHT: I will. I'd need to.

MR LARKWOOD: Right, off you go.

BELLE MACKNIGHT: Well, I don't know where to begin.

MR LARKWOOD: Well, let's see . . . Had you told them the whole story at work?

BELLE MACKNIGHT: No.

MR LARKWOOD: Where did you stop?

BELLE MACKNIGHT: Oh, right. Well, the war is over, that's the war between the Yankees and the South, and Tara, that's Scarlett O'Hara's house, is still standing, although the whole place is in ruins. And then Ashley Wilkes, he's married to Melanie, but Scarlett, she was always in love with him, he comes back, and he was on the side that was beaten. And he comes back and he's reunited with his wife and the baby he's never seen. But Scarlett, she still fancies him and she goes after him and she gets him to kiss her, 'cause from the very minute she first saw him she always wanted him –

'By now,' reported the *Belfast Telegraph*, departing at that point from the transcript form in which it had daily reported the trial, 'a theatrical hush had fallen over the courtroom and even his Lordship seemed entranced. The witness transformed the witness box into a miniature stage, from which she beamed her light. She ceased to be a Belfast mill-girl in a correct hat and costume. Her demeanour became that of Scarlett O'Hara in a way that would not have shamed the renowned Miss Vivien Leigh. To emulate the stars of the film shedding tears, she whipped a handkerchief from her cuff and sniffed into it, sobbing convincingly; to display defiance, she flung out a perfect hand and flicked a wrist. When portraying disdain, she tilted her chin haughtily, and by magic the familiar accents of Belfast became the musical and deep tones of the United States' deep South. The courtroom must undoubtedly have burst into an ovation of applause – risking the wrath, no doubt, of his Lordship – had the witness been allowed to continue uninterrupted. But at that moment a greater drama superseded.'

ACCUSED: [interrupts: shouts] No, Belle! Don't!

MR LARKWOOD: What –?

BELLE MACKNIGHT: Oh!

LORD CHIEF JUSTICE: Silence! Silence in court. You are not allowed to speak.

ACCUSED: [shouts] He's tricking you, Belle.

LORD CHIEF JUSTICE: If you are not prepared to behave, then you will be taken downstairs to the cells.

MR LARKWOOD: Thank you, m'Lord.

ACCUSED: [shouts] Belle, he's trying to make you look like a fool, like someone who makes things up.

BELLE MACKNIGHT: Oh! [sits]

LORD CHIEF JUSTICE: Take him downstairs. We will pause for a moment, Mr Larkwood.

MR LARKWOOD: Very well, m'Lord.

[court resumes after three minutes]

MR LARKWOOD: Thank you, Miss MacKnight, that was most entertaining, I'm sorry about the interruption. Now – let us go back. You saw the prisoner listening to you as he stood in the doorway – you know, the day you first saw him. Is it fair to say that you noticed him?

BELLE MACKNIGHT: I did.

MR LARKWOOD: I beg your pardon, I didn't hear you.

BELLE MACKNIGHT: [louder] I did.

MR LARKWOOD: Did you from that moment think about him?

BELLE MACKNIGHT: I don't know.

MR LARKWOOD: I beg your pardon, I didn't hear you then either.

BELLE MACKNIGHT: [louder] I don't know.

MR LARKWOOD: But you did begin to think about him, didn't you? You are on oath, remember.

BELLE MACKNIGHT: Yes.

MR LARKWOOD: Yes, what? And please speak up.

BELLE MACKNIGHT: Yes, I did think about him.

MR LARKWOOD: I'm not surprised. He's a good-looking man. Did you have a boyfriend then?

BELLE MACKNIGHT: No.

MR LARKWOOD: Did you ever have a boyfriend?

BELLE MACKNIGHT: No. A bit of a one, once.

MR LARKWOOD: But no real boyfriend?

BELLE MACKNIGHT: No.

MR LARKWOOD: Then you saw this man again and again at work, in the distance perhaps? Is that how it was?

BELLE MACKNIGHT: Yes.

MR LARKWOOD: And then one day he asked you to walk out with him?

BELLE MACKNIGHT: Yes.

MR LARKWOOD: And naturally enough you said yes immediately?

BELLE MACKNIGHT: Yes. He helped me. Gordon Blackwood at the mill –

MR LARKWOOD: [interrupts] Don't digress, please. He asked you to walk out with him. Yes or no?

BELLE MACKNIGHT: Yes, but it was because young Blackwood –

MR LARKWOOD: It was really because he saw you looking at him and you were a good storyteller?

BELLE MACKNIGHT: No, it was because –

MR LARKWOOD: Please! I don't want the story of your life, I just want the answers to questions. Now – you described this evening you and the prisoner had together in Madden Park. Was it your idea to go there? A nice, secluded nook?

BELLE MACKNIGHT: No.

MR LARKWOOD: Whose idea?

BELLE MACKNIGHT: His.

MR LARKWOOD: So he knew it?

BELLE MACKNIGHT: Yes.

MR LARKWOOD: But he was a stranger to Belfast?

BELLE MACKNIGHT: [silence]

MR LARKWOOD: Don't you find that interesting?

BELLE MACKNIGHT: [silence]

MR LARKWOOD: Well, don't you? [voice raised]

BELLE MACKNIGHT: I don't know.

MR LARKWOOD: He's been in Belfast a matter of weeks and he knows a park hardly anyone else knew existed it's so small. And it just happens to be beside where a murder is about to be committed, where a frail and nice old man is about to be bombed and shot. Oh, come along, Miss MacKnight. Really? And with your powers of imagination?

BELLE MACKNIGHT: I don't know. I don't know.

MR LARKWOOD: [shakes his head] Really. Now – you said in evidence to Mr MacMahon, this is what you said: 'We had our arms around each other all the time, he couldn't go away without taking me with him.' That's a romantic little scene. You like romantic little scenes, don't you?

BELLE MACKNIGHT: No.

MR LARKWOOD: Oooh, aren't you pushing it for a woman on oath? Do you or don't you? There's nothing wrong with it, all women like romantic little scenes.

BELLE MACKNIGHT: I do.

MR LARKWOOD: That's better; let us continue to have the truth, shall we? Then you went on to say, what? About 'leaving' and about 'a bang'?

BELLE MACKNIGHT: I said, 'Just as we were leaving, 'cause 'twas getting cold, I heard a bang.'

MR LARKWOOD: Indeed you did, those were your words. Mr MacMahon asked you, 'What kind of a bang?' And what did you say?

BELLE MACKNIGHT: A real bang. I said, 'a real bang'.

MR LARKWOOD: Indeed you did. Now can you remember what you said next?

BELLE MACKNIGHT: I said, 'Jesus. What was that?' And then I said, 'That was a bomb, and there was no air-raid warning.'

MR LARKWOOD: And Mr MacMahon said to you, 'And Mr Comerford – did he say anything?' And you replied – ?

BELLE MACKNIGHT: He said, 'No, there was no aircraft noise.' And then he thought and he said, 'Oh, maybe there's some old bomb or a mine or something that didn't go off when it landed and they're blowing it up.'

MR LARKWOOD: Then Mr MacMahon said, 'What happened next?' And you said – ?

BELLE MACKNIGHT: There was a second noise.

MR LARKWOOD: That is exactly what you said. Can you remember what you said the noise was?

BELLE MACKNIGHT: A gunshot.

MR LARKWOOD: And Mr MacMahon asked you, 'How do you know it was a gunshot?' And what did you say?

BELLE MACKNIGHT: I said – 'I hear them in the pictures.'

MR LARKWOOD: [throws his notes down] Now, Miss MacKnight, you have repeated word for word what you said to Mr MacMahon. According to my notes – and I am sure the shorthand-takers around this court would verify if asked – you did not differ by so much as a word. Not one word. How long did it take you to make up this story?

BELLE MACKNIGHT: I didn't make it up.

MR LARKWOOD: And how long did it take you to rehearse it. I mean – we have seen that you are a practised story-teller?

BELLE MACKNIGHT: What I said is true.

MR LARKWOOD: Every lawyer in the country will tell you that it is perfectly natural for a witness when repeating something to change a few unimportant words here and there – but you have not changed one single word.

BELLE MACKNIGHT: They're all important words. That's why I had to remember them.

MR LARKWOOD: Why did you come here to testify?

BELLE MACKNIGHT: I was asked.

MR LARKWOOD: You could have said no.

BELLE MACKNIGHT: It was the right thing to do.

MR LARKWOOD: Oh – are you going to tell us what the right thing to do is? What is your address at the moment?

BELLE MACKNIGHT: [silence]

MR LARKWOOD: It is Crumlin Road prison, isn't it, on a charge of murder, I believe, and you purport to tell us what the right thing is to do? I put it to you that you are a fantasist?

BELLE MACKNIGHT: [in tears] I don't know what that is.

MR LARKWOOD: Someone who makes up stories. This man is the first boyfriend you ever had. It may yet be proven on another day in this very court building that because of your obsession with him, you –

LORD CHIEF JUSTICE: [sharply] Mr Larkwood!

MR LARKWOOD: Sorry, m'Lord. You are, I repeat, a fantasist, and the story you made up about Madden Park and the loveydovey arms about each other is as much a fantasy as all the other stories you have been spinning every day of your life for years.

BELLE MACKNIGHT: No.

MR LARKWOOD: You are still obsessed with this man who is the only boyfriend you have ever had – and you're, what – twenty-four? I bet most of your colleagues are married and have children at your age, and so you decide you will show your love for him by coming here, having memorised his story to the letter?

BELLE MACKNIGHT: Not true. Not true.

MR LARKWOOD: Absolutely. 'Not true. Not true.' Now you are telling the truth. At last. No further questions, m'Lord.

LORD CHIEF JUSTICE: Prosecution and Defence summing-up tomorrow morning.

CLERK OF THE COURT: Court will rise.

20

In the last hour of daylight, Gene walked through the high door into the small yard. A winter sun blinded him for a moment and he flung his hands up to shade his eyes.

'Sure. No bother,' Charlie Gilbert, the new warder said, when Gene had asked for some exercise. No other prisoners exercised out here: they used a bigger yard, on the other side of the high wall, and he could hear them when they talked and shouted. This afternoon – not a sound: he might have had the prison to himself.

'They call it "solitary confinement",' he had told Master Kane on that single visit, 'but I'm talking to people all the time.'

Gene walked across the yard, flexed his fingers to the wall, turned around and began to touch his toes.

'That was not so intelligent,' said Mr MacMahon downstairs, where they had put Gene in the holding cell. 'You could have got yourself done for Contempt of Court.'

'What's that?'

Mr MacMahon explained, and went on to say, 'Although at the same time, it might have gone down well with the jury.'

'Why do you say that?'

'My esteemed rival was livid. He thought we pulled it as a stunt. Deliberately.'

'No?'

'Yes – which means it might be a good idea if you were to apologise tomorrow. I'll work out a short form of words and give it to you in the morning.'

Gene touched his toes ten more times and stood to stretch his arms above his head. The door from the yard stood open and empty; Charlie Gilbert had gone back inside. As Gene stretched, the warder reappeared and walked across in his thin little lope.

'D'you want long out here?'

'I wouldn't mind a good few minutes – but if that's not right?'

'No, no, it's not that. The Governor is here and he has somebody with him to see you. Is it all right for you to meet them out
here?'

'Yes.' The warder loped back, heel to toe. Gene looked at his
departing uniform, puzzled. A moment after the man vanished
into the dark slot of the door, another figure appeared, hesitantly,
then bolder. She walked, hands by her side, across the yard.

Gene stood stock-still.

'Hallo,' she said.

'Belle!' He dropped his shoulders back against the wall, and
looked to the blue sky.

'How are you?' She held out her hand.

He shook it, then dropped it.

'Fine, thanks. And yourself? How did you get in here?'

'I live here.' She shrugged, and made an embarrassed *moue*.

'I didn't know. Until – recently. I mean, how did you get in
here, to this yard?'

Belle said, 'I didn't know, either. They told me first you were
out in the ship, out in Belfast Lough. And now that man said, the
Governor, he said I could meet you. We've all to keep it a secret.'

Gene said, 'They told me you were in Armagh. Only in the
court did I know you were near me.'

'I was in Armagh. They moved me.'

'When?'

'Just before Christmas.'

Gene said, 'God, so we were only a few walls away from each
other all the time.'

'Aye.'

Belle stood in front of him calmly, hands dangling by her sides.
'How are you anyway?' she asked.

'I don't know where to start to say what I want to say,' he said.

'Neither do I.'

Gene smiled. 'Maybe we'll say nothing.'

'Maybe.'

'There's one thing, though – thanks for today. In court.'

'You're welcome.'

'Would it be any good if I was to do the same for you?'

Belle replied, 'I don't know. I'll ask.'

'When are you up?'

'The beginning of March, you'll be out of here by then and away.'

'I hope so.' Gene indicated with a hand – 'Will we walk around the yard?'

'Okay.'

They walked in silence once around the yard, exactly side by side, keeping slow step, never touching. As they passed the door, both glanced: nobody stood inside watching them.

At length, Gene said, 'Mine should be all over in the next few days. So they tell me. They have to sum up now, and the judge has to do the same, and then the jury decides its verdict.'

'Right.'

'When I get out again – can I, would you like me to – come and visit you?'

'Yes,' said Belle.

Gene began to speak again. She interposed. 'No. Don't say anything to me today.' She put a finger to her lips. 'Not today. There's a lot to say. But I can't say my bit yet, and I don't want to hear your bit until I'm ready to say mine.'

'Okay. Okay. I understand.' They walked on.

Gene said, 'I have to say one thing. Can I say it? Just one?' Belle smiled gravely and nodded.

Gene blinked. 'No, no. You're right. I'll wait. I can't say it anyway.' He thought for a moment. 'But will they let us meet again?'

Belle replied, 'They will.'

They walked one more circuit of the yard in silence, and when they came level with the door again, Belle said, 'I'll go now.'

'Oh. Well, yes. Sure.' He stood, looking at her hair, hands in the pockets of his prison trousers. 'Belle,' he said, but the inflection did not require an answer.

As she stepped away he said, 'Belle, I'm – I'm frightened outa my skin.'

She looked back and paused, nodded, then continued her journey to the door. Before she slipped inside, she turned and waved her white hand like a wing from the gloom of the doorway.

Gene said to the warder, as they walked back the short distance to the cell together, 'Mr Gilbert, I never asked this until now, but what d'you think is going to happen to me?'

'Listen, Gene. See me? I'm the wrong one to ask, I never know what's going to happen, that's what has me as I am.' He paused at the cell door, holding it open. 'And listen more. Call me "Charlie". Except when your man Allison's here, or Headcase, and then I'll have to call you "Comerford". But it's nothing personal.'

Each barrister's summing-up turned into a performance. The Lord Chief Justice did not intervene or curb. Perfectly trained and highly experienced, both retraced the lines of thought they had opened in their examination and cross-examination. Declaration, amplification, resolution, conclusion: each phase became a short oral essay, in language beautifully judged to presume the jury's intelligence, never to estrange them with big words. Ernest Larkwood addressed them from the floor directly beneath the judge's position; the small acre of highly polished wood became a stage for him, and his voice the music of the morning. It rarely moved more than half a spoken register up or down, but every word could be heard, and having analysed the pedigree of every juror, he knew precisely how far up the scale he should take it in the accents of wealth. Should he sound too upper-class he might alienate them – yet he must strike the employee chord in them all, must play that class difference that brought obedience, rather than obeisance, because in Northern Ireland obeisance soon turned into rebelliousness. Furthermore, were he to use too rich an accent – to sound like the judge's society, for instance – how then could he make that swift occasional swoop into knowing mateyness that he would need with a jury so hard-faced?

He walked them through all the witnesses, reminded them, asked them: 'Now you will, for instance, have asked yourselves about the fingerprinting testimony of Mr Wheaton, whose intelligence, I must say, I found impressive, too.' He was known for that trick, that 'too', joining the jury into his way of thinking, flattering them into the momentary belief that, well, this is a man I can understand, this is someone who certainly knows his onions. When it came to retracing for them – or as he put it, 'Let me now discuss with you' – the testimony of Judy Cruiseman, he began with an apology.

'When I went home that evening, I said to my wife, "I do hope I didn't overdo the rudeness today, but I get so irritated when I see people manipulated into telling what they think is the truth, but is actually a pack of lies invented for them by some unscrupulous person." You may say to yourself, now, that I shouldn't be discussing this with my wife, but whatever you may think, I am human. Barristers are. Even Mr MacMahon over there is human.' He waited for their smiles to subside. 'What is inhuman is the taking of another's life.'

One by one, he then took apart the witnesses for the Defence, and when it came to Belle he reminded them.

'Didn't she look lovely – up there in the witness box? And wasn't she marvellous at telling the pictures? Better than the real thing, I should say.' He stopped, whirled on his shiny shoes (he had worn dark socks since Norman McCullough's gibe) and pointed at himself.

'But I too have a daughter and one day I hope she will fall in love. But I do not want her to meet a man who will use her to cover up for him.' He continued to tell them, 'That was a sweet girl and look at the dreadful mess she has got herself into, or, I should say, she has been got into.'

The Lord Chief Justice coughed, and Ernest Larkwood took it as a warning that he had sailed too close to blaming the accused in this trial for the murder of Noreen O'Connor as well.

'Nor do I want my daughter's innocent love betrayed when she falls in love with some man.' He pointed to his adversary. 'Mr MacMahon will shortly tell you that this girl is the key to the correct verdict in this trial. He will tell you she swore on oath that she was with the accused all the time, that he never left her sight. I suggest the poor girl does not now know what she believed – and who can blame her?'

Close to the end of an hour and fifty minutes on his feet, Mr Larkwood then moved on to the state of affairs within Northern Ireland, which he described as the 'real business we must attend to'. In full flow, while checking each juror's face carefully, he reminded them that the authorities believed the greatest danger to Ulster, even during this terrible war, came from within the island of Ireland. 'God and Ulster' was the phrase he used: eleven times in his last five minutes he used it, and he told them he would ask for the maximum penalty 'for God and Ulster'. He did not say 'the death penalty'; he did not mention the word 'hanging'; he did tell them they must not be squeamish, but must reach their verdict like Ulstermen.

'If you believe that in these times, a man who comes into this city from the Free State, where our greatest threat arises, a greater threat to us than Hitler, a greater threat to us than Mussolini – if you believe that a big, strapping man comes into this city, and within weeks of his arrival here, has found the secluded little green and peaceful corner of Belfast, where one of our most distinguished old soldiers lives, a place many people who have lived in Belfast all their lives had never heard of. His room is stashed to the ceilings with money – cash. A mill-worker? He can miraculously get hold of a motorbike to take his "girlfriend" down the country – and to where? Into south Armagh, famous as the hidey-hole of the Irish Republican Army. And this stranger's fingerprints are then found on the barrel of the gun that fired the fatal bullet – the slug of lead that bored, that seared a tunnel, straight as a die through this gallant, dear man's frail old body. And this stranger, that man sitting over there, the accused, even admits to being there that night, on that street at that time – if you believe after all that that he is innocent – then, of course you must acquit him. That, as honest Ulstermen, is what you would and should do. For God and Ulster. But if you believe, as Christians loyal to the Crown, that this man is also part of the enemy burrowing beneath our very houses, infiltrating our society, seducing our pretty and innocent young working-women – then you must for God and Ulster, for Ulster and God, take the correct decision.'

As he returned to counsels' table, Adrian MacMahon murmured savagely to him, 'You are disgusting.'

The Lord Chief Justice said, 'An appropriate moment for lunch, I think?' The court rose.

Downstairs, Gene said to his solicitor, the hurrying Mr O'Connor, 'That was awful.'

'You'll feel better when you hear your own side put.'

Gene did feel better; he said so, as he and Mr MacMahon parted company.

'I liked your – soberness,' he said.

Adrian MacMahon replied, 'I think I went on too long, but there was a lot to say. We'll have a fair idea how we're doing when we hear the judge's summing-up in the morning.'

The fact that one of the jurors had nodded off, or seemed to, during Mr MacMahon's summing-up did not seem to Gene a good omen. Nevertheless, the court had been presented clearly with the facts over and over again. First of all, Gene would have had to have judged accurately the height of General Knowles, and then stooped to adjust to it in order for the bullet to make the die-straight wound it did. Secondly, Gene had no record of any kind, nothing but reports of excellence in all he did. All his references, his employer, his employer's reports of how colleagues saw him: this was not some vagrant coward, not some vagabond man of death. Thirdly, most cast-iron of all, he was with a witness when the murder was committed, a witness who swore on oath, a God-fearing Protestant girl. Mr MacMahon told them they would be asking themselves what was Gene doing associating with IRA men? He was from the south, they would have sought him out, he spoke Gaelic. Should a man be condemned to death for speaking Gaelic?

Downstairs, when Gene had left, Mr MacMahon said to his junior, 'No bets on this one.'

As they drove away from the court, Gene asked, 'What is all that for?', indicating the intensive police activity on the street. As usual nobody in the police van answered.

Gene told Charlie the main points of the two summings-up, with emphasis on his own defence.

'And then he said that there was no doubt. He said I had never been in trouble of any kind, that I wouldn't know what General Knowles would look like if he walked up to me and shook hands.'

'How d'you feel?' asked Charlie Gilbert.

'Confused. And dog-tired.'

That night at seven o'clock, Nesbit Blackwood held a meeting in his office at Rufus Street. No Gordon, no Desmond, no Heck-wright: Nesbit sat alone at the head of the boardroom table, two men on his right, two on his left, all senior overseers including Bingham. Nesbit took an envelope from his pocket on the back of which he had written a number of details.

'This, men, will be the last check. "Retail is detail," my customers say, and even though Blackwoods isn't in the retail trade we still have to look to the detail.'

The men smiled as Nesbit smiled. 'Start with you, Mr Bingham. You're reasonably sure?'

'Aye, I am, sir. I went through my list again at home last night, sir. I made sure to see everyone. I was lucky, like. I knew my three, and knew them well, like, even though none of them was related to me.'

'And?'

'They was all very glad to get your good wishes, sir.' These men worshipped Nesbit Blackwood, even more than their fathers had worshipped his father: Nesbit made an easier idol; he mixed relaxedly, could stop and discuss pigeons, or football, or, his own great interest, health.

'There isn't a difficulty you see, then, in your lot, Mr Bingham?'

'No, sir, oh, no, sir; mind you, I think we'll get an approach for a job for his daughter from one of them, she's near leaving school.'

Nesbit looked benevolent and grave. 'And isn't that what Blackwoods are here for, Mr Bingham – to give people jobs?'

'Sir, them's the words I said, I said you'd say, "And isn't that what Blackwoods are here for – to give people jobs?" And they was glad to hear it, sir.'

Of each man Nesbit asked similar questions. Each of the four had been sent to visit homes, talk to three men. He had briefed them carefully, and in the briefing had never referred to the current civic duty in which each man they were visiting had become embroiled. Nesbit's instructions had been along these lines: 'I hear that man Agnew up in Clongall Street, I hear he's a very good man altogether. I know he's retired from the shipyards, but in this business you never know when you need someone. I wonder now, Mr Bingham, if you could find a way of telling Mr George Agnew that I have a high opinion of him.'

One by one, Nesbit had distributed the list – by neighbourhood rather than alphabetically: it could not have been as simple as giving Agnew, Cresswell and Harris to Mr Bingham; Hastings, Livermore and Luckman to John Cridemore; Medcalf, Orpen and Pattison to Alec Nairn; Rees, West and Wraight to Mr MacGuckian. When checking the jurors' addresses, Nesbit matched each overseer to three men living roughly within the overseer's area.

He brought the meeting to a close by telling the overseers how well they had performed in a difficult year for trading and told them they had the half-year's accounts confirmed that very morning.

'Each of you gentlemen will be finding something extra in his pay packet this coming week,' he said. 'I could not function at this mill without the staunchness of men like you. You're the kind of men beat the Kaiser.'

When the glowing men left, Nesbit made a telephone call.

'Nicholas? Nesbit Blackwood. How are you, Nicholas? I'm very well, very well indeed, well, I'm not, I have a touch of that old sinus thing and I have to keep out of certain areas here, but otherwise I'm fine. Yes, yes, I'm still working, what's that sign in Liptons, "The business on which the sun never sets". No, Valerie says that too. I never heard it myself, although it stands to reason, friar's balsam always works, if the sinuses go haywire altogether. And yourself? Good. Good. I can see that you're busy. Yes, yes, well, you'll be glad when that's over, yes, yes. No, I saw Ernest, what, a couple of weeks ago, we haven't spoken since, no, no. I gather he's in good form. Yes, yes.'

Clumsily manhandling a cigarette and match around the telephone, Nesbit lit up, and then said, 'Nicholas, it's not that but this, as they say. You may by now have heard. Yes, yes. That's right. And he seemed pleased? Good, well there's a lot of work to be done and whatever else he is Eric Heckwright is a capable man. Oh, yes. Yes. Yes. Yes, that's true. Anyway, the point is, that incident is now closed. No, not at all, not at all. No. Oh, no. Good, well, I'm glad. I'm glad. What? No. Definitely not. The only indication he ever gave in front of other people was he said in front of my brother Desmond and his unfortunate wife – yes, isn't she, I know, I know, but we must be broad-minded – Eric said in front of her and Gordon, my lad was there, Eric said that there was also "a VIP" there – but we managed to fudge that over. Not a soul. No, she doesn't; no, no, yes, she has a mouth as wide as the mouth of the River Lagan. No, no question. Pleasure. A pleasure. Nicholas, when you've this sorted, and of course I'll know from the papers – yes, definitely, definitely, it's been too long. Good man, good man. All right, then, Nicholas. Yes, yes. Good. Okay. Okay.'

Next morning, the Lord Chief Justice of Northern Ireland, Sir Nicholas Bowling, addressed the jury. The *Belfast Telegraph* reported it as 'One of the shortest-ever summing-up addresses by a judge in a murder trial'. It took ten minutes.

'Gentlemen of the jury, it is my intention, once you have reached your verdict and therefore discharged your duty, to render you exempt from jury service for the rest of your lives. Even if that were not my intention, it is my plain belief that never again in a jury room would you have so clear-cut a case to consider. The counsels for the Prosecution and the Defence have done their jobs admirably, and have laid the evidence out in front of us all so clearly that we can survey it and reach a decision. You have to decide whether the accused man, Eugene Patrick Comerford, fired the shot that killed Brigadier-General Knowles, or was implicated in a way that makes him as guilty as if he did fire the fatal shot.'

The judge did not direct them to ignore any part of the evidence, merely highlighted several aspects, notably the fact the accused himself had chosen not to give evidence, his right certainly; and whether the testimony of Belle MacKnight could be regarded as reliable. The accused's character had been the subject of testimony by a distinguished woman, wife of a magistrate. The jury would have to make up its mind, no matter how ungallant it felt, as to what was the reason for that woman testifying. Could the testimony be counted valid? When is character evidence useful, when is it invalid? Obviously a man going for a job will never offer a character reference from his own wife or girlfriend, and counsel for the Prosecution was at some pains to point this out. It goes without saying that character evidence is at its best when the witness does not have some sort of feelings for the person for whom he or she is testifying, that was the Prosecution's case.

He described the Defence case as short and to the point – and repeated the words. The ballistics people had ascertained beyond any doubt that the fatal bullet came from the rifle on which the accused's fingerprints had been found, nor had the Defence challenged the ballistics evidence. The Defence had challenged the fingerprinting evidence and with some success; but care must be taken when considering that challenge. Even though the Defence had ascertained that there were other fingerprints on the barrel of the gun, it never challenged the presence of the accused's fingerprints.

At seventeen minutes past ten o'clock the jury retired to consider their verdict, and the judge left the courtroom.

In the public gallery people stood, stretched, looked at their watches. An air-raid warning sounded and somebody remarked that it was the first they had heard during the entire fortnight of the trial: nobody made any attempt to leave, or to clear the building. The buzz of conversation mounted until the Clerk of the Court had to ask people to remember they were still in a courtroom. Mr Larkwood and Mr MacMahon, backs to each other, talked to their juniors; Mr O'Connor, leaning on the rail of the dock, asked Gene had he heard from Thomas Kane, the letter had never arrived? Unseen by Gene, the Governor of Crumlin Road sat at the back among court officials; Lennie MacKnight sat there too, hair gleaming with oil, a sad expression on his face.

Gene replied, 'I feel very sick in my stomach.'

Mr O'Connor said, 'Would you prefer to go downstairs?' Gene nodded and with the permission of the Clerk of the Court – who had to dive behind the scenes before he came back and said 'yes' – Gene was led out of the courtroom.

Below, they permitted him to sit on a chair outside the holding cell. He sat with his head against the wall, eyes closed, face white, blue-ish at the eyes.

At a quarter to twelve, the usher at the door to the jury room answered the knock from inside. His head and shoulders disappeared into the open doorway, obscuring him from all but the Clerk of the Court. He reappeared, and nodded to the Clerk of the Court, who sent an usher to fetch the judge. The word spread to the people ambling or talking or smoking in the hallways and corridors, and the courtroom filled with a rush. Gene was reintroduced. The jury-room usher held the door almost shut.

'All rise.'

The Lord Chief Justice swished in, and the legal representatives bowed; the Clerk of the Court nodded to the jury-room usher, who opened the door and beckoned; the jury filed back into their oaken corral. Eleven of them sat.

'The prisoner will rise.' Gene stood in the dock, hands behind his back, eyes fixed, bright terrified points of light, on the foreman of the jury, who stood.

'Gentlemen of the jury, have you reached your verdict?'

'We have.'

'Do you find the prisoner, Eugene Patrick Comerford, Guilty or Not Guilty?'

Somewhere a door slammed and people jumped at the sudden noise. The jury foreman, in a brown suit, raised his chin, and answered, 'Guilty.'

Some applause broke out, and moans; some cries of 'No, no,' answered by cries of 'Yes, yes.'

The judge called, 'Silence!' After a general muttering, everyone slowly froze.

The Clerk of the Court reached to the floor beside him and lifted a white, rectangular box. From it he took a black square, and handed it to the usher, who had sidled briskly along the bench to the Clerk's desk. The usher sidled back again, and climbed the steps to the pathway behind the judge's chair. He draped the black cloth over the judge's head and patted it diagonally into place on top of his abundant curling wig.

'Eugene Patrick Comerford. You have been found guilty by a jury of your peers of the charge of capital murder. There is only one penalty prescribed by law. You will be taken from here to a place of execution and you will be hanged by the neck until you are dead. May the Lord have mercy upon your immortal soul.'

In the outburst of noise and agitation, Mr O'Connor said, 'You can sit down now, sit down.'

'I can't, I'm not able to move,' said Gene, out of breath.

The barristers approached the bench to begin the legal argument for appeal. Warders held Gene under each arm and steered him from the dock. In the back of the van, the police who had driven Gene silently to and from the prison throughout the two weeks of his trial, now grinned at him and winked.

Malcolm dropped into Rufus Street to give Janice the news. Sent for, she met him in the entrance hallway, and they stepped outside.

'What's up? Where's the ghost you met?'

'I'm after coming from the court. Your man's guilty.' Malcolm cut his hand-edge across his throat.

371

She began to clap her hands with delight, and he caught them. 'Hold on, Janice.'

'But that's great, Malkie, that bastard, and what he did to our Belle.'

'No, Janice, listen. If he swings – you know what, don't you?'

'What are you saying?'

'You know what I'm saying.'

She looked at him. 'Come on, Malkie. What are you saying?!'

'An eye for an eye, Janice.'

'That they'll hang Belle?'

'That's the talk, Janice. You see why. The Roman Catholic bishops is expected to make a statement. That's why I called to tell you as quick as I could. So's the girls and you in there, so's you don't all go cheering or that, so's things don't get inflamed.'

'What am I going to do now? Go in there and tell them not to smile in case Belle gets hammered for our being glad a murderer is going to swing? Jesus, Malcolm, where's that fair?' She pushed back her turban-headscarf and said, 'Come on, Malkie, tell me where's that fair?'

'Janice, fair's nowhere near this. Now what I'm going to tell you now you have to keep shut inside you. I'm only telling you so's you understand.' He rubbed his nose with the back of his hand. 'Your man, Belle's fella, the Taig, he never done it. And they all know down the station. He only handled the gun 'cause somebody tricked him into handling it at a meeting. Belle was telling the truth. He never done it, they know who done it.'

'And why – ?'

''Cause your man that done it's away down south. And the IRA's not going to say a word. 'Cause if your boy here is hung, they'll come out and say, "See – there's no such thing here as justice." That's what's going on.'

'Jesus, Malkie.' Janice started to whimper. 'Belle. Belle. Our own Belle. They'll not, will they? They'll not?'

'Sit you down there,' said Charlie Gilbert very quietly. 'Here, take off them shoes, your feet must be tired, all that standing.'

On the Governor's orders, they gave Gene a sleeping draught that night, the only one he would receive. When the watch changed in the morning, Headcase looked in and saw Gene

372

sleeping peacefully. He opened the door and shook him, waking
Gene up an hour before it was necessary – and later said he had
made a mistake. At eleven o'clock, the Governor came to the
cell.

'I have had a call from Mr O'Connor. He wants to come and
see you. Naturally enough there is an appeal being lodged.'

Gene said, 'Yes.'

'How are you feeling?' asked the Governor.

'I don't know.' He sat up. 'When I woke up I knew I had been
dreaming. And then I knew I hadn't.' He drew a deep breath that
was like a gasp. 'Will they really do that, what he said, "to a place
of execution"? Will they actually do that?'

The Governor said, 'You must be prepared for anything.'

'What place? Where would it be – ?'

'Here. Inside this prison.' The Governor sat beside Gene on the
bed, not touching him. 'If there is any comfort I can give you –
say so.'

Gene dropped his head to his hands, never said a word.

'Terrible trouble in parts of the city, if that's any comfort to
you,' said the Governor. 'Fires. And riots. A lot of people believe
you're innocent.'

'So do I,' said Gene.

'What about visitors now?' asked the Governor.

'I don't know.'

'What about the visitor from "inside"? It is very much against
regulations – but then a lot of things are.'

Gene nodded.

The Governor said, 'You have to have warders here all the time
now. That's the rule. Three shifts. Six to two. Two to ten. Ten to
six overnight. There's games – draughts, Ludo, dominoes. We
have a pack of cards. This door. There will be extra people on it
now, that's the way the rules are. But I'll give an order that the
key will not ever be turned in the lock, don't pretend you know,
and when you have visitors, the warders will have instructions to
move out of earshot. I'll arrange that visitor for you now.' He rose.
'My wife would like to come and see you. Is that all right?'

Gene had not moved; he sat upright, inert. When Belle came in,
she walked over, sat beside him and stretched one long arm along

his shoulders. They sat there for several minutes, not saying a word. Gene looked down, began to pick at a nep of thread on the prison blanket. Charlie Gilbert read a book in the corridor.

'The other day,' he began eventually.

'Shhhhh.'

He turned his face up, and closed his eyes, and tears slid down from under his eyelashes. 'No, the other day, I want to say this, when you came into the exercise yard. What I wanted to say was, d'you remember I said there was something I wanted to say? What I wanted to say was – and I didn't know how to say it. I was planning to get you away with me. I had tickets enquired about. I knew how fond of you I was.'

Belle said, 'I know. I knew. I didn't know then, but I did afterwards. I mean about the fond, I didn't know about the tickets.'

'The ticket agent, he has a brother, a policeman –' Gene began to wheeze. 'That's how they –'

'Yes. Shhhhh.'

He said in desperation, 'But we both told the truth.'

'I know. My turn's up next.'

'Oh God. Oh. God. I know. Are you afraid?'

'Desperate,' said Belle. She clenched her teeth, drew her lips back in a rictus.

The fires smouldered all morning in west Belfast; one linen warehouse which had once belonged to the Blackwoods; a lock-up premises thought (mistakenly) to belong to a relative of a jury member; the smaller Bairds carpet showroom; one small office block – gutted, it was claimed later, to destroy the records of a debt-collecting firm.

Judy Cruiseman telephoned Rufus Street.

'Is it true, Nesbit? You know we have no newspapers down here and our wireless has broken. Is it true?'

'There will be an appeal, Judy.'

'Bother the appeal. Chappie had to sit there and listen to that. Hee-hee!'

'Judy, I have to go, I'm starting a meeting.'

'You mustn't relax now, Nesbit.'

=

374

Gene fell ill two days later. Mr O'Connor was the first to notice when he came to brief Gene about the appeal.

'They want us ready in about ten days, we're trying to stall for time.'

'Don't stall, get it going as quick as you can.' Gene sighed.

'Are you sickening for something? You are. You've to watch your health now, this is a time you could get very sick.'

'What matter would it be?' asked Gene.

'Oh, now, oh now! Don't let me hear you talking like that. While there's life there's hope.'

'How many times have you had to say that?' asked Gene unbitterly.

Mr O'Connor busied himself with the briefcase. 'All the same, you have to be fit and well to fight them.'

By nightfall Gene had a high temperature, and the prison doctor wondered if he should be moved to an outside hospital.

'Problem there too,' murmured the Governor in a low voice outside the cell. 'Same problem as the sick bay here, it's full of quite hard men at the minute.'

'Keep him here, then,' said the doctor, 'but I'm going to have to see him every day to begin with.'

21

No minutes of meetings, no notes of interviews, no records of conversations: if you go looking today, in Belfast's archives or in London's, you will find no trace of any of the myriad discussions that took place in that four weeks. 'Balance' became the key word: 'Balance'. The Civil Servant later told the whole story to his daughter, and with his ordered mind set it out chronologically:

> The Comerford trial ended on Monday, 4 February.
> After notice, an appeal was lodged on Wednesday, 6 February.
> Hearing date for appeal set for Monday, 18 February: after strenuous objections from the Defence – 'unseemly speed', Mr MacMahon called it – this was put back to Monday, 25 February. Pending the failure of appeal an execution date was set for Monday, 18 March.

To the Civil Servant fell the responsibility of organising the date for the trial of Belle MacKnight, the second of what the newspapers had called The *Gone with the Wind* Trials. He chose Monday, 4 March, reasoning successfully to his superiors that if the trial opened any sooner, it would interact unsatisfactorily and confusingly with the Comerford Appeal.

Next, the Civil Servant persuaded the Home Secretary for Northern Ireland to meet the small delegation of Roman Catholic bishops and senior clergy. On the appointed day, the Home Secretary declared food poisoning, and a Home Office Minister took the meeting. The reverend gentlemen put their case forthrightly. They could not guarantee to have any further influence with the mainstream, non-IRA Catholic community if a Catholic generally believed to be innocent, and known to have no IRA connections, were hanged. The Minister made an insensitive remark, when he said, 'Are there such people as non-IRA Catholics?' The clergy, observing the flurry of Civil Service notes passed to the Minister, chose to observe yet ignore his discomfiture, a Vatican-taught ploy. Indeed, they went on, Thomas Williams, hanged last July for the killing of that unfortunate policeman, was later found to have been less guilty than charged.

Then they put the hypothesis on every lip: supposing Eugene Comerford, innocent, well, a matter of opinion, but certainly never seen firing a shot, ever, anywhere, supposing he is hanged, and this MacKnight girl, actually seen by hundreds doing the deed, is not hanged and it was a Catholic she killed – what then?

The Minister had the good grace to assume a grave expression. 'Then, gentlemen, I see your problem. And you see ours. Imagine Mr De Valera's words.'

'Not to mention,' they said to him, 'the Vatican and the Americans.'

'No, not to mention them indeed.'

The Civil Servant insisted that meetings took place between the Home Secretary and the Lord Chief Justice and Mr Ernest Larkwood, who later became Attorney-General for Northern Ireland. Not that they could be called meetings, of course. They met for lunch, 'as it happened', and they talked of many things.

Did they talk of 'Balance'? During that short, wild period, the Civil Servant murmured many times, 'Minister, there is of course the matter of "Balance" between the two communities'; or, 'Home Secretary, I feel certain the Chief Constable will want to talk to you about "Balance"'; and with the Chief Constable discussed the need for 'Balance'. The Chief Constable, a pragmatic man, whom many felt too weak for the job, said, 'If we have a second death sentence, Kenneth, then we must have two commutations.'

'Yes,' agreed the Civil Servant, 'both sides of the scale absolutely balanced.'

'Aha, but which scale? Blind Justice?'

As the Civil Servant said to his daughter, 'I bit my tongue, Diana, but I should have spoken the words in my mouth – "No. Not blind justice. Blind prejudice."'

The Chief Constable helped the Civil Servant work out the ideal schedule of developments.

'Given the ferocious independence of the Lord Chief Justice – he has now, finally, insisted on taking the second trial, no joy along that route, Kenneth. And Larkwood's instructions – he's also to seek the maximum penalty in the MacKnight trial.' They stopped and pondered.

'Therefore, Kenneth,' said the Chief Constable, 'we have two hangings facing us. Now, what's the logic to be?'

'The logic is – it stays at two death sentences – only. Let's not talk of hangings, just yet. If I know Nicholas Bowling, I cannot see the MacKnight trial producing anything other than a death sentence. Look – you have reams of statements from witnesses who actually saw the girl doing the stabbing. So, Guilty – and sentence of death. Therefore, we have a draw, so to speak. Therefore, there will almost certainly be a commutation in the girl's case, and if there is a commutation in the girl's case, there will have to be a commutation in the Comerford case. Good result – especially as almost everybody in the province, with the exception of the hardest hardliners, believes the bloke is innocent.'

A skein of ducks flew low over the Botanic Gardens as the men's breaths puffed smoke signals in the frosty air.

'Yes,' said the Chief Constable, 'yes – and a commutation robs the IRA of their propaganda. There is only one thing that worries me and that is the timescale.' He stopped walking and the Civil Servant stopped with him.

'Suppose,' said the Chief Constable, 'the Comerford Appeal fails?'

'As it almost certainly will,' interposed the Civil Servant.

'And supposing the MacKnight trial has not ended by the time of the execution date?'

'Yes,' said the Civil Servant. 'I've been worried about that too. Unfortunately, the timescale has gone to the courts now.'

'No.' The Chief Constable shook his head. 'The MacKnight trial is very short. Open-and-shut if ever there was.' He paused. 'One last scenario, Kenneth – the danger that both will hang? I will have hell on my hands. I will lose more than one or two men on the streets.'

'No. That, oddly enough, worries me least. They will not hang a woman and they'll certainly not hang a Protestant woman.'

The Chief Constable said, 'You see, that is where I disagree with you. I told you before – I know some of those boys up in Stormont better than you. And have you seen the girl? She is pretty – and she's buxom.'

'There is another problem,' said the Civil Servant. 'If the girl hangs, Nesbit Blackwood says he will not be able to control the workforce in Rufus Street. And if that happens we're playing dominoes. If they riot, will Blackwoods be burnt? If Blackwoods is burnt that workforce is on the loose and resentful. There will be Protestant arrests and no end to the hoo-ha.'

'Oh, Christ,' said the Chief Constable. 'This bloody place.'

Gene developed an influenza that grew bronchial. The prison nursing staff prepared poultices for his chest, and kept bathing his forehead and torso with tepid water to get his temperature down. Charlie Gilbert fussed like an anxious parent. Headcase, however, furtively dampened the sheets and pillow with the coldest water he could get and then said, 'The prisoner was sweating awful hard in the night.' On the fourth day the doctor sent one of the other warders for the Governor, who peered down at Gene.

'Yes, even I can see that. Not good. Not at all.'

He and the doctor repaired to the corridor.

'What I need,' said the doctor, 'and I don't mind trying it, I'm sure the patient would be agreeable, is the penicillin.'

'Well, I'll ask,' said the Governor. 'We've never been allowed it before. In fact since it came in, we haven't had it once here. But I'll ask.'

When the official reply came back that afternoon – 'We haven't got enough for soldiers much less a convicted murderer' – the doctor said, 'Tell him.'

'What?'

'Tell him. Tell the patient.'

'Why?'

'Tell him they want him to be convenient for them.'

'Oh,' said the Governor, 'I see.'

He walked over and bent down. 'Mr Comerford. You won't like this. My masters won't let me have the medicine the doctor says will make you better. I think they're hoping you will make things easy for them. Do you mind my saying that?'

Gene, bleary, smiled, teeth coated. 'Dth, dth. Whuw.' He blew a small breath. 'No. They'd like that . . .'

=

379

The Governor's wife took over the nursing. In her loud voice, she ordered the warders to hang blankets either side of the high window where crevices in the wall had sent stilettos of icy air straight into Gene's sleeping eyes, making them bloodshot and sore. She requisitioned two extra chairs, one soft and comfortable, 'for when you're sitting up again'. She spoke to him all the time, unheeding of whether he replied. Soon he got the hang of her, and stopped making the effort to answer everything.

'You know we'll be sacked if this ever gets out, we have now broken I think it is eleven rules of things like fraternisation with a prisoner, allowing another prisoner to fraternise, allowing a prisoner of the opposite sex to fraternise, exceeding the prison supplies to give a prisoner favoured treatment, favouring a prisoner; my husband looked them up last night, that is just what he's like but I was an army nurse in the last war, that's what made me as hard as nails, dried up my tear ducts by the way, and I don't care much for their regulations, and I broke every rule in the book in those days; if a young soldier was dying d'you think I'd stick to regulations and deny him a little bit of comfort, I would do no such of a thing, the things I've seen, and that is how I met my husband, through breaking rules; he pretends to keep every rule meticulously and when he's making his reports every week he always refers to the rules but underneath it all he's a man who loves to break the rules, that's why him and me get on so well together, I'm here now in your life and here I stay one way or the other; I think it is dreadful what's going on, I could tell by looking at you that you haven't an ounce of bad in you, in fact if you have any bad in you, the bad is that you can't take a good decision on your own behalf, although that might not be true now that I think of it, and what's more if you get out of here and I hope and pray you will, you must marry that girl the two of you were made for each other take her off to Canada or New Zealand or America the southern Irish do well in America my family's all from County Longford we even hid men on the run in 1920 that is of course if she gets out as well, yes Canada, I'd say, and if the war ends soon it could change everything in all our lives. Now – how are you feeling?'

The regulations inside Crumlin Road prison had become a tense and complex matter. Wartime internment inflated the prison population to a point the Governor considered dangerous. He complained repeatedly, without a note of complaint in his voice. Two inspections took place in the winter–spring of 1942–3.

One Member of Parliament raised the question of 'the province's most famous inmates', and asked could he see where they were being held.

The Governor shook his head. 'I will show their separate cells to you on a map, but I'll not take you there.'

'Why not?'

'Perhaps Mr Lewis here doesn't feel he's running a zoo, John,' said a fellow MP.

The enquiring Member replied, 'I heard a rumour, it's supposed to come from a constituent of mine who works here, although I haven't spoken to the man myself, that these two prisoners were allowed to meet. And frequently.'

The Governor said, 'Will you allow me to answer that question after you've viewed the prison in general? We're a little behind time.'

The party set out; the Governor showed the MPs the inadequate and filthy sanitation; the cave-like, reeking damp on the walls; the wire edges of the window grilles on which prisoners sawed their wrists; the dark patch on a corridor wall where two convicted IRA prisoners had hammered out a warder's brains the previous year while trying to take the man's keys from him; the corner of the balcony where three months earlier a prisoner had prised the wire netting apart, and dived head-first to his death.

A cell had been cleared of inmates, to allow the party of six to visit. They entered and stood.

'God, this is claustrophobic,' said one.

'Count the bunks, gentlemen,' invited the Governor.

They counted – seven.

'You mean,' asked the MP who had asked about Gene and Belle, 'that seven people sleep in this cell?'

'They don't *sleep* here, they *live* here,' said the Governor.

Back in his office, he addressed the Member for Belfast East.

'Now you were asking about my allowing prisoners to meet each other? I have to make all kinds of judgements every day. What was it you wanted to know?'

The man said, 'I didn't realise that running a prison was such a difficult job.'

The Governor told his wife that evening, 'I feel a little freer in some aspects of the daily tread. Why don't we work out a timetable?'

Initially, therefore, Belle came to see Gene every evening at six o'clock. Usually he had been asleep for an hour or so before she arrived. The first day, Headcase turned Belle and Jeannie away; 'The Boss says he's to have no visitors the day.'

Neither woman questioned – but the Governor did. He sent for Headcase and asked him one question, 'Who is your Member for Parliament?'

Headcase blushed and said he did not know.

Next day Charlie Gilbert nodded Belle through and sat to talk with Jeannie in the corridor.

'You're very pale.' Belle felt his forehead. 'You're as hot as hell.' She pulled the chair forward where he could see her clearly.

'I've no news, much, I'm afraid; they're going to tell me tomorrow when I'm up. They think the fourth of next month; it can't be much later than that. My mother came in. She baked me a lovely currant cake, and somebody took it, 'tis gone out of my cell, otherwise I'd have brought you a piece. Does your mother and father know you're sick?' Belle smiled a little and said, 'Did you hear that the newspapers said I was like Vivien Leigh?'

He smiled as much as he could. 'You're better than her.'

'I've no green eyes, but.'

He put out a hand along the grey prison coverlet. Belle took it. Gene closed his eyes and dozed. When he opened them she was still sitting there.

'Were you dreaming?' she asked.

'No, I don't think so.'

'I was remembering the day you took off your shirt. D'you remember? Down in Armagh. I pegged it out on a branch, as if the oul' tree was a clothesline.'

He smiled.

'D'you know that was the nicest day I ever had in my whole life?' said Belle.

'I never knew I'd like someone as much,' said Gene.

Belle stroked the back of his hand. 'Them pyjamas in here is terrible,' she said.

'All the clothes are.'

She said, tentatively, 'Do you know that you're entitled to ask for your own clothes. I mean – you couldn't before, but you could now?'

He brightened.

The commotion at the door meant the Governor's wife had arrived.

'How's the patient? No. Put that hand back where it was,' she bossed, when she saw Belle withdraw her hand from Gene. 'Touch is the most important part of healing.'

'He'd like his own clothes,' said Belle.

'What a good idea,' said the Governor's wife. 'What a good idea.'

That night, Charlie Gilbert, who volunteered, called to Mrs MacCartan for Gene's clothes, to be told by the woman, embarrassed but stone-faced, that she had given them all away.

Gene did not recover in time to attend his own Appeal, although by the end of that week he was up and sitting, and walking up and down his cell very slowly. With any warder except Headcase on duty, he also walked in and out of the cell into the corridor. The architecture of that corner – an angle turned blind at the end of a long corridor – made his situation comfortably remote, so long as nobody occupied the other two cells. Nobody would – but Gene did not know that and did not know why. He found out while attempting to make conversation with Headcase one day.

To try and break down the man's hostility, he made an observation on the position of the cell.

'You'd have to know this cell was here in order to find it,' Gene said.

'Aye, that's why 'tis the condemned cell.'

'Condemned? You mean this part of the building is unsafe?'

'Cop on, didn't you get the smell? Everyone in this cell spends most of their time boking.'

'What's "boking"?'

'Puke. Throwing up. Vomiting.'

'Why?'

'The condemned cell. The "Top Hat" they calls it as well. You're only put in here when you're going to be topped. That's why the window in the door is so big, so's the man in the brown coat can guess your weight without having to shake hands with you.'

'But – I was here since the day I was arrested?'

'Course you were, course you were.'

The Governor's wife told her husband that night, 'Mr Comerford's had his first attack of nausea.'

Mr MacMahon, in his opening ploy, said, 'My client is rather ill, m'Lord. He certainly can't be here and therefore I wish to apply for an adjournment. I have asked the doctor to write out in detail what exactly is the matter.'

The Appeal Judge said, 'Were you going to call him?'

'Yes, m'Lord.'

'New evidence?'

'Not materially, m'Lord, but he did not testify before, so in that sense it will be new evidence, yes.'

'But Mr MacMahon, forgive me – he did not testify before because he chose not to.'

'That is so, m'Lord.'

'And now he chooses to. But will he be saying anything that your case has not already said?'

Mr MacMahon paused, then answered slowly, 'No-o, m'Lord, but his presentation of his own evidence is, I think, important.'

'Mr MacMahon, I have to disagree with you. If it were that important you would have called him. You're saying that his change of mind, or indeed your change of mind on his behalf, makes a material difference to the evidence on which this case was decided?'

'Well, yes, m'Lord.'

'I'm prepared to listen if you can cite.'

'Unfortunately I am not aware of a precedent, m'Lord.'

'H'mm.' The judge rubbed his chin. 'This is, as we all know, a most important case, with already civil unrest. Therefore I am bound to take your proposal very seriously indeed. And even though I do not like adjourning, what – ?' – he looked at his watch – 'fifteen minutes after we have started, I feel I must. A ruling on this after lunch.'

This, and every ruling of the Appeal, went against Mr

MacMahon. On Friday afternoon, the Appeal was denied, and the date of execution was set for Tuesday, 19 March at seven o'clock in the morning. The Civil Servant's calculations had been a day out; feverish lobbying for a reprieve or commutation began.

That night, Edith and Lennie sat at their kitchen table. The outcome of the Appeal had come down in time for the latest editions, and Lennie had bought a copy on the way home. They propped the paper where both could see it.

'What d'you think's going to happen now, Leonard?'

'I don't know, Mam, I'll have to ask Malcolm.'

'I don't know if I'm ever going to get tireder than this.'

Lennie said, 'What's Belle going to say?'

'Oh, God, you reminded me. She asked for your Da's old jumper, the one that was new and he died. Her place's awful cold.'

Lennie said, 'I'm cold every night in my bed these nights.'

'That's nothing to do with being cold, Leonard, all this is what's making us cold.'

They ate in silence for some minutes. Then Lennie came forth with one of his bursts.

'Mam, what's going to happen to us? Here's me, and I'm amazing myself, for I don't want to see your boy swing, he's a working-man like myself and if we wasn't taught to hate him, and if his crowd wasn't taught to kill us –' He shut up abruptly, having run out of words.

'Your father used to say, we was kept at each other's necks, so's the politicians could get on with making their money, but I always told him to shush himself, 'cause that talk's going to do nothing but trouble. I'm thinking of Belle tonight, she likes him, Leonard, she likes him, and look what's going to happen to him.'

'We should go away out of here, Mam, we should go off to Canada or something.'

'We've no money – though Jed and Sandra's going.'

'No!?'

'They came in this morning. He's that upset about Belle he can't go and visit her.'

Gene recovered slowly. The Appeal decision did not bring the setback the doctor had feared, and he formed the view, which he voiced to the Governor, that Gene must be experiencing some kind of resignation. The Governor accepted the opinion without comment.

Gene played cards with Eustace, the other warder, but not with Headcase. Father Egan called every day.

One morning, he said to Gene, 'Will we say the Litany again?'

Gene wrapped his arms around himself tight and muttered with a gasp, 'I forget the words.' Father Egan caught him as he fell forward: it took an hour for Gene to stand upright again.

Next afternoon, Belle, sitting by Gene, opened the brown-paper parcel.

'Look. This was my father's, it'll keep you warm.' They fought it on over his head. 'And it fits you.'

'Big.' Gene fingered the sleeves.

'He was. And a bit fat.'

Gene said, 'Terrible what happened to him.'

Belle remarked, 'I could never forgive my mother for never telling me.'

'I suppose she wanted to – save you the pain.'

'Aye, but the Governor's wife, she said the right thing, she said I was as entitled to feel pain as to feel happiness.'

'When did she say that?'

'We're having these what she calls "talks to each other", we had two of them, I'm having another after I walk out of here in half an hour. She's awful nice. You know her brother's the minister my Mam's friends with, and she's not a bit like him, he's a long drink of water.'

'She's very bony,' said Gene.

'And God, isn't her voice loud,' said Belle. 'And she talks all the time.'

'Tell her *Gone with the Wind*.' Gene smiled. 'That'll keep her quiet.'

Belle smiled too. 'I never thought of that until this minute,' she said.

'Do you, are you, telling them over – over with the women?'

'No.' Belle smiled sadly. 'I don't think I'll ever do that again.'

'Don't be rueful,' he said.

'"Rueful". That's a nice word. Where did you get it?'

Gene said, 'I found it in a book.'

'What does it mean?'

'It means, being sad in your regret. Doleful.'

'What book was it in?'

Gene said, 'It was called *The Water Babies*. It said, "And they looked very rueful."'

'Do we look "rueful"?' Belle asked. 'I was thinking the other day – I'm beginning to feel like a child again.'

Belle then fell silent. For minutes neither spoke; in the corridor outside they could hear Charlie Gilbert coughing again. Off somewhere else, a door clanked and clanged.

'Gene?'

'Yes?'

'Should we be talking about – ?'

'About what?'

'About – what's going to happen?'

'Not yet.'

Belle laid her head on his shoulder, so that her eyelashes brushed his neck.

After some silent minutes, they kissed, as tender and clumsy as children, and Belle sat up and said with a touch of forced impishness, 'I'm off to my talk.'

'I'll count every minute until I see you again,' said Gene, 'and I mean that.'

'Do you like porridge?' she asked.

'No. I hate it. Why?'

'Good, I was never any use at making it, all lumps,' Belle said. She waved from the door.

The couple's meetings became the means by which each avoided lapsing into catatonic silence. Belle had associated so little with the other female prisoners that she might as well have been in solitary confinement. She spent long periods looking at the wall, sometimes in tears, sometimes with eyes shut. Any work she was asked to do was performed efficiently and quickly but without communication. She walked carefully, now, the hippy, sexy swing had gone from her step, and she walked with her feet pointing straight ahead. Since Gene's sentence, nobody from Rufus Street had come to visit her.

Gene, now moving about his cell but medically not yet allowed outdoors into the exercise yard, had tried to give himself a routine; without a watch, he measured periods of the day by small chores. Exercise – a hundred gentle arm-lifts; food – eaten in a rhythm of chewing. He shaved elaborately, counting the strokes of the razor and trying to complete the exercise in fewer than thirty strokes each morning: he had managed a record of twenty-two. Shaving proved the most difficult emotionally: every time he touched his Adam's apple, he flinched, and often had to squeeze his eyes tight to stop tears.

The Governor's wife said, 'The last time you were here, you were talking about your friends at the mill.'

'They all say they like me – but they're the ones convinced me that she, that girl . . .' Belle stopped.

'She,' interjected the Governor's wife. 'What was her name?'

Belle shook her head.

'We will come back to that,' said the Governor's wife. 'Do you think your friends were fond of you?'

'I don't know. If they were they'd have been glad to see me happy.'

Mrs Lewis smiled. 'What makes you think people like seeing other people happy?'

Belle said, 'In the pictures, people are always – always, well.'

'Always what?'

'I was going to say,' Belle raised her head, 'that they're always nice to each other.'

'But they're not?' said the Governor's wife.

'But they're not,' agreed Belle.

'But you might be. I mean – you might be nice to everyone. Has that occurred to you?'

Belle said, 'I am now so mixed up inside myself that I don't know.'

Mrs Lewis said, 'You know you have a big ordeal ahead of you?'

'I do.'

'We have to prepare for that, don't we?'

'What can I do? Them solicitors that come in to see me, I know they're supposed to be for my side, but they frighten me.'

Step by step, Martha Lewis coached Belle in how to behave in court. She showed her a way of sitting with her head held untiringly high; a composed way of holding her hands in her lap, out of sight beneath the rail of the dock; they discussed whether Belle should wear lipstick, and Martha Lewis decided against it. Above all she instructed Belle to answer every question clearly and truthfully.

'That way is the only way you will be able to feel any comfort when you come back here every evening.'

Belle said, 'For years if anyone said anything to me, I used to feel my face go all sore. That's coming back now.'

The Governor's wife said, 'When I was Martha MacCreagh, before I became Martha Lewis, I used to think men looked away from me when they saw my face. And I thought as well that I had a smell off me or something.'

Nesbit closed the small suitcase that contained his trowel and apron; other Lodge members yawned.

Peter Derrymore said to him in a stage whisper, 'This must be the most boring way of giving money away that I have ever heard of.'

Nesbit smiled. 'That's only on account of Donald's chairing. Donald is the only man I know who can fall asleep during his own speeches. Oh, will you excuse me, Peter, there's a man I want to catch. Ernest!' he called.

Ernest Larkwood turned and grinned. He shook Nesbit's hand.

'What is it they say, "You did bravely," Ernest.'

The men smiled at each other.

Ernest Larkwood said, 'It wasn't difficult. Jesus Christ would not have got past that jury.'

'Well – well done anyway,' said Nesbit.

'Now the real fun starts,' said Ernest. 'You know I'm doing the MacKnight trial?'

'Speed is the thing apparently,' said Nesbit, 'if it can be finished in time for a verdict by the date for our friend.'

'Yes. Two commutations, I believe?' said Ernest Larkwood. 'It seems okay.'

'So – nothing to be done, then?' asked Nesbit.

'No.'

22

Belle's trial began with advance warning of procedural difficulties – forty of the mill-women wished to give evidence for the Defence, who had taken statements from them all. But the same women had given statements to the police, and the Prosecution wished to call them as witnesses. The women themselves had no interest whatsoever in the legal niceties: they had determined to appear in court and since Christmas they had worked like dervishes on their outfits.

Enid Mulcaghey, who actually cut and tailored a new coat for herself of navy barathea that she got in the Co-Op, which often had better material than clothes, broke the news.

'D'you hear what?!' They gathered. 'D'you remember them statements we gave to the polis? They want us to go into court and back them up – but against Belle.'

All railed furiously.

'I told him he could fuck off, he was a real young fella and he didn't know what to say. I told him I wasn't going to say a word against my friend Belle, and who the fuck did he think's leg he was pulling, and the other one with a big fucking bell on it dingdong? Eh?'

Four constables reported identically to their superiors, who reported it to the Prosecution office. The Chief Constable roared with laughter.

'Now what? I wouldn't take them on. They're the ones should be let loose against Hitler.'

Ernest Larkwood smiled broadly with him. 'Poor Mr Jameson said he would issue subpoenas against them all. And then he was told that they said they would all go to jail, because if they were forced to go into court and speak against their friend they'd just stand there with their faces closed.'

The Chief Constable laughed again. 'Has nobody explained to

them the nuances of Examination and Cross-Examination?'

'Mr Jameson,' Ernest Larkwood chortled, 'it seems got one of them in, a woman called Byers, and she told him that she wasn't going into the witness box to say anything bad about her friend. He asked her, "But didn't you see it happening, weren't you right there at the time?", and she said to him that was none of his effing business.'

The Chief Constable laughed again. 'Now what?'

'You may well ask. The things I do for you. We're going to let them appear for the Defence and then I'll cross-examine. A prosecutor's life! Who'd have it?'

'And what colour socks are you going to wear?'

Ernest Larkwood said, 'I wish I had some of those women's vocabulary.'

On Sunday evening, Gene said to Belle, 'I wish I could go with you tomorrow.'

Belle said, after some moments, 'Have you any news?'

In recent days, Gene had cared less about showing his dismay. 'No. Just – petitions. For reprieve, and all that. There's over a hundred petitions.'

Belle said, 'If they didn't believe me about you, then I've no chance at all.'

He grabbed her hand so tightly it hurt.

'They can't, I mean. There's a natural thing, fairness, and that.'

Belle said, 'My father used to say, my Mam was reminding me, I think she meant it well, my father used to say, "Fairness emigrated from here years ago."'

Next morning, Nesbit Blackwood telephoned his wife.

'You would not believe it. The Long Room is nearly empty, there's only about twenty women in there. It is like a morgue. God, this is irritating! Is this going to go on while this trial lasts?'

Sir Nicholas Bowling, the Lord Chief Justice of Northern Ireland, looked astounded.

'Is this a circus I'm presiding over? If there is even as much as a voice raised where it should not be, this case will be conducted with an empty public gallery.'

There had been wild cries, of 'Hallo, Belle'; and 'Belle, look, it's me'; and 'What about ye, Belle'; and 'Belle, look, it's me'; and 'Hey, Belle, we're all here'. Long Room women, not asked to testify, overwhelmed the courtroom.

The Prosecution and the Defence had arranged a preliminary meeting the previous Thursday and agreed on the following witnesses for the Defence: Acheson, Anne; Byers, Anne; Craig, Gloria; Gillespie, Janice; MacKechnie, Alice; Millar, Edith; Mitchison, Jane; Mulcaghey, Enid; Stevenson, Anne.

'Nine,' said Ernest Larkwood, 'will nine be enough for you? Are you calling the lady herself?'

'Oh, yes. And keep your sarcasm for the courtroom, Ernest,' said John Rudden, KC.

'I'm going first,' said Alice MacKechnie to John Rudden, 'I don't care about the alphabet, 'twas never any use to me.' He had packed the women into the small meeting-room off the entrance hall.

'We're only trying to do it in an orderly fashion,' he protested.

'We'll be orderly,' said Janice, 'but Alice has the most experience of court.'

'Aye, my young fella, he's up in court twice already, and up again next month, and I do have to talk for him, 'cause he has a stutter, so I know the procedure, like, so I'll go first. He's my second, he was awful sick when he was born, we thought he was going to die,' she told John Rudden.

They agreed an order of appearance – rather, the women told John Rudden the order in which they wanted to appear. Various factors shaped it – for example, Janie Mitchison not wanting the sun in her eyes and what time would the sun be shining in, and Anne Stevenson saying, 'She only wants us to see the new dye in her hair' – to much laughter.

As they left the room, John Rudden grinned to his junior, 'I cannot wait – I cannot wait – to see Ernest dealing with this lot.'

Belle, as instructed, pleaded 'Not Guilty'. The police, pathology and forensics took from Monday morning until Tuesday mid-afternoon. The Lord Chief Justice adjourned slightly early, with a mild complaint to the two barristers that it was going too slowly. Next morning, Bingham, the overseer, with his glossy, black, narrow sideburns, gave the factual evidence for the Prosecution; a woman muttered aloud, 'We'll not forget this for you, you bastard.'

Others remarked, 'D'you notice no Blackwoods is here?'

Bingham described what he saw happening, what he found when he pushed through the crowd. Ernest Larkwood took him patiently through any possible doubt that Belle MacKnight might have committed the killing, and Bingham pointed out that the murder weapon still hung from Belle MacKnight's waist on a string when he reached her: he identified it as the weapon now exhibited in court.

John Rudden's brief cross-examination dealt entirely with Bingham's reaction when he got to the actual scene. Did he think Belle looked calm and deliberate? Did he think she looked wild and distraught? Was she the woman he normally saw at work? Or had she taken leave of her senses? All the time the unofficial jury, that is the tribe of women sitting all together in the public gallery, nodded in agreement or shook their heads or gave as large a flounce as they dared, or spoke none too *sotto voce*. With pathologist's and other evidence, the first day passed.

Belle found Gene in a considerable emotional state the evening of the first day of her trial. She hugged him.

'No, no. Easy. Go easy on yourself. Here, come here with your head.'

He allowed her to hold his head on her shoulder and she negotiated a sitting-down on the edge of the prison bed.

'What's up?'

Gene did one of his gasps for air, then straightened up and ran a huge hand through his hair.

'Two weeks tomorrow – is my last dawn,' he said, 'this day fortnight will be the Monday before the nineteenth of March.' He began to slap his face and she grabbed his hands.

'No, no, hold on, no. Don't be hitting yourself.'

He dropped his head to her shoulder again and she rocked him back and forth.

'This is what my father used to do to me if I fell,' said Belle.

'My mother to me, too,' he said. 'Belle, I'm finding it hard even to write a letter.'

He did not tell her that Headcase had come into the cell and, pointing to Gene's fountain pen, said, 'Can I have that eventually? As a souvenir? I have souvenirs from them all. I got your man Williams's rosary-beads. And me a Presbyterian?' He laughed. 'They'll keep away the devil.'

On the way back to her own cell, Belle said to her wardress, 'Gene was so bad, Jeannie, he never asked me about my own troubles the day.'

'How would you know?' was Alice MacKechnie's first answer to Ernest Larkwood. He had asked, 'Belle MacKnight – now she was a well-liked girl, wasn't she?'

The Lord Chief Justice intervened calmly, 'Mrs –' – he checked his book for the right name – 'Mrs MacKechnie, you are supposed to answer the question.'

'Yes, but he wants me to say that I'm only here because Belle was my friend, and that I'd do anything to help a friend, and that's not why I'm here, I'm here to see youse does fair play.'

To Anne Stevenson, Mr Larkwood said, 'Was she passionately in love with this man, Comerford?'

'What business of yours is that? That's her private business.'

'Mrs Stevenson,' said Sir Nicholas Bowling carefully, 'Mr Larkwood is trying to establish a motive. He wants to find out the reason for any alleged action Belle MacKnight took. If she were passionately in love she might have been jealous.'

Anne Stevenson replied, 'I wasn't inside her head or her heart, was I?'

Janice, with Malcolm watching her from the public gallery, gave calm, reasoned evidence to John Rudden.

'Yes, I was surprised. I was shocked.'

'Why was I shocked? Because that girl wouldn't hurt a fly.'

'No, you're right, she wasn't herself.'

'No, she was like that for a few days. Moody, like, and quiet.'

'I'd say she couldn't stop herself. Who'd blame her?'

Ernest Larkwood walked right up to the witness box. 'Miss Craig, you sat beside the accused every day.'

'Sit,' said Gloria.

'I'm sorry?'

'I do sit beside her every day.'

'Well, you don't at the moment. She's lodged in Crumlin Road prison.'

'She wouldn't be if youse was doing your job properly.'

Sir Nicholas Bowling glowered at the laughter in the court.

Edith Millar had cautioned Enid walking to work that morning. 'For Jesus's sake, Enid, watch your tongue, won't you? No dirty words. I mean that crowd'd throw you into jail yourself for only swearing.'

'They can fuck off if they try'n' to do that to me,' said Enid.

The women of Rufus Street linen mills had long habituated themselves to dealing obstructively with superiors, especially those with educated accents. Dismayingly for him, they disrupted the Civil Servant's neat timetable further. They so harried Ernest Larkwood that he took his own perennial advice to his own witnesses, and slowed down. On the Tuesday lunchtime of the second week, Sir Nicholas sent for both counsel.

'Is there any way of hurrying this up? No, Ernest, do not raise a disapproving brow. This is not a complicated case.'

Matters quickened only slightly thereafter.

Each evening, Belle gave Gene a full account. She made him smile and even laugh at the answers and rebuttals of the mill-women, all of whose accents she could mimic. But then, Gene took to lying down, and at the beginning of that second week, when she walked into his cell, he lay rigid, arms stretched stiffly along his sides.

With a wild eye he said to her, 'I'm practising for how to lie in the coffin.'

Belle began to cry, and backed out of the cell.

Hands on his hips, standing behind his desk, the Chief Constable said, 'I'm worried, Kenneth.'

'I'm worried, too.'

'Christ, what is Ernest Larkwood playing at? He hasn't even cross-examined the bloody girl yet? That could take three or four days, if he's going to go at this pace.'

The Civil Servant, not sleeping very well these nights, said, 'Apparently she's on tomorrow.'

'Jesus, Kenneth, tomorrow's Thursday.' He tossed a folder across the desk. 'See. I've taken that out.'

'Will it come to that?' The Civil Servant picked up the dossier: *Government of Northern Ireland: Emergency Measures: Implementation of Curfew in Belfast and Londonderry.*

'Of course it'll bloody well come to that.' The Chief Constable whipped hard enumerations across his fingertips. 'Tomorrow Thursday, the girl is examined. Tomorrow afternoon if we're lucky – IF we're lucky – Larkwood begins his cross-examination. Will it go to the jury by Friday? You tell me, Kenneth? And if it does, will we have a verdict by Monday evening – the last possible moment for a reprieve?'

The Civil Servant rubbed his tired eyes. 'What's your best estimate?'

'That's my best estimate.' The Chief Constable reached across and tapped the file. 'My best estimate is a bloody curfew on the streets next week with my young constables getting themselves shot.'

He softened and sat down with a thump.

The Civil Servant said, 'What about a stay? A stay of execution? Would that help?'

'On what grounds?'

'I could invent something.'

The Chief Constable asked, 'What's the state of play on the reprieve anyway?'

'No sign one way or the other. My guess is that if nothing dramatic happens they will commute the sentence. That is if Mr De Valera does not inflame matters. And then they can all put themselves in the advantageous position of having to reprieve the girl. So, they may reprieve him – in order to free themselves to reprieve her.'

'You credit them with more intelligence than I do, Kenneth. Any chance of a Not Guilty?'

'No. None.'

'Even with that jury? Eleven grandfathers and one young fellow who keeps making sheep's eyes at her in court?'

'No.'

The Chief Constable asked, 'Go back to that idea of a stay of execution. How would it work? I mean – we need at least a week. Larkwood is not exactly speedy.'

The Civil Servant said, 'Can I use your telephone? You'll have to leave the room.'

When he went to the door and beckoned the Chief Constable back in, he said, 'No stay. No grounds.'

'Christ Almighty!' said the Chief Constable. 'How am I going to cancel all police leave without people getting to know?'

He rubbed his hands.

'We have met before. Belle, isn't it?'

She did not reply.

'Well, now, Belle – you are on trial for murder. You are charged with taking someone's life, the life of a girl who was your friend.'

She looked at him.

'With your "pickers", I believe it is called? And we have it here, with a little piece of white tape around one handle and in your handwriting, I believe, the letter "B" – "B" for "Belle", in, what, it looks like nail varnish. The colour of blood. The colour of Noreen O'Connor's blood. Your friend's blood.'

'Remember what I said. Keep your hands folded in your lap,' the Governor's wife stood at the door of the car. 'I find it very calming.'

'Don't let him rise you,' said John Rudden, KC. Therefore Belle listened.

Ernest Larkwood lifted the 'pickers' by its tag and walked over to Belle, displaying the instrument before him as if it had been a dead frog he was holding by one leg.

'This is yours?' he asked with an affirmative nod.

Belle looked, and turned her head to address the judge, 'My Lord. It is.'

Ernest Larkwood walked slowly back to the exhibits table, rested the instrument there, and, his hand still resting on the table beside it, looked at Belle, his head angled, and asked, 'Why did you do it, Belle, why did you kill Noreen? Why did you drive that into her neck and then her stomach, her breast?'

John Rudden, coaching her that morning at half-past eight in the cell downstairs, said, 'Remember – you are in a kind of shocked

397

state on account of what is happening elsewhere in your life. You are distressed. Therefore, only give short answers and do not answer immediately. And especially do that with Mr Larkwood. It will help if you turn to the judge each time and address him as "My Lord", it will give you time to breathe.'

In answer to the powerful question, Belle now turned to the judge and said, 'My Lord, I do not know why I did it. I still do not know. I did not mean to do it.'

Mr Larkwood smarted after the many humiliations and disrespects heaped on him by the women.

Anne Byers said, 'Any man who believes that that girl over there, who never harmed anyone in her life, who only knew loss and sadness, would go out and do such a thing deliberately, any man who believes that is no more man than a wee pig.'

Edith Millar said, 'I never seen her like that before, and I never want to see her like that again. She was out of her head so she was.'

'So you don't deny you did it?' spat Ernest Larkwood.

'My Lord. Nor nobody ever did deny, me included,' said Belle.

The cross-examination of Belle MacKnight by Ernest Larkwood made legal folklore in Northern Ireland. It turned the barrister into a kind of celebrity, not a well-loved one, but a man who generated enormous interest and comment. He became a public figure by default – because, as his many detractors pointed out readily, he was cross-examining a relatively simple girl, uneducated, immature emotionally, who knew little about anything apart from the pictures to which she went three times a week. Not only that, he was dealing with a witness there should have been no need to cross-examine at all. Abundant evidence existed: she had been seen by hundreds in the act; the murder weapon had been taken from her hand by witnesses who said so; she did not even deny.

Others then widened the debate to try and understand why Larkwood's cross-examination had gone on so long. When the tussle had ended, the various camps had their say. Had he fallen in love with her, the romantics asked, had he been hit by some foolish flash-flood of obsession? Conspiracy theorists said, 'No, he was playing some deeper game, he was trying to manipulate the reprieve system in some hidden way, settling a few scores, showing them he could dictate the game.'

A generation later, in his memoirs published when he had long retired, Sir Ernest Larkwood, KC, devoted a whole chapter to his encounter with Belle. He too called it by the name everyone remembered, *The Gone with the Wind Trial*, and it made the book newsworthy, because Sir Ernest divulged sensationally that he had almost given up halfway through his notorious cross-examination.

It was late in the afternoon, and I was debating within my mind whether to open the new line of questioning I had prepared. My hesitation came from the knowledge that the Lord Chief Justice liked his court to rise as punctually as it sat. I glanced up from my table at the witness and I remember as clearly now as on that March day in 1943 what went through my mind. As she stood there (she had refused a chair throughout her testimony), she seemed again not as roughened by her mill work as I would have expected, and with a good bearing. She held her abundant hair pinned, and I observed the calm and decency in her eyes, untroubled after all the revelations and dreadful events of her recent life. I began to quarrel with myself. I knew that it was my task to annihilate her case. I had already attempted to do so during the earlier trial, in which she testified on behalf of her IRA lover. Yet, for the first time in several years I asked myself the question so dangerously sympathetic whenever it surfaces in a prosecutor's life – if our legal system can violate such a human being, then mustn't the old saying be true: 'The courts do not dispense justice, they dispense law'? I told His Lordship that I wished to ask no further questions until next morning and I spent a troubled night. Next day, the due process overcame me, and the trial continued.

Moments when humanity and duty confront each other abound in the life of every younger advocate. One naturally expects to dismiss such impostures so that they never again threaten. In the cross-examination of a female witness the added difficulty of one's natural chivalry must also be dispatched, because the intrusion of the subjective always undermines the objective pursuit of law. Across forty years in wig and robes at the Northern Ireland Bar, I cannot recall such a clearly visible challenge to my professional impartiality, or one that so haunted me for so long.

In effect, Larkwood the autobiographer was attempting to cover his tracks. His memory had become faulty, as evidenced by the insistence that Belle had stood throughout – when she had taken to the letter the advice of the Governor's wife. The truth was – he misjudged Belle, and then became dislodged when none of his ploys worked. Sarcasm, friendliness, sympathetic understanding, aggression, undermining, disapproving, smiling, sharing, approaching, sitting down, turning his back on her, yawning, laughing derisively, shouting – he tried everything. Belle answered his questions in the same tone of voice, and from time to time she took noticeable pauses before answering.

All the questions turned towards the same point. Did Belle kill Noreen? Answer: Yes, I did. Did you deliberately murder her? I don't know. The reporting, as seen now in the *Belfast Telegraph* files, seems not nearly as comprehensive as that of Gene Comerford's trial. One explanation given suggests that the reporters, and those others taking the shorthand notes, became too absorbed. Be that as it may, only one piece of transcripted exchange was published next day.

MR LARKWOOD: How did you grip your pickers?
BELLE MACKNIGHT: My Lord, I held them in my fist tight.
MR LARKWOOD: Show the court.
LORD CHIEF JUSTICE: [to witness] A gesture will do.
BELLE MACKNIGHT: [gesturing] Like that.
MR LARKWOOD: That's a practised grip. Is that how you usually held them?
BELLE MACKNIGHT: No, my Lord, I usually hold them like this. [gesturing]
MR LARKWOOD: Usually 'held' – if you don't mind. Past tense. You won't be holding any such weapon again. So you had a special grip for holding them?
BELLE MACKNIGHT: No, my Lord. I did it automatically.
MR LARKWOOD: Quite the little murderess, aren't we? You did it 'automatically'.

BELLE MACKNIGHT: I mean, my Lord, I didn't think it up.

MR LARKWOOD: But it is very difficult to kill someone. You must have practised – or perhaps been shown by your murderous boyfriend.

BELLE MACKNIGHT: He is not murderous, my Lord.

MR LARKWOOD: The court says he is. A jury of twelve honest men like those over there, they said he is. Are you going to go against all of that?

BELLE MACKNIGHT: I can only say what I know.

MR LARKWOOD: Did he teach you how to kill? Did he? Did he?

BELLE MACKNIGHT: My Lord –

MR LARKWOOD: Come on! Did he teach you how to kill? Well – did he?

BELLE MACKNIGHT: My Lord, I'm trying to answer –

MR LARKWOOD: Oh – trying to answer? But not answering.

BELLE MACKNIGHT: [silence]

LORD CHIEF JUSTICE: Mr Larkwood, the witness is attempting to answer the question. [to witness] You may answer.

BELLE MACKNIGHT: Gene Comerford never killed anyone.

MR LARKWOOD: And that is the level of value we may place on your testimony. A convicted murderer, who next Tuesday will hang by his neck from a noose, and so he should having killed that defenceless old man, and you say in your little-girly voice, 'Oh, Gene never killed anyone. Oh, no, oh, no.'

BELLE MACKNIGHT: [in tears] My Lord, I don't know how to answer these questions except the way I'm answering.

LORD CHIEF JUSTICE: Mr Larkwood, I require some moderation from you.

MR LARKWOOD: I apologise, Belle. I got carried away. Please forgive me. But I have to ask you how you learned to stab like that? It's important. The jury needs to know. Can we approach it another way? These pictures you go to? Could you have learned it there?

BELLE MACKNIGHT: No, my Lord.

MR LARKWOOD: Why did you go to them anyway, I mean why so often?

BELLE MACKNIGHT: Because, because, my Lord, they – took me out of myself.

MR LARKWOOD: Out of yourself? What do you mean?

401

BELLE MACKNIGHT: They gave me enjoyment, my Lord, and there wasn't much of it at home.

MR LARKWOOD: Why not?

BELLE MACKNIGHT: Because, my Lord, it's a gloomy house, ever since my father was killed, and I enjoyed the pictures, they were full of stories.

MR LARKWOOD: Murder stories?

BELLE MACKNIGHT: I never went to them, my Lord, I didn't like them.

MR LARKWOOD: Is there someone stabbed in *Gone with the Wind*?

BELLE MACKNIGHT: No, my Lord.

MR LARKWOOD: But there is someone killed – a soldier is shot, is he not?

BELLE MACKNIGHT: Yes, my Lord.

MR LARKWOOD: And by a woman with a gun. Would you like to tell us that bit of *Gone with the Wind*?

BELLE MACKNIGHT: No, my Lord.

MR LARKWOOD: Why not, you've entertained whole fleets of women with it, and they're all here – they will applaud you?

BELLE MACKNIGHT: No, my Lord.

MR LARKWOOD: Why not? Come on, Belle, you're wonderful at it, you're famous for it by now.

BELLE MACKNIGHT: No, my Lord. I don't tell the pictures any more.

(Beside this paragraph of the newspaper file at the *Telegraph* offices in Belfast, someone has written the word 'Bastard' beside Ernest Larkwood's name.)

When the first day's cross-examination ended, John Rudden patted Belle on the shoulder downstairs, and told her how well she had done; the wardress passed her a note signed by all the girls, with messages like 'Good girl, Belle' and 'We're keeping your chair warm'; she fell asleep in the van going back to Crumlin Road.

While Belle was having her supper, the Governor's wife came in.

'But how are you, my dear?'

'I don't know. And I don't know how I can last through any of this.'

'My dear,' said Martha Lewis, 'human beings are extraordinarily durable. You'll do.'

On Friday morning, the Lord Chief Justice asked, 'Mr Larkwood, when do you think you will have finished your cross-examination?'

'By lunchtime without fail, m'Lord.'

'I shall hold you to that.'

Larkwood began again. Belle sat as before; nothing changed. It became a battle between a middle-class, educated man, who lived in great comfort, and a socially deprived girl who had nothing but her instinct for survival, an instinct she did not know she possessed. Of the two, her behaviour grew closer and closer to a definition of human dignity, his drew farther and farther away. He abandoned the cross-examination when, in answer to the question, 'But you are a known associate of a known murderer?', Belle, after a moment's pause, replied, 'My Lord, I know that I would never have anything to do with a murderer, and that's the other reason I know that Gene Comerford, the man I'm fond of, and will marry if I can, is innocent.'

When the Lord Chief Justice said to her, 'You may step down now, Miss MacKnight,' the courtroom broke into spontaneous sustained applause.

'Ernest, there are still bounds of decency in this profession,' said John Rudden in the robing-room. 'Is there any chance at all you might observe them?'

'It is a murder trial, you know,' said Larkwood, now infuriated.

'Well, I hope you show a little modesty during the summing-up. You've gone round and round and round, and you've got nothing.'

23

On Saturday morning, the Governor himself, who had been on the alert, answered the telephone.

'Yes, it is. Oh, hallo, and how are you? Have you been well? Yes, yes, thank you, although as you can imagine, it is not wonderful here. Yes, she's well, thank you. Yes, yes, fine. I see. That leaves tomorrow night? Fine. And you'll be in – what? First thing Monday morning? Have you booked a berth for yourself? Oh, good, good. Same arrangements as before, I suppose, yes, the car will be there. And I suppose you know there are moves towards a reprieve. Or the Royal Prerogative. Yes, yes, of course you do, of course you do. Very well, I shall see you then on Monday morning.'

Gene and Belle agreed, in halting words, they could only spend minutes at a time with each other, then had to part.

'Sheer pain,' said the Governor's wife on Saturday afternoon. 'Look, how would it be if we set up the cell next door for her?'

'Oh, I really will be sacked,' said the Governor. 'No. But she can visit as often as she likes.'

'Or is able,' said Martha.

To Belle, she said, 'This is going to be very difficult. This is going to be the most difficult thing in your life.'

Belle sat straight, as she had recently been taught.

Martha, who always seemed to have a part of herself to scratch, continued, 'I'm going to ask you to pretend to yourself that you don't exist, that only one other person exists.'

'Gene?' asked Belle.

Martha said, 'Gene.'

'Oh, God, oh, God! Is there no reprieve?'

Martha tightened her lips and shook her head. 'But it's often a last-minute thing.'

Belle gasped, 'But if Gene goes –'

Martha repeated her husband's favourite phrase, 'We'll cross that bridge when we come to it. For the minute, be kinder to him than you ever were to anyone.'

Belle replied, 'The only one I was ever so fond of was my father.'

She walked into Gene's cell. Charlie said, 'He's only waking up. It takes him ages.'

Belle sat on the bed and cradled Gene's big head. 'I'm here, Gene, it's Belle, I'm here.'

He opened his eyes.

For an hour they sat, touching, saying nothing, occasionally weeping into each other's sleeves. Gene said eventually, 'This is all wrong. The whole thing is wrong. I knew it when I came to live here. They control everything by pretending your people are better than mine, when they keep you poor as well.'

'Shhhh,' said Belle. 'Hug me, Gene, hug me.'

On Sunday morning late, two men with overcoats folded over the handlebars of their bicycles cycled down the Springfield Road. They dismounted casually, and went up the small path to a house. To answer their knock, a man stood in the doorway, the suspenders of his uniform trousers falling happily at his waist, his collarless shirt open a few buttons. In his arms, a small boy in a Sunday-best sailor suit sat with jam-stained mouth, holding what remained of a bread crust and smiling, saying, 'Me. Me.' The two cyclists shot the man in the face twice, one shot each. Then one squeezed off a second shot, but the man was falling backwards, and the bullet hit the fourteen-month-old boy in his tiny right nostril, killing him too. The IRA later issued a statement apologising 'for the regrettable death of the child'.

During the summing-up by Ernest Larkwood on Monday morning, the car drove into the prison yard. The Governor stood to greet the occupant, a brown-eyed man in an expensive but discreet coat. The driver fetched the man's two large suitcases.

'Alone?' asked the Governor.

'Home Office economies,' said the visitor.

'A second breakfast?' asked the Governor as they walked indoors.

'Oh, yes, thank you,' said the brown-eyed man, 'but I think I'll do my calculations first.'

He and the Governor breezed along the corridor.

'I've put my best man on today,' said the Governor. 'He will be with him now. Same window as before, same yard.'

The brown-eyed man and the Governor looked down at Charlie Gilbert and Gene in the sunshine of the small exercise yard.

'Hm, big fellow, isn't he? Ye-es,' said the brown-eyed man. 'He's what? Six three, fifteen, no, fourteen stone, call it fourteen and a half for safety.'

The Governor said very quietly, 'He's six foot two and three-quarter inches, and he weighed fourteen stone eleven pounds the day he was sentenced.'

'Oh, thank you. And they say this one really is innocent.' He grunted as he wrote the figures in his notebook.

'He is passionately innocent,' said the Governor, 'and when this is over, I am retiring.'

The man in the brown coat looked at him with sympathy. 'I know, I know, there are some jobs I just would never have the stomach for and yours is one of them. I could never be someone's jailer.'

The jury retired to consider the verdict in the case of *Rex versus MacKnight* at half-past four on Monday afternoon. At six o'clock the court was informed that they did not expect to reach a verdict that night and the necessary hotel arrangements were made. Belle returned to the prison at just before seven. She found Gene lucid and walking up and down in his cell.

'I can't explain it. I suddenly seem to have come to life.' His words hit her like a broken glass in the face, and she crumpled. 'Oh, Belle, no, no, what I meant was, I'm resigned. Father Egan has been here. I made my Confession. I am peaceful for the first time in months. I want to talk to you, Belle, for hours.'

They walked up and down the cell, turn and turn about.

'I want to tell you all the news,' said Gene. 'Do you know who came in?' Gene said. 'Ernest from the lappers' room. I was asleep but he left them this to give me.' Ernest had copied out the words of 'The Old Rugged Cross', the hymn that Gene had liked. 'And he gave me this. Don't know if I should show it to you. Montana

Campbell sent it.' It was a crude drawing of an angel with bare breasts being chased by a man, and underneath Montana had scrawled, 'There's no sin in Heaven, Geney boy. I'll never forget you. Your old lapper friend, Derek (Montana) Campbell, Giddyap!'

Belle said, 'Gene, I can't get my breath.'

'Of course you can.' He put his arm around her shoulder. 'Of course you can, my love, my little Lagan Love.'

'Sing it to me again, you old crow,' she said, 'you old crow.'

'Where Lagan's streams sing lullaby.' Gene stopped. 'Belle – if we got out what would we do?'

'We'd go down to your house, Gene, and we'd meet your mother and father.'

'Will you do that anyway? And clip that youngest brother of mine around the ear.'

At that, they both sat separately down on the hard floor of the prison corridor, and leaned against the wall weeping.

'No, no, let them alone,' whispered Charlie Gilbert to Jeannie, who had wiped her eyes and walked forward.

In a few minutes, Gene sat up and wiped his eyes. He wheezed so much he could barely speak.

'Belle, tell me the end of *Gone with the Wind*. Will you? From Clark Gable is in jail. And give me the full thing.'

She looked at him and stood: he sat on the floor of the corridor looking up at her.

'All right. Clark Gable is in jail.' She wiped a tear and smiled. 'And he's playing cards with the officers who's guarding him.'

Gene said, 'I should have played cards with Headcase and cheated him.'

She braved and braved. 'Gene Comerford, did your mother never put manners on you? Stop interrupting me.'

He mimicked her accent. 'Did your mother never put manners on you?'

'And Clark Gable he's sitting there. And someone comes to the door and says to him that there's a woman outside to see him – noooooooooh!!!' Belle howled, doubled as if in pain.

Gene jumped up. 'Hey, Belle, Belle, Belle.' He grabbed her and Jeannie rushed forward. They helped Belle to Gene's bed, and laid her down.

'I'll sit here.' Gene perched on the edge of the bed, his eyes glittering bright.

'And I'll sit here,' said Jeannie, drawing in a chair. Belle subsided.

'What happened to you at all?' said Gene.

'I just remembered.' Tears flowed.

'What? What, my love, my only love, my wee love as you'd say yourself?'

'The last line.'

'What last line. What last line?'

Belle stumbled and stuttered. 'Scarlett. When Rhett's gone – she. Awwwww! Jesus! Jesus!' She wailed.

'Come on, Belle, say it.'

'When Rhett's gone and they're all gone, and her child's dead, and she hears all their voices – I can't say it, I can't say it!'

'Yes, you can, Belle, you can do anything, you can do anything. You can say it for me. Tell it me.'

Belle gulped and said, 'And it – it's the very last thing she says, she says – Scarlett says it. She says it at the very end. "After all – tomorrow is another day."'

Gene and Charlie sat and played draughts.

'What time is it, Charlie?'

'I told you, Geney boy, I left my watch at the mender's.'

'Charlie, how old is your daughter?'

'She's eleven, Geney.'

'And fair hair?'

'Like straw.'

Gene stood up halfway through the game, coughed and said, 'Oh, Charlie, I'm sorry.'

Charlie looked up quickly. 'What is it?'

'My bowels. They're gone.'

Charlie rose, saying, 'No, no, 's okay, Geney. I've towels and you've clean trousers, 's okay.'

He changed Gene as he would a baby.

Headcase came back from the canteen. 'Well, the bag of sand dropped all right,' he said out loud.

'Shut you up!' said Charlie.

'Bag of sand?' asked Gene, almost unconscious with apprehension.

Before Charlie could stop him, Headcase blurted, 'Aye, they tested the rope with a bag of sand your weight.'

The Governor stayed up all Monday night. At six o'clock in the morning he telephoned the Civil Servant, who had not slept either. No, not a word. Royal Prerogative?

'It will not be exercised,' said the Civil Servant.

Nesbit Blackwood went to his doctor on the way home.

'No, completely blocked up now.'

The doctor said, 'Any pain, sinuses are painful?'

'No, not this time.'

'Otherwise, I must say, Nesbit, for a man your age.'

On Monday night at ten o'clock, Judy Cruiseman abruptly said goodnight to her sister Blanche who had come to stay for a long weekend. On Tuesday morning at five o'clock, Judy Cruiseman rose, donned a warm dressing-gown and in the hall downstairs put on a heavy wool ulster coat with a plaid lining. She opened the door on to the terrace and walked slowly parallel to the house. A cold breeze ruffled and lifted her hair. She walked by the rockery and into the kitchen garden by the side entrance. At the far corner of the kitchen garden she jerked open the stiff door of the summer house, then banged it to behind her; she sat on the seat that ran from one wall to the other. Her silver-topped cane fell to the ground. Minutes later, she stood, lifted her skirts and urinated, letting the water flow over her ankles. Then she sat again. From the floor near the widening pool she picked a small piece of old slate, and holding one arm up so that the sleeve fell back, she began to hack at the soft white underside of her forearm with the slate's edge. When she stopped after three or four slashes, and began to feel the pain, she screamed. Richard heard, woke and found her: Blanche did the bandaging.

'Not serious,' they agreed.

'Nasty fall,' said Richard.

At a quarter to seven, Father Egan and Gene rose from their knees. By the door of the cell, the Governor shook hands with Gene, looking up at him and blinking. The hands parted and suddenly the Governor reached out a second time and shook hands with Gene.

Charlie said, 'I'm awful sorry, Geney, but I have to put these straps on your hands behind your back.'

'No, Mr Gilbert,' said the Governor, 'no need this once.'

In the corridor, Charlie Gilbert said, 'Do you want to go first, Geney?', and the little procession moved off, Gene ahead. He walked without assistance.

'This way?' he asked, and climbed the short stairs; he did not look around him.

The man in the brown coat waited formally by the door, his foot near the base of the green-painted wooden structure. In the small, overheated room, Gene did not look up. The door clicked shut behind them. Still looking down, guided by the loving hand of Charlie on his shoulder, Gene walked forward.

'Is this where I stand?' he asked.

Charlie patted him. 'Come on, Geney, that's grand.'

Gene turned around and shook Charlie's hand, and then Head-case's and then Father Egan's, who made the Sign of the Cross on his forehead, and said, 'Incline unto my aid, O Lord. O Lord, make haste to help us.'

Charlie said softly, 'Look, I have to put this oul' hood on you, Geney,' which Headcase handed to Charlie – who then whispered, as he stood behind Gene, 'Listen, I brung a soft bit of cloth here for your neck, like, I'm going to smuggle it in here under your collar,' and he arranged a thick wad of linen on the skin of Gene's neck. 'Best Belfast linen, Geney,' Charlie said. 'And this is awful but we have to tie your hands. And your poor feet.'

The buckle on the strap pinioning Gene's ankles took ages, pricked Charlie's finger.

'That's it, Gene, that's all we'll have to, have to, h-h-h-ave to – do to you, my old segocia.'

He reached on tiptoe to whisper in Gene's ear, 'Keep your head a wee bit to one side. That's the man, that's the man.'

He patted Gene on the shoulder one more time.

Charlie stepped back, took the noose forward in his hands, arranged it, then allowed the brown-eyed man to inspect it – who then nodded and stepped back to the lever.

Father Egan had stopped praying, because his voice had grown desperate; shiny tearstains spotted his black soutane. Headcase muttered, 'Wait,' and stepping forward took the wad of linen away from beneath the rope, which he then tightened a little to Gene's skin.

A commotion at the door of the room caused everyone to pause: footsteps could be heard on the stairs. The brown-eyed man held up his hand to halt the proceedings, and the Governor opened the door to the knock, but prevented the caller from seeing the scene inside the chamber. Outside stood his wife: she looked bleak and old. Martha shook her head from side to side several times, her mouth of long teeth wide open, and walked back down again. The Governor closed the door and nodded, looked at the hooded, pinioned man whose head was raised as a blind man seeks the sun; then the Governor put a hand over his own eyes.

The brown-eyed man pulled the lever. Gene Comerford fell vertically, very fast, down, down, like a statue dropped from a sheer, if tiny, cliff.

At half-past seven, it took Jeannie and another wardress up to an hour to mobilise Belle: her sedation had been particularly heavy.

'No rules in these circumstances,' Martha Lewis said the night before. A new difficulty arose. The crowds outside the prison had not dispersed: Catholics remained on their knees praying, led by several priests; Protestants had not cheered in the way they had done at past hangings – nevertheless the police feared an ugly mood. Belle had to be taken along a laneway to a car at another exit. She did not walk very well, and all morning needed assistance, from the car into the court building, to the holding cell, and finally when the call came just before six o'clock in the evening that the jury was returning its verdict, she had to be assisted up the stairs and back into the dock.

All the Rufus Street women had gathered. The ushers, double in numbers, had great difficulty in restraining the noise. When the Lord Chief Justice did eventually enter, the jury came back into the morbid room.

At Crumlin Road prison, under the wall, the workmen patted the last anonymous swards of turf into place over the uncoffined body of Gene Comerford, whose death certificate had been signed two hours earlier. The man in the brown coat caught the night boat to Liverpool.

'Gentlemen of the jury. Have you reached your verdict?'

The foreman answered, 'Well, we have and we haven't,' and, seeing the eagle head of the judge about to strike, said, 'but we can reach a verdict, my Lord, if we know the answer to one simple question.'

'What is the question?'

'Do we have to give a verdict according to the charge?'

'I am not sure I understand you,' said the Lord Chief Justice.

John Rudden, KC, did understand, and beamed broadly.

'Can we say, for example – she did it all right, but she did not mean to.'

Nicholas Bowling said, 'The charge before you is murder. What you are describing is manslaughter.'

Someone in the court whooped, and was shushed by the thronged hisses.

The foreman, a tenacious person, persisted, 'Well, your honour, that's what we're thinking – that it should be manslaughter.'

The judge said, 'No. You do not have that right. The charge is murder. You cannot suddenly take it into your hands to alter the charge. The accused is charged with murder, and you have to find a verdict of Guilty or Not Guilty.'

'Right, my Lord. We'll retire again,' said the foreman.

They returned in ten minutes: other than the judge, the court had not disbanded.

'The prisoner will rise.'

Nicholas Bowling surveyed all. The murmurs died.

'Gentlemen of the jury. Have you reached your verdict?'

'We have.'

'And do you find the defendant, Isabel or Belle MacKnight, Guilty or Not Guilty of the capital charge of murder?'

'Not Guilty.'

When the cheering and weeping subsided, the Lord Chief Justice exonerated the jury from all future jury service and left the court. A surge forward began as the public began to reach towards Belle. The ushers could not stop them, and Alice MacKechnie, Anne Byers and all the others – Janice had not turned

412

up – grabbed Belle and began to embrace her. They managed to outflank the ushers and the police, whom they abused so heavily the men fell back. Belle, half-faint, was propelled to the door and in the street they raised her shoulder-high. Someone lit a flare.

The size of the crowd outside indicated either a high level of organisation or some leak from the jury as to their intentions. Blackout, or no blackout, the street was alight with flaming tar-barrels; Belfast, for a moment, had been lit like a triumphal Rome.

The women from Rufus Street lifted Belle on their shoulders; the police shrugged and stepped back. Singing and cheering, the women bore Belle in procession down the streets of the city. At the corner of Pretoria Street they deposited her, and Malcolm reached in to take her, and shelter her from the crowd.

'Did you see her face? Tears of pure joy,' said Anne Byers (who always got everything wrong).

In Belfast, in 1942, lived Belle, a mill-girl with a gift. Every morning at work, she enthralled people with the story of the film she saw last night. In her apron and turban-tied headscarf she climbed on the table of the spinning-room in Rufus Street, and dramatised, in her own sharp accent, the passions of Hollywood. With her wide eyes and her wit, and her hands weaving gestures like a magician casting spells, she pierced the overcast of their long, dirty workdays . . .